· ESSIEN OF ALKEBULAN ·

DESCENDANTS OF
FIRE & WATER

ALKEBULAN

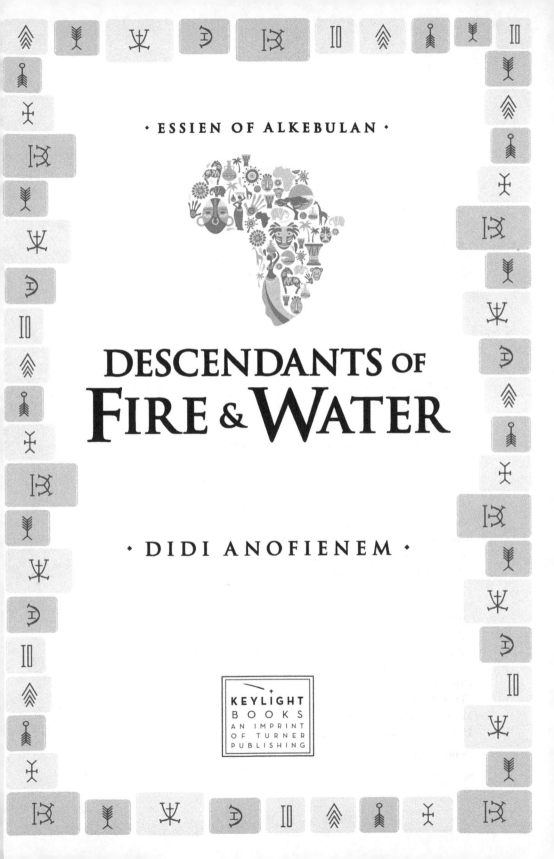

· ESSIEN OF ALKEBULAN ·

DESCENDANTS OF
FIRE & WATER

· DIDI ANOFIENEM ·

KEYLIGHT
BOOKS
AN IMPRINT
OF TURNER
PUBLISHING

KEYLIGHT BOOKS
AN IMPRINT OF TURNER PUBLISHING COMPANY
Nashville, Tennessee
www.turnerpublishing.com

Descendants of Fire & Water

Cover and book design by William Ruoto
Cover and map art by Alexis Seabrook

Library of Congress Cataloging-in-Publication Data

Names: Anofienem, Didi, author.
Title: Descendants of fire and water / Didi Anofienem.
Description: Nashville, Tennessee : Keylight Books, [2023] | Series: Essien of Alkebulan; book 1 | Audience: Ages 12-15. | Audience: Grades 7-9.
Identifiers: LCCN 2022058180 (print) | LCCN 2022058181 (ebook) | ISBN 9781684429905 (hardcover) | ISBN 9781684429912 (paperback) | ISBN 9781684429929 (epub)
Subjects: CYAC: Ability—Fiction. | Magic—Fiction. | Sex role—Fiction. | Family life—Fiction. | Blacks—Fiction. | Fantasy fiction. | LCGFT: Fantasy fiction. | Novels.
Classification: LCC PZ7.1.A57 De 2023 (print) | LCC PZ7.1.A57 (ebook) | DDC [Fic]—dc23
LC record available at https://lccn.loc.gov/2022058180
LC ebook record available at https://lccn.loc.gov/2022058181

Printed in the United States of America

This book is dedicated to the nation called Africa and its revolutionary leaders, whose efforts to unite the continent under a common purpose, a common government, a common culture, and a common currency, ignite dreams for a resurrected Africa that will never die with them.

The child in each of us
Knows paradise.
Paradise is home.
Home as it was
Or home as it should have been.
Paradise is one's own place,
One's own people,
One's own world,
Knowing and known,
Perhaps even
Loving and loved.

—Octavia E. Butler, *Parable of the Sower*

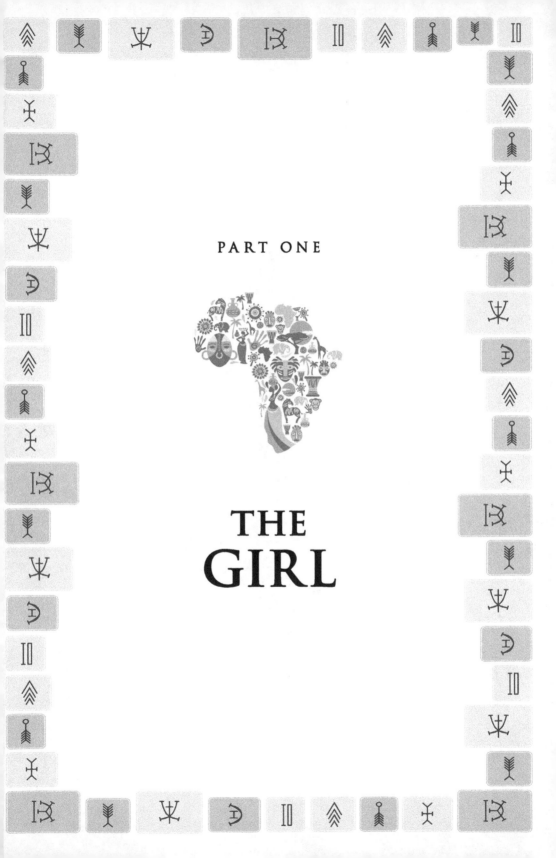

PART ONE

THE
GIRL

CHAPTER ONE

◆

A LL VILLAGES ARE UNIQUE IN THEIR OWN RHYTHM, AND EV-
ery village has steps and patterns that it follows. The dance is familiar, and the people of the village perform it beautifully. Each step in the
rhythm accounts for and leads to all the others. Where one rhythm be-
gins, another ends, and there is always another one just behind it. Some
villages are comprised of metal workers crafting beautiful, intricate pieces
from gold, silver, and copper. Other villages have sculptors, using clay or
stone to mold and carve statues and buildings. Yet other villages began as
gatherings of woodworkers or were the creation of seafarers. No village is
more important than another, but each village depends on the others for
needs that are not met by the local industry. The metal workers depend on
the metallurgists to mine for precious metals from deep within the land's
womb. The woodworkers depend on the woodcutters for wood, and the
seafarers depend on the shipbuilders to secure their catch of the day. And
of course, no village survives without its farmers. So, every village must be
in perfect rhythm to keep all the others dancing, too.

Essien was a farmer's daughter in Igbo State, where the Capital of Alkebulan was not quite three thousand stadia away, but it might as well have
been a different world entirely. Since she was a young girl, she had been
hearing stories of Akukoifo, mysterious beings who roamed Alkebulan before there was forever. Stories that kept her up at night, huddling beneath
her covers, both afraid and fascinated at their possibility. But she knew
Akukoifo were real, not a myth; she could see them and hear them, but she
was almost certain that no one else could.

On this day, Essien walked along the well-worn path that led into the
village center. Her mother had sent her to pick up a few items for the week,
and Essien had wanted to walk alone instead of waiting for the youngest
of her older brothers, Femi, to return and take her. The path led along the

edge of a deeply tangled jungle, where no one in the village ventured under any circumstances.

Fairytales warned them about the jungle, horror stories that stayed with her every time she laid eyes on that tangled thick of trees. She'd heard one story about a man who lived in the middle of the jungle, at the bottom of a lake. The man could use water like a wall or as a shield. In times past, he had pulled the waters up around Alkebulan like a curtain made of foaming waves. The water walls stretched up higher than the tallest mountain. With water, he'd kept invaders out and kept the occupants of Alkebulan in, so that the country remained rich and fertile, unbothered by outsiders for millennia.

It is for that reason that Alkebulan was covered in endless stretches of sand that went on and on in microscopic particles farther than anyone could walk in one day. When the water rose up to meet the sky, the people had to worship the man for ten thousand years, so he might release the waters again. Essien had taken a school trip to see the Nahla River, and she'd stood at the base of the sand mountains leading into the Land of Sheba. The Nahla River flowed like a trickle of thin fingers so close to the desert and its parchedness, but it roared and raged in other parts of the country that it touched.

Essien heard squeals and screams from up ahead. As the dirt path ended, she saw a large group of children jumping around excitedly. Little boys and girls of varying shades of skin tones in playing clothes, most with no shoes. Two girls who looked older than the rest had two pieces of rope stretched between them. As Essien watched, they began to turn the ropes. The other children quickly formed a line. Then one by one, they ran swiftly toward the turning ropes and jumped in. The girls holding the ropes spun them faster and faster, shouting a chant as each rope hit the ground and stirred up dust. As she watched, Essien remembered playing stockings. She had never been any good at it.

One little girl, a bright lemon yellow in the sea of browns, saw Essien from her spot in the line and shouted out, "Essien, how now? Come and play!" It was Nneka, her best friend Ntoochi's littlest sister.

Essien smiled and waved back at the girl. "Next time, next time!" She held up her market basket, so the girl would see she was in the middle of running errands. Essien remembered the first time she had met the little girl, when Ntoochi had invited her over for an evening meal. The little girl had stared at her openly and then sidled up to her and said, "Why did the Mother bless you so much?" Essien had laughed and rubbed the little girl's cheek. Essien knew the girl was talking about the color of her skin, a deep, dark, shiny brown that glistened in sunlight like obsidian stones.

There was one story of Akukoifo, about a woman, Anyanwu, who could turn night into day with a flick of her eyebrows, and kept it daytime for ten thousand years. The fairytale said that she made herself a throne of flames, and she sat on it next to the sun, high in the sky, lording their height and light over every person and plant on the blue planet, Ala-ani. The sun beat down relentlessly for so long that everyone's skin in the country of Alkebulan was shaded and colored to varying degrees of darkness. Anyanwu, the woman on the throne, reserved the deepest, darkest shades of brown for the most beloved. In Essien's own family, everyone was the same deep, nighttime shade of brown that reflected the sun and the moon.

As she got closer to the village center, Essien said hello to a group of nnennas, elder women of the village, who were sitting on stools before a wooden storefront. They were using large wooden nwaodo to grind melon seeds into egusi powder. Essien loved egusi soup with stockfish, the salty aged fish that smelled and tasted of the sea. Her mother only made it on her birthday and for the new year because her father hated both the smell and the taste. Her mother's favorite meal was pepper soup, and Essien could not stand even a spoonful of it. Every time her mother made the soup, Essien would protest having to eat it and her mother would chastise her for refusing to eat the soup, saying Essien would never grow old.

In these instances, Essien would remember another Akukoifo fairytale about a little child who lived forever, never growing older or dying. If the little girl touched anybody, they would immediately shrivel up into an old thing, all gray and lifeless, but they wouldn't be dead. The heart would still beat, slow as death and thick as bee's nectar. The gray shrivel would stay like that forever, until the girl touched it again. Then it would be like her, eternally young, never dying, the heart a gray husk behind their ribs.

Essien's walk had brought her to the bustling and raucous village center that served as a central gathering for vendors. There were storefronts in assorted sizes, crafted of wood, stone, and glass. In front of each, there were wooden stalls lined up in rows, and customers and vendors haggling spiritedly. There was an entire section at the farthest end of glass stores that housed government offices. Essien had learned from her mother which stalls had the best produce. Her mother most often bought from the vendors who leased out land from the stadia her father owned. After shopping for what she needed at select stalls, Essien paid for the items and turned to head for home.

As she headed back to her family's compound, she heard a shrill whistle, the sound of the wind turned into a sharp point. She looked up, beyond the trees lining the footpath, and viewed a flickering in the bluest part of the sky. As she did, a wavering figure of iridescent shimmers floated down in front of her. Essien smiled and reached out her hand to touch the figure. When she withdrew her hand, it was wet. The Akukoifo bobbed in front of her for a second and then disappeared.

Essien recalled when her mother had told her the stories of Akukoifo, and her voice filled with warning that let Essien know her mother could not see them, as Essien eventually realized she could. Her mother had told her many stories of caution and concern, including one that said if children completed their levels at school, they were protected from the girl, and they would grow old like their parents. Essien knew she looked older than she was. Her mother had said that Essien would one day look younger than the years she had lived, because she was loved most by the woman on her sun throne, as evidenced by her dark skin. Her mother had also told her that she was protected from the man at the bottom of the lake, as long as she stayed out of the jungle. Essien believed the stories she'd heard, especially the scary ones—and it was the scary stories her mother had warned her not to repeat in the light of day or the dark of night.

As she walked along the edge of the dense forest of snarling trees, recalling stories from her past, she remembered one that her brother, Femi, had once told her that entranced her more than terrified her. He'd said the man who kept out the water was still alive, floating deep at the bottom of the lake that was located at the center of the jungle. At the time, Femi had shown her a path that went into the jungle, and she passed it now as she approached the back gate of her family's compound. It was only a slight opening between the encroaching trees, eerily straight and smooth, but narrow, like someone had taken care to both reveal and hide the entrance. She stood looking into the darkness just beyond the opening of the path. It seemed to glow with a pulsing silver-blue color. The first time he'd taken her to the hidden path, she'd shaken her head and rejected Femi's dare. She wouldn't be the one to get into trouble for disobeying her parents, her grandparents, her teachers, the elders . . . everyone had warned them never to go into the jungle, especially not alone. If there was a man in the lake—and she didn't believe there was—she would not be the one to find him. But there was something intriguing about the pulsing silver-blue glow, calling to her as she stood there staring past the tree line into its depths . . .

WHEN HER TENTH YEAR OF SCHOOLING BEGAN, ESSIEN STARTED the next levels with the fifteen- and sixteen-year-olds. Ntoochi was still her closest friend since first level. This year, they only had Cosmology together. It was Essien's favorite class of all the required courses, such as Modern Math, Ancient Writings, and Contemporary History. In Cosmology, she learned about the gods of Alkebulan who reminded her so much of Akukoifo. She always paid attention during the lessons, no matter how much Ntoochi tried to distract her with her silly boy-mindedness and fatuous ways. Essien would stay up late at night reading her texts, long after she should have been asleep. If there were more stories of Akukoifo, she wanted to know them. She kept comparing the stories to what she knew of real life. Some of it matched the stories she'd been told as a young girl, such as the stories about Oya, the warrior goddess, and Yemaya, the goddess of the ocean. But she also learned new stories, such as the one about the Mothers, immortal goddesses who could become women in human form, at their will.

Her teacher, Ara Isikwe, liked to include her own opinions tucked into the crevices of her lectures. Everyone knew that the last outspoken head teacher had been driven from the village with nothing but the tunic on his back. He had been teaching students in level twelve about pre-unification and condemning the War of Unification as a mistake.

Pointing to pictos of hundreds of bodies being prepared for burial, Ara Isikwe said, "Twelve million lives were lost in the War of Unification. Many believe it was the flow of blood seeping into the mud and polluting the rivers that finally persuaded the Mothers to act on our behalf and bring peace to the land."

Essien wondered how "peace" was defined and when it was determined that the country was no longer at war. Essien had not seen any military engines since last year, and there had been no word from her parents about the state of the country either. She often asked her father about the war, and he only answered that farmers did not do the jobs of military men. In other words, he would not talk about it with her. She couldn't talk to her parents about the war, and she couldn't talk to them about the Mothers. As a rule, her parents did not believe in "imaginary celestial beings," as her father had called them, although her mother believed in Akukoifo, but that was the extent of her beliefs.

The teacher told them, "The land and its people are protected by the Mothers. There is a way to contact them if you are of the land. But you must be willing for them to take possession of you. You must allow them to become your life, down to your very soul. To contact the Mothers, you must travel back to the beginning of human existence—to the bottom of the lake at the center of the jungle."

Here, she stopped and looked right at Essien. Essien dropped her eyes to the floor and then snuck a glance around the room. Ntoochi stuck out her tongue from her seat near the back of the class. Essien's teacher was still staring at her when she turned her head back around. *She must know about the Akukoifo, too*, Essien thought.

After class ended, Essien shooed Ntoochi out of the classroom and waited patiently until everyone else had gone. She put her fingertips on the edge of her teacher's desk and waited for her to look up. No one else spoke about the Akukoifo like they believed them. Instead, stories of Akukoifo were used to threaten and scare children. Nobody mentioned them in any other contexts, especially not at school. And until a few minutes earlier, Essien had never heard any adult speak about the lake in the middle of the jungle.

In a faint voice, Essien greeted her, "Ara, abeg, please tell me, do you believe in the Akukoifo?" Essien flicked a glance as her teacher looked up at her face. Her teacher had round brown cheeks with light brown eyes and long, curling lashes that reminded Essien of a bee's wings. She was wearing a light green tunic with darker green embroidery. She was not smiling, but Essien got the feeling that her teacher was glad to see her.

"Essien, must I always remind you? Call me Abara. We can be more friends than teacher and student."

Essien nodded but waited for her question to be answered. Abara smelled of burning sandalwood this closely, and Essien leaned away slightly.

"Do the Mothers really live at the bottom of the lake? Has anyone ever found them?" Essien wanted so badly to believe in a world where men were made of water and where women could smile in their knowledge of flames. Essien wanted to know those unspoken secrets that couldn't be talked about when the sun was up.

Abara smiled at Essien, the movement of her lips making her face appear to beam with genuine sweetness.

"The Akukoifo are true, young one. Why is it so hard to believe?"

Essien shook her head, "It's not hard for me. I believe. I just want to know more. I can feel that there's more out there to know."

"You need not ask me what you will one day come to know, Essien. Trust yourself. The Akukoifo will be very valuable for you someday." Her teacher began to stack her folders and papers before placing them inside a canvas bag.

"The Akukoifo . . . can you . . . can you see them?" Essien stared hard into her teacher's eyes. The woman's head tilted, and then she smiled.

"You don't need to see Akukoifo to believe. They are there whether we can see them or not. The same with the Mothers. If you believe, that is enough."

Essien held her tongue about her own Akukoifo sightings. After a moment, her teacher smiled and beckoned her. "Come Essien, we must go for our evening meal. I'm sure your mother is waiting to hear about your day."

Essien followed her teacher out of the room and watched her walk down the path in front of the class building. Her teacher walked slow and methodical, each step placed exactly in front of the other. Essien imitated her walk, which made her thick ropes of braided hair swipe side to side across her back. Essien preferred wearing her hair in braids because it kept her thick, curly hair out of her face and protected. Her mother oiled and braided her hair every two weeks, and Essien only wore her hair out in all its coiled splendor for special occasions.

Her teacher continued along the path, nodding and smiling as she caught up to and passed Ntoochi, who had taken a seat on a bench near the school entrance. Ntoochi's skin was a bright yellow shade of brown, and her hair was sandy red. Her mother nearly always kept Ntoochi's hair arranged in scalp braids that hung down to her shoulders. All of Ntoochi was thin, from her face to her legs. And, although prohibited, Ntoochi was known to roll the waistband of her uniform skirt to make it even shorter.

Essien slowed as she approached her friend. As she did, Ntoochi stood up, and Essien noticed that she was holding two coconut bowls of papaya cubes. Ntoochi handed Essien one of the bowls.

"What did you stay and talk to that one about?" Ntoochi pointed at where Abara was walking away from them, her sandals swishing against her long uwe. She disappeared beyond the stone wall surrounding their school.

"I asked her about Akukoifo."

Ntoochi rolled her eyes dramatically. "You and the spirits of the sky."

Essien closed her mouth. Now she understood her teacher's reluctance to talk about the Akukoifo. Essien wanted nothing more than to share what she had been thinking. She also knew that she was not supposed to talk about Akukoifo where the sky could hear, but most people didn't care about spirits, and that included Ntoochi. She typically only cared about conversations involving which of the local boys she might end up marrying.

They ate their cubes of juicy fruit as they walked down the path that would take them to the motorbus. The next bus was ambling up as Essien and Ntoochi reached the stop. They boarded with the other passengers, which included a group of teenage boys with their neckties and overcoats dangling from their necks and arms, a grandmother with a small sleeping baby tied on her back, and an old man with a bag of rice on his shoulder. Essien sat near the front of the motorbus, next to the window, with Ntoochi beside her. The motorbus traveled down a gray stretch of roadway that connected the outer villages with the main village center. Green and golden-topped crops rolled along beside the roadway, dipping and rising as they did. They had just barely begun their journey home when low, gray clouds began to float toward them from up ahead. There was a dark line of the same dark clouds rolling low to the ground as far as they could see, with a layer of orange and yellow glinting beneath all the shifting black and gray.

"How now? You see fire, too?" Ntoochi asked.

Something was burning up ahead. It looked like it was coming from the fields where some of the farmers of the region grew their fruits and vegetables, providing food for families in more than just Essien's village. The black smoke was like a never-ending blanket covering the entire space of fields, which stretched for hundreds of stadia. The motorbus kept driving alongside the growing stretch of black smoke and sun-colored flames. Essien stared, her mouth open in horror, as fire stretched and yawned over all that was once green. The motorbus driver suddenly pulled over and stopped.

"We can't go any further. The smoke is getting worse," he announced, over the questioning clamor of the passengers' voices. Essien peered out the front window and saw a line of motorbuses, double buses, two-wheelers, and wheeled engines stuck and unmoving in the lane up ahead.

"My Nne is already fainting, I can now imagine."

"How do we get home? We can't go into the jungle, and there's no other way around."

"Maybe the smoke will clear?"

Other passengers were already getting off the bus. The baby on the granny's back began to screech, and the older woman carefully pulled her back bundle to the front. Essien glanced again at the fire burning the earth, trying to follow it to its beginning, but there was just the blanket of black and the rows and rows of vehicles. She and Ntoochi stepped off the motorbus and attempted to use their hands to cover their eyes and mouths.

"Should we be standing so close?" The fire was moving, but Essien couldn't tell if it was moving toward them or away from them.

"We start walking," Ntoochi said. "Maybe we pass a motorbus heading our way."

Essien wanted to stay with the rest of the passengers, but the driver had already pulled out his pocket dialer and was focused on making a call, more than likely to the transportation company. No one would be driving anywhere until the fire was under control. But how did one control a fire that large and massive? Were there water buckets large enough to hold enough water? Essien thought again of the Mothers and the man at the bottom of the lake. He could put out that fire. For someone capable of controlling water, dropping a ton of water on that stretch of burning field would be as simple as breathing.

Please let it rain and put out the fire in the fields, Essien wished. *Please, let it rain.*

Essien followed Ntoochi as she began winding her way through the nearby vehicles. The fire was a distant redness eating at the farthest fields to the left. The gray layer of smoke moved toward them, showing the advancing fire. Essien couldn't yet smell the burning smoke. They had barely reached the crest of the hill they were climbing when lightning ripped through the sky in multiple directions, and within seconds, small drops of chilly water were pelting their heads and arms.

"Rain?" Ntoochi asked, holding her hands out to catch it. "During a drought?"

Essien tilted her head all the way back to stare up at the sky as it dropped water. Essien looked back at where they had just come from and wondered at how it had begun to rain only seconds after she made her wish. It felt like an ihebube, a gift from the Mothers. She started to tell Ntoochi.

"I wished for rain," she said aloud, looking at the back of Ntoochi's head as she was staring up at the sky. As Essien looked up again, a single droplet landed in her eye. She squealed and blinked it away.

"How now, don't boast," Ntoochi said. "Give thanks to the Mothers."

Essien thought silently, *Thank you, Mothers*, as she put her hands straight up toward the sky. "Thank you, Mothers," she then said aloud.

Ntoochi joined her elations, shouting out, "Thank you, Mothers!"

As the rain fell, and the girls continued walking, Essien let an amused grin play over her face. If she could wish for rain, what else might she wish for? She wanted to ace her levels this year; last year, she had just barely passed. Her father had promised to take her on a tour to see the pyramids in Sheba and Nubia if she got a high score. She would wait to make that wish. If she truly had a power, she wanted to be wise about how she used it.

Essien smiled wider as she thought about how many wishes she might be granted.

The rain kept pouring down upon their heads and on the fire in the fields to the left of them. Essien had never walked home from school, but she knew the way. It wasn't a short motorbus ride, so it was surely going to be a long walk. They trudged onward and upward, over a hill and down the other side, around a curve, and down a bend. They kept walking, and it kept raining. The fire burned in the farthest fields they could see, but it was getting further away rather than coming closer. Essien could see that the rain was beginning to extinguish the fire. Patches nearby were smoldering white. The walking path widened, and Essien began to walk beside Ntoochi.

"I wonder what caused the fire," Essien said. She knew her father kept fields in this part of the countryside, but she couldn't be sure if these were his fields or not.

"Probably some lousy farmer," Ntoochi said. "Or maybe it was Aku-koifo." She made a scrunched face at Essien, who laughed and pushed her gently against the shoulder. Ntoochi believed in the Mothers, but Aku-koifo were outside the bounds of her imagination. She'd listen to Essien's stories, but she never added any of her own.

The further they walked, the closer what remained of the fire appeared to be getting, until at last they reached a blazing bright patch that wasn't receiving any rain. The road turned, and Essien saw a truck parked near the side of the road. There were empty black buckets turned over in the middle of the roadway. As they approached, Essien recognized the beat up dark blue truck as her father's. There was an emblem of a produce basket painted on both side panels, with an image of all the produce her father grew— plantain, grains, leafy vegetables, green vegetables, melon fruits, citrus fruits, red fruits, pineapple, papaya, coconuts, mango, and nuts. The details of the basket grew sharper as Essien sprinted ahead. She was hoping to see her father perched on the back of the vehicle. Maybe he would give them a ride and then return to check on his fields. The stalks near the truck were still burning, but the flames were short and getting shorter as she watched. Essien was nearly soaked completely through, so it wouldn't be long before the fields were completely awash, too.

Her father was not sitting on the back of the truck, nor was he inside it. Essien scanned the area and couldn't see him anywhere along the sides of the field. The flames were still eating at the tops of the crops, like someone had touched the top of the green stalks and vines with a match and lit them all at once. As Essien continued to scan the area for movement, Ntoochi caught up to her.

"I don't know why my nna would leave his truck."

"Do you think he ran into the fields?"

Instinctively, Essien slid down the side of the embankment, hurrying into the bottom of the ravine. The hay was soggy under her as the rain continued to fall. She could distantly hear Ntoochi yelling for her to stop and calling her crazy. She ran to the edge of the field, mud squishing beneath her feet, and feeling the press of the fire. It was a greater heat than any she'd ever felt from the sun. She could see a trail that was likely used to trek in and out of the massive acreage. Essien started to edge her way toward it, and a stalk of burning leaf fell down upon her head. She was able to dodge its slow descent, but she realized if she slowed, she might never reach her father. She knew he was in there; she could feel it. She ducked her head and dashed down the lane.

She hadn't run for long before she saw the body of a person collapsed at the side of the trail. The person was on their side, empty black buckets overturned beside them. Essien knew it was her father from the dusty dark green coveralls he wore, and the brown sandals that had fallen off his feet and lay nearby. Essien also knew her father was too heavy for her to carry or drag. She reached him, sobbing his name and rolling him over. He flopped over into her lap, but he didn't stir. She would have to carry him out of those fields before the fire and smoke killed him. She didn't stop to check if it already had. Pushing her hands under his arms, she lifted her father, bracing with her knees like he had taught her. He was so heavy that she dropped him almost as soon as she felt his weight. She kept trying, using her knees, and steadying against thick stalks of grain beside her. Surprisingly, she got her father standing and leaning against her. He was so heavy and completely unconscious.

This must be what people mean when they refer to "dead weight," Essien thought as she tried to walk a step forward, but they both crashed to the ground again. Her father never opened his eyes.

She felt a hot drop hit her face, and at first, she thought it was fire. She screamed, and it pushed her to rise again and get her father's arm slung across one of her shoulders. She didn't know where the strength came from, but it was there. She tried to run, and she could. Her father was heavy, and he weighed her down, his feet dragging behind them, but she could run. It was slow and painful, one slow step at a time, but she was running. She kept feeling those drops now on her hand and her cheek. They were hot drops of water, not fire. She kept running, her father a lifeless sack across her neck. It felt like she wasn't moving at all, like her feet were trapped in blocks of sticky sand that sucked up every step before she made it. She could see the ditch up ahead, and she could feel the water growing warmer and warmer as it poured down upon her. "Keep going," she told herself. "Don't stop." She felt herself getting weaker, and her father's weight getting heavier. She slowed and almost stopped. *Please*, she thought again. *Help me save my father, in the Mothers' name!*

She was wheezing for breath, and each step felt more difficult than the last. By the time she got her father safely into the ditch and halfway up the side of the bank, all of her strength was spent, and she collapsed. She could go no further. Ntoochi was yelping from the top of the road, dripping water as it rolled down her face.

"Emergency vehicle is coming!" she was shouting. Only then did Essien look at her father's face, darkly still, his eyes closed tight, his lips parted and ashen. She touched his neck and felt the artery slowly give out a thump and then another one. She put her ear against his chest. Her face rose and fell with the rhythm of his breath. Her father was unconscious but still breathing. He had not yet passed on to be with the dead. Essien stared up at the storming clouds as water poured down now in a solid sheet, running into her eyes and her mouth.

THE NIGHT WAS PITCH DARK WHEN THEY FINALLY REACHED their village. Essien could see the outline of a group of people waiting at the entrance gates. Her mother's tall stature made her easily stand out. She stood with her arms crossed over a dark red uwe, her hair covered in a silver and white wrap. Ntoochi's mother was standing next to her, short and the same yellow-brown as Ntoochi. Both their faces softened with relief at the same time and in the same way. Hugs were exchanged between them before Essien could open her mouth to say anything.

"What happened, Essien? Why were the fields burning? Where is Nna?"

Essien started to shake her head, and then she was wailing out the words she only just that moment let sink in. "Nna is in hospital, Nne. He almost died in the fields."

Her mother's wail was almost instantaneous, matching Essien's in a grateful sorrow, tempered with caution. Even Essien knew that going to hospital did not always mean salvation. Sometimes, it meant quicker death.

The roads had been cleared of motorbuses, engines, and cars, so they were able to travel to the hospital with quick speed. As they did, Essien's mother held tight to Essien and wiped tears from her eyes with the edge of her headscarf. When they arrived at the hospital, they found her father was lying in a bed with his eyes closed. His skin looked dusty, his hair looked crispy, and his lips were cracked at the corners. There were clear tubes and patches on his bare arms and chest.

The doctor came in, a woman with fuzzy gray hair and yellowed eyes. "The good news, he's alive. He kept breathing even after passing out. The bad news, his lungs were filled with smoke. One second longer in the field, and he might be dead now." Essien's mother held her tighter, one hand gripping her father's arm.

"He will need to rest for months," the doctor told them. "He may never be healthy enough to return to his fields. If you don't have hired help, now would be a proper time to get some."

Essien's mother only nodded and covered her entire face with her head wrap. Mother didn't like to cry in public. She always said it shamed her. Instead, she laid her head against her husband's slowly rising chest and let the tears seep into him.

THAT NIGHT, ESSIEN FELT A DEEP HOLLOW INSIDE HER STOMACH. As she was getting into bed, the feeling welled up inside her, and the weight of the emptiness made her drop to the floor. Her knees cracked against the wood. She dropped her head against the bed and recalled her mother's tears seeping out of her eyes. Essien began to pray a silent prayer to the Mothers, and then she said another one to the God-man who controlled water and had made it rain upon the fields when she asked. The hollowness slowly began to fill, as if a cup tilted under a spigot. Essien began chanting words, and she only half deciphered their meanings. A fountain of words spread cool, clear water over her. She couldn't hear her mother crying anymore. So profuse was her gratitude, for her father's life, for the pure feelings welling up through her, that she vowed in the dark silence of her room that she would do anything asked of her.

"I am Yours to use," she whispered aloud, wiping at the tears streaming down her cheeks.

The Mothers had spared her father, and in return, she would become their most devout believer. No more doubts would come from her about their existence. They were just as real as the Akukoifo she had witnessed with her own two eyes.

CHAPTER TWO

◆

WITH HER FATHER ILL, ESSIEN LEFT SCHOOL TO HELP TEND to things at home. Her mother said it would only be temporary. Essien's father had hired men from the surrounding areas to help plant seeds and bring in his harvest, so there was little concern that the fields would continue to be well taken care of. They were all family men, one of whom had six small children—sextuplets. At the end of each week, the men came to give her father an accounting. They kept meticulous records and counted out the money they were owed with careful precision. Her father paid them generously, despite having taken a loss because of the fires. He was grateful for the help and for the men's company. The men would often stay with them for the evening meal, and they liked to sit with her father on weekends as he sipped his mint tea and breathed his herbs.

While the group of men attended to the fields, Essien concentrated her efforts on the small family plot. Feathery leaves and bright fruit lined up in rows in the small patch of fertile dirt. Essien learned to tell the ripe fruit from the unripe fruit and how to pull or cut green shoots so that they continued to grow. On occasion, her father would attempt to kneel beside her, fondling the leaves, and prodding gently at the fruit. He helped her as much as he could in those days after she left school, but eventually, his breathing would become a struggle, causing him to slow and then stop altogether. He would kneel on the ground, his head down, his hands clenching and unclenching around fistfuls of dirt. Then Essien would help him rise and shuffle slowly into the coolness of their house. She would bring him a cup of cool water and light the dish of licorice root and eucalyptus leaves for him to inhale. After ensuring that her father was comfortable and properly convalescing, she would return to her work, the fragrant smoke following her outside.

Sometimes she stood on the granite walkway and stared down at the dirt, not wanting to go back to weeding. She had taken on the task with perseverance of spirit, but inside, she complained vehemently. Once, she had even expressed an inner rage at her father for collapsing in the crop fires. She had caught herself and apologized to the Mothers profusely. It wasn't her father's fault that he had been injured in the fire. He had been trying to save his crops. Even though the fire cost him over five hundred thousand naira, he was optimistic that the fire-fertilized ground would produce a harvest ten times what he had gathered previously, during the drought years.

On this day, Essien sighed and prepared to kneel again in the weeds of the garden. Suddenly, the iron gates at the back entrance showed a blur of motion outside. She thought at first someone was running back and forth in front of the gate. She walked down the flat granite stones that made a path down to the gate from their back door. Her eyes were tracking that odd spacing of motion as it clipped through the iron bars, a quick streak, then nothing, then another fast streak.

She pushed open the gate, and the joints squealed in a high-pitched shriek. She stopped short and looked back at the compound, its windowed eyes staring blank and empty. A trickle of sweat began to slide down the back of her neck, and she wiped the trail away with dirt-grimed hands. She would not be missed if she stepped away just to see what those streaks were. Her mother rarely came out to check on her anyway, and her father would not move from his spot near the herbs that were burning to provide therapy for his lungs. So she pushed through the partially opened gate, stepped over a few more slabs of granite stuck deep into the red dirt, and ducked beneath the hanging vines of the weeping willow trees lining the street.

She pushed the thin green vines to the side and looked up to see a line of sand-colored engines barreling past in a camouflaging column that stirred up dirt and dust as far as she could see them. She covered her mouth and nose with the collar of her tunic. She stood at the edge of the dirt road and watched them roaring up out of the jungle surrounding the village. A fire pincher bit her ankle, and she squished it between her fingers, then scratched the place that had been bitten. She moved further down the street to get a better view and to avoid more ant bites. At the edge of the road, she could feel the heat of the engines and smell churning rubber.

Beyond the engines, the sun beat down with squinting heat, and Essien put a slanted hand up in an attempt to block the intense rays. She had never seen this many engines driving into their village in the long year and a half that the country had been fighting the war. Essien was unsure if the country was actually fighting a war or negotiating peace for the war. The last year and a half had seemed like a confusing mixture of the two, with engines passing through in trickles and surges and then trickles again. Essien heard village elders discussing the war not far from her in ways her parents never did. She overheard them scoff that rebels who didn't want to be united with Alkebulan were making demands, burning villages and planted fields, and killing people. They said it was rebels who set fire to the crops that had injured her father. As a result, the government was trying to squash the rebels with the rows and rows of engines Essien now saw before her.

Essien didn't understand why the rebels wouldn't want to be united. The country was better now than it had been in her parents' day; she'd heard them say this too many times. People were happier and healthier, and girls could go to school at least. There were countries outside of Alkebulan, countries where girls had to hide their faces and have babies when they were young, countries where men were locked in cages and forced to work for little money. Alkebulan wasn't like that at all. She tried to imagine what might happen if suddenly the states were not united anymore. She would never be able to see the pyramids in Berber and Maasai states. She wouldn't be able to go to the Bush festival down in Khoisan State. She wouldn't be able to visit Bantu State and its lush wildlife preserves or take a trip to Hausa State and get her arms and legs painted in sacred black and red script. If the country wasn't united, she'd have to stay in Igbo State forever. *How boring!*, Essien thought to herself.

Her father used to say that the country had been at war since its beginnings because it was war that had brought it into existence. Whatever that meant, she knew the engines passing could mean the start of another battle or the end of the last one. The engine's tall wheels kicked up more and more dust, turning the air hazy red, and causing the dust to dampen the sun's rays.

There were so many engines already filing into the city that their progress had slowed to a barely moving crawl. As one of the trucks passed, a face wearing a helmet and goggles turned its head to look at her. In that brief instant, she could clearly see the tint of goggles, dark skin, a man's bearded face, the shadowed interior of the truck, and dark gloves gripping the steering wheel. The truck was gone past before she could do more than stare. She put her hand up and waved as an afterthought. The man in the next truck caught her waving and put his gloved hand up to wave back at her. She let her hand drop to her side. The military men in the photos with her great-grandfather were stern and fierce with slim weapons that looked like dangerous points of thin knives. Soja men couldn't possibly be friendly and nice to kids, not when they had to kill people and defend the country against rebels trying to undo progress. The man who had waved tossed something out of the window at her before his truck lumbered on. It landed a few feet away in the road, sparkling golden in the red dirt.

"Essien?" She heard her name being called from behind the wall. It was her mother's voice, an irritating tickle in her ear. She still had weeds to pull, and she had vegetables to clean, peel, and soak, and then she had to study three books her mother had picked for her that day. Essien hadn't been back to school since her father's accident, but that never mattered to her mother at all. She still made Essien read and write essays and recite historical facts. Every day was the same—read, weed, cook the evening meal, read, write, recite, clean, sleep, wake up, and do it again.

Femi never had to weed. He had other chores, and he often went into their father's fields. But those were the chores she would prefer: going into the heart of their farmlands to harvest the vegetables and fruits, then taking a trip to the market to sell what they had picked. Femi could leave the compound alone to visit his friends, but she had to get permission, and then her mother would accompany her and pick her up.

Standing outside idly while there were chores to do wasn't permitted, her mother had told her. Wanting to do what men did was not appropriate, her father had said. Girls do not play with boys, her brother had told her. Girls do not pee standing up, her mother had chided her in the toilet room when she'd tried to pee the way she had seen her brother. Girls do not go to war, her father had told her as they watched the news reports of war recruiters in Igbo State. She had said she wanted to be recruited, too.

Hearing all those thoughts as her mother's voice rang out her name, Essien moved closer to the street. The hanging vines of the willow tree would obscure her from the gate, at least for a little while. She kept facing out at those engines as their fast travel blew gritty wind over her. Essien looked up, a shimmer of blue directly above her head catching her eye. Akukoifo floated around the sky above in a lazy oval, iridescent blue outlines of figures higher up than she could reach.

More and more engines were coming in from the jungle where Essien wasn't allowed to go. If she were in the Soja, she could be on those engines going with them. She looked toward where the engines were going, and the line continued its endless movement into the heart of the village. The line of engines stretched as far as she could see. If she stood there all day and night, it might never end.

"How now, Essien, you still have weeds to pull! What are you doing?"

Her mother loomed over her, taller than her father, but with softer hands and a softer face around the jaw and eyes. Her mother had skin the same dark mahogany as her father's, only her hair was grown out longer and protected in thick, shiny braids pinned back into flat ropes wrapped around her head. Both her parents had the same thin, elegant fingers that could gently caress an obedient child or harshly snatch a defiant one. Essien—curious, willful Essien—more often experienced the harsher grips than the soft touches. She knew her mother would give her at least two chances before she needed to make her point in Essien's skin, but her father, his tolerance for her was endless, up to a point she had yet to reach so far. If it had been her father to catch her standing on the street at the back gate, he would have stood with her and watched until all the engines had disappeared. He would tell her what the engines passing meant. He would have watched the street while she ran out to get that gold medallion.

Essien heard a high, girly shriek. It was Ntoochi with her middle sister Obechi. They stood on top of their stone wall and waved their arms at the passing engines. Their spindly arms and legs moved in wide circles as they hopped up and down. They were both wearing thin house tunics that whipped in the wind. Essien's mother watched them, too, as they pointed their tongues, pulled their faces, shook their hips, and shouted out rhyming chants. Essien was worried they would fall off the wall, just as they had fallen out of her father's mango tree last year. The girls were always this loud. Essien could sometimes hear them yelling at each other from inside her room when she had the window open. Their shouts echoed and made some of the military men honk horns and wave back. The girls laughed loudly once they'd been honked at and clapped for themselves. Through gaps in the engines, they saw Essien standing in the shadows across the street and beckoned her over with fast-waving arms.

"Come now, Essie! Come see! Come here!"

Essien smiled at them and waved back, but she shook her head. Her mother's lips pursed, but she didn't say anything about Essien's friends.

There were too many engines to count as they rolled by, and she hadn't thought to begin counting them when she first saw them. More and more faces turned to look at her or across the street at her friends, but most of them kept their eyes glued forward at the truck in front. She knew the engines had somewhere important as their destination, or they wouldn't all be traveling at once. The urgency had drawn other children and some adults out into the streets along the path. She hoped no one else would see the gold medallion before she could dart out and grab it.

"Where are the engines going?" she asked aloud but didn't expect her mother to answer. Her father was stern but talkative. He loved telling her stories about when he was a young boy growing up in Fulani State with his mother's grandmother. Her mother never shared such stories about her childhood in this very village. She looked soft, but she wasn't gentle at all.

"Sojas are recruiting in all the villages. They have come from the Capital." Her mother let her eyes follow the engines. She looked and then scrunched a deep indent into the bridge of her nose. "The war is over, so the news reports say, and Sojas will get to return home, but still, they recruit our sons. And stirring up dust like this in the day, ehn-ehn! They should have passed in the early morning hours or at night after we have gone to bed." She used the hem of her uwe to fan the air around them and cover her nose.

Like all of the others, this war had begun before anyone realized they were fighting an active enemy. Maybe there was always war, and everyone lost the ability to tell the difference between each of them. Maybe this war was a continuation of the war before it, the one that Essien had learned about in school. The one that popped up in information bubbles on the smart screen that told her the War of Unification was first fought in year 1492 and the Battle for the Capital was finally won in year 1787. That war was long; the information bubble calculated the years, and Essien couldn't imagine anything taking more than a century. Essien had not been born when those wars had been fought, neither had her parents, or grandparents, or any of their parents or grandparents. But here she was, standing on her own street in front of her parents' compound, watching history storm by on tall, rubber wheels.

The capital city, located on Capital Island, was almost three thousand stadia away. It was off the coast of Lagos, with only one bridge connecting it to the mainland. She had never been to the Capital or to Capital Island, but Femi had been once with their father. It was for some reason, which he could not remember, and so he never said. Femi's descriptions of the Capital were plain enough that she always suspected he made the entire story up just to taunt her. Whether the engines were going to the Capital or not, she wanted to follow their stream of rumbling engines and wear those onyx-colored helmets with the dark goggles. She didn't want them all to disappear before she got the chance to . . . to do what? She imagined herself rolling along in that eternal parade, traveling in a procession of hard metal, hawkish eyes, and harsh-sounding engines.

She wanted to be rolling along with them wherever they were going. She wanted to carry a rapid-fire slung across her back and wear a glare across her face. She wanted to be a Soja. She wanted to have stories to tell her brothers that would match theirs in importance. Only, her stories would be real and true. Essien knew it was impossible, and yet still, she wanted it. More than she wanted to start the next levels at school or to visit Khoisan with her father for the Bush Festival this year. When she was five, she'd asked for a younger sister, but this was something she wanted even more than that. To do what everyone said she couldn't do. Essien couldn't state this feeling in words, but she felt it settling down in her belly as she stared at the glistening gold medallion still lying in the dirt, just out of reach.

"Come, Essien. You still need to finish weeding, and then I need your help with the okra. Evening meal won't prepare itself."

Her mother turned her back and began walking toward the compound gate. Essien watched after her for a second, noticing how fast her mother moved with her feet barely kicking up any dust. She wore closed sandals to keep out the skin fleas that she constantly warned Essien would burrow in between her toes and have babies if she did not wear sandals with no holes in them. Her uwe swished around her ankles in deep reds and soft yellows but managed to avoid scraping in the dust. As Essien watched, her mother's perfectly postured form disappeared through the gate.

Essien turned again for a final stare after the last few engines as they barreled away. There was an end to this procession after all. She watched in the direction that the engines had come with a hopeless expectation. Another truck might roll up over the crest, bringing with it a space just for her, with a uniform and helmet to put on over her printed pants and tunic top. A rapid-fire to sling around her shoulders. Or maybe she could carry it in two hands the way she'd seen some of the men doing as they sat inside the engines. She waited longer, staring into the hollow of trees.

"Essien!" the shrill tone of her mother's voice made her startle. She darted out into the street, her sandals kicking up flecks of red dirt. Her fingers dug into the grit, getting more dirt underneath her fingernails, retrieving the medallion into her palm. As she wrapped her fingers tightly around it, she was surprised at how cold it felt against her skin.

Essien turned back toward home, opening her palm briefly to glance down at the object she had snatched from the road. It was shiny and smooth with an image of a raindrop engraved on it. She flipped the medallion over and viewed an engraving of flames on the other side. As she walked briskly down the path toward home—in response to her mother's urgent prodding—she flipped the coin over and over, viewing each side again and again.

Why had the Soja thrown this coin out of the window? Where had he gotten it? It looked like real gold, and it wasn't like any of the paper money she had ever seen used.

Essien put the medallion in the pocket of her tunic and scrambled through the gates into the walled garden. Her mother stood at the door, her hand on her hip and her mouth set in a firm line. Essien had reached the end of her mother's tolerance for the day, she knew. She would not be given any more reminders to obey. Her mother would simply grab the nearest piece of meat she could reach on Essien's body and make Essien squirm for her disobedience. Only, she would never feel she deserved it, and she would rub her arm and keep her back turned to her mother for the rest of the evening. Essien stared down at the dirt patch not even half weeded, the pile of pulled weeds not even a quarter of its usual. She could see the roots of weeds sticking out of the dirt as if they'd crawled back into their former homes while she'd been idling.

"Finish weeding and come to the kitchen," her mother said, her voice a low and dry command. "And hurry. How much time have we wasted watching wheeled engines go by? Sojas will not come and make your father's meals."

Essien kneeled near the basket she had left and began snatching weeds again. Her fingers sank into the dirt, and she felt the grit like jagged spikes under her nails. She thought about the men who had turned to stare at her, especially the one who had waved and thrown the gold coin to her.

Two of her eldest brothers had joined the military after secondary school and served for the required time to appease the Family Service Rule. As a result, none of the three middle brothers had needed to serve. In all the pictures she had seen of her brothers and her great-grandfather in dark uniforms and stiff stances, there were no women. Women were not fighters or warriors. Women couldn't protect anything, least of all themselves. Women were wives, and wives were important. Women were daughters, and daughters were useful in small numbers. Women were cooks and cleaning ladies; those were the women that were allowed in military compounds. But there were no women commanders, no women Sojas, no women officials.

Essien thought again about the rumble of ton engines shaking the ground and the deep black of uniform boots and helmets. She imagined herself leading those men, her engine leading their progression to the Capital, her own rapid-fire shooting before anyone else's in battle. Essien scraped a line of dirt from underneath her nails, drawing a small prick of blood, and then put her hand in her pocket and ran her fingers along the edge of the double-sided gold coin.

CHAPTER THREE

◆

THE SPREAD OF NEWS WAS A SPARKING MATCH SETTING FLAME to tinder throughout the villages, stretching fiery fingers out across the land. The flow of information was impossible to contain from household to household, and from village to village—whether via news reports on screen projectors or the movement of conversations passing across vendor stalls. Yet, the information was rarely consistent or complete, and what was first told was likely to have morphed completely in the retelling. Essien's family had stopped watching the news reports when her father got sick, and they somehow never returned to the practice.

It was a cool morning when Essien and her mother headed out to the markets. Essien's mother moved methodically from vendor to vendor, filling their bags with ingredients for the week's meals. As they shopped at one of the larger vendors, containing numerous rows of displays, they noted bits of conversation as it floated toward them like embers.

Someone behind them remarked, "The President might not see another term after the legislation he has just passed. Lifting the ban on women in the military? After what happened the last time it was tried?"

Her mother laughed and said, "Any woman who attempts to join the military would be very brave. There are many who will not accept this new change."

"But what if she felt obligated to serve her country?" Essien asked, ignoring the reprimand she knew could follow. "What if she made it about serving and giving back?"

Her mother smiled at her, the gentle movement of her mouth making her face seem happier and much less stern. "Women feel duty the same as men, Essien. When your father became ill, you did your duty by staying home to help."

"I don't like gardening, but I like staying home." Essien held the bag open as her mother placed red vine fruit still on the thorny vine inside.

"We know you have missed your friends. Your father and I were thinking that you might want to finish out your final years at formal school. We thought it would help you with getting into some university. Perhaps for medical school?"

"What if I don't get into medical school?"

Her mother paid for the produce in the bag before she responded. She handed Essien the canvas, and Essien slipped it over her right shoulder, her mother carrying two other bags.

"You have always done well in your levels, Essien. There is no reason you wouldn't get in somewhere."

Essien nodded and reached into the pocket of her tunic to rub her fingers over the cool surface of the gold coin. When it wasn't in her pocket, the coin stayed in a small black bag underneath her bed square. The coin was always cool when she caressed it. She had shown it to Ntoochi, who said Essien could probably get several thousand naira for it from the precious metal vendor. But Essien liked the way the coin felt pressed between her fingers. She particularly enjoyed repeatedly rubbing her thumb over the raised surface on each side, as she flipped it.

As they prepared to leave the village center, Essien noticed a group of her agemates across the wide street, standing in front of a technology store, each of them clutching the latest telecommunicators. An elderly man in a yellow hat and blue trouser suit was shaking his hands emphatically, the gnarled brown knuckles standing out against his time-worn fingers. "What will become of our homes?" he shouted. "How will we get our meals? Who will be raising our children? This is a mad thing that has been done!"

An elderly woman in a faded pink uwe nodded solemnly and crossed her arms. "This President has come to bring us ruin. In office for only a few years and look! Who here voted for him? You, sir, you were a staunch supporter this time last year. Do you support this latest plan?"

The man she had pointed to was passing by with a large black portfolio under one arm. The man frowned at the older woman and then removed his cap. "Nobody asked me. I see my daughter's face, and I think of what a mistake I have made. This man should never have been voted President!"

A young man with a young woman behind him stepped up next to the old man and with the woman's hand clutched tightly, he said, "No women from this village should join! Any woman caught joining the military should be stripped of her status and declared outcast."

But a young voice rose up above the rest, and the crowd parted. It was a girl wearing a flouncy black skirt and white knee socks. "That's not fair. What right do we have to say women cannot go to battle when we send women into the fields and the factories every day? Women don't just tend your children and make your meals. They pick your food and melt your metals and sew your fabrics and do just about everything else they aim for."

The old man responded with a lower voice, his tone much calmer. "You didn't see it, young one, but the War of Unification cost us a great many mothers and daughters. We were left with so few women."

"Men died in that war, too. Fathers and husbands never came home. Who is suggesting men should be barred from joining? Why is the military free to recruit men and not women?"

The elder woman leaned in toward the girl from behind. "Many of your young women haven't even given birth yet, girl. How can they deprive their families of the opportunity to grow into the next generation?"

The crowd was starting to shout over the girl.

"There is more to women than giving birth. A death in war is an honorable death."

"We cannot bury more of our daughters and mothers. This village at least will not allow it."

"The views on women in this village are backwards!"

People began to shout the girl down. Older men angry and foaming white froth at the corners of their mouths, older women covering their faces and fanning the air with white squares. Young men steered their women and children away from the gatherings with firm grips. There was Essien, watching the girl walk—nearly run—away from the village center, and wishing she had been the one brave enough to shout those words.

ESSIEN HEARD THE GIRL'S VOICE IN HER HEAD THE NEXT MORN-ing as soon as she opened her eyes. "There is more to women than giving birth."

Essien knew girls her age were eager for marriage and babies, especially Ntoochi. It was sometimes all she wanted to talk about when they met up on the street behind their homes. But children had never been her interest. She secretly thought it was absurd that anyone would want to have children as she had always found them to be annoying and nettlesome. Her eldest brothers had children, some older than her, but she had never spent much time with them. That same morning, her mother reminded her that her father had his check-up at the doctor's, and they would be gone all morning. They left before the sun was up.

Struck with an idea like a lightning bolt ripping through the sky, Essien quickly got dressed and headed out to the nearest motorbus stop. She knew there was a military recruitment center in the village center, but she didn't dare go to that one. The furthest one she'd heard of was on the next to last stop she could reach by motorbus. It was several thousand stadia away from home, taking her all morning to reach, and she hoped no one would recognize her. With the words shouted in that village square still rattling around in her head, Essien boarded the motorbus.

The early morning journey took her over innumerable hills and past extensive green fields comprised of tall, waving stalks. Essien watched with a mixture of excitement and caution and was soon lulled to sleep by the motion and views. She awoke just as the motorbus rolled to a stop on the edge of a village center that she was unfamiliar with. She'd never ridden the bus this far.

She disembarked from the motorbus and found herself standing outside a rusty gray building. As she stood watching the doors of the building swing open and shut with each entrant, she saw groups of young men, loudly cajoling and back-slapping each other. They would wrench open the doors and strut right in. But none of them came back out. She also noticed groups of older men entering the building, grayer, and shuffling slowly inside the same doors, but those didn't come out either.

The day was growing later, and the sun stretched overhead as she tested her courage again and again. In the two hours she had been standing in front of the building, she had seen dozens of men arrive, some in pairs, most in large groups, only a few by themselves. She'd arrived early, before the doors were unlocked, but she hadn't been able to will herself inside. She held the doorknob in her hand, unable to twist it and step through.

What are you afraid of? What is the worst that could happen? she chided herself. She imagined them laughing at her and telling her there was no chance she'd be admitted. She imagined being turned away at the door. There was a lot to be afraid of; this was the easy part. Yet, she continued to stand outside in the blazing press of heat.

Hours passed. The street was empty, and the sun was now high up in the sky. She continued to watch the gray building. A lone female appeared and walked slowly to the doors. Essien realized instantly it was the same girl she had seen defending the ban lift in the village center. She was wearing the same black school skirt, and, this time, she'd added a vest and a white necktie, done up sharply against her throat. She was carrying her school bag over one shoulder, her hair in small braids hanging straight down her back. She approached the door of the gray metal building, and her shoulders moved up and down with her breath. She gripped the door handle and started to twist it. Then she stopped in mid-motion. She dropped her hand from the door, and then her head dropped a second later.

Essien stood up from where she had been squatting and watching, her eyes intent on the girl. *Go inside*, she said inside her mind. *Go inside. What are you waiting for? Go inside, so I can follow you.* The girl grabbed the door handle again. She started to turn it. Just then, a jostling group of teenaged boys rounded the corner behind her. They weren't wearing shirts, and sweat glistened on their muscle-defined stomachs. Without hesitation, they shouldered past the girl, pushing her out of the doorway. All of them disappeared inside, loudly chanting a song about shooting rebels and going home to their women covered in blood. The last boy pointed a finger at the girl and then made his hand into a fist. The girl waited until the boys had all gone inside, and then she took the door handle again, clutching the bottom of her skirt tightly in the other hand.

Essien watched as the girl's shoulders deflated almost as quickly as they had risen. The girl turned away from the door, her head down, her feet kicking up dust. She was going back the way she had come.

"Wait!" Essien heard herself yelling. Then she was running across the street. A horn blared at her as she darted in front of a moving engine. Essien tossed a hand over her shoulder in apology.

The girl stopped walking and watched Essien as she trotted closer with a frown on her face. Her lips were pulled tight together. She eyed Essien up and down, from her dusty sandals to the large braid hanging over her shoulder.

"I saw you yesterday in the village center. I heard what you said."

The girl cocked an eyebrow up as if saying, "So what?"

Essien didn't know what else to say. She had spent the last few hours trying to come up with something to say to herself. Instead, she'd sat mute and immobile. She didn't know why she had to stop the girl from leaving, but she had felt it hammering in her chest as she watched her start to go. She watched the girl struggle visibly with a decision she herself had struggled with for weeks now. She could see the intimidation and the fear on the girl's face; her lips rolled under, and her eyebrows almost met in the center of her indented forehead.

The military isn't for women, she had heard when the decree lifting the ban on female military recruits was first announced. She imagined a picture of the President smiling and regal with his voice in a sound recording: "The strongest people I know are women. A woman can do anything a man can do, only better. It is time Alkebulan stepped into the new century. Women are warriors. Women are fierce. I want Alkebulan to be defended by our fiercest people, and there is no one fiercer than an Alkebulanian woman."

"Women should not be in uniform," her father said when her mother shared the news.

Her mother had glanced at Essien before replying, "Women are more important caring for their homes and their children, not fighting with rapid-fires and steel."

"If girls fight next to men, they will be slaughtered," her brother Femi told her the day after she and her mother had been to the village market.

"Any woman from this village who joins the military will be disowned by us all," she heard a village elder shouting during that week's festival.

"Imagine how smelly it would be," Ntoochi told her as they sat outside eating red fruit. "Imagine having to bathe next to a boy and him seeing your jigglies!"

Nobody around Essien thought it was a good idea for women to join the military. Essien had heard what they had to say. She had heard and listened, but she had not agreed. She could not let everyone's opinions stop her. She had already made up her mind. She remembered the military procession that rolled through her village and the Soja who had thrown the coin from his window. Seeing how vehemently her family and the entire village opposed it meant she'd be going against everyone she loved and respected.

She and the girl eyed each other. Despite all they had heard, they had persisted. Staring into the girl's dark eyes, Essien knew that this moment counted for something.

Thinking of all the obstacles still piled up in their way, all that they would need to endure to enlist, Essien looked deep into the girl's face and said, "I'll go in if you come in, too."

The girl stared back at Essien, her face blank as she tried to decide. Essien didn't know if the girl was to be her salvation or her damnation.

The girl loosened her grip on her school bag. "I'm Ngozi," she said.

Essien introduced herself, and they touched palms.

"Why did you turn away?" Essien asked.

Ngozi shrugged. "I heard my mother's voice calling me home."

Essien nodded. "My mother, father, and brothers have been yelling inside my head all morning."

"I don't know how to open that door," Ngozi admitted, staring down at her shoes.

"You take the knob and turn it."

Ngozi almost let her lips spread into a smile but stopped herself. In one motion, she turned, gripped the handle, and pulled the door open. She walked in, her skirt flouncing. Essien walked in after her.

A small smile started to grow, but she clenched her lips to keep it hidden. She had walked inside, finally, and they were so much closer to signing up. The happiness she felt in that moment took her back to the day the doctor had released her father from hospital. A sweet relief mixed with excitement and a small feeling of fear.

"Ehn, see now? The first two women today? A record!"

Essien saw a low table with three men sitting behind its wide span. They were all village elders wearing the signature gold cap of the holy men.

Behind them, a cavernous room spread out and up. There were men running around an indoor trail, other men lifting heavy stones of different weights, and even more men being examined and weighed by physicians. Essien watched it all, amazed and temporarily stunned.

One of the men with a big, round belly and brown sandals waved one hand at them. "Young ones? Are you here to try out? You have to sign papers and qualify for tests. Are you ready to give away your life to Alkebulan? Hello?"

The other two men behind him chuckled and turned their attention to the men already trying out behind them.

Ngozi and Essien looked at each other. Ngozi shook her head. Essien watched her face with her eyes stretched wide and showing all the whites. She could hear the voices getting louder in her own head. *Girls don't; women shouldn't; you can't!* As Ngozi backed up a step, her skirt flounced and lay still. Essien stepped closer to her, a pleading look on her face. She didn't know how to put it into words, but she needed the girl to stay in order for her to go on. Coming through that rusted door was only the beginning of their battle.

With one hard shake of her head that made her braids swing back and forth over her shoulders, Ngozi turned and started to walk back toward the door they had come through. Essien grabbed at her arm, desperate to keep her. She didn't want to make a scene, but if Ngozi left, how could she stay?

Ngozi easily wrenched free from Essien's grasp, and looked briefly at her. "I cannot, nwaanyi, but I know you can. You don't need me."

The door thwacked closed, and Ngozi was gone. Essien turned back around to see the men near the door staring at her. Some smiled, but they weren't friendly smiles. Most of them scowled.

The man with the round belly held up a pamphlet and shook it at her. "Best to follow your friend out now, young one. Better to end before you start."

Essien put her hand in her pocket. The metal of the gold coin was a cool salve against her fingers. The symbols on both sides gave her something to smooth across. She flipped the coin over and over, rubbing both sides between her thumb and index finger.

"Essien Ezinulo. I'm here to sign up for the Soja."

The man with the round belly said, "Such confidence from one so young. None of the others announced themselves with such flair. They slunk in like guilty cats and sulked out just the same. Remember the one who came with her mother?"

All three men burst into a merry laughter. The man with the pamphlet tipped his head back and chortled to the ceiling. Essien tried not to smile with them, suspecting she was the foot of their joke. She stepped up to the table, picked up the ink pen, scribbled her name in tiny block letters, added her date of birth, and then gave her signature. She had been practicing signing her name in notepads, going over the Es again and again. She breathed out the air she'd been holding in and tossed the pen down. The men weren't laughing anymore, but the man with the pamphlet snatched the paper away as soon as he could and stared at her name written there with his mouth open. He turned his head to look at her and swallowed.

"We must let you in now, young one. You will be off like all the others. None has made it through as yet. I don't see you being the first." He shook the pamphlet toward the rest of the space behind him. "Join the line in back. They'll weigh you and get you a registration tag." His voice sounded like a robot, and he kept staring at her with wide eyes. Like she was a floating apparition, and he was reciting prayers to keep her away.

Essien feared it would get back to her parents at some point. There weren't any faces she recognized in the building, but that didn't mean there was no one who recognized her. Nna wasn't an important man, but he traveled far and wide. Perhaps she had not traveled far enough from their village in coming there. Essien cast her eyes to the ground and headed toward the short line near the back of the large warehouse space, the activity of the men training around her still humming in the air.

Surprisingly, there was a woman behind the canvas curtain at the very back of the gym. The woman looked just as surprised at the sight of Essien. Her eyes quirked up, and her mouth made a small "O" of surprise. She had on a white tunic with a heavy black shawl wrapped around her head, shoulders, and her middle section. She held out her hand and touched palms with Essien.

"Very happy to see you," she said, her voice high and light. The woman was cordial and professional, but the smile on her face was wide and intrigued. Her hands were busy pointing Essien to the scale, to be weighed, and to an X on the ground, to be captured on a picto. Her eyes kept trying to make contact with Essien's. She seemed as though she were holding her mouth closed, her lips pinched tight together. Essien moved where the woman pointed, grateful that at least this part was being conducted by a woman. She knew this might be the only woman she would ever see in the military.

The woman smiled and told her, "Weight is good. Height is shorter than average, but the muscle to fat ratio is perfect. You are within qualifying metrics." When she stopped smiling, her eyes still sparkled.

"Qualifying metrics?" Essien realized that she had no idea what the process of joining the Soja would be like. It made her feel silly for a moment as she thought of her two eldest brothers who had joined the military. She could have asked them if she hadn't been so worried about keeping her audition quiet. She already knew the backlash she would receive from the village elders if and when they found out. She imagined her nna's face, . usually soft and gentle, turned to the rigid stone of her nne's countenance. Essien stared down at her feet and wanted the sign-up process to be over.

"Here is your military registration." The woman handed Essien a small square of black with raised white letters spelling out her name, followed by a series of numbers, and her home village and state. There was her picto in a smaller square at the bottom. She looked like her brother Femi—dark brown skin, shiny black hair, narrow jaw, wide nose, thick pink lips in a perpetual pout. Only her long braid hanging over her shoulder told them apart. On the back of the card, there was the seal of Alkebulan, a raised engraving of an outline of the country like a raised lion's head. Essien smoothed her finger over the surface and clenched its straight sides tight into her palm.

"Wait outside in the line until you are called. You will receive further instructions there." The woman was all business, but Essien could feel her bubbling excitement in the movements of her hands, her words, and her quick steps around the curtained room. She waved Essien back into the larger room. The woman's energy trailed with Essien, so that the large room full of men didn't seem as daunting anymore.

IN THE EZINULO HOUSEHOLD, NO ONE EVER GREW BEYOND THEIR parent's dominion. There were mornings Essien would awaken to find seated at the table a brother whom she hadn't seen for the better part of a year. The two eldest, Idara and Malachum, came home the least. They both had families of their own. Idara lived in the Iroquois Nation, all the way across the Atlantic, a trip Essien had never made. Malachum lived in Mesopotamia, and her father traveled to see him at least once a year. Essien didn't have any memories of the two eldest brothers until she was ten years old when Idara had come home to introduce his children to the family. His wife was a woman from Iroquois, and she looked so different from the women Essien had seen all her life. Idara's wife, Alliquippa, was the color of pale red earth, and her hair was straight and black, falling like a curtain. Essien had asked her question after question, inquiring about all the things she had read in history books and seen on screen projectors. Her eldest brother had encouraged her with a smile that showed all his teeth, set in a face so much like their father's.

The two middle brothers, Manai and Chukwu, had been university students for most of her childhood and only appeared for Equinox and Solstice Festivals, along with the occasional Turning Year Celebrations. They, too, had families now, but both still lived in Igbo State, just a half-day's drive from home. Essien saw these two more often than the eldest as they often came to help their father with his government filings for the farm or to bring some newly discovered electronics. The last time he had come, Chukwu had brought their father a breathing machine that vaporized herbs into a gentle mist that floated throughout the house and made it easier for her father to inhale deeply.

Femi, the brother six years her senior, had been a helpful yet annoying presence throughout her life. He was enrolled in university, working toward a degree in agricultural studies, so he was home more often than any of the other brothers. Her father was proud and made mention of Femi's studies at every evening meal, but her mother wanted another daughter-in-law. There was no chance she'd be getting a son-in-law at any point in the near future, and so she nagged her youngest son because she couldn't yet bother her only daughter.

Even though Essien was in her final year of adolescence, her brothers remained distant older men. At the family gathering for the Turning Year Festival, they all made her feel silly in her unimportance. It wasn't that they didn't love and care for her. They doted on her and babied her with wet, sloppy kisses on her forehead and tight hugs that smothered her. They were just like her father. They had the same face—sharp features cut into onyx, hair the same shiny jet black with tiny curls. They were all tall, but none was the tallest with her mother in the room.

Idara and Manai were loud and boisterous, rarely stopping their mouths from competing to tell stories except to shovel food in. Malachum was mischievous and loved to play tricks on Essien and their mother, like replacing the boiled eggs for the moimoi with raw ones from the neighborhood coop. Chukwu was quiet and gentle, but his eyes were stained yellow, and he drank cup after cup of palm wine, barely touching his food. Femi was like Malachum, a jokester with a big ego who liked to brag. He became even more full of himself when the older brothers were around, trying to prove he was old enough to have their respect.

The wives of her brothers were pretty, each in their own way. Idara and Malachum had both married women from Iroquois. Both women had long black hair and golden red skin. They had brought Essien a cape made of soft gray feathers and a headdress made of iridescent beads. Manai's wife was from San State, and her sandy yellow skin and closely shaved head stood out amongst the other women. Chukwu's wife was from Nipon, a country east of Alkebulan. Her skin was pale white, like sea foam, and she had small, thin fingers that could play any instrument placed in her hands.

Essien had lots of nieces and nephews. In fact, there were too many to fit in her nne and nna's home, so they had to stay at local rooming houses. The oldest niece was four years older than Essien, and the youngest nephew had recently turned one. When they all went out to explore the neighborhood, Essien did not go with them. Instead, she preferred to stay home and talk to her brothers.

"Idara, can you answer a question?"

Her older brother smiled, "What question?"

"What was it like being in the Soja?"

His smile drooped a little. "Thinking of joining, nwanne?"

"Not necessarily," Essien quickly replied. "Did you enjoy being in the military?"

"I did not. Malachum did."

At the sound of his name, Malachum walked over.

"I liked getting to use rapid-fires."

Essien smiled. That was part of what had made her want to join, too. The rapid-fires looked dangerous and lethal. They could be used to protect the innocent or destroy the wicked. If Essien had a rapid-fire, she might use it to hunt the people who had set fire to her father's land. They, or others like them, were still burning land across the country, and the government did not seem to be doing anything to stop it. Essien had made up her mind already. The military registration card was a slick hard fact, but she couldn't say any of her thoughts out loud.

"Why do you want to know what the military was like?" Idara asked. Essien looked at him, and his eyes were serious and direct.

Essien shrugged. "You've never talked about it before. I wanted to know."

Malachum sat down next to her. "The training was hard, one of the hardest things I've ever done. I was injured in my third year of serving, but I made the decision to stay enjoined after my injury healed. I served a total of fifteen years. I wanted to join The Guard, the Uzo Nchedo. Those are the Sojas selected to guard the President, but I did not pass the qualifying metrics. So, I resigned, and now the President pays me to stay at the ready should he ever need my services again."

Essien looked over at Idara. He wasn't smiling at her anymore. He was staring at the ground, a frown formed between his eyebrows.

"I joined because we were duty bound, but I would not have joined otherwise. I served five years, since that was before they wanted you to serve for half of your life. When I got out, I went to the senior academy. There I learned to plan budgets and coordinate projects, and that became my expertise. I didn't have to fight in the field. There were other ways I could use my talents and training. I wish more of the Soja knew that."

Idara sat back and eyed Malachum. "Would you return?" Malachum asked. "If they called you to serve again, would you return?"

Idara was already shaking his head. "The children and my wife need me more than this country does. Alkebulan is running over with agile, untethered youth. It is their turn to serve."

Essien looked back and forth between Idara and Malachum. She wanted so badly to ask them what they thought of the lifted ban. She hesitated, and not only because she might out herself without meaning to. She wouldn't want to learn her brothers' true thoughts if they were somehow against her decision. She eyed their faces. Malachum might give her a positive reaction, but neither of them could be held to secrecy. They would most surely tell their wives, and their wives would tell her parents. Instead, Essien held her tongue with her teeth, deciding that silence was her better option of the moment.

CHAPTER FOUR

◆

A VILLAGE THAT CLOSES ITSELF AT NIGHT BECOMES A SILENT fortress. All are safe inside, gates locked, families tucked away in comfortable beds. The home becomes a stalwart against the outside world and the creatures that might roam. It was said that Akukoifo were most active at night, when humans were safely out of eyesight. The Akukoifo rose up from the waters and drifted down from the trees to slink in and out of unprotected souls. It was believed the Akukoifo could siphon off the energy of anyone who did not protect themselves. The people prayed to the Mothers, and the Mothers offered their protection. Where one prayed, all were protected, and so the protection of the Mothers was an absolute. So, in essence, it is the family bond that holds the village together, and the family is a fortress surrounded by the protective walls of the Mothers.

When her brothers and their wives went away, the house was empty and forlorn. In those times, Essien spent as little time within the compound walls as she could get away with. It was much harder for Essien to go unnoticed when she was the only child at home. The secret she was keeping had turned her into a hard-edged, tight-lipped, sharp-eyed recluse. She was not even spending time with Ntoochi anymore. Essien had returned to school for her final year, and she only needed one final class to complete her secondary studies. After school, she bolted out of the classroom, not waiting for her friends to catch up, changed into running shoes, and ran home. The time and distance seemed much quicker and shorter now. Upon returning home, her first stop was to check the mail to try to intercept anything addressed to her from the Capital. Then, it was off to weeding, harvesting, and preparing the evening meal.

After her chores were completed, she changed into dark clothes and heavy boots, and disappeared out the door. Her nne was too busy caring for her nna to ask her where she was disappearing.

Essien headed swiftly to the village center to catch a motorbus. She had to be careful as she made her way because she had caught Ntoochi following her more than once. The motorbus ride was far enough that everyone she knew would likely get off of the motorbus before her. But, on the outside chance that were not the case, Essien had a plan. If there was anyone she recognized by the time her stop arrived, she would ride past it and get off a few stops further away. Her trek was furtive, and no one could know where she went and what she did. The peace and calm of her life at home depended on it.

This evening the journey had gone quickly and without incident, and Essien soon found herself at the gray building where military recruitments had been held. The warehouse was less crowded at this time of day. The running lanes were empty, and there were scatters of other Sojas lifting stones and practicing plyometrics. A few men glanced her way and began talking amongst themselves. Essien ignored them, as she always did, and used the curtained room near the back of the warehouse to quickly change into her uniform and running shoes.

Essien didn't mind training with the men, most of whom left her alone, and the company helped make the training more tolerable. Essien really hated the running. There was so much running. They would run long distances to increase their endurance. Then they would run to an area where they would lift stones of increasing sizes; Essien learned to lift with her legs and not her back. After that, they would run some sprints. It was exhausting. And yet, for Essien, it was not over.

After training, Essien quickly changed back into her clothes to make the return trip home. She exited the warehouse through the back entrance, just in case she ran into someone she knew. If all went as planned with the motorbus trip, she'd be able to slip in the door of her home, eat dinner by herself, and then hole up in her room for the remainder of the night. Though the days were blurring into each other, and the schedule was arduous, Essien felt like she was floating rather than touching the ground. She was withdrawing from everyone, but the path she was on felt like one she was destined to travel.

It wasn't long before her mother noticed her absence and reticence. She began knocking on Essien's door in the early mornings to hug her and ask if she needed her hair re-braided. Essien would smile and hug her mother tightly, but she never shared anything with her mother. And her father was too busy struggling to breathe to inquire much of Essien.

When she returned home one night, her mother tried to coax her with gifts. "Essien, we invited the seamstress to fit you for gowns. Would you like that?"

Essien had murmured a response that her mother took for agreement. When the seamstress arrived later that week, Essien chose dark fabrics layered on top of darker colors to assemble trousers and ankle-length tunics.

Her nne poked her head in the room as the seamstress was leaving. "Essien, my sister, your nwanne nne, wants us over for an evening meal and social gathering. Your cousins will be leaving soon, so it's a sort of sending off. Your father won't go, but you and I can take the truck and arrive together."

Essien frowned immediately. "Do I have to?"

Her mother made a sound with her mouth, "There will be others your age, including my sister's children. You can make some friends. Ntoochi can't be your only friend forever."

Essien wanted to decline, but she had only disobeyed her parents once. She lived in fear every day that they would find out about her registering for the military service. Her mother looked at her with such delight on her face that Essien found herself nodding.

Her mother's sister lived not far from Essien's home, and although her mother knew how to drive her father's truck, she did so with tight knuckles. When they arrived, Essien entered the red stone compound behind her mother, and she noticed immediately that the front room was full of teenagers, some of whom she recognized from school. A few of them recognized her and called out greetings to her.

"How now, Essien?"

Essien did not return the greetings because she could not recall their names. Her levels were almost complete, and she did not need to attend school daily anymore. When she did go, her mind was barely there. She stuck around long enough to attend her lone class, and then she spent the rest of her days at mgbati training. She did not even know anyone in her levels because she had not taken the time to meet anyone.

Essien hugged her nwanne nne, who was just as tall as her mother but pale. Her skin and hair were completely white, not a freckle or brown mark anywhere. Her eyes were a colorless gray that made her look blind. She was what they called palbinos. Essien's great-grandfather, her mother's grandfather, had been palbino, too. Her twin cousins, Okeke and Nkechi, were next in line for hugs. They had graduated the previous year. They were both short, like Essien, and had a similar deep brown color, with more red than blue undertones. They were both wearing matching dark green uwes with ruffles and pleats. Essien had always protested wearing an uwe because she preferred pants, but she wished suddenly that she at least owned one.

Essien hugged both of her cousins and asked them about their plans since graduating school.

"We're going to Nipon in a few months," Okeke said. She clasped both Essien's hands in her own. The smile on her face was wide and crinkled her eyes almost shut.

"And Hangul this summer. We want to study Eastern fashion," Nkechi said.

"Essien, had you thought of traveling east?" her mother asked. "You might visit the girls and see if you like it. Medicine in the east is far superior to medicine in the west. You might find a doctor to study with."

Essien shook her head and didn't elaborate. Her parents had been insisting she become a doctor ever since she was in sixth level and Essien had asked for a microscope for Winter Solstice. She'd gotten the microscope and used it to observe leaves, strands of her hair, and a prick of her own blood. But she had lost interest in being a doctor before she had discovered the military. The secret she was keeping beat like an echo of her heart as she continued chatting with her aunt and cousins, delivering her responses in staccato fashion.

"School is almost over for me, too. I've learned so much about Alkebulan, the history of it. I don't plan to go to university, but maybe I'll change my mind. The military has universities in Ibadan and Nsukka. My father's lungs are still so weak, but the herbal treatments have been helping some. No, I haven't met my eldest brother's youngest child yet. Yes, I had heard about his oldest son joining the military. Idara was very disappointed, but I'm proud of my nwa nwanne. When you're in Nipon, you have to stop and visit Chukwu and his wife, Myako. They are having twins!"

After enduring the peppering of questions and providing the requisite responses, Essien hung around her aunt as she finished up the final preparations of food. She watched the older woman slice peppers to top the indomie and then pour cups of ice with hibiscus fizz. When her aunt was done, Essien helped carry out platters of sliced fruit and sweet fried dough and place them on the table.

Soon the food was being served, and the questions and chatter mostly stopped. Essien remembered growing up and hearing the saying that during mealtime, "quiet mouths are happy mouths," because the mouths are busied with eating delicious foods rather than talking. And yet, in what would seem a breach of protocol, a girl approached Essien. She was plump all over, with chubby cheeks and chubby thighs. She clapped her chubby hands together and beamed.

"Your hair is beautiful," the girl said. For the occasion, to do something different, Essien had decided to wear her thick, black hair fluffed out into a cloud. Essien smiled, but failed to say thank you. She always felt so awkward in social situations. Sometimes, there were things she wanted to talk about, but she was never sure of their interest to other people her age. Truthfully, she wanted to talk about the President and his new international policy that might open up Alkebulan to more foreign tourists. She wanted to talk about Akukoifo and how she had been trying to make her wishes come true again, but they hadn't yet. She wanted to talk about the secret she had been keeping for several months that no one else knew, which would probably have her exiled from the village if anyone found out.

Instead of talking, Essien quietly sipped her hibiscus fizz. Noting the lack of interest in engaging in conversation, the girl quickly excused herself and withdrew.

After eating, Essien walked around, floating from room to room. There was the large front room with the seating chairs and the plush rug in a creamy yellow. There was the back room with the kitchen and table seating for meals. There was a fenced area in the back of the compound with a lush, green garden. Stairs outdoors led up to the second floor. Essien didn't climb the stairs, but she knew from previous visits that there were four bedrooms situated around an inner courtyard where sun pooled during the day. Essien floated back to the front room where everyone had gathered. There

were at least twenty teenagers in different groupings, some sitting in the
chairs and others hopping from place to place.

Essien sat down near the very back of the front room. She drank
a second fizz, taking a long sip that burned her throat and made her
eyes water.

"I never see you at parties, Number Six." It was Mmeka, her brother
Femi's closest friend. He was wearing a black tunic and loose slacks embroidered all over with shiny gold thread. He took off his matching cap and sat
down on the floor next to her chair.

"I never go to parties," Essien said. She sipped from her drink, taking a
smaller portion of the sugary beverage, and holding it beneath her tongue.

"I'm glad you came to this party, then."

Mmeka had been friends with her brother since before Essien was born.
Mmeka's mother was an nwayi nke nēle ime and had helped to deliver Essien and all of her brothers. Mmeka called Essien Number Six, but in years
past, she had been Sister Brother, Daughter Son, and even Girl Boy.

Essien knew that she would probably get up and walk away soon,
even if he tried to be nice to her. She knew he made fun of her and
called her weird names because he wanted her attention. He'd been
doing it since she was little. He'd started calling her Number Six just
a few years ago. Perhaps he liked her, she reasoned, but she quickly
brushed the thought from her mind. Femi's friends were not allowed
to look at her in any way besides as a little sister. She'd overheard him
threatening his friends with bodily injury when she had begun to grow
mounds on her chest and a rounder backside.

"You look pretty with your hair done like that, Number Six. Like a
queen." He looked her in the eyes for longer than he ever had, and the joking was suddenly gone, replaced with something much darker and foreign
for Essien. She rose quickly from the chair, the edge of its wooden surface
scraping the back of her knee.

"Thanks," she said softly as she walked away, favoring the leg that had
been indented.

Essien entered the back room and saw her mother gathering bags of
prepared meals in glass containers. She wrapped her head scarf around her
neck. She was giving her sister a final hug.

"Nne, leaving so soon?" Essien admitted that she wasn't ready to leave. Nobody had left yet, and she didn't want to be the first. She'd thought for sure her mother would want to stay with her sister until the party ended.

"Nna called me. He is having trouble breathing. He could hardly talk over the phone. I want to get home to him. But stay longer, Essien. You can ride home on the motorbus or walk if you like. Some of the others will be riding with you."

"I can come home now," Essien said. She felt guilty for being out while her father was home alone and suffering.

"No, Essien. Nna wants you to stay, too. He was happy that you came tonight. He wouldn't want to ruin it."

"Stay, Essien," her aunt chimed in. "We will make sure you get home safely."

Essien shrugged and agreed. In the front room, music started. Essien walked in as everyone was fanning out into a circle. She did not join in as they began dancing steps in a coordinated rhythm. The bass got into Essien's spine, but she pressed herself against the back wall. Only her foot tapped out the instruments' time. Her aunt came around with more fizzy drinks. Mmeka came to stand near her.

"Want to dance?" he asked, looking out at the dancing circle.

Essien shook her head. "I don't know the dance they're doing."

"It's easy to learn. Come on." Mmeka grabbed her hand and tried to pull her in toward the circle of dancers. She snatched her hand away so hard it made her drink slosh over the sides of the ice. Essien withdrew to the shadows and comfort of the wall, embarrassed.

Mmeka gave a soft chuckle and joined the circle of dancers. He was a good dancer. He was able to jump right into the group and imitate their movements. Essien swore to herself as she watched him that she would go back to avoiding parties and ignoring boys. The music changed again and again, and the dancers followed its sounds. Essien sipped her drink and watched Mmeka. His forehead began to glisten with a sweaty sheen. Wearing a grin, he looked over at Essien. She felt embarrassed at getting caught staring. She wound her way through the bodies to get out of the room. It was much cooler in the kitchen. She sat at the table with her aunt and listened to her chatter away about her daughters and their upcoming trip to Nipon.

When the music stopped, and it was time to go home, she met Mmeka again. He had put an overcoat in the same gold embroidered black fabric over his tunic. His cap was on, and he looked serious.

"Your auntie asked me to make sure you get home," he said.

Essien looked down the street that she had to walk to reach the motorbus. It was that, or she could continue down the street on foot for half an hour to get back to her home. She looked up at Mmeka's face, but it was hidden from her in darkness. She started to shake her head even though she did want him to walk with her. He moved around in a half circle, so the light from the compound behind them slashed over the top half of his face. His head looked disembodied, floating out of the thick darkness.

"It is my duty to get you home, Number Six. Femi would have my head if I let you get home alone at night."

Essien knew the threat of Femi, her father, and her other brothers would be enough to keep Mmeka in line. She nodded her head slowly. "Agreed."

They made it to the motorbus stop. The darkness around them felt like a bed cover folding them into each other. While they walked, Essien heard herself starting to talk.

Mmeka asked her, "What will you do once your levels are complete? Plan to take over the family business and be a farm boy?"

Essien wanted to reject the remark and push back with something spicy after he had referred to the potential of her being a farm boy. But instead, Essien watched her feet kicking up red dust while she heard herself begin to tell him the secret she had been keeping from everyone.

"I'm training to be a Soja. Instead of coming to parties or hanging out in the streets, I go to the mgbati ahu to lift stones and run on the indoor trail." Essien thought of how much stronger she was becoming. She could run faster and further than ever in her life. She could lift heavier and heavier stones. She still ran with rivers of sweat each time she exerted herself, but she could feel her body getting used to it. Even as she walked, she felt lighter on her toes.

Mmeka laughed out loud, the booming sound echoing back to them from the sky.

"Your parents aren't suspicious?"

Essien shook her head. "Not at all. They trust me. I've never been a problem child. Unlike you and Femi. I only tried to run away once, and I wasn't even successful."

"Running away? No way. Not you. You're an angel."

Essien laughed and rolled her eyes, "When I was nine years old, I threatened to run away, so I wouldn't have to pull weeds anymore. Nne just smiled and told me to go into my room and begin packing. I did it, feeling righteous in my anger, of course. The lock on my door was installed on the outside of my room, and I hadn't even considered that. So, you can guess what my nne did. I spent the rest of that night locked in my room. Never tried to run away again."

Mmeka was bent over laughing. "Aren't they suspicious of where you go?"

She shook her head. "My parents never ask me where I'm going in the evening. They probably assume I've been with Ntoochi."

It was often well after dark when she entered through the back gate of the compound. Her parents were almost always asleep in their rooms, or her father would be sitting up in a chair with his breathing apparatus strapped over his mouth and nose.

Mmeka didn't ask her anything else, so she stopped talking, letting the night sounds push them down the path in their own silent musings. She regretted telling him then.

"Keep your mouth tied about it. If my family finds out, I'll know you told."

"How can you join the Soja without their permission? Isn't that . . . illegal?"

It was Essien's turn to laugh. "Everybody was so busy being upset that women could join the Soja that they didn't even realize so could pre-adults. Pre-adults are sixteen to eighteen years old. That was something else in the President's plan that nobody was paying attention to."

Mmeka looked at her sideways with his head tilted over. "Femi's sister is all grown up? News to me."

Essien rolled her eyes. "I'm serious, Mmeka. Don't let a word of it slip to Femi."

The motorbus ambled up to where they were standing in wait, so they both boarded and found seats near the front. Mmeka sat next to her, but he stayed silent on the ride to her village. He was silent as they walked down the village streets that would lead to her home. She began to speed up, putting distance between the two of them due to her swift pace.

"Thanks for walking me. See you around."

She prepared to dash away, but Mmeka caught up to her and grabbed her arm. She looked back at him, but his face was completely obscured. Before she could see what he was doing, he was kissing her, his mouth finding hers in the darkness, as he held her tightly. She pushed him away, but he followed her, his teeth biting, and his tongue wet. She punched him in the gut and kneed him between his legs. He let go of her with an *oof* and held himself. She ran.

"Wait, Essien! I'm sorry! Don't run off!"

She could hear his feet pounding after her. She pushed herself to run faster. She realized that even if she made it home before he caught her, she would still have to open the gate. She kept running.

Of course, he caught up to her, grabbing her again, rougher this time. Essien whirled around and aimed a punch at his face. He blocked her with his forearm.

"I'm only going to walk you home, Essien. That's it!"

She stopped trying to fight him and stared up at him in disbelief. Mmeka wasn't safe anymore.

"That's all I wanted you to do in the first place," she shouted into his face. She felt like crying but kept blinking fast. "You're a bastard, you know that?"

"I'm sorry," he said. "I just . . . you asked me not to tell him about the military thing, so I figured you wouldn't tell him if I—"

Essien punched him in the jaw, and he wasn't expecting it. The punch landed at the tip of his chin, just hard enough to knock him down. Essien watched him fall and stepped back into a protective stance she had learned. She expected the punch to feel good, but the hit reverberated up her arm, and her knuckles throbbed. She turned to walk away, and he let her go.

Mmeka slunk after her, and she knew he wasn't going to say anything at all. He'd get a worse beating than she would. The thought made her smile. When she entered the back door, the sight of Femi sitting in the gathering room made her frown. He was supposed to be away for at least another week. She glanced back, and Mmeka was walking through the door behind her.

"My brother, Mmeka, good of you to bring Essien home. Have a drink with me."

Mmeka smiled and touched palms with Femi, his eyes wide when they looked at her. Do not tell him, they begged. Essien frowned and turned up her lip at him. *Don't* you *tell* him *either,* her eyes said. Essien disappeared down the hallway into her room.

CHAPTER FIVE

◆

ESSIEN WAS ABLE TO KEEP THE SECRET OF HER MILITARY EN-listment for six whole months. By the time she graduated, she had already made a formal application through the military commander who came to the mgbati ahu to train them. She was wondering to herself how she might tell her parents. Perhaps she might wait until her bags were packed, and she was being shipped off to military academy at the nearest university. There'd be no objection they could make at that point. Instead, it was her father who found out first.

"Essien, what is this?" Her nna held a plain white, almost pale pink, sheet of paper in his hand. There were blocks of writing on one side and the seal of Alkebulan on the other. The letter's package was held in his other hand, ripped open despite Essien's name present on the front in squat, black letters. He stepped further into her room. Essien had been sitting on her floor with a history book spread open and a notepad beside her. She'd been writing down all the military officials of each state. She knew there would be written exams to pass once she was fully enlisted, and she wanted to be certain to pass that part with ease. The plain white walls and the white rug on the floor made her room feel larger than it was, and yet her father appeared to encompass the majority of it, towering to the ceiling from her vantage point.

Despite looking as though he was cut from harsh stone, her father always had warm smiles for her. His smiles would curve his face into something gentler and more patient. His smiles always seemed to swell up from the goodness of his soul. But at this moment, he wasn't smiling as the paper hung in the air between them, pinched tightly between two of his fingers.

Essien sighed. For the past several weeks, she had been trying desperately to intercept the mail. The delivery arrived every day in a dark blue truck with bushels of letters and newspapers that were set out in front of each neighbor's door. Every day so far, Essien had been able to catch the mail the minute it sank into the rusted metal box at the front gate. She had slipped her hand easily into the slot, sieved out any letters addressed to her, and took the remaining inside. She would then drop the mail into her father's lap. He would look down at the mail and then busily go about opening the letters that arrived. He didn't know her reason for delivering the mail to him all of a sudden, and he didn't ask. Some days, his lungs were clear, and he would stand in the garden outside taking deep breaths of clean air. Some days, he hacked and spewed all day long, having to wear the breathing machine for hours. On those days, her mother said it was the dust from the east stirred up into the air that compromised her father's breathing. Essien dropping the mail into his lap every evening was a relief. On the days when he couldn't draw much breath into his lungs, just taking the short walk out to the back garden left him struggling for air.

Unfortunately, Essien hadn't gotten to the mailbox in time on this day. She'd been too busy making a chart of the current military officials after learning that she'd need to memorize them all for her military exams. She'd been consumed with studying the history book and writing the names over and over. She forgot about needing to get to the mail before anyone else did.

Now, here he was waving the letter around. She hadn't wanted anyone in the family to see it until she was ready to tell them. She knew they would open her mail if they saw it. Even letters from her brothers were slit open and read before she could get to them. Any money in them would be extracted and stowed away for her. The only other mail she had received was a wedding invitation from one of her nieces, Adamma, Idara's oldest child. Adamma was four years older than Essien, and she was to be married at the end of the year. Of course, her mother and father had opened both invitations, the one addressed to them and the one addressed directly to Essien. Essien knew her niece had wanted an invite sent especially for her because when Adamma was ten and she was six, Essien had taunted her niece that she would get married first. Essien had not seriously considered marriage since she was twelve. She had expected the wedding invitation to be opened, but just this once, she had been trying to keep something to herself.

"Essien, did you hear me?" She looked up at her nna. He was flapping the letter to catch her attention. "I know you are almost grown in your own eyes, but seventeen is still a young girl in this household. Did you enlist in the military without asking us?"

"Essien got into the military?" Femi's voice reached her before his head ducked around the corner of her door frame.

Essien smiled, the anger she felt at her father washed away by the chance to embrace rivalry.

"What are you doing home?" Essien asked. Femi's face was shiny, his coily hair too, and he was dressed in a red and gray tunic and slacks. He was supposed to be starting his new job in Kano, a city nearby.

"I'm finished at work for the day, and I wanted to check on nna," Femi replied as he peered over their father's shoulder, squinting his dark eyes and making his nose look wrinkled.

"May I read the letter, Nna?" Essien had been waiting to hear back from the military for months now. Her father looked down at her and then huffed out air between his two front teeth, so that it whistled in a shrill tone. He let the paper fall from his hand, and Essien stretched out over the pile of books to reach it before it floated to the ground.

"What does it say?" Femi came to squat down beside her. He was peering over her shoulder now, feigning interest. She let him lean closer, her eyes on the lines and trying to work out what they meant.

"Qualifying scores . . . passing school marks . . . hearing interview . . . military academy . . ."

The paper was snatched with a quick swipe of Femi's hand. "I'll read it," he said.

Essien stood up but didn't try to regain the paper. Besides, she couldn't get the words straight in her mind because she was too excited about what she thought they meant. Had she really been enlisted? Were her eyes telling the truth?

"Well, that's it," Femi said, pressing the letter up to his chest like a blanket. He was smiling, and Essien knew he was about to make a joke. "My sister has beaten me into manhood. I will never live it down once the brothers hear."

"Don't kid, Femi. Is that what it really says?" She tried to reach for the letter, but Femi spun out of her reach.

"Has Nne seen this? Nne, you must see!" And he ran out of her room with her letter in his hands, shouting for their mother.

"What is it, nwanne nwoke?" Essien heard her mother say, and she stepped into the doorway as Femi showed the paper. Her mother looked up, and before she had time to repress herself as mothers are wont to do, before she could resort to her usual firmness, before she had time to disremember her girlhood, her eyes widened, and her lips spread outward just the slightest.

"Essien got into the military, Nne. Look at Nna. He is too stunned to even move."

Essien looked back at her father. He was still standing in her room, both his hands planted at his sides like a statue of stone disdain. She knew he was thinking of how to discipline her and whether he'd really be allowed to keep her from a government-assigned position. Her father wasn't a government man; he had said so himself. He had land that he paid men to work for him, and he loaned out his unused harvesting equipment. He farmed because his father had farmed, and his father before him, and so on as far back as any of them cared to recollect. Even after being injured and losing naira in the field fire, he still farmed.

Femi continued his teasing, "The daughter of Buchi," he pointed at her father, "and Nneka," and he pointed at her mother.

Her father seemed to shake himself out of his trance. He looked at his wife standing in the hallway, and Essien knew in that moment that there was something beyond her that even he feared. Essien walked toward her mother with her hand out.

"Give me the letter, please." Her mother looked up at her with an arched brow. The paper swished, and then Essien was holding it. She took the time to read it again, to be sure. Every word she read the first time was there. She was going to be a Soja. Essien folded the letter without trying to read over it again. She slipped the square into the pocket of her tunic.

"Well?" she asked, turning from her mother to her father. Her father had moved finally to stand at the doorway of her bedroom. He was leaning one shoulder against it, and his face told her his angst. "Will either of you force me to disobey my President's orders?"

She knew they wouldn't, couldn't. Once an individual was conscripted into service, they could not be released, unless given written and

pre-approved permission. Other new laws the President had passed included an increase in the minimum time Sojas must serve, which was the
average life expectancy times one half. The military wanted thirty-five to
fifty years from every enlistee. Essien herself was still just seventeen, so she
would spend the better part of her life serving.

Essien tried to explain, "When I signed up—"

"You did so without our permission! Does your precious Soja know
that?" Her father had found his voice, but it wasn't one he was used to
directing at her. His sweet, beautiful Essien, his only daughter among so
many sons. His sixth born, but not a boy. She knew he would try to be stern
in the face of this disappointment.

"I'm legally an adult, Nna. I did not need your permission."

Her mother's face looked upset; her brows dented into a sharp V that
made her look older.

Her father's outburst echoed through the hallway. "They allowed
women, but we were not expecting them to allow our children, too!"

Essien felt she needed to raise her hand to speak again. "I won't fully
enlist for two years. I'll keep training this summer and attend the military
academy for two years. I'll be able to take my final enlistment tests after
two years of study. I'll be twenty when I finally become a Soja."

Her mother put out a hand and touched Essien's shoulder. "What about
doctoral studies? I thought we agreed—"

Essien shook her head and pulled away from her mother's touch. "We
never agreed."

There had been discussions, which consisted of her parents telling her
how she should spend her academic years after she completed her levels. They
wanted her to practice medicine, and Essien had only silently resisted. Until
her recruitment, Essien wasn't fully sure or convinced of what it was she
should do. Go against everyone and serve the country, or remain here in this
village and become a doctor. That square of folded paper was her certainty.
The golden double-sided coin in her other pocket was her motivation.

Her mother's voice was choked and halting, "You are in the wrong this
time, Essien."

"How am I wrong, Nne?" Her eyes were starting to sting, and her
throat ached. She had hoped her mother would be joyful with her. That

smile, before her father started to talk, had been real, and a moment Essien would never forget. She blinked, and a water droplet fell.

"You went against your family's wishes. You disobeyed what we told you to do."

"You never told me not to join the military."

That was true; they hadn't told her specifically not to follow her dream, but that's what they would be doing if they kept her from serving in the military, shoving that younger Essien into a coffin before her time.

"You did not consult with us before making that decision, Essien. You took your life into your own hands."

She could not argue with her mother; she had been raised to accept her parents' authority without question. She had made a conscious decision not to tell anyone her plans because she knew they would try to stop her. In her mind, she was right to do what she did. No one should get to keep her from that conviction she had inside her. The blood pumping through her had become consumed with a dream she had seen while wide awake.

Essien looked back and forth between the both of them. She saw their resignation in the slump of her father's shoulders, lower now because of the smoke in his lungs. She noticed it in the smoothness between her mother's eyebrows, her face as still as polished obsidian.

"Which of you will force me to disobey the President?"

Essien had never felt so bold. That square of paper had given her confidence like nothing she'd ever experienced. She had been enlisted in the military. She would finally get to join the Soja, wear a rapid-fire slung across her back, and the stiff formality of a black uniform. Neither of her parents said anything, so she retreated back into her room and closed the door to shut them out as they stood watching her on the other side. She didn't have a lock on her door—the working lock was on the outside—or she would have locked everyone out. Essien stared down at her history books in a forgotten pile and put her hand in her pocket to twirl the gold coin between her fingers.

CHAPTER SIX

◆

ESSIEN DREAMT OF A HIDDEN ENTRANCE INTO THE JUNGLE. Femi stood just beyond the line of trees and beckoned to her with both hands. A blue-silver light flashed from his eyes. Essien turned and ran in the other direction, but everywhere she turned there was the entrance to the jungle right in front of her.

She sat up in her bed in the dark, hearing a loud ringing sound that went away as soon as she opened her eyes. The room seemed to glow with a pulsing blue light. Essien looked up at her ceiling and saw an Akukoifo bobbing in a corner. She felt relieved, a soft happiness spreading over her. How long had it been since she'd seen one?

Essien slipped out of bed and pulled on her overtunic and boots, led by some residual force in her dream-like state as she dressed, pulling on her pants with the letter still folded in the pocket. Essien remembered vaguely that she was going to be a Soja. Now she felt there wasn't anything she couldn't accomplish. A trek beyond the thick, tangled tree trunks of the jungle that backed the family compound would be an easy thing compared to what she'd already accomplished. She had already overcome her own fear and the threat of exile from the village. She'd overcome her parents' disapproval. Seeing the jungle entrance in her dream had opened up a challenge in her. One that her remaining fear wouldn't let her ignore. There was nothing else that made Essien afraid except the thought of failing her exams.

She remembered Femi's eyes flashing blue, and shivered. That had scared her even in her sleep, but not the thought of traveling into the jungle in the middle of the night. She looked up at the Akukoifo, casting blue slivers of light around her dark bedroom. Now that the thought was in her mind, she realized that this might be her last chance to explore the unexplored before she was shipped off to military academy. She would probably attend the university in Ibadan as the closest military school, but it was still over five hours away from home. If there was anything else that scared her, Essien wanted to find out before then.

Part of the urge to explore was feeling emboldened by her enlistment. The other part was wanting to see if she was as brave as her dreams wanted her to be. If she couldn't withstand the fear of going against all she had been taught, she wouldn't be able to withstand even one day of what awaited her in the Soja. Everyone had always told them: never go into the jungle. It was a village command; the jungle was off limits to everyone. They'd said the same thing about the military for women, and so Essien was ready to break even this rule, too.

IT WAS EASY GETTING OUT OF THE COMPOUND. NO ONE EXPECTED her to be sneaking around after dark, so there was no one watching to be sure she didn't. Even the lock on the back door remained unlatched. The gate screeched as she pushed it open, and Essien slipped out through the small opening without a glance back. The blue shimmer followed closely behind her.

The moon slid gentle palms over her as she crept along behind compound walls. The jungle butted up against the edge of the village with a road that ran parallel to its border. She came to the entry point that Femi had shown her years ago. The trees seemed to be growing into each other; they were so close together. The space for her to enter was tight, but she could fit. She put one foot in and looked back. Silence, stillness, and the silver moon watching her overhead. That glowing circle in the sky stained the ground, trees, and air like the kiss of a glowing goddess, swirling in low-hanging fog. Essien took in a deep breath and pushed through before she lost her resolve.

She crossed over logs and brushed against shivery, wet leaves and branches. She trusted her retinas to see by the little light sifting down through the tightly packed canopy above. She stumbled once and caught herself in the squishy, swampy ground, taking a moment to scrape off leaves and dirt and a beetle shell onto a supportive tree. She glanced back down the trail, but it seemed like the trees were closing behind her, their limbs hugging each other tightly. A whistling wind made her shiver, and she turned to keep going. As she walked, she began to smell a sweet, powdery scent, almost like the smell of marshmallows drying in the fire pit.

"You come here to die or to live?" said a voice in the wind, which she heard both outside and inside her head. It made her afraid, a scared pulsing against the inside of her chest. The voice sounded like herself, only it was coming from the air whistling by her ears, and from the tree branches swaying near the sky. *Just a few steps in*, she had initially thought. Just to do it and satisfy that dream, which had come from nowhere. *Just a little way into the jungle and then turn back.*

But she didn't turn back, and now it was probably too late because she had already come so far in. She realized as she squished on that she wanted to find the lake in the middle of the jungle. She didn't think it existed, not really, but here she was, trudging on through the silvered darkness. She was trying to find that lake to prove to herself that it existed, and that maybe, just maybe, Akukoifo were real after all. Since her father's near death, she had made more wishes, whispering fervently in the dark, but none had come true. Well, except for being admitted into the Soja, but that was her own doing. She had wished for her father's lungs to be healed, and sometimes, it did seem that he was getting better, but then he'd have a coughing fit and be back to where he started. She had wished to be accelerated into the early graduation program, but the headteacher had rejected her request on the condition that she wanted Essien to finish with her starting class. Essien had wished for Femi to never invite Mmeka over again, but there he had been, smiling sheepishly, almost every other day.

Despite those unfulfilled wishes, tonight she could prove to herself and everyone else that the Akukoifo were real. The trees were getting spaced closer and closer together the further she trekked. She had to step over their bases and find another way around when they were too close for her to squeeze through. She felt them pushing her back, the trunks seeming to squeeze closer together to keep her out. She had to walk in a sideways direction for a long time, and she lost track of how much time. Perhaps an hour had passed, maybe closer to two. She had to wiggle sideways through a stand of trees that was thick and choked no matter where she tried to push through.

On the other side of that thick, a clear mirror of water reflected back the eerie shine of moonlight and the dark lines of thin, closely tethered trees. *This must be the lake!* She couldn't tell if she had walked far enough to reach the middle of the jungle because this was territory she had never been in. She glanced around and could only see thin trees stretching up to the night sky. There was no end or other side to the lake that she could see. Essien shivered and wished that she had brought Femi with her. No one would believe that she had come here without proof. She walked up to the edge of the water, and her boots splashed up little kicks, which disturbed the water in rings, pushing out and out.

A wind blew the sweet smell of marshmallows and rotting wood into her nose and mouth. She waited, though she didn't know what she was waiting for. She wondered what it might look like in the daytime. Would the lake seem to heave and sway toward her like the top of a nectar pudding? As she was staring at the lake, its surface began to rise out of the rolling stillness.

Essien's chest clenched as she watched the silvery figure materialize in the sheen of lake water pooling at its feet, if it had feet. It loomed above her so that she had to crane her neck. She could feel the thump of her blood flow in her ears as she swallowed hard standing there on the edge of the mirrored lake. Essien could now see a man—*was it a man?*—standing in the middle of the lake, clothed in water that dripped off him in rolling droplets.

"You come here to live or to die?"

That voice again, rumbling toward her like thunder over a mountain, only it was coming from the figure now. Her heart slowed; she could feel its pounding stutter before beating once and going still. She breathed around the vacancy in her chest and thought that she should scream. But who would hear her? Nobody but the man at the bottom of the lake.

Essien stared into the face of the being and knew she was afraid by the stillness of her heart, as if her very soul had left her body. But, then again, if she was so afraid, why had she remained there and not run in the opposite direction? Instead, why did she feel her foot stepping closer, almost into the lake, and her hand reaching out to touch that silvery, shimmery spread of lake water wrapped around a solid figure that stared down at her with no eyes? She was afraid, but she knew that it wasn't a real fear—not like getting in trouble with Nne or making Nna upset. This was a fear in the hollow of her chest where her heart wasn't beating, in the back of her throat, which wouldn't let her swallow anymore and felt like a heavy stone rooting her to the spot.

"To live or to die?" the voice repeated, surrounding her and tasting of a gentle bitterness, like the feel of black soap scrubbed against sensitive skin.

"Live or die?" The figure was floating closer, making the rings in the water shift and move in different patterns. In the moon's milky beam, she could see through the figure, like it was made entirely of water through and through. Yet when the night shifted, obscuring the moon's beam, she stretched her fingers out a little further. If she could touch it, then she would know it was real. If she could lay her hand against that impossibility, she would believe in all things as possible.

"To live," she whispered.

Her voice seemed so loud in that silent place of lapping water and a figure made of waves. She stepped onto the water, and it held up beneath her. Each step she took toward the floating figure made splashes beneath her feet, as if she was walking in shallow puddles, but still the water held her up, and still she moved forward.

Surrounded by the cool night wrapped around her, aware of the fear paralyzing her chest, Essien reached out her hand in an attempt to touch the figure's body where its chest would have been. She saw and felt her hand go into, not against, the figure. She felt her hand surrounded by water. It felt hot, so hot, and she tried to snatch her hand back. But the water surrounding her hand wouldn't let her go. And then, suddenly, she found her entire body being sucked down into the water below her, like an irreversible magnet, swift and without sound. She didn't even have time to fill her lungs with air or thrash against the force of the pull. Just as quickly as it began, it was over, and Essien was swallowed into the depths below. The ripples on the surface of the water went still.

CHAPTER SEVEN

◆

ESSIEN AWOKE IN A PUDDLE OF SWEAT, HER SOGGY NIGHTDRESS sticking to her thighs and stomach. She quickly realized that she had sweat through all her bedclothes and would need to flip over her bed square. She rubbed a hand across her forehead, and it came away wet, while she tried to remember what it felt like to touch the man made of silver water. There was no memory where a memory should have been. There was only her hand reaching out to touch him and then waking up in her bed.

Essien put both hands on her head and pressed, trying to will herself to remember. She could almost feel the figure against her palm, hot and quivering. Then nothing. She sighed and threw back the dripping bedclothes.

She opened the window behind her bed. Pale blue light let her know it was still early morning. She stripped the wet covers and tossed them in a pile on the floor. The gray cotton of the bed square had an outline of her body in a dark stain across the length of it. Heaving it by one side, Essien managed to flip it over to the dry side. She quickly dressed in her uniform and grabbed her school bag.

When she approached the front room, she saw her father seated at the table with a scowl on his face. Her mother was seated next to him, a hand resting on his arm. Essien mumbled a greeting and dropped her glance when they looked up at her. She could feel their disappointment clouding the air, and it was difficult for her to breathe normally. Yet, Nne had taught her that breakfast was the most important meal of the day. She knew she must eat to have strength for the day ahead.

As she dished up her morning porridge, Essien replayed her trek into the darkness of night. She kept flashing on seeing the man made of water rising up from the surface of the lake. She desperately wanted to go back into the jungle again to see if what she remembered had been real. Instead, she spooned hot porridge into her mouth and avoided her parents' stares.

She would go again, she decided, before night fell, to get a better view and to know for sure that she had actually seen what she thought she had touched.

"Your Nne and I need to talk," her father was saying, staring down at his hands spread palm down on the table.

"Go to your room, Essien," her mother told her in as gentle a voice as she had ever heard.

Essien frowned, "I have school."

"We will get an excuse."

Essien didn't say anything back but stood from the table and walked quickly down the hall. She needed to pack a small bag with her picto capturer. She would want to document what she had seen, to show others who wouldn't believe her otherwise. If she had proof that Akukoifo were real, and there was a man who lived at the bottom of the lake, in the middle of the jungle, what could they say? She would become an overnight sensation.

Of course, her parents had been calmer that morning than she'd imagined they would be. She knew she could go into the jungle again, and they would never know until she told them. Besides wanting to prove to them and to everyone that she was worthy of her enlistment, something else thumped inside her like an echoing refrain: *You come to live or to die? To live or to die? To live or die? To live? To die?*

She closed the bedroom door on her parents still sitting at the table down the hall. Her mind was already trying to retrace her steps and remember how far she had gone before she'd reached the lake. She hadn't taken a straight path in but had to turn many times to avoid the tight spaces with the tree trunks blocking her way through. It was no matter; she would find it again. Maybe her footprints would still be visible in the wet ground, and she'd be able to see them by the light of day. If it was too dark in the jungle, she could use her light beam.

Behind her, she heard the peculiar, rusty creak of an unused lock turning, and she whirled around. She tried the handle, but the door did not open. She glanced over at the window, but there were window bars on the outside that only her parents could unlock. Essien sat down on her bed and stared at the door. She had forgotten about the lock on the outside of her bedroom door. She did not leave her room that day.

When they let her out the next morning, her mother and father stood side by side in the hallway dressed in fancy agbadas, her father's suit a sand color, and her mother's a light rose.

"We are going to petition the President." Her mother's voice was gentle.

Her father said, "No daughter of ours will be in the military, and that is final. We will have your enlistment reversed." His lips were set in a thin line, and his eyes were red. Her mother silently followed him out of the compound, with a scarf wrapped around her face.

CHAPTER EIGHT

◆

I N THE DAYS THAT FOLLOWED, HER PARENTS ONLY SPOKE TO
her to remind her that they had petitioned the President for an enlistment reversal. Every day, her mother went into the village center to check
for an official reply. Each day, her father checked the mail for a letter in
response. No replies came.

Essien continued going to training, leaving each morning after an intense interrogation from her mother until she was finally allowed to leave
with a bag full of gear tucked over her shoulder. When Essien passed near
the jungle, a chill of shivers went over her, and she hurried by. Essien was
afraid to go back to the lake. Now that she'd had time to sit and stew on
it, the empty space where a memory should have been made her feel more
anxious than eager to explore. She had gone in once, and that was enough,
she decided. She couldn't risk getting caught now.

Weeks passed, and her eighteenth birthday came and went. Every other
member of the family had been given a grand birthday celebration for their
eighteenth birthday, but no one even mentioned planning one for Essien,
not even to observe her maturation rites. There were also university appli-
cations to be completed, but neither of Essien's parents brought it up to her.
She was finished with school, and there was nothing further to be done except wait for her final marks and her certificate of graduation to be released.

It had been a month since Essien had been to the lake, and she still
dreamt of the man made of water. They were dreams she couldn't quite
remember, as if her mind erased them, but she kept the sense of something
having been there just moments before. In one dream, Essien was made of
water, too, and it made everything she looked at glint like diamonds. She'd
woken from that dream with her palms sweating.

Summer was ripening and growing into an exhausting heat when a
summons finally arrived in the mail. Her father sliced the letter open and

read it slowly. Essien watched his face as his eyes moved down the page. What began as a lighthearted hope quickly turned into a sedated gloom. Essien knew the letter was not the news he had hoped for. He turned to her mother and handed the letter off. He steepled his hands and put them over his mouth. He stared at Essien, and the look in them made her stomach feel heavy. She looked down at the table. She did not want to hurt her parents. She wished this did not disappoint them so much.

Her mother let out a short gasp and dropped the letter. Essien stared at the paper, which she couldn't read, knowing that it was good news for her. She picked up the letter and fought an urge to smile. In the end, to stifle the smile, she had to bite down hard on her lip. Military academy was to start in two weeks. She would need to meet the caravan at the village center motorbus depot. Essien wanted to squeal and shout, but the air in the room made her hold herself in restraint. She folded the letter into a square and tucked it into her pocket.

"I'm sorry, Nne. I'm sorry, Nna. I did not mean to upset you this much. I just . . . I just wanted to shoot a rapid-fire . . . and I wanted to help protect this country from the people who wish us harm . . . Like the ones who burned your field, Nna. I hope I am not exiled from your home, but I plan to follow through with my enlistment."

Her father started to say something, but when he opened his mouth, only coughing came out. He waved her away as his chest and shoulders heaved up and down, and he wouldn't look at her. Her mother helped him up from his chair and led him toward the back room where his breathing machine stayed. Essien wanted to follow them but knew talking would only make his breathing worse.

THE WEEKS PASSED SILENTLY, AND IT WAS TIME FOR ESSIEN TO leave. Her mother was gracious enough to help her pack her belongings into a large cargo bag. Femi drove her to the village center. He hugged her tight and didn't make any jokes.

"Travel safely, nwanne. You will always have a place in my home."

He was cordial, but he did not wait with her until the military transport arrived. There were others milling around—all men—but Essien recognized no one. She found an empty bench and waited for the engine to arrive.

This was it.

This was the start.

She wanted to be excited, but her family's disappointment twisted like a knot in her throat and made it hard to swallow or take a deep enough breath.

CHAPTER NINE

◆

EVERY DAY OF THE MILITARY ACADEMY WAS LIKE AN UNREAD book flipped open, bringing a new chapter. When she'd first arrived, she'd been awestruck by the number of buildings so close together. The buildings were white, red, and brown brick, and she eventually grew to know her living hall—the short, squat red building—from the university library—the tall, white stone building—from the hall where her classes were—the long brown building with lots of windows. The campus was beautiful to walk through, with lots of foliage and places to sit for study groups and conversations.

At the military academy, every student was given a uniform. The uniform was comprised of a pair of stiff pants with many pockets, an overcoat with more pockets, and heavy, waterproof boots. In addition to the uniform, she was also issued a stack of textbooks and numerous study manuals. The books and manuals were just as integral to her training as her uniform. New recruits were meant to become scholars of the nation before they could become fighters.

Madam Abiola was house nurse, and she carried the title with great import. She taught second-year classes, and she monitored the dorm floor where Essien was assigned. She wasn't very tall, but her head wraps gave the impression that she was larger than she was. Her voice was very soft, but she had a way of squinting her eyes and pursing her lips that conveyed a subtle strictness. She never let a stain or a wisecrack slide.

Essien roomed with one other girl—Anuli. Their room had loft beds with desks and cabinets placed against all four walls. Anuli was fast and observant, with a quick mouth. She had a piercing in her nose connected to a chain that wound around her neck and disappeared into her tunic. Anuli should have been in her second year, but she became pregnant the first time around and had to return to her village to give birth. The baby had not survived, and rumors followed Anuli about how the infant had perished.

In the first week of the term, Essien tagged along with Anuli as she made her way to their first morning lecture. The classes began with a recitation of the nation's anthem. All who were present stood, while the students sang the tribal song, including chants for each of the tribes of Alkebulan. Then the gathering began to take their seats in order of status, with military academic officials and their military decorations sitting first, and then the military academic administrators, followed by the teachers, house nurses, second-year students, and finally the first-year students.

Essien watched as Anuli slipped out of the row and stepped back once, twice, three times, meeting up with a few other girls at the door to the back entrance. Anuli smirked at Essien still standing in her row, and then the group of them disappeared through the doors. Essien sat down, but she didn't hear a word of the entire lecture because she was thinking about what the girls were up to.

After the lecture, all the military cadets filed out of the auditorium and walked to their assigned study halls. The halls were silent. Essien powered up her personal screen projector and started on three chapters of *A History of Military Conquest*, followed by a series of articles written by the current leader, President Gabriel Ijikota, on Alkebulan's military prowess. Essien devoured the texts with ease. She wanted badly to know all there was to know. In her vast knowing, she might finally learn something more about Akukoifo. She had not seen them at all since the night at the lake, and she felt a pinch in her chest, like missing an old friend.

AS ESSIEN LAY IN HER SINGLE COT IN THEIR SHARED ROOM, SHE wondered if Anuli and her friends would stay in the Soja. It was obvious they did not feel as Essien did. She seemed to be the only one among them who took her studies seriously. It made Essien feel scabbish and judgmental, like she'd spent her early years inside a convent, sequestered from the world. She wondered about the girls' incessant need to disobey. Essien felt embarrassed that she didn't act the same, as though she were a prude. Here were girls whom she should have everything in common with, and they were nothing like her. It made Essien feel sad and wish for home, feeling more and more alien and alone as the days passed. She wanted more than anything to be able to control what happened to her in life. She had been able to save her father's life through Akukoifo and the Mothers, and she wanted that power back again. She thought about the lake and grew still. She remained unable to remember what exactly happened that night—or how she had gotten home—but she knew that something had happened, and it gnawed at her knowing that whatever it was, she might never find out.

Essien had started wearing the gold coin from her pocket in a small black bag hanging around her neck under her top. She'd wanted the coin to be placed on a chain, but she couldn't bear the thought of drilling a hole into it. Instead, she used a small black bag made of velvet cloth that her mother had once stored buttons in. Now, lying in her bed, she took the small black bag from around her neck. She slipped the golden coin out of the bag and let it rest in the middle of her palm. It was cool and heavy in her hand. She smoothed over the raised symbols on each side, water on one side, fire on the other. She twirled it between her fingertips and tossed it back and forth between her hands. She let it spin on its edge. She flipped it into the air and caught it. Heads, fire. She flipped it again. Heads, fire. Every time she flipped the coin, it landed on the flame side.

That night, Essien dreamt of the man at the bottom of the lake. She was in her room, asleep, when she felt water splash against her face, like someone had dumped a bath bucket over her head. She startled awake, expecting to find Anuli and her friends playing a joke on her. The room seemed to glow with blue lights that flickered and danced around the walls and up near the ceiling. An instant smile spread her lips wide when she realized the Akukoifo she had seen as a child was there in her room. She sat up and reached out her hand. The Akukoifo came to her, floating through her palm and winding itself around her arm. The feeling of cool air blew over her as the figure danced in and out of her chest, coming out through her back to float above her head.

"I have missed you," she whispered, not wanting to wake Anuli still sleeping across the room. The Akukoifo bobbed away from her, the light seeming to dim. Essien threw back her bedcovers and set her feet on the floor. "Don't go," she called. The blue light suddenly flashed bright, like staring directly into the sun with eyes wide. Essien turned her face away until the light dimmed. When she looked back, the man made of water was standing in front of her, shrouded in clear, moving liquid that dripped puddles and left wet footprints across the wood floors he crossed to reach her. His voice was like the falling rush of a waterfall.

"Our time is coming, young one. Be patient. Have faith. The water will be with you until the fire comes."

Essien couldn't understand the meaning of the words, and there were no lips on the figure for her to read. She wanted to ask questions, but the sternness of the figure towering over her was a restraint. The puddle at their feet grew until she realized it was up to her knees and continuing to rise. One second the figure was in front of her, and the next, she was inside the figure, the water enveloping her like the arms of a lover. Essien screamed, but the water rushed down her throat and into her lungs.

Blinking awake into sunlight streaming over her, Essien sat up in bed-covers that were soaked through to the bed square beneath her.

ONE NIGHT WHEN SHE AWOKE, JUST A MONTH INTO THE SESSION, Essien found Anuli in her bed, rolled up into her covers, still and quiet. Essien usually tried her best to ignore or minimally acknowledge the times when Anuli would suddenly and unreliably be present in their room. A brief exchange of pleasantries when Anuli entered, or an even briefer forced smile. On this night, she could feel Anuli's eyes on her, but she didn't make eye contact.

"You have beautiful hair," Anuli's voice came out muffled.

"Thank you," Essien replied, as she stroked one of her braids with her hands. Earlier that day, when Anuli had not been present, Essien had used a small bottle of soybean oil to gloss her hair strands and braid her hair into two braids. Essien glanced over at Anuli in her bed but saw only the mounds of her cover and a small sliver that might have been eyes.

"My friends were caught stealing. They are being expelled. I was given a warning."

Essien stopped fussing with her hair and moved closer to see Anuli better. "Did they do something drastic? Beyond the usual?"

Essien had wondered how long they'd be allowed to break rules and show such disregard for their position. They were among the first of Alkebulan's women to reach that much closer to the military, and their behavior was that of scandalous schoolgirls, even though Essien knew that saying this would make her sound like her mother.

"They never wanted to be here. This *was* their something drastic."

"Why did they even come, then?"

"The military is the only free academy in all of Igbo State. When the military opened the academy to women, it became the only chance for many families' children to get a proper education. Most of them hate it; I know you've heard how they are. But what can they do? My family could not afford any other school. I imagine it is the same for many of the other girls here."

Here was Anuli, balled up into her covers, and seeming like a small child afraid of the dark and monsters under the bed.

"I'm sorry. I know they were your friends."

"Weren't they yours?"

Essien shook her head, then said, "Do you want to be here?"

Essien could see Anuli frown as she hesitated to form a response to Essien's question.

"My father is dying, and my mother is already dead. I didn't have anywhere else to go."

"I'm sorry."

Anuli turned over, so that the mound that was her head faced the wall.

"You didn't kill my parents," Anuli mumbled. "Why do people always apologize?"

"It's the thing we say when we feel bad . . . we should come up with better sayings."

"I prefer it when people say, 'Damn you, Death!' That always makes me feel better."

WHEN SHE HAD THE TIME, ESSIEN SPENT SOME MORNINGS WRITing letters to her nna and her nne, even though they had not yet written her back. Time seemed to move faster at the academy than it did anywhere else. The days were a constant stream of classes, exams, assemblies, lectures, and physical conditioning. Essien felt robotic in her plodding along, and the thought of the rapid-fires that awaited her was a constant motivation. Somehow, holding that weapon in her hands felt like the key to avenging her father. The rebels who'd burned the fields had never been captured and were probably out there somewhere still burning fields.

After the evening meal together, Anuli pointed out a boy named Chike as they were passing between academic buildings. He was tall and almost double her size. He had skin the color of dark red sand, and his head was covered in low-cut blond fuzz. He had a point of reddish-brown hair on his chin that he kept winding around his pinky finger. The boy stared at her as she passed, and Essien stared back at him. The boys surrounding him were eyeing her, and one of them shouted out greetings to Essien and Anuli. Chike smiled, and Essien looked away. Anuli playfully hid laughter behind her hand.

"Do you know Chike?" Anuli asked, her nose chain jingling. Essien had no idea who the boy was aside from this first glance. "He's been telling everyone that you're going to be his girlfriend."

Essien frowned and kept walking. "No. I don't know him. I'm focused on getting my final enlistment certified. Chike is nonexistent on my list of concerns."

Anuli rolled her eyes. "Do you know how popular he is? You haven't seen how the other girls are with him. Somebody will snatch him if you don't."

Essien shook her head, "I'm not interested." She remembered Mmeka and shook her head again. She wanted nothing to do with boys after that experience, and she'd never told anyone about it either.

"Shh, shh, he's coming this way," Anuli chattered excitedly. She wandered off, leaving Essien alone.

"Hi Essien," she heard from behind her. Essien turned, and there was Chike. A feeling of pleasant thrill surged through her, despite her protestations to the contrary, although she still took a step back to maintain adequate space between them.

"Sorry, I hope I didn't startle you," he said. He was wearing a plain gray tunic and slacks. He kicked the toe of his boots into the dirt. "We're both first years."

"I know," she said. Essien turned to look for Anuli, but she was already in a conversation with boys Essien did not recognize, probably second years. "How now?"

"Would you like to get some puff-puff? I know a good confectionery here."

"I don't like puff-puff."

"What about a fizzy drink? They sell lots of different sweets."

Essien wanted to decline, but the offer seemed genuine. She could at least turn him down politely. But she had meant what she said to Anuli; she was not interested.

"I'm with my roommate today," she told him, turning and pointing toward Anuli.

Chike's forehead was slowly creasing into a frown. He opened his mouth to say something, but Essien said, "I should get back to her. We'll probably be leaving soon. Nice to meet you." She walked toward where Anuli and the boys were still talking. Essien gripped her hands into fists and hated that she felt so shaky and nervous.

As they walked back to their room, Anuli said, "So, what did Chike say?" She had a wide smile on her face.

"He wanted to take me out for dessert."

Anuli squealed. "Why didn't you go? I would have waited."

Essien shook her head and said, "I don't want to be distracted. We are here to train and prepare for the military. Chike is a nice boy, but I don't see—"

"What a prude. The boy is handsome. Every girl wants him. And he wants you. If you don't act, some other girl will claim him," Anuli tsked.

Essien felt chided but said, "What are we here for if not to focus on our education?"

"You're too young to sound so old, Essien. Lighten up. You might end up marrying and then you won't need to join the military after all."

Essien had to laugh. "That's your dream, Anuli, not mine. I dream of rapid-fires."

CHAPTER TEN

◆

ANULI WAS FAST, AND ESSIEN WANTED TO LEARN HOW TO BE faster. When Anuli went out to run at the end of the week, Essien followed her, unsure of why she felt too bashful to just ask to join her. Anuli exited the dorm building and turned left down the stone pathway bordered with orange and yellow flowers. Essien followed at a distance, keeping a few people between them. The stone pathway curved around a large open field edged with trees where some were playing a game of football.

Essien had hoped the more intense physical trainings would have begun by now. As yet, all she had learned were facts and statistics. She knew how many people currently lived in Alkebulan. She knew how many states there were and how many tribes within each. She knew the names of the major military officials. She knew the ranking of each of the Tribal Council Members, but there were other things she wanted to learn. She had come to learn how to shoot a rapid-fire, and she had yet to even hold one.

Anuli glanced back at her, startling Essien. "Nobody has ever followed me all the way out here," Anuli said casually. Essien walked closer, taking Anuli's glance as an invitation to come nearer. Anuli stopped walking and set her bag down on the ground in the roots of a tree.

"I thought you were coming to run. I want to learn how to run faster. I'm too slow. Everyone always beats me."

Anuli pulled her racing shoes from around her neck where she'd tied them together and dangled them. She used one foot to push off the other loafer as Essien set her own bag down.

"You lift heavier than me."

"That's all I practiced. I thought it would count more that I was strong, but fast is important, too." Essien had come out in her running shoes, so she didn't need to change.

Anuli stretched her arms over her head and then down to touch her toes. Essien copied her. Anuli grabbed one ankle and folded her leg behind her to rest near the top of her thigh. She repeated on the other leg, and so did Essien.

"If I teach you to run faster, then will you spot me when I lift?"

Essien broke out into a grin. She put out her hand. Anuli touched her palm to Essien's and then gripped tightly. "Of course."

A few minutes later they had both finished stretching. Anuli jumped up and down a few times and then set out at a run on the grass and dirt trail. Essien kept up with Anuli's pace until she kicked up her speed a few minutes into their run. Essien lengthened her stride, but still she trailed behind. After a few paces of the faster speed, Anuli slowed down a touch, so that she and Essien ran at the same speed.

"I'll push us faster every few minutes. Try to keep up with me." She wasn't even out of breath.

Essien felt her lungs protesting, aching at the fullest point of each deep breath. She fought for control of her breathing, in and out, and her arms, back and forth, and her legs, out and in, and her toes, down and up. Anuli kicked up her speed, and Essien was right there with her. Now she was on Anuli's heels. A few more rounds of slowing and increasing their speed, and Essien was running alongside Anuli just fine. Her lungs still hurt, but the pounding vibration of her foot every time it hit the ground sent thrills of glee through her. She was running faster than she'd ever run before. And for the first time, she was enjoying it.

THE NEXT MORNING, ANULI SKIPPED MORNING LECTURE AND study hall again. Essien got through her essay exams with barely enough time to finish her second writing. She had been distracted, worrying about Anuli and hoping she was okay. There were only so many exams a student could miss, and Anuli had already been warned.

By the evening meal, Anuli had still not been seen. Madam Abiola came around to their empty room later that night. She stood near Essien's desk and turned her nose up at the other empty bed.

"If it were up to me, there'd be only girls like you. Quiet, studious, do-gooders. We let in the rabble, and girls like you won't join anymore. Keep going your way, young one. The military will be good to you, yet."

ESSIEN WOKE UP TO THE SOUND OF RAIN AGAINST THE ONLY WINdow in the room. She almost jolted out of her skin as she glanced around in the darkness. Anuli was standing next to her bed, a shadowy figure that made Essien remember her dream several nights ago. Essien sat up, afraid.

"Anuli? What's wrong?"

"You were screaming in your sleep. I thought I should wake you."

"Sorry. I don't remember. Probably a bad dream." Essien lay back, and Anuli walked across the room to her bed. "I've been dreaming of—something weird . . . a man made of water . . . He—this lake—and fire . . ."

"I'm leaving tomorrow," Anuli said flatly, cutting her off.

The news hit Essien with a jolt, and she sat up again. "Where did you go today?"

"To visit my nne's grave. I wanted to talk to her."

"Why didn't you get permission? I would have gone with you if we'd gone on the weekend."

"I wanted to be alone. When you asked me to teach you to run faster, I didn't tell you 'no,' or that I prefer to run alone. Here, we're always surrounded by somebody. We never get any privacy. I should never have come."

"Maybe you can plead your case?"

"Abiola already made arrangements. She said my work was subpar, and they have given me the limit of warnings."

Essien felt her eyes begin to sting enough to cry. She felt a pinch in her nose. "I'm sorry, Anuli." She was going to be alone now.

"They're sending me to my aunt's in Iroquois. She has seven kids, plus my brother. I don't want to go there. I won't be able to visit Nne."

Then, Anuli started to cry too, but she rolled over to face the wall and let the tears silently wrack her.

As Essien turned on her side, she noticed wet footprints on the floor that crossed the room to her bed. There were no footprints leading out of the room.

CHAPTER ELEVEN

◆

IT IS KNOWN THAT THE MOTHERS CONTROL BOTH AKUKOIFO and the passing of time. Akukoifo always bow to the Mothers and lay aside their reckless ways in favor of the Mother's divinity. There is no one before the Mothers. It is said that the power of the Mothers is infinite, going back to the time before man, even before Ala-ani was a planet. When the galaxies were still swirling purple ribbons of gas and dust, the Mothers were there, stirring that primordial soup, adding just enough seasonings and sauces to bring creation to life. A power that large would need many containers to fully hold it all. So, the Mothers search and search for those containers with enough durability to hold their fullness. It is often the container who comes searching for the Mothers, and They are glad to fill these seekers up to overflowing. Besides their powerful army of magical beings, they can slow down time to extend a moment into eternity, stretching it out until it is a thin string connecting all of time in a twisting and turning line. Infinity can also pass by in the winking of an eyelash, and seasons flow into each other unmarked and unobserved. Time in the Mothers' hands is a smooth and perfect sea pearl with marbled colors swirling in its depths. One flick of a wrist, and that pearl scatters and rolls in every direction.

The rest of the first year was a blur for Essien without Anuli, and Essien thought about her old roommate every day. Reading her assigned readings, there were thoughts of Anuli taking over her mind, so she often had to re-read again and again. Writing her essays, she wondered how she was doing in Iroquois and felt sad knowing she had no way to contact Anuli across the sea. Eating her meals alone, watching the others talking excitedly together, she felt a loneliness swallowed down with every bite. Her first year ended with a prayer for Anuli and gratitude that she was not her.

The year was over, but Essien did not want to go home. Her nne and nna had not replied to any of her letters, though they had not returned any of the letters she had written either. Essien knew they were still disappointed, but their silence made her feel an even deeper sorrow that she refused to cry over. Femi wrote her back twice and invited her to come and stay with him for the equinox break. She had also received a letter from Ntoochi asking her to travel to Bantu State with her. Essien had options, but she realized that none of them were what she truly wanted. She doubted she'd feel welcome at home or in her village, especially if they found out about her enlistment. It was curious that her parents had so far kept it a secret from everyone, including all her brothers besides Femi. Essien thought about what she wanted, and it finally settled in. She wished she could continue to train on campus to be ready for her second year.

"Madam Abiola?" Essien stood at the doorway of the house nurse's offices. Madam Abiola sat behind her desk writing in a ledger. A cluster of low, green chairs were set in a half circle near the door. The walls were held up with bookshelves, some of the shelves so full that books were stacked on top of books.

"Come in," Abiola said smiling.

Essien walked closer to the desk. Madam Abiola's desk was clean and bare except for the large book she was writing in. Essien stared down at the house nurse's hands where they rested on top of the ledger. Her fingers were thick and solid, with a plain gold band on the left ring finger. "I wanted to know if I might stay on campus over the break. I'd rather not go home."

Abiola frowned. "Something going on at home?"

Essien could feel her eyes starting to sting, but she sniffed and shook her head. "My parents have not been supportive."

"I see." Madam Abiola sat back in her seat. "Essien, you are among the first women to attend this academy with the goal of joining the military. That is a brave feat. What you are doing will change this country forever."

"I wish it could change my parents, too."

Abiola nodded and then stared at the floor as she seemed to think. "We usually close the living halls over the break for cleaning."

Essien felt her stomach deflate hollowly. She would have to go home.

"But I often open my home to one or two students during academic breaks. Would you like to stay with me?"

Essien was already nodding before the woman could finish her sentence. "Thank you. Thank you so much."

Essien wrote a letter home asking after her nna's health and her nne's extended family members, letting them know she had decided to remain at school for the equinox break and would likely see them once she had finished her second year. A letter came back to her written in her mother's light, curving script. Her nne was thankful for the letters keeping them updated, and she had missed Essien over the many breaks and holidays. She did not invite Essien home, but she ended the letter with "Your father sends his blessings."

AT A MORNING MEAL THE FOLLOWING WEEK, MADAM ABIOLA handed Essien a letter in an official envelope with the President's seal affixed. She slid a thin nail under the seal and opened its contents. It was a letter from the Committee of Women's Affairs in the Department of Military Recruitment. She read the letter in a hurry and then again more slowly. She was to have a hearing in a few days at the Capital in response to her parents' complaint against her enlistment. The military had finally gotten around to hearing their request. Her mother had not mentioned their complaint in her letter. The summons went on to tell her that the full Military Council would be present for her hearing, and her parents would not be allowed to attend.

The President's own signature was upon it.

CHAPTER THIRTEEN

◆

WEEKS PASSED, THE SECOND YEAR BEGAN, AND THE MILITARY finally sent a truck for her, a shiny black one that rolled up in front of the residential hall with all the fanfare of a military motorcade. She climbed into its tall frame by herself, and she watched out the window as the academy rolled by in a red and yellow dust cloud. It was a short trip compared to the traveling Essien was used to, not quite three hours. The scenery and the other drivers were her entertainment in the back of the swiftly traveling vehicle.

The Capital was as lively and bustling as Essien had imagined it. There were buildings of brown and gray, slate black, and shiny black, and she felt tamped down by their height and slick surfaces. The streets weren't sun-baked dust as they were at home, but rather a dark shade of gray, some concrete and others smoky quartz stone. At the space of every intersection, vendors gathered and sold items of necessity, which lack of preparation would demand: a meal of fried breads filled with seasoned meat and vegetables, or cubes of red and yellow fruit in wooden bowls, or sticks of cane in a nature-made gourd of young coconut juice. People stopped at the vendors to make their purchase and walked away with greasy packets or wiped dribbled juice from their chins. As she watched it all play out through the back window of the truck, Essien mentally kicked herself for not accepting the offer of porridge from her house nurse. Doing so would have given her a feeling of fullness to last the entire ordeal.

"First time in the Capital?" Her driver glanced at her in his rearview mirror. He had golden eyes that smiled at her. Essien nodded. "Nice place to visit in summer. Much to see and eat. Best to bring a friend. Women don't travel alone."

Her driver's accent sounded foreign, like someone from Aborigine or maybe he was from Tear Drop Falls, the southernmost island. He spoke in clipped tones that chopped off the endings of most words. He kept talking, pointing out buildings and streets, telling her why they were important. Essien just nodded. She was thinking about the hearing. There was no chance that her parents' complaint would be successful, so she wasn't nervous. It was more a type of sadness, like a wound that had healed over but still ached. She had wished her parents would accept her decision. It did not look like they would, especially once Essien pled her case using the laws of the country in her favor.

She watched out the window as the buildings grew shorter with every passing block. The food stalls became more and more sparse until there were none. The same dark concrete stretched on for endless stadia ahead. The truck finally stopped at the side path of a long, low building made of light brown stone. Her door was opened for her. She straightened the lapels of her black uniform jacket, flexed her toes in the tight, black boots, and exited the vehicle. She made herself meet the eyes of the man who walked up the path to receive her. He was short, but felt large in size and presence, wearing a pearl gray suit and white undertunic. She shook his extended hand, which was coarse and dusty, and made herself repeat his name back, "Antonious Nakanri," following with stating her own.

He motioned for her to follow, so she did. Her boots thudded every step she took, while her driver remained with the truck. She walked down a lighter gray side path up to the front door of the building that was taller than it had appeared as they drove past. A cool wash of air brushed over her as she entered, and the scent of jasmine made her smile. Noticing the smile on her face, Antonious replied, "Imported scent oscillator. It cools the air, scents it, and circulates it throughout the building."

Essien didn't respond, but the smile stayed on her face as she followed her guide through long hallways made of polished concrete.

They rounded a corner, and there was a man walking toward them, surrounded by other men in the black uniform of the military. Essien's eyes locked on the man in the middle. He was President Gabriel Ijikota, the President from Igbo State. The men around him were carrying their rapid-fires in both hands, held tight to their chests. They all moved in sync. When one's leg lifted, all of their legs lifted.

President Ijikota's eyes stared straight into hers, holding them like magnetizing glimmers. His suit was shiny in the bright lights of the dark corridor. Essien felt herself slowing down in anticipation of the moment he would stand beside her. She practiced deep breathing as she had been trained, but the scent of jasmine was thick and clogging in her throat. She couldn't look away, not until he had passed her with a snap of air that clung and stretched between them. Essien could sense him walking beyond her, like a wall of climbing flames. She looked back and saw only the tail end of his Guard as the cyclone of energy moved away and faded.

Antonious had walked much further ahead of her, almost turning the next corner. She quickened her pace to catch up. The President in the flesh. Antonious had made so little fuss of their passing that she wasn't quite sure at first if that man had been the President of Alkebulan or not. Essien whipped her head around to look behind her, but there was no one in the endless hallway. She stopped, the delayed shock halting her steps with a discordant stumble of her boots on the concrete floors. She had just walked past the President!

Antonious was at the end of another long hallway, already waiting at the doors there, looking back at her with the patient glance of a grizzled grandfather. The doors she walked through were heavy steel with black handles. Two Guard held them open for her, and she looked up at all the rows of people, men and women, who had come to view her hearing. She had known she would be interrogated, but she had not known they would do it before such a large audience. Why had her family not been allowed to attend, or at the very least, one person permitted to accompany her?

There was a path of dark wood between the rows stacked up high on each side. She entered first with Antonious now trailing her. Her name was on a shiny copper label on the table next to a clear cup of water. She sat down and kept her back rod straight. She had been so busy tracking her eyes up over the rows of people sitting in the stands that she only just now faced forward to meet the table of sinister eyes.

Occupying the central seat of the panel was the man she had seen storming toward her in the hallway. Essien's brow indented deeply as she tried to make sense of how the President might be in two places at once. On both sides of him were more men, all much older and grayer. She did not recognize any of them, but she knew their names upon hearing them. They were members of the Military Council, the men holding the highest positions in the military from each state. Essien thought their faces were all slanted toward instant dislike. Their noses were slightly flared, arms crossed, and most of them looked down at her over the vision correctors each wore.

At first, the proceedings began rather sociably, and Essien felt confident. Antonious asked her the questions from a podium off to the right of the panel.

"Please state your name," his dry voice intoned.

"Essien Ezinulo."

"Place of birth?"

"Delta River Village in Igbo State."

"Mother and father's names?"

"Nneka Ezinulo and Buchi Ezinulo."

It was straightforward and seemed customary. Antonious held his hands at his sides with the palms facing forward. He looked stuck in a habitual motion of casual shrugging.

"Do you support the Unification?"

"Of course."

"What do you think of the rebels?"

"They must be stopped."

"Would you be willing to travel outside of Alkebulan?"

"I've always wanted to visit Nipon and the Iroquois Nation."

"Do you speak any of the regional dialects?"

"Igbo is my first language, but I'm fluent in Yoruba, Swahili, and English. I know conversational Arabic, Amharic, and Hebrew. I have had beginning lessons in Hangul and Nihongo. I was learning some of the Iroquoian languages just before I left school—Onondaga, Susquehanna, Cherokee."

"Have any of your family served in the military?"

"Many. My great-grandfather, and my grandfather, and my two eldest brothers, and my oldest nephew."

"So there was no need for you to serve under family obligation?"

"That's correct. I wanted to serve voluntarily."

"What did you hope to accomplish in joining the military?"

"Stopping the rebels."

"How do you think of the President?"

That question stopped Essien, and she stared into those eyes and couldn't answer. She wondered suddenly how old the President was. Perhaps he was younger than he looked because she didn't think him to be older than forty by his unlined face, and that was young for a President. Yet, she'd seen him when she was a younger girl as he passed through the streets near her home. He felt older in her head, like he'd gathered the weight of many decades of life in his time.

"Respectfully, sir."

There were several snickers from the stands behind her. Antonious cleared his throat but moved on.

By the end of it, eight hours had passed. She was so exhausted her legs and fingers trembled, and she still hadn't eaten anything. They had kept asking their questions, droning on and on, and when she wasn't answering, she'd sat there in a silent trance, her eyes staring into the President's, unable to look away. Then it was over, and Antonious stepped into her line of sight. It was he who escorted her silently back down the concrete hallway to her waiting driver and truck. The driver tried to talk to her, but Essien fell asleep with her mouth hanging open. She dreamed of two chips of black diamonds floating in front of her face and then disappearing down her throat when she opened her mouth to scream.

CHAPTER FOURTEEN

◆

W HEN ESSIEN RETURNED FROM THE CAPITAL THAT NIGHT, a replacement for Anuli had been assigned to her dorm room. The new girl was a transferred second year who was serious about the military, a welcome change from her previous dormmate. Her name was Folashade, and she was from Igbo State too, and short like Essien. Folashade had a softer brown skin tone than Essien and had golden brown hair that was done in thin locks down to her waist. Nurse Abiola introduced Folashade to Essien and tasked her with orienting the new girl to the academy. Essien wanted nothing more than to be alone to think, but she wasn't going to get the chance. Folashade stepped forward and touched palms with Essien. "Folashade Iziduko, but you can call me Shade."

Essien showed her the cabinets where she could store her belongings and then let Shade pick which loft bed she'd prefer. After that, seeing as how it was late, Essien said goodnight and went straight to bed. As she lay on her bed trying to fall asleep, she kept replaying her hearing over and over again. She wondered if she'd said the right words and made the correct impression. She thought about the President, and envisioning his face in her mind sent thrills of girlish pleasure down into her fingertips and toes. She rolled over to face the wall. *I can't bear being forced to leave and return to my family's home when I have only just started*, Essien thought. She could already imagine how happy her nne and nna would be if she were kicked out of the military. How their faces would spread in smiles across their cheeks, how they'd welcome her with warmer hugs than they'd given her before she left. Essien tossed and turned all night with worries about the possible end of her military career.

The next morning, Essien showed Shade around the floor of their dormitory, with its wide-open windows at each end of the hallway, and then took her on a tour of the academic building, lecture rooms, study halls, and the fields where they had physical conditioning.

Shade was excited and lively but kept asking Essien questions that had nothing to do with their training. "People are saying you and Chike are a couple," Shade said, leaning in close with a knowing smirk. "They're all jealous of you."

Essien let a frown form. "Chike is not even my friend. We are not a couple of anything."

Shade said, "He's the finest Soja at the academy. All the other boys are peasants next to him. Or so I've heard."

As they were arriving back to the dorms, they noticed ahead of them, in the middle of the path, a large gathering of students arranged in a dance circle. They were clapping their hands in a choppy rhythm and stomping their boots. Two people were in the center of the circle, gyrating their hips to the makeshift music. The boy was tall, and the girl was very pale. She looked palbino. The pair in the middle turned, and Essien saw that it was Chike with another female Soja whom Essien did not know. She must be new, too. Chike saw Essien at the same time that she saw him. She dropped her eyes to the ground and sped up to go around the large group. They had to pass them to get back to their dorms.

"How now, Essien! Stay and dance with us!"

It was Chike. He had become so boisterous, calling her out publicly. Essien wanted nothing to do with him. Not if it meant him making a fool of her or embarrassing himself in front of everyone. Chike started to step out of the circle, and the girl reached out for his arm. Chike shook her off without glancing back. The girl's irritation was written across her furrowed forehead as she glared at Essien. The girl was a pale white, almost translucent, and her hair was cut low to her head. Bald heads on girls were common in many tribes. She might be from Khoi San or Xhosa States. Essien didn't like seeing the girl's face as her smile dropped and she stared after Chike. Shade poked her in the back, and Essien turned to see her. She was smiling and smoothing her hair between her hands, back and forth.

"He's coming over here." At hearing that, Essien was more annoyed than eager. She didn't need to be in competition over Chike, and she hoped everyone would soon realize it.

Chike trotted over to them. He had a grin on his face, and Essien noticed that he had a double indent in one cheek. His grin was lopsided, with one side not coming all the way up. His eyes were sparkly, and he was breathing heavy.

"Hello, I'm Chike," he stuck his palm out to the new Soja. "You must be new here."

Shade stepped forward and grabbed Chike's hand. "Folashade Iziduko, but you can call me Shade. I transferred from a different university."

Shade was smiling wide, showing all of her teeth. Chike nodded and tried to take his hand back. Shade's smile turned into a grimace as she tightened her grip to hold on to Chike's hand. He politely extracted himself and turned to step close to Essien. He whispered in her ear, "I would love it if you stayed. Send the new girl back to the dorms."

Essien barely heard him because she pulled away from him and turned her back. She did not want anyone to believe the rumors. She and Chike were not a couple. It was obvious he wanted them to be, but Essien was here for a purpose, and she could not get distracted.

Besides wanting to shoot a rapid-fire, Essien longed to find and stop the rebels that were still burning across the country. Not enough was being done, and rumors reached them even at the academy. Rumors of more fields being torched. It incensed Essien, and she thought of her nna. She was suddenly angry at everyone and everything. She brushed past Chike and walked right through the middle of the still-dancing circle.

BACK IN THE DORM, ESSIEN WENT TO BED EARLY WHILE HER NEW roommate talked quietly to other residents in the hallway outside their room.

The next morning, Chike found Essien after morning conditioning. He had his usual grin plastered on his face, and he stood very close to Essien as they filed out for weapons training. Essien noticed that he smelled nice, like amber oil. The smell tickled her nose. She found herself leaning into him to get a better whiff. The pale girl from yesterday kept her eyes on them, and Essien noticed her leaning over to whisper into the ear of the girls standing next to her. Chike chattered on, oblivious.

"Stop following me, Chike," Essien told him when they reached the weapons training room. His smile wilted one side at a time.

"We're partners. Have I done something wrong?" he asked. His forehead indented. He rubbed a hand over his head and tugged on his goatee.

"I don't like the rumors. We both know they're not true."

His smile lit up again. "They are not rumors. You are my girl."

Essien stopped walking. It was her turn to glare. "No, I am not," she seethed between gritted teeth.

"Don't play shy, Essien. I know you like me."

Essien started walking again, feeling eyes turning their way. "Leave me alone, Chike. I want nothing to do with you. There are many others here who would like to be your girl. I am not one of them."

Essien hated how she always had to defend herself against boys. They could like her if they wanted, but that was not her problem. She hated that they always tried to make it her concern.

One of the coaches began to instruct them in retrieving rapid-fires from their sleek metal cases and loading them with handfuls of silver bullets. Chike stayed beside her at the stall next to hers, despite her telling him to go away. He kept trying to talk to her, but she was concentrating completely on her weapon. After her first year spent waiting and hoping, she was finally holding a rapid-fire! She was consumed with nervous excitement, afraid of dropping the weapon or messing it up. When given the instruction to do so, Essien put the weapon to her shoulder, lined her eyes up with the sight, and began firing at her target. The paper exploded with bullet holes all concentrated at the major markers on the paper, the target's head and chest. She was a natural! It was like she had done it before. The fired shots, and the dropping cartridge casings made it loud enough that Chike had to stop talking to her altogether. She wouldn't have heard him over the clatter of spent rounds. *If only I could keep shooting this rapid-fire forever*, Essien thought to herself.

Essien knew she didn't need the problems that boys caused. She had seen girls in her village drop out of school with their bellies beginning to show beneath their tunics. She knew of one girl who had been forced to marry the boy who made her pregnant with a child. The girl had always looked sullen and miserable, waddling back from town with a basket on her head. She had gone to the Capital to give birth, but when she returned, there was no baby with her. Her mother told Essien's mother that they had put the baby up for family transfer. The baby had been given to another family but not one in their village. The girl ended her marriage, moved to Oromo State with her grandparents, and went back to school. At least, that's the version of the story Essien's mother told her. No, Essien knew too well the risks of having a boyfriend at a young age. Just because Chike was handsome and smelled sweet didn't mean she had to return his niceties.

WEAPONS TRAINING WAS HELD EVERY DAY, AND AFTER A FEW weeks, Essien began to excel. She only felt like a Soja when the rapid-fire was in her hands. When she held it, she forgot everything and everyone else except the solid thrumming of rounds projecting out of the weapon, and concentrated on the thought that she could one day bring down the rebels who'd scorched her family's land with her father lying half-dead on it.

Essien looked through her sight viewer and fired. The kickback was less obvious to her now, or else her shoulder had gotten stronger. She hit one target, and it exploded. Another target slipped into the space, and she hit it and each of the next targets in turn. The final target shattered, and Essien let her arm rest, a smile breaking across her face. She happened to glance down the row and saw Chike. He looked forlorn. Even though he still trailed after her like a stray cat and still tried to talk to her as often as possible, Essien ignored him as best she could. It didn't make sense to her why he was preoccupied with her, but she'd done her best to make her point to him and to ignore his attention.

"You're breaking his heart," Shade told her that night when they were back in their room. "His boys asked me to convince you to let him take you out."

Essien scoffed at the remark. "Take me where, eh? We're in the middle of nowhere. Where could he possibly take me?"

"It's not nice to reject him and make him so sad," Shade said.

Essien laughed, but she didn't say anything. Chike's sadness was not her problem.

She was getting ready for bed. She'd already bathed and washed her hair, the coily strands dripping water into her eyes and on the floor. She added shea butter cream that Nurse Abiola sold in clear glass containers and used wooden hair teeth to detangle the fluffy mass. As she and Shade talked, Essien braided the thick strands of her hair into two braids that trailed down her back. Lastly, she slipped the small black bag holding the coin over her neck and put it beneath her sleeping tunic. She put her hand over heart, pressing the bag tighter against her chest. She could just barely feel the edges of the coin through the fabric.

"Maybe you could talk to him. Just hear what he has to say."

"I don't care what he has to say," Essien said, climbing into bed. She curled up under her bedcovers and scrunched her eyes closed. She hated that the situation with Chike had become a topic of conversation with everyone. It wasn't her fault that he was lovesick. He should've chosen one of the other girls who drooled after him. It was his fault for thinking like a sexist. She did not owe him a conversation nor her time.

Essien remembered Mmeka and how he had tried to kiss her, how he'd tried to get her to do something she did not want. She recalled that even after she had made her lack of interest known to him, he'd kept hanging around their family compound, hoping to catch her alone. Essien had avoided him in much the same way she was avoiding Chike. She considered for a moment that perhaps her experience with Mmeka was making her react so strongly against Chike. They were two different people, but in Essien's mind, they were just the same. She wouldn't be the one to go home with her head hung in shame because she'd been caught up with a boy. Essien had one goal: to get into the military and become a Soja. That was why they were all at the academy. Perhaps the others could remember this goal, too. Chike could choke on a chinchin.

CHAPTER FIFTEEN

◆

I T WAS THE FINAL MONTHS OF ESSIEN'S SECOND YEAR, AND SHE was busy training and studying for her qualifying tests. In their final term, second years were freed from attending classes and physical conditioning. Instead, they were to devote their days to preparing for the qualifying tests. The tests consisted of a body exam, an endurance run, hitting a required number of targets in shooting and knife throwing, and a four-hour academic exam on the history of Alkebulan. How well a student prepared was entirely up to them, but if they wanted to pass, they would do well to take it seriously. In Essien's case, she turned into a hermit in preparation.

Surprisingly, she found that she was quite adept at throwing knives. They were small and light, balancing across her palm. Essien soon found she could whip them at targets with a trained flick of her wrist. The sharp end stuck with a *thwack* and winked at her with a glint in the lights. Machetes were heavier and not as balanced, and the longer swords required her to hold them with two hands. She had used knives and machetes in her life, helping her father in the garden and around the house, but swords were new and scary to her, with their dual sharp edges and heavy-weighted hilt. Essien practiced slashing at sand-filled canvas bags with various-sized swords, the biggest almost longer than she was tall. She also learned to use an ax, which was good for both throwing and hacking, but the instructor explained that it also worked well as a secondary weapon. She practiced hacking off the head of a life-like mannequin until she could do it with one blow. Fake head after fake head went rolling until her hands and arms were slick with synthetic blood, and blisters formed on her palms.

Essien still kept to herself, but being from Igbo State gave her and Shade an unspoken bond. Shade was serious about advancing into the military. She asked Essien during one study session how she had learned to aim so well. Essien had subsequently been excited to show Shade how to line up both eyes with the sight on her rapid-fire and confided to Shade that the secret was to never close one eye. She also demonstrated to Shade how to completely exhale just before shooting, so her body was still, and that nothing interfered with the pull of the trigger. The time spent sharing and learning from one another improved their bond, and soon Essien and Shade began starting their days together at sunrise by going for a run. They kept each other fast, pushing against one another's tiredness, and encouraging the other to go a little further and faster. After their run, they went to the weapons lab. They were allowed to check out any weapon they wanted, except rapid-fires. They had to wait until the afternoon training to practice with the rapid-fires. The house nurses did not trust them with weapons alone, so they had to have an instructor present.

"Let's practice sword fighting," Shade tempted her.

Essien laughed, but it turned into a frown. "It's not allowed. We could get in trouble . . . or hurt."

"You always do what you're told?" Shade taunted. She flipped her locks behind her back and grabbed one of the swords. The light hit its edge, showing how sharp it was.

"We could accidentally hack each other to pieces," Essien half laughed. She grabbed one of the swords and hefted its weight in her palm.

"When I was twelve, I watched one of my aunts chop her husband into pieces because she'd caught him with a woman in her bed. He was unfaithful to her a lot, but that was the last boat."

"What did she do to the woman he was unfaithful with?" Essien inquired with shock in her voice.

Shade smirked, "She cut off one of her boobs and chopped it up, so it could never be repaired."

Essien put the sword down. "You look far too happy about that story."

"The swordswoman was my favorite aunt."

Essien hesitated and then turned away. "Let's just practice knife throwing."

THAT AFTERNOON, ESSIEN AND SHADE WERE THE FIRST IN LINE for rapid-fire checkout. They took their rapid-fires back to booths at the very last stall in the row. Targets were already set up for them. Essien was a far better shot, but Shade was seeing improvement as she and Essien met more often to train together. While she could hit the majority of her targets with the first shot, Essien always hit all of hers.

"Don't squint your eyes," Essien told her as she stood beside her and repositioned her firing stance. "Keep your eyes open. It changes your target when you squint." *Thwack*, the target shattered. "Relax your shoulders." She pressed down on Shade's collar bones. Shade cringed but tried to relax her neck and back. "Keep your back straight." Essien pressed Shade's sides to straighten her up. "Widen your stance. It helps with the kickback, so you don't fall over on your backside." *Thwack, thwack, thwack.* With each day of practice and each shot fired downrange, Shade was getting better—with Essien's help.

After rapid-fire shooting, they took their weapons back to the weapons lab. Chike was there with the pale girl. They were checking out weapons even though there was just a half hour left to practice. Chike carried both their weapons slung across one shoulder, leaving his other hand free to hold the girl's hand. She looked at Essien with a bright smile, her lips spread wider than Chike's familiar grin, which he wasn't wearing at that moment. He didn't even glance at Essien, keeping his eyes in front of him.

CHAPTER SIXTEEN

◆

THE FINAL WEEKS OF THE TERM PASSED, AND THE DAY OF THE
qualifying tests soon arrived. On the day they were to begin, Essien
awoke to sharp pains in her palms, like knives shoved between her tendons.
She stretched her fingers out and rubbed each palm in turn. She'd spent
only a few hours practicing the day before, so it was strange to wake up in
pain. She massaged her palms, going back and forth between both hands.
She had been up late the night before practicing throwing knives, but she
had gone to bed at a reasonable time. She didn't remember injuring her
hands during that practice. She felt good about everything except her han-
dling of those small-pointed weapons. At yesterday's practice she missed
most of her targets, no matter how much she practiced. Shade was just as
terrible, so she couldn't help.

Surprisingly, Chike was great with throwing knives. Essien couldn't ask
him for help after the way she had forced him to leave her alone, not when
he was finally ignoring her back. It would be cruel to tell him she needed
him to teach her now. She watched him when he was up at the throwing
line. He stood with one foot slightly in front of the other, his body angled
to one side. He pulled his arm back beyond his shoulder, almost leaning
backwards before whipping his hand forward. The knife flew, and his arm
kept rotating, down and around, his back foot coming up with the force
of his throw. The knife sank precisely into the wooden target, proving his
prowess with throwing the blade.

Essien tried to duplicate Chike's knife-throwing style. She set herself
up in the same way. She closed her eyes and felt the metal between her fingertips like a thin needle set to pierce a piece of cloth. Then she wound up
and threw the knife, following the force of her arm with her whole body.
The knife hit the bottom of the target and bounced off. She kept trying,
each of her throws getting closer and closer to the target's center. She'd felt

confident about her ability to at least pass the knife-throwing part of the test. She didn't even bother to practice with rapid-fires.

Sitting in her bed the morning of the exams, Essien felt hot all over and threw her covers off. She soaked her hands in cool water from the faucet. She splashed her face, and the heat of her hands made her recoil from her own touch. She dumped the coin out of its bag into her hand. Today, the edges seemed to grow soft as she clutched the coin back and forth between her palms. She went to see the house nurse who looked at her hands and told her she was fine.

"But, Auntie, feel." She placed her palms against Nurse Abiola's cheeks. The nurse jumped back and then held her own hands against her face.

"You must have a fever. Here, take some eucalyptus and mint extract. Drink it with coconut water."

Essien watched the house nurse use a grinding stone to pulverize several sprigs of mint and dried tea leaves of eucalyptus. The smell alone made her feel calmer. The green pulp was added to the bottom of a glass and clear, cold water from a fresh coconut was poured over it. A wooden spoon stirred it into a clear green swirl, and Essien took the glass with gratitude. She drank the concoction and felt an icy sting burn down her throat and into her chest. It spread down to her toes and up into the top of her head.

"Thank you," Essien said.

Nurse Abiola took the empty glass back. She looked down at Essien and smiled gently. "Try not to be nervous. You've been preparing for this for two years already. It's time. Trust yourself."

Essien took those words with her out into the sunshine. Her palms were still so hot that she couldn't touch her skin. Morning meal was being served, but Essien couldn't think about eating. Her hands were bothering her like a gnawing toothache that was growing duller and then sharper with every passing second. Essien made her way out to the furthest field on the campus early. She sat on the ground to stretch out the tension in her back and her legs. Her hands were still aching, so she plunged them into the dirt at the base of a tree. It was wet and clung to the lines in her palms. The coolness finally made the pain start to recede, a numbing constant that she could ignore for a while.

When it was her time to run, Essien was so hot that she began to sweat instantly, the sweaty flame in her hands spreading to the rest of her body. Lined up at the starting line with the other cadets in her heat, she could see the short distance they would have to run. It was only about twenty-four stadia, but they were expected to run it as fast as possible. When the whistle sounded, Essien pounded her way through the course trail.

When she was finished, she had only bettered her previous best time by one-thousandth of a second. Essien collapsed in the grass, exhausted and burning up. She closed her eyes right there, resting her eyes and her body, and hoping that her hands would soon cool down.

The tests after that were a blur of checking the clock and trying to beat it. Next, they sat for their exams on paper. Essien was assigned to a room in the academic hall and led inside with a line of other cadets. The clock whirred on the wall, and Essien's hands seemed to smoke with heat. In spite of her efforts and studies, she found herself frequently losing her concentration. Throughout the exam, she often looked down at her palms and wondered if she was dying of an infection that was torching her insides even as she tested, her hands as hot as if they were aflame.

The questions were simple enough, and she felt she knew the answers to most of them. She smoothed her hands over the test booklet and clenched the pen tightly, glancing around the room where there was only silence and the shuffling of paper. She tapped her feet, bouncing one and then the other, trying to breathe around the pain. She finished the final question just as the instructor called time.

They were allowed to change into their ceremonial uniform for the remainder of the tests. It was only the second time she'd worn the white tunic top tucked into white slacks with black boots, shined to the glossiness of tar. Her hair was pulled back into a single braid and rolled into a pinwheel bun. She filed out of her dorm and lined up with the other second years. Essien kept rubbing her palms against the sides of her legs, and they seemed to get hotter the more nervous she felt.

The rapid-fire test was after that. They were led to an open field that had been transformed into an outdoor shooting range. There were tables and targets set up for each student. On Essien's table, there was a box of rapid-fire parts and a box of rounds. The instructor blew a high-toned whistle to signal the start of the exam. As the last note of the whistle faded, Essien dumped her box of parts on the tabletop so she could see each piece clearly, visualizing a mental map in her head of the completed rapid-fire. After quickly making her assessment, she began grabbing the parts to assemble it. It didn't take her long, and the last part soon clicked into place with a satisfying sharp sound. The bullets were next. They weren't allowed a loading tool, and so each round had to be inserted manually, one by one. Essien nicked her finger loading the last round, but her rapid-fire was loaded and ready to shoot. Other shots echoed hers, moments before and after she fired her first round. She shot all the targets, shattering them with a precision she had come to expect. Essien put her weapon down and stepped back from the table. When she looked up the line, Chike was the only other cadet with his weapon not in his arms. He noticed her looking and wasted a smile on her. She looked away.

When everyone had finished their turn up at the shooting stalls, the rapid-fires were switched out for knives, and new targets were posted. Essien heard the whistle signaling to begin, and she lifted the first knife. It was shiny and slim. She had to grip the handle a few times before making her first throw. As she threw the knives, she found they were going everywhere but into the targets. Essien kept trying, using everything she knew about knife-throwing to get at least one of the knives to hit the target. Her manual aim was terrible. Essien threw the last knife and knew it wouldn't be enough. She didn't want to glance at anyone else, but she could see that those nearest her had several knives sunk deep into the targets. Essien was among the first to leave the field, walking fast to avoid being asked how she had performed.

During their break to have an evening meal, Essien sat near Shade. They weren't allowed to speak, and instructors roamed among them to be sure they did not talk. Essien tried to think over her performance so far. The rapid-fire had definitely been her best test. The knife throwing was dismal, but perhaps her skill with the rapid-fire counted for more. She couldn't be sure how she'd done on the written exam. She picked over her meal, not caring that it was the last meal of the day.

The walk back to the dorm hall was excruciating. All the other second years were too exhausted to speak, so there was a silent hush over the crowd.

Essien could feel her blood pounding into her hands and making her fingers throb with heat. When she made it to her room, she soaked them in the faucet again, cupping water and rubbing her hands together under the stream. But doing so only made her hands ache worse, like all the blood was rushing into her fingertips, and it was hotter than the blood anywhere else in her body. All the tension of the day seemed to well like needles piercing deep into her skin. Essien was worried, but she didn't know who else she might seek out for help. *I wish I could talk to my Nne*, Essien thought. *She'd know what to do.* As she got ready for bed, all her thoughts were replaced with the beating of fire like a drum in her palms. She doubted she'd get any sleep.

She dreamt of the lake again. This time, the figure on the lake was already standing there waiting for her. It didn't beckon to her, but Essien knew it wanted her to come closer. She stepped up to the shiny surface of the water. Her feet kicked up waves at the edge, and the water invited her into its cool depths. She ignored the figure floating closer and sloshed her way into the water. As she began to sink down, letting the water come up over her thighs, her waist, her shoulders, and eventually coming to her neck, she felt that her hands were cooled. She swirled her hands around in the water, and they felt normal again. She laughed out loud and then floated onto her back, staring up at the sky. For the first time in a long time, she saw circles of Akukoifo floating above her. She smiled and rotated her head to see all of the sky. There were no flashes of blue, but she could see that some Akukoifo were tinged red, and others were black. When the water sucked her down below the surface, she felt peaceful and welcomed it this time.

CHAPTER SEVENTEEN

◆

T HE NEXT DAY, THE SECOND YEARS WERE CALLED INTO THE grand assembly hall in the administrative building to receive the results of their qualifying exams. Nurse Abiola handed out their results in sealed cream-colored envelopes. Essien's legs started to shake, and she had to sit down. This was it. This was the moment that she had both dreamed of and dreaded. She slowly slid her finger under the flap and felt the paper rip. She closed her eyes and took in a deep breath. Her eyes scanned the lines quickly.

At first, her chest rose into her throat because she had failed knife throwing. Even though she had known she was going to fail that part from the moment the first knife left her hands, it still startled her. She had come here to be a top contender, yet with knives, she was mediocre at best. Then, she saw her scores on the rapid-fire test and the written exam. She had passed those two with very high scores. She was ranked second on rapid-fires and first on the written exam. She wondered who had beaten her with rapid-fires. Probably Chike.

Two out of three tests so far. Did that mean she would be allowed into the military? The officials had said they needed to pass all of their tests. But when had she ever seen a Soja use a knife? Never, now that she thought of it. Maybe the knife throwing was just a formality. Surely, they could teach her how to throw a knife properly once she was enlisted. Essien's hands were heating up again.

Around her, Essien could vaguely hear people celebrating tinged with others moaning of sadness. She kept scanning down her own results and tried to blot out who else might have gotten in or done better than her. She'd passed her running time, but just barely. That was three tests out of four that she'd passed. What did this mean?

At the bottom of the letter, there was a date, time, and location listed, which pertained to the cadet's pending departure and destination—typically associated with their first assignment location. The date and time listed at the bottom of Essien's letter was for tomorrow. That was much sooner than she had thought it would be. The time was scheduled for early morning, which didn't concern Essien, since she had grown used to rising before the sun. The location was familiar to her, and for a second, she was confused by why it was listed as her pending destination. It was a destination she was extremely familiar with, in fact, as she'd been sending unanswered letters there for the last two years.

And then it hit Essien . . . she wasn't being sent to the nearest military base—or even to the furthest—she was being sent back home. There was nothing else on the bottom or the back of the paper.

Essien let her hands fall, the letter dangling between two fingers of her left hand. Her hands gave a deep throb, reminding her that she was in pain. She didn't see or hear anything else around her. Shade tried to grab her attention, but Essien shook her off and raced toward her dorm room.

She wasn't going to be a Soja.

She was being sent home.

PART TWO

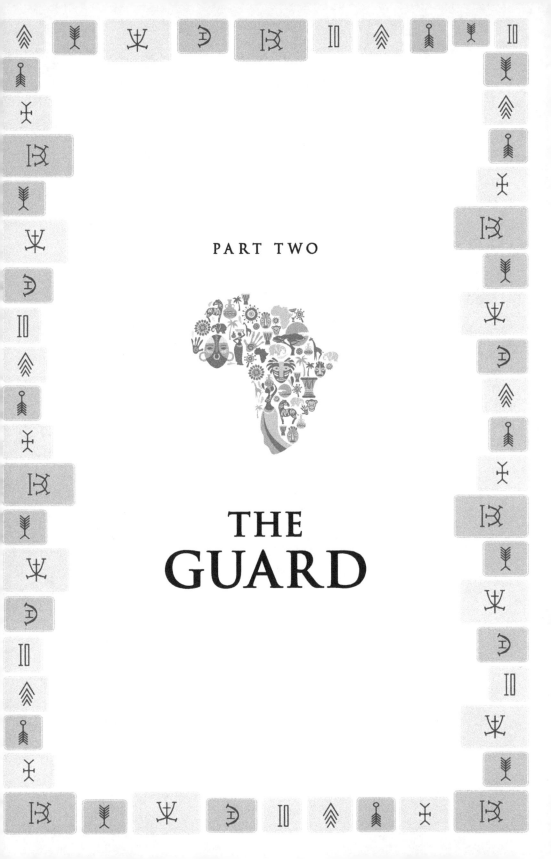

THE
GUARD

CHAPTER EIGHTEEN

◆

I T IS SAID THAT AKUKOIFO ORCHESTRATE THE MOTHERS' WILL, bringing men and women into alignment as easily as chess pieces are placed in their rightful squares. Their magical maneuverings are said to topple nations and win wars. A blessing from the Mothers is enough to set one up for eternal grace. It's also said the Akukoifo follow the Mothers' divine orders, and there is a great gathering of Akukoifo that occurs once in a millennium. The Akukoifo gather to share their tales of magic and to share their power with others in an electrified loop of creation energy. A human touched by such energy would combust or evaporate. The Akukoifo use their power to turn the tides of man or to stem them, depending on the Mothers' guidance. Any power known to man comes from the Mothers, and the Akukoifo are their odibo, their most faithful adherents, serving them in eternal fealty. Any who seek power must seek it first from the Mothers. It is known that any whom the Mothers bless will have what they desire, even if they at first feel doomed and cursed.

For Essien, doom was having to take that engine ride back home to her family's compound. She had been back home for a week, and she kept thinking about the lake as she gathered food from the garden for the evening meal. On this day, Essien's brothers were set to arrive that evening, all flying in on the same route. Her parents would be picking them up and bringing them home with a hired engine. That morning, her father had been cheery and bustling, even smiling and kissing Essien on the cheek. Her mother, on the other hand, had tasked her with preparing the evening meal before the sun had even risen above the horizon. Her mother had left her detailed instructions on how the final stew should be prepared, with guidance not to prepare the pounded yam until they had returned, so it would be fresh.

Essien snapped gungu beans off their vines and dropped them into her basket. She pulled red fruit, seed fruits, and different herbs with a satisfying snap of each. She ate a sprig of mint wrapped around a piece of red seed fruit, the juice bursting on her tongue and rolling down her chin. Essien hated gardening as a young girl, but now, it brought a small slice of peace. It gave her something to do with her hands, which still seemed hotter than anywhere else on her body, even a week after her qualifying exams. She had mentioned the burning, and her nne gasped and let her hands go when she had held them out to her. "Soak them in ice water," she'd said. The ice had only made them hotter, as though her hands were in boiling water, no matter how freezing. It left her fingers stiff and bruised for hours afterward. Thinking of the burning made her hands suddenly spring red while she was putting vegetables in the almost-filled basket. She plunged her hands into the dirt, breaking up clods with her fingers and squeezing piles into balls before sprinkling the dirt into the wind. It was the only time the heat in her palms lessened at all.

She washed the fruit and vegetables and used a large knife to peel, chop, and slice them into different multi-colored piles. The crisp slice of the knife reminded her of the knives she'd thrown, that didn't come anywhere near their target. Sighing, she put the knife down. Essien pulled the lid off the large stewing pot. Steam and the rich aroma of spices bubbled up into her face. She added the vegetables and herbs and stirred the mixture with a long wooden spoon. She covered the pot again, and the mixture bubbled merrily.

Essien heard the front door open, and a booming voice announced, "Number Six, come out! Number Six, One through Five have arrived!"

A reluctant grin widened Essien's mouth. She put down the bowl where she'd been measuring out the yam flour. She wiped her hands on a towel and made her way to the front of the house.

The first brother she saw was Femi. He was the same old Femi, only he looked taller now, and his head was full of frizzy coils that hung almost down to his ears. Next to him, Idara's shoulders seemed to take up all the space in the room. Malachum was a towering statue next to him with a shiny bald head. Manai and Chukwu, the identical twins, had always been hard to tell apart, but now, Manai's hair was cut low and Chukwu had grown his hair out into short locks. She felt almost overwhelmed by their height and their sternness, and the fact that all of their faces looked almost the same, with only the slightest variations between them. A thinner chin on Idara, a wider forehead on Malachum, high cheekbones on Manai, and a set of dimples on Chukwu. Femi was the shortest brother, so Essien had no trouble setting him apart. Her mother and father stepped into the door behind the bunch, and Essien was glad to see something familiar.

Suddenly, she felt shy and didn't know what to say. She gave out hugs to each of them. She tried to give a weak half hug, but one after the other, each of them wrapped her up into a tight embrace that squished her face into their chest muscles or their abs depending on how tall they were. She laughed and frowned and didn't try too hard to make them let her go.

Finally, after hugs had been dispensed, and the brothers had crowded into the now too-small gathering room, Essien stood back while they all stared at her, and she knew what was coming next.

"I see you've given up your dreams of joining the Soja," Femi started. Essien rolled her eyes.

"I didn't give them up," she said. "They sent me home."

"Good for them. No women should join the Soja," Chuwku spoke up.

Essien didn't roll her eyes this time. Femi was only six years older than her, but the other brothers were much older. Essien had grown up showing them a deference that she had never shown Femi. They were like her father in Essien's eyes.

"There were twenty-nine other women admitted into the Soja," Essien said. There had been a news article about the new enlistees. The enlistees included Shade. Some women had made it past the training, but Essien wouldn't be among them.

"We wouldn't be able to live with ourselves if our baby sister had been admitted into the Soja," Malachum said. "We would have gone into mourning. Imagine my baby daughter fighting to protect me. Chineka, I would not have it."

Essien squinted her eyes and squeezed her lips together. Seeing the look on her face, Idara spoke up, his voice gravely husk. "In Iroquois, women have been fighting in wars for centuries. In many cases, the women lead the battles with the men following their leads and taking their orders. It is a normal thing in the Nation."

Essien started to smile at her eldest brother but kept her face stony and silent.

"See now, it is not just Iroquois," Manai joined in. "Women in Palestine and Catalan have been fighting alongside their men since at least the 900s. It is only here in Alkebulan where we attempt to hold on to backwards belief systems."

Femi tried to make a joke. "Essien is one hundred percent a progressive. I thought for sure they would admit her as their Soja."

Her mother smiled and said, "She has been dragging around here like the dead. I almost wish she had been admitted. It would have spared us having to see her so depressed."

Her father spoke up, "Better depressed and safe than dead and gone from us forever."

Essien turned her head. She had hoped her parents wouldn't notice her decline in demeanor. The thought of an endless chain of evening meals put a salty taste on her tongue. She couldn't see herself doing what her mother had done: finding a husband and rearing a half dozen sons. It would drive her into misery. She was already miserable.

ESSIEN DISHED UP THE STEW INTO LARGE BOWLS. SINCE THEY had returned sooner than they had thought they would, her mother had helped Essien prepare the pounded yam. It came out of the large fufu pot steaming and smelling of fresh dough. Essien carried bowls of stew to set in front of her father and brothers. Her mother brought out the fufu platter with balls of rolled yam and served each of the brothers a ball. Essien went back into the cooking room several times for bowls of water. She placed the bowls beside each of her brothers. In unison, they all rolled back their sleeves and cleaned their hands by dipping them and scrubbing them in the bowls. After cleansing his hands, her father dipped his damp fingers into his yam, pulling a piece of the warm dough and forming it into a ball between his fingers. Her brothers followed his lead, pulling their pieces of yam and rolling them to cool them down. Essien watched her father dip the yam into the bowl containing stew, gathering pieces of meat and vegetables onto the dough before sliding it into his mouth.

"Delicious," he said, smacking his lips. "Nice and spicy."

"Good job, Essien," Femi said, and the smile on his face let her know he was going to make another joke. "You're in the right place, nwatakiri. You make a mean stew."

Essien didn't feel hungry. She stared at the white mound of yam, steam wafting off its roundness. The oil slick over her stew spread and then congealed in one spot. But nobody noticed that she wasn't eating as they cleared their bowls of stew and the mounds of yam disappeared.

SLEEP WAS IMPOSSIBLE FOR ESSIEN AS SHE LAY IN BED LISTENING to her brothers loudly joking and chatting in the other room. When she got up to use the private room, she could see that her parents were still up, participating in the fray with her brothers, and happier than she'd seen them in years. She couldn't blame them. All six of their offspring were under one roof. They probably felt such peace and joy that they rarely experienced.

Essien tossed and turned. Her hands seemed to blaze to life. She held them up in front of her and tried to understand why nothing else hurt except the palms of her hands. She couldn't touch them, and pressing them against her bedcovers did nothing to relieve the sting. She took the gold coin out of its bag and smoothed her fingers over both sides. The coin was still cold to the touch, but the heat of her hands overrode its cool comfort.

As if by an intrusion of memory, Essien remembered the lake in the middle of the jungle. She had dreamt of dipping her hands into the water and immediately feeling relief. Perhaps those silver-blue waters could calm the sting. There was only one way to find out for sure. She was desperate for any relief, even if it came through putting herself in danger by going back into the jungle. Essien threw back her bedcovers and began pulling on warm clothes, slipping the coin into the pocket of her pants. She grabbed a light beam.

Outside her room, her parents were now loudly singing the Igbo tribal anthem with her brothers banging on pots and tabletops in time. Essien peeked her head around the doorjamb into the front room. Her mother had her hands raised, her eyes were closed, and she was singing the words up to the ceiling as a vein pulsed in her neck. Her father was sitting in his chair with his eyes closed and his head nodding in time to the beat. Her brothers were all in various throes of ecstasy as they belted out the words as loudly as they could. It sounded terrible and lovely.

Essien crept around to the back room using a side hallway that led between her parents' room and the back of the house. She got to the back door and waited for the shouting in the front to reach a fever pitch. The pots were banging so loud, she could feel it echoing in her chest. She eased the back door open and slipped outside. She ran down the path, and the back gate squealed open. She slipped between the space, and the gate squealed closed. She didn't wait around to see if anyone heard her.

On light feet, Essien ran down the dirt lane behind the family's compound. It was so dark that she clicked on the light beam to guide her. She passed rows of other compounds and soon the lane ended, and grass began. When she got to the edge of the jungle where the trees pushed up against each other in a line, the opening was smaller than she remembered, but it had been a few years. She had to crouch down and wiggle in sideways to fit. The jungle was deathly silent. She heard water droplets falling and the wind playing in the leaves above her in the canopy. She picked her way through soggy undergrowth and around densely packed trees. She could not remember whether this was the way she had taken originally, but it seemed to lead in the same direction.

As she made her way through the lush vegetation, she thought of how hopeful she had been to join the military. She had been so sure of her enlistment. She'd taken her studies seriously, and she'd been serious about everything she learned. Essien found herself reminiscing but not emotional about it all. She hadn't intended to come into the jungle to cry, and since being home, her emotions had been as dry as the Nahla River during the drought that always hit Northern Alekbulan every year. Even as a child, she had not cried or been overly emotional. She felt numb and shocked, but the sadness had yet to fully reach her.

Essien soon approached a cluster of trees that were impassable, and they served to remind her that she was close. She used the light beam to find an opening and shoved her way through. The familiar smell of marshmallow was strong in her mouth. The water was still, as it always was. As she was standing on the shore, Essien let herself remember the water man she'd seen both times she'd come. He was always taller than her, wider through the shoulders, and he had a strong masculine air, as though he could command her to do anything, and she would gladly do it. Her palms gave a heated pulse that reminded her why she'd come. It wasn't for the man at the bottom of the lake, although she glanced out to the center of the still surface. If she put her hands in, would it disturb him enough to rise out of the depths and face her again? Essien didn't care, as long as her hands would stop searing her night and day.

The water was cooler than the last time she'd stepped into it. She swirled her hands around in the clear water and felt instant relief. She sighed and sat back on her haunches while gathering pooled water into her palms and letting it run through her fingers. As she did, Essien felt the coolness spread and the searing pain cease. She then pushed her hands into the water up to her elbows. The coolness seemed to spread up her arms and into her heart, which was beating fast, happy at her discovery. Even if the water helped cool her palms, she couldn't risk coming back to the lake every day. It was still forbidden. Essien was about to reach into her bag to grab the flask she had brought with her, when she felt something graze against her fingertip. The water was clear as a cloudless sky, and there was nothing for her to see. Essien started to pull her hands out of the water when suddenly, she felt two hands grab her around the wrist and pull her headfirst into the water. One second she was looking down at the glassy smooth surface, and the next second she was underwater, breathing in liquid and thrashing against the hands that pulled her down.

Essien tried to scream, air bubbles exploding out of her mouth soundlessly. Looking down, Essien couldn't see anything, just water that grew darker and murkier the further she was pulled. There was no sandy bottom to land on. She closed her eyes and continued to tug her wrists against the force dragging her down.

CHAPTER NINETEEN

◆

WHEN ESSIEN OPENED HER EYES, SHE WAS INSIDE A STONE room. The room shined brightly, but there were no lights in the space. The walls climbed up high and disappeared into a darkness hovering above. There were no doors or windows. Essien looked down, and she was wearing a gauzy black gown. Her hair was down, the shiny tight curls hanging to her waist.

She walked to one wall and touched it to be sure it was real. Then she turned and let out a gasp that was the only sound in the room. There was a black stone table and behind it three women sat like regal statues on thrones made of the same stone. The woman on the far left was a palbino, her skin as white as iris blossoms. Her head and the entirety of her body were covered in black, so that all Essien saw was her face, a round light orb floating out of the darkness. The woman in the middle had brown skin the color of tree bark, and her eyes were a fiery red. She also had golden rings in one of her nostrils connected by a thin gold chain to the middle of her bottom lip. The woman on the right was a deep black, the color of night massaged with oils and sculpted down into flesh. She had a white covering over her head, and the contrast against her skin was blinding.

Upon seeing their faces, Essien fell to her knees, her forehead pressing into the stone ground. She knew that these were the Mothers.

"Oh, bless me, Mothers. I have transgressed. Please forgive—"

"Sssshhhhh," all three of the women seemed to silence her with a whistling of wind. Essien stopped talking but kept her face on the ground.

"Stand, young one."

Essien slowly got to her feet, but she kept her eyes down. According to the Akukoifo, the Mothers were the creators of the Multiverse and all that was in them. They had been before, and they would be after. There was nothing else but them.

"Look upon us, sweetness. We mean you only good tidings."

Essien didn't want to look, but she trusted them. The Mothers represented all that was good and holy about life, the world, and all the worlds beyond. They had created the Akukoifo to be men's guides on Ala-ani. They had created Ala-ani to be the habitation for mankind. It was by their grace that mankind continued. When Akukoifo got out of hand, it was the Mothers who brought them back to heel.

When Essien looked up, the women all had smiles on their faces. They were pleased with her. Seeing them smile made Essien's lips spread easily in a smile back at them. They were beautiful to behold, and she was not afraid.

"We have brought you here to deliver a message," one or all of them said. Essien didn't want to look directly at their faces again, but she had the urge to do it so badly. She looked at their hands, covered in cloth, and their lips, pursed or half open. She glanced at the stone room surrounding them, empty and without light, yet seeming to shine and giving sight so that she could see.

"You have not been forsaken. What you seek is fervently seeking you. Your hands are burning now, but they will not burn you always. Your anointing will come through blood. Do not let yourself become a sacrifice. Strike when you can, but hold your peace when you can't. We are with you always. He will be with you soon. You already know the costs. Have you a fitting sacrifice?"

Essien remembered the coin in her pocket, her fingers reaching to find it. She twirled the coin around in her hand as she pulled it out. She walked toward the table, her hand held out. All three Mothers reached for her at the same time, their hands superimposed one over the other. She didn't feel their touch as the coin appeared in all their hands. It shined and glowed, the solid metal sinking down into a melted puddle as Essien watched. The gold seemed to absorb into their hands, the liquid continuing to sparkle beneath their skin.

As the Mothers faded in the brightness of the gold flowing into their veins, their words seemed to embed themselves into her memory, repeating over and over, the echo circling around in her head even as she listened. Essien wondered who the "he" was that they referred to, perhaps the water man. Maybe she'd get to meet him after they let her out of this room. The room around her began to grow darker. As their words faded into her memory, she couldn't see anything at all.

"Mothers?" she called out.

Essien blinked, and when she opened her eyes, she was standing on the shore of the lake. She sat down on the sandy beach, rocks poking into her, and focused on her breathing.

She had met the Mothers. There was nobody on Ala-ani that she could share this with. She could be cited or fined if she told anyone she had come here. Excitement and apprehension tingled in Essien's fingertips. The fact that her palms no longer ached was a grateful afterthought. She thought of the coin, how it had disappeared right before her eyes. She already felt the lack of it twirling between her fingers.

Essien sat on the shore for a long time, the gentle light of the morning sun beginning to peek over the edge of the trees in the distance and rousing her from her trance. She could walk out of the jungle in the middle of a crowd, and something in her knew that nobody would touch her. She had met the Mothers. Essien felt a burst of joy well up from the place where sadness and disappointment had been waiting to bubble up. She felt there was nothing she couldn't do. The sun was already starting to climb for the day when she finally stood and began to make her way out of the jungle.

CHAPTER TWENTY

◆

The brothers remained with them for a week, and Essien knew it would feel hollow and lonely when they finally left. They were up early and loud everywhere they went. In just four days, they had eaten all the meat stored in the ice cellar and cleared out almost all of the fruits and vegetables from the garden. Her mother quietly mentioned that she would go into town for shopping, not wanting to draw attention to the brothers' hearty appetites. Her father was still happy and excited, but he now sat down in his chair more often, and he listened to his sons speak more than he took his turn. Essien heard him coughing late into the night, and she wondered if happiness was its own kind of stress.

Her mother reached for her overcoat, but Essien stopped her by standing up from the table.

"I'll go for you, Nne. I can shop much faster. Stay with Nna. I will be back within the hour."

She took her mother's pocketbook and canvas bags to carry everything in, setting out with boots and an overcoat over her plain pants and tunic. It was warm out with a breeze blowing away the heat from the sun. Essien walked quickly, her head down. The village center was only twenty-four stadia away, barely three miles. She could have driven her father's truck and arrived much faster, but she wanted to walk. She missed the physical activity of the running she had done almost every day at the military academy, the feel of sweat pouring down her back and the aching grind of her muscles wanting to slide off her bones. She also missed the taste she had gotten of what it might be like to be a Soja. Essien set off at a run, her boots kicking up dust behind her. She could still run. Nobody could take that simple pleasure from her.

Essien slowed to a walk and approached the displays to do her shopping. Her mother had given her a list of items to get. There were bright red tomatoes still on the vines, white chicken eggs in little straw containers, and root and seed vegetables stacked in colorful pyramids. After acquiring everything on her mother's list, Essien paid, and bagged her items. She was looking down at the stuffed canvas bags, and preparing herself mentally to heft them onto her shoulders for the trek home, when she heard someone call her name.

"Essien? How far, Essien?"

The woman Essien looked up at was unrecognizable at first. Her hair was done in a twisted updo, and her eyes were surrounded by eye kohl done thick and dark around her lids. It made her eyes look big and bright. She was wearing a colorful pink floral tunic with a red sash wrapped around her middle several times and sandals.

"How now? Do I know you?" Essien asked. The woman's face was long and angular with high cheekbones and a pointed chin.

"Ngozi," the woman said. "From the recruitment center."

Essien gasped. Ngozi looked much different. She was larger, for one, with a big bulge at the front of her belly. She had a large bundle on her back with little legs peeking around her waist. Essien realized it was a toddler, asleep in a wrap.

Essien couldn't help her mouth hanging open as she took in Ngozi, who'd raised her voice in the village square, then left Essien to fend for herself at the Soja sign-up. Now she was a mother. There would be no military for her, not now or in the future.

"Two babies?" Essien exclaimed before she could stop herself.

Ngozi got shy and turned to the side so that Essien could more fully see the baby. It was a girl, Essien could tell by her pierced ears and the eye kohl around her closed eyes. Ngozi put her hand underneath her bulging belly.

"This one is a boy. My husband wants a soccer team before we are done."

What a change two years had made. Essien tried to think of something to say.

"It's nice to see you again," she managed. "You look lovely."

She really did. Ngozi got shy again and shuffled back and forth on her feet, wafting the hem of her uwe around her legs.

"What are you doing here?" Ngozi asked. "I thought you were joining the Soja."

Essien looked away. "I didn't get in."

"Why not?"

Essien shook her head. "Not good enough."

"How could you not be good enough? I remember that you wanted it badly."

Essien shrugged and started to lift one of the canvas bags onto her shoulder. It was heavy, and she staggered.

"Let my houseboy help you," Ngozi said. "The baby and I are walking out to the next motor stop. We can accompany you." Ngozi put her fingers in her mouth and whistled. A tall boy came hustling over with fluffy sandy brown hair and a long-sleeved overtunic and pants.

"Idee, help my friend carry her things. We can go now."

As they walked, Essien tried to ask Ngozi about her life, but she just wanted to talk about the Soja and what it had been like at the military academy.

"Did you get your hands on a weapon?" Ngozi asked. "Oh, that was my dream. To hold one of those weapons and feel powerful. Did it feel as powerful as I imagined it would?"

Essien nodded and looked at the ground as they walked over it. "We didn't shoot anyone, but I was good with rapid-fires, really good."

"So good, but they didn't let you in? Surely, there must have been some mistake? Did you inquire at the Office of Women's Affairs?"

Essien shook her head, "I accepted their decision. I didn't try to fight it."

"At least take my chances for me," Ngozi insisted. "Try again. Work harder next time. If you try, they'll see your dedication. They'll have to."

Essien felt bad for Ngozi. She was about to be a mother of two. She'd never get another opportunity to become a Soja. She'd forever be wiping dirty bottoms, changing soiled clothes, and feeding greedy mouths. It almost made Essien want to cry, and then she remembered her own condition, and her eyes began to sting.

Ngozi was right. She needed to try again.

"How did you come to have two babies? And married?"

Ngozi looked away, pretending to scan the storefronts they passed. She patted the baby's leg with one hand and held the bottom of her stomach with the other.

"Arranged," she whispered. "By my mother. A deal made when they learned I wanted to join the Soja. I was to be married to a boy from the village near hers. They sent me on a trip to visit my nnenna, and when I arrived, there was a wedding party already underway. I had no idea it was an arrangement for me. I thought it was for my younger sister."

"They tricked you?" Essien began to feel as horrified and angry for Ngozi as the woman had felt for her just moments before.

"At first. You should have seen me ranting. But I saw my husband again afterward and fell in love. He's nothing like the horror stories we've heard. He's kind and gentle. He has money, so I can buy whatever I want. He works long hours, but we have servants and cooks. I don't have to work at home at all. He lets me visit my mother whenever I want."

"He lets you?"

Ngozi had a look on her face now. Defensive, drawn in, hard lips. She was holding her belly with both hands now.

"The baby will be due soon. Having two babies will be hard, but I'm confident in myself as a mom. I was never confident in myself becoming a Soja."

At the motorbus stop, Essien prepared to take the bags from the house-boy, but Ngozi stopped her with a fluttering of her fingers.

"Idee will walk with you." She sat down on the wooden bench to wait. She pulled the baby around to her front and nuzzled her forehead. "I will wait here, Idee. Go quickly and come back."

"It's nice seeing you, Ngozi. I hope everything goes well with you . . . and the babies."

Ngozi smiled and rubbed the baby's back. "I will see you again, Essien."

Essien's mind was a storm of thoughts and confusion. Ngozi seemed happy. Who was Essien to decide that motherhood and marriage were beneath a woman, especially if it was what a woman wanted to be doing? Essien was not in a position to judge anyone, especially not someone who was better off than she was.

At the turn to the front entrance of her compound, Essien saw the military engine parked in front of her family's compound. It was a large, over-sized engine, shiny and black, with wheels almost as tall as she was. Essien ran down the lane, not bothering to wait for Idee. She got to the front gate, and it was sitting wide open. The front door was closed, and there was a military official standing outside the door wearing the black-on-black uniform of the Soja. Essien skidded to a halt at the door, afraid to go into her own home.

The front door opened as she was preparing to take the handle into her own hands. Another military official stepped out with her eldest brother Idara escorting him out.

Idara looked at her, and he was frowning. "Essien! How now? We all thought you were not enlisting, but apparently that decision has been revoked."

The news made Essien gasp and cover her mouth for a second time that day. She looked from her brother's angry face to the military official's stoic, expressionless one.

"Soja Ezinulo?" the official asked. Essien could only nod. "You are remanded to appear at the start of your placement with the closest military base at one quarter and one-fourth tomorrow morning. A military engine will be your escort."

Essien nodded again, wordless. The military official handed her the summons, then stepped around her and trotted down the lane, opening and closing the gate behind him. The rumble of the engine's motor echoed noisily out of sight.

Essien walked through the front door that Idara held open for her. Her brothers were all standing around the room, their faces in different configurations of disappointment and disgust. All their talk would have to go unheeded. Essien could not disobey a government summons now any more than she could have two years ago.

Her eyes fell last upon her parents. Her mother was leaning against the side of her father's chair where he sat. They both looked once at her face and then looked hurriedly away. Her father threw a blood-stained square across the room; it was the rag he used to cough into when his lungs were at their worst.

Essien wanted to shout with joy, but seeing the blood sprinkling the white turned the mood in the room into one of mourning. They were mourning her, but she hadn't yet been lost. She was mourning her father and only slightly regretting that she would be leaving him again. She folded the letter and held in her joy like a repressed smile. Her father leaned against her mother, and there was nothing else to be done about it. Their daughter was joining the Soja after all.

CHAPTER TWENTY-ONE

◆

THE DAY SHE ARRIVED AT THE KEDI EGWU MILITARY COM-
pound of Igbo State, Essien was assaulted with an odor she had been
smelling faintly every day of her life: maleness. It was musty and suffocat-
ing and made it difficult to breathe in closed buildings. Her brothers had
this same smell under their expensive scenters, but she had never lived with
all of them at one time, so she never had to walk into a room that smelled
of stale sweat and unwashed armpits.

She was shown to a long, empty room with a few rows of double beds
stacked one on top of the other. There was a rusted bathroom space near
the end of the room, no walls, just the repositories and bathing stalls
along the wall, out in the open. The women's barracks, she'd been told.
She was the only occupant in the echoing, hollow space. Essien was to be
the first woman to join the Kedi Egwu compound.

"Eh, is this her?" she heard as she entered the meeting hall. There were
so many men sitting, standing, and hanging around the door, that she
couldn't tell which of them had said it.

Essien let her eyes skirt over the mass, not glancing at any one of them
for too long. This was to be her first assemblage of all the Sojas at the Kedi
Egwu military compound. This was the second military compound she
had been shipped to. At the first, Ihe Egwu, a senior official on site had rejected her admission, claiming that he had reached a maximum number of
women allowed, and there was no space for another. Essien had spent two
days in limbo at a nearby military transport station while another position
was found for her. She learned on the way to Kedi Egwu that every Soja in
the entire compound had been lost in a surprise attack by rebel soldiers. It
was suspected that there had been a traitor among them, and many were
saying the attack had been achieved largely with inside information on
Guard rotations and how to disable central communications. As a result,

an entirely new class of Sojas, fresh out of academy, had been shipped in to begin specialization training. Essien's reinstatement made sense as she listened to the military officials decide where to send her. Kedi Egwu had put out a call for any and all enlistees within a four-state area. It had been a necessity for the military, failing scores notwithstanding.

As Essien had unpacked her belongings in the long, empty barracks, she had hoped there would be other women among the newly recruited. Seeing the empty room made her feel deflated. She felt suddenly nervous and doubtful of herself and her ability to belong. The two days without a position had made her feel worthless and more ignorant than wise. She hoped that the Sojas at Kedi Egwu would welcome her.

Essien stood in the doorway of the large room and perfected the art of glancing over a room without seeing anyone in it. She saw a mass of bodies, all in the stark black of the military uniform, but she avoided making eye contact, except for one—she noticed Antonious almost immediately. His short, wizened figure stood at the front of the room on a viewing platform with a voice amplifier pulled down to his height. He seemed to be wearing the same gray suit that he had worn during her hearing almost a year ago. He placed his hands palm down on the mantle where he stood and called for silence and for the gathered crowd to settle.

Essien walked quickly toward the front and sat in the very first seat, keeping her eyes on Antonious as she could feel eyes gather on her. She sat with her back straight, her hands on her thighs, her feet together. On the platform, Antonious was giving an introductory speech.

"Welcome to the first day of the next thirty-five years of your service. You will be tried beyond your strength. You will be tested beyond even your endurance. Only the strongest, bravest, fastest men—people—will be given the uniform of the elite fighters in the Soja. Many of you will be gone by tomorrow."

And here, he looked down at Essien. With that glance, he seemed to be daring her and everyone else to prove him wrong.

THE FIRST TRAINING SESSION WAS HELD IN A GYMNASIUM MORE than twice the size of the mgbati ahu Essien had practiced in back home.

There were various pieces of machinery placed around the room, with cords attached at different angles. Essien had never seen or practiced on much of the equipment that she saw surrounding her. However, there was some equipment she was familiar with, such as stones and jumping ropes, organized on a shelf near the back. There were also shiny swords hanging in a glass cabinet near the doors.

The other Sojas were outfitted in the gray of their practice uniform, spread around the room, and lined up along the walls in various stages of interest. Every eye turned to stare at Essien when she entered the gym. She stood just inside the door and stared back. She breathed shallowly, so she didn't get lungs full of that smell that made her feel nauseous. And then there were hands on her back, pushing her to walk into the room. She whipped her head around and came face-to-face with Antonious. The same short height, the same gray suit, the same eyes staring into hers with deep knowing.

"You've almost made it, Soja," Antonious said as he pushed her to walk into the mgbati ahu. "Be sure we keep you this time."

The edges of her lips quirked up in the smile she wanted to give him but knew she couldn't. He could probably figure out how much his presence meant to her, but she would need to learn to exist without him. He seemed to be her ally, but he wouldn't always be there to save her from feeling isolated among the men. The nervousness Essien felt thrilled over her skin, and she shook out her hands to dispel the feeling.

Antonious clapped his hands as he entered the room and walked toward the front. "Today, you begin training to join the Soja. Nobody will be given a pass. Everybody will be expected to meet qualifying scores to move on. First task—putting you in your training groups for the next two years of your initial enlistment. Pay attention as you will be asked to remember each other's names, faces, and eventually, your ranks."

Antonious began listing the Sojas off in groups, and Essien tried to listen closely for her name. She looked around the room and couldn't help looking at faces. One man sitting next to her had yellow eyes like citrine crystals. The man on the other side of her had his hair in thin locks down to his shoulders.

". . . And Essien," she heard Antonious call out. She realized she had been distracted observing the Sojas around her and hadn't been listening at all. Antonious was on to listing the other groups, and she had no idea which of them was hers. Once Antonious had finished calling out the groups, the men around her began moving toward their teammates with introductions and touched palms. Essien stood by herself, looking around, trying to decide if she should approach Antonious for assistance.

"Essien, right?" A soft, gentle voice behind her. She turned and looked into the lightest pair of brown eyes she'd ever seen. They were more gray than brown. It was a man almost exactly her height with a closely shaved head and a thick patch of hair on his chin.

"Enyemaka," he pointed at his chest with a thumb. "You're in my group." There was no vexation in his voice at all as he motioned a hand for her to follow him over to a group of men already gathered. Maybe Enyemaka had no issues with her being on his team, but by the looks on their faces, the other men surely did. Two were tall, taller than her mother for sure. They both had dark skin, almost blue-black in darkness. The other four men were medium height, taller than Essien, but not as tall as the giants. One had dark reddish-brown skin, another was the color of sand with short locks, and two were the pale white of palbinos with white hair and red eyes. Essien put out her hand for each of them to shake. Most of them returned her handshake politely, except for the two palbinos. They had stared down at her hand with their nostrils turned up, and then turned to each other and spoke in a dialect that sounded vaguely like the language of the San tribe.

The man standing closest to her laughed and said, "Those hands are for cooking and cleaning, girl, not for shaking as equals." She let her hand fall from its outstretched position and felt the embarrassment flame into her skull.

"You're fortunate it was a handshake I offered and not a fist," Essien retorted. That earned her a few chuckles from the other men in the group. The two palbinos seethed a deep red.

After that, Essien stood quietly at the back of their group, with her hands in her pockets, trying not to appear as ego-bruised as she was.

Enyemaka was the smallest among them, but he slipped into a natural leadership role that everyone accepted. "Military base training is not like military academy. I've been studying the manuals for years, so I think we'll have an advantage. All of us will need to score high to get our team into the top spots. Any team members who consistently rank poorly may be discharged."

Here, Enyemaka turned to address her directly. Her spirits swelled slightly at finally being noticed and included.

"With you on the team, we'll have to work harder to make up for it. Try not to score too low on the board. You'll probably be going home first, so be prepared for that."

They were all looking at her now. The palbinos were smiling. She could agree with them and let them think that it would be her who would bring the team down. She could say nothing as she had stood there for almost another hour and said nothing.

Instead, Essien parted her arms from where they had been wrapped tight around her. "I don't plan on bringing this team down." She felt defiant, but it was an untried rebellion. She wasn't sure how long she could hold it up. "I'm going to be the reason this team gets in the top spot and stays there." The men were already laughing out loud before she'd gotten to the part about earning the top spot.

"You have a man on the scoring squad already, ehn?" said Akpari, one of the taller of the palbinos. He had a jagged, bright pink scar running down the middle of his forehead, through his left eyebrow, and down the side of his cheek, disappearing along his jawline. Essien looked full on at his face for the first time and knew that whatever his problem was, it wasn't her at all. She was just the physical embodiment of his own demons. She cringed with thoughts of how he'd gotten that scar. Maybe his mother or his sister had done it. If it weren't for the scar running across his face, Akpari would be handsome. She stared at the scar openly, trying to decide if it should make her feel sorry for him. Maybe if she felt sorry for him, he wouldn't hate her.

"I bet it will be Antonious. He is the President's press man," Keesemokwu, his second pale shadow joined in. He had a bald head to Akpari's pale-gold curls. "He will do what looks good for the news reports."

"Like what you see, akwuna? I can give you a close up, ehn?" Akpari started to move forward, but his colorless shadow put a hand up to block him. Akpari didn't try to fight that hand, settling back where he'd been leaning. They smiled at each other, and it was a smile meant to make her feel beneath them, like meat on a platter.

"They want her here," Keesemokwu said. "I don't know why they let women in so often now, but they do, and they want her here. Antonious will be the one to rig her scores, so she stays." They had all nodded at each other in agreement like their half-truths and rumors were somehow factual, and then they looked at her again.

"Don't worry about me, umu nwoke" she said to their mockery. "I will show you what having me on your team will do." That seemed to end the discussion for the moment.

Antonious wrapped up the introduction and training assignments, and then led them through a tour of the military base. The buildings spread out along angled pathways that led into the heart of the military compound. Each building had a name that Antonious mentioned as they went along, but Essien didn't recall any of them later. She remembered only where her barracks, the dining hall, the meeting hall, and the mgbati ahu were. There was a running trail surrounding the compound, bordered by trees with small ponds in hidden coves. The tour ended back at the mgbati ahu, and Essien stood alone, thinking about running and trying to ignore the feeling of foreboding she felt.

CHAPTER TWENTY-TWO

◆

T HE NEXT WEEK, THEIR TASK WAS TO NAVIGATE THEIR TEAM through a jungle labyrinth to reach the top of a mountain on the other side. To do so, they had to locate a map, a key, and a chalice along the way to the finish line, all hidden around the labyrinth. All teams started at the same time and the winning team was the one that crossed the finish line with the chalice first.

Essien and her team were transported to the beginning of the exercise by skycraft. They were all blindfolded, and Essien could feel the air whipping around her body as she sat quietly and patiently with a parachute strapped to her back and a satellite map in her jacket pouch. When they reached the jump site, there was a shout, rough hands removed her blindfold, and she was tossed out of the moving skycraft.

Essien landed in a thicket of trees with branches slashing at her face. She cut herself free and rappelled down to the ground, the intense, earthy smell of jungle life filling her nostrils. Essien looked around her vicinity, but she appeared to be alone. She pulled out the satellite map and began planning her course as it beeped to life in her hands, displaying her first set of coordinates. She had to meet her teammates at an assigned rally point where they would find another set of coordinates to enter into their maps along with instructions to locate their key and chalice.

For a myriad of reasons, Essien wanted to be the first one at the rally point. If she could find the location first, she could get a head start on the rest of the team. If she could get a head start, she wouldn't have to worry about them hassling her along the way. She knew deep down that if she tried to work with them, she would only be excluded. So the only alternative was to try and reach the location before anyone else did.

According to the rally point indicator flashing on the digital map, and the indicator of her current position, Essien determined she was eighty-four stadia away. So, without delay, she set off in the direction indicated, at an urgent pace.

The trees surrounding her were tall, and they created a canopy above her that housed brightly colored birds flying from tree to tree and small monkeys shaking the leaves. Although they had not been told beforehand, and had been blindfolded on the flight to the location, Essien knew they had been dropped in the Black Jungle in the land of Sheba. She had visited a reserve on the edges of the Black Jungle during a school exploration in tenth level. They had not ventured this far in, but she remembered the waterfall to the north, which was shown on the digital map by wavy blue lines. From the other blinking black indicators on the map, she knew that she had been dropped closest to their first set of coordinates. She couldn't tell which black dot was which of her teammates, but she was the shortest distance away. She began to run; the faster she traveled, the faster she'd get there.

She stopped once to check the coordinates. She was almost there, and the other black indicators were much closer now. They must have sped up their progress in response to how fast she was moving. Essien's hands clenched around the device as she saw the other dots getting closer and closer to their destination. Her blood pulsed in her veins, trembling with a sudden nervousness she hadn't felt just moments before, when she'd been so sure that she would arrive first, victorious even for just this leg of the race.

Essien put the map away and sped off in a full-out run, hopping over fallen limbs and skirting around tree trunks, leaves and branches crunching under her boots, the monkeys watching her curiously. She couldn't see anyone approaching when she looked around the flat clearing with a wide tree in its center. She'd reached the coordinates first.

The map was rolled up and hanging from a tree branch. She took a picto snap of the map, which activated the next set of coordinates. She knew that they were expecting her to wait at the first set of coordinates for the rest of the team to reach her, so they could plan and strategize together, but she had already decided she would complete the task on her own. Looking at the map, she would have to run between two of the black dots on the map in order to reach the next spot.

She didn't care how reckless she was being; she just wanted to beat them all to the finish line. She wanted to make it before any of them did, even Enyemaka with his gentle eyes and his quiet mouth. Nothing in the rules forbade her working alone or acting in her own best interests. So, she ran as fast as she could, dashing through the thicket as her heart pounded in her ears, directly through two of the blinking dots on her map. She couldn't tell which of her teammates she'd passed, but she didn't care.

She reached the second set of coordinates, her chest heaving from the exertion of running under the hot sun through steaming humidity of the trees around her. The coordinates, she saw, led to a sandy pit between large rocks blinking from just inside the pit as the sun overhead beat down on her back. Essien jumped down into the sandy mound and started digging. She didn't have to dig long before she found a large black pouch. She didn't even bother to wipe away the sand before reaching inside the pouch, and a golden key spilled out. Essien took another picto of the golden key glinting in the blinding sunlight, and noticed that her map had updated with the third set of coordinates. A golden marker blinked over the wavy lines she'd noticed earlier. The last set of coordinates were near the waterfall.

Essien sprinted until her lungs beat frantically against her rib cage, and her legs ached to stop. The ground beneath her began to rise, and the incline grew steeper. As Essien continued to run closer to the waterfall, she heard the song of rushing water falling into a deep tumble. The roar got louder as she ran. She could smell the water, a marshy brine in the air. She felt invisible droplets hitting her skin. As she neared the location, she realized the chalice was *in* the waterfall.

The blinking gold cursor hovered over a spot below her in the crashing cascade of water that she could feel even from hundreds of feet above. The line of trees broke, revealing the side of a tall, gray cliff with crumbling rocks leading down its steep sides. She stood on the edge of the highest point looking down on the mouth of the thundering waterfall. The roar was loud and monstrous this close, the vibrations of it thrumming under her soles.

It was a dangerous drop and a deadlier dive. No one in their right mind would attempt such a feat. No one . . .

She could see the black dots getting closer to her, two of them overlapping each other as they galloped toward her own black circle on the map. She turned around, expecting to see them rushing her, but there was no one. The black dots on the map seemed to be right on top of her, but when she looked up, there was no one but her.

She turned back to the edge with the thunderous sound of water just below. The rocks along the edge were wet and slippery. Even if she tried to climb down, she might still slip and fall, never to surface again from the pull of the water's current or be killed instantly if her head hit the jagged edge of one of those monstrous rocks. She heard baritone shouts behind her, but she didn't dare look back. It was now or never.

Essien stepped back and took a running start, jumped, and regretted the decision the moment her feet left the ground. She fell faster than she'd planned for, and the frigid water splashed in her face as she crashed through the tumbling waterfall, down and down. Essien could see the water like a blue iris, unusual and rare, deadly even. She slammed into the water below headfirst, the force compressing her lungs, and she didn't know which way would send her back up for air. The press of falling water pushed her down until she hit the rocks on the bottom. The pressure would have held her there if not for the opposing current just beneath. She found herself being dragged by the water, scraped against the rocks, and she felt something metal against the back of her hand as she tumbled. Somehow, she managed to grab hold of it, and determined it was a handle that was connected to a wooden slab. She held on, and the slab moved with her. Essien realized she was holding a box, and she wrapped her arms around its sides. It wasn't that heavy, so she and the box swirled with the water, pushing and pulling and occasionally bumped against jagged rocks. Essien squeezed her eyes shut in fear, then forced them open to reorient herself to a sense of direction. Unable to determine which way was up, she exhaled a bit, and noted the direction the bubbles went, and began kicking in that direction. A few short strong kicks later, she could see the sky.

The air tasted of ice candy when she sucked in her first breath. She looked at the box in her hands. It was made of burnished metal on all sides with a wooden door that had a golden keyhole melded into it. She shook the box and something heavy rattled around. The chalice must be inside!

She let the water float her downriver, the metal handle gripped tightly in her hand. She knew this river led to a reservoir and the end of a dam and that the waters moved swiftly, but not swift enough for the crocodiles and snakes that populated the slower shores. She would have to let the waters whisk her almost into the dam and make her escape from the water that way to avoid their snapping bites. Then she could map out how she might get back to their finish line. It hadn't even occurred to her how she might get out of the water once she'd gotten into it. And she hadn't thought about the dam, a wall of concrete with all this swiftly flowing water pushing her straight into it and over the edge with those voices shouting behind her.

The dread of being slammed into the dam made her finally turn onto her stomach to regain control of her body and direction. That's when she noticed the triangles of gliding water moving swiftly toward her from the shore. Essien imagined being eaten by sharp teeth snatching at her underwater in the Black Jungle infested with crocodiles. She thrashed against the current, trying to reach the opposite side. But the water was moving too swiftly. She was pulled along quicker than she could swim.

As she kicked and thrashed, the box still in one hand, the thick ridges of the crocodiles' backs glided toward her, navigating their way to her more effortlessly than she could ever manage her way to the shores. She gulped in water that made her choke, adrenaline racing through her in sheer panic. Eyeing her hunters, Essien was so worried about being eaten by a crocodile that she wasn't paying attention to where the stream was taking her. When she finally looked ahead, she saw a churning hole where the water disappeared into the dam. A wire net covered the hole, so that only water was allowed to get through.

As she got closer to the dam, the water got stronger and pushed her forward like enormous hands. She tried swimming to shore again, but the current was too much for her. She was going to be swept into the wire and cubed by the force of the water pressing against her.

Essien was about to close her eyes and submit to her end, the crocodiles on either side changing course to follow her direction, when she saw a flicker of blue tail dangling down into the water. Looking up, an Akukoifo, the same one that had come to her in her dream, bobbed over an edge of stone jutting out over the dam. The ledge was connected to a wall that ran the entire length of the dam. It looked big enough to walk across and reach shore and low enough that she thought she might be able to grab it. If she missed, she would be pushed through the wire and that would be her death.

She would only have one shot at grabbing it and holding on. The Aku-koifo flitted down to her, so that as the water rushed her forward, she felt herself passing through its translucent body. For a moment, her eyes flashed with blue light, and there were strong arms pushing her up out of the water.

It would have made more sense to drop the box, but she couldn't come out of this ordeal with nothing to show for it.

Clenching the wooden box in one hand, she let herself be propelled out of the water by those hands, kicking her feet to help with the momentum. She had just one hand to grasp with, but the blue light that covered her and made her blind was stronger.

CHAPTER TWENTY-THREE

◆

T HE RACE WAS OVER TWO HOURS LATER WHEN ESSIEN dropped the opened metal box onto the finish line. All of the other squads were there in the huge clearing, waiting for her, scowling and empty handed under darkening skies.

She didn't smile. She couldn't, still angry with herself for diving into a waterfall without planning for how she might get out. It had almost killed her. There was also a blue haze over her vision, and no matter how much she blinked and shook her head, it wouldn't go away.

Antonious separated himself from the huddles of men, and there were bright spotlights set up in the clearing to illuminate his face. The scoreboard was held up by two military instructors behind him, and there was a whistle like an applause of windy notes that shut off abruptly. There, at the top of the board, was just one name in tall, bright red colors: Ezinulo.

Essien stared up at herself, and it felt like someone else's identity, not her own. She wanted to feel pride in what she had just done against all odds, but she felt defeated by her own accomplishment. Not just defeated, afraid. She hadn't been meant to win; none of them had been meant to win single-handedly. So, how had she done it? *Had* she been able to do it without the Akukoifo?

She felt guilty, and it was a new feeling—like she'd violated much more than the code of brotherhood. Like she'd gone against something much more instinctual and primal. She imagined being bitten in two by a crocodile, and it made her shiver with a fear she hadn't felt even while neck deep in the water with gliding figures moving toward her.

Behind her, a voice fused with scorn and malice. "Akwuna proves she's crazy, and we all sit by while they hand her pity points. She breaks the rules, doesn't work with the team, and they let her win?" Akpari didn't even bother looking at her, but his voice was loud enough to carry.

Her win was a win for the team, and his first words to her weren't even a parody of gratitude.

As everyone turned and walked away, grumbling to themselves, Antonious watched on from afar as Enyemaka held her up with a hand on her shoulder. He held out his hand, and she touched palms with him.

"You think you achieved something back there, do you?" His eyes were serious and hard. "All you achieved was showing your own naïveté. It was stupid, Essien. It was blind. You wanted them to see some stellar performance as proof of your worth to us, to the Soja. But all you achieved was putting a target on your back, making them hate you more."

Essien jerked her arm away from him. "If they see me that way now, then that's how they've always seen me, Enyemaka. What else could I do but try to prove them wrong?" Essien ignored the shake of his head and pressed on. "Getting my name up on that board forced them to finally acknowledge that I'm as good as I claim. I'm a top competitor, and now they all know it."

"Essien," he groaned, "you want them to submit to you, to trust in you, but they will not. They will never. The only thing they will think now is that a woman has beaten them. These men who believe that women are for dominating—you think they will respect that you've outrun them, outthought them, embarrassed them? These men are seething," he jabbed the air between them. "Maybe they wanted you for themselves, or even suspected the next man did—but now you've *beaten* them, and they won't forgive that. These men do not deal with women as equals, do you not see? All you've done is sealed your fate— your fate that they will destroy you."

Essien felt those words like a chilled knife through her heart, but she would never show him that. She pulled her chin up in defiance and stared Enyemaka right in the eye. "I didn't ask for their forgiveness, so let them keep that. What I asked for is their respect."

"Look, Essien, I won't doubt you again. But to them, no matter what? You're still akwuna, and that's not something you can ever change."

His attempt at solidarity, however misguided, made Essien feel a small slice of home for the first time since she'd returned to the military.

Akpari and Keesemokwu lurked just outside of their hearing, talking to each other about her, she guessed. That made Essien's stomach do a flip up into her throat, and she walked briskly away.

"Maybe so," she said to herself. "But if anything else needs to be proven about me, look at that scoreboard. It has already been proven."

CHAPTER TWENTY-FOUR

◆

Two days later, in the darkness of night, Essien was startled out of her bed in the lonely barracks by clanging bells. She quickly dressed, and when she exited her room, a military instructor greeted her by shoving a rapid-fire into her arms. Essien was too startled to ask any questions as she was pushed along with the rest of the entire compound.

The Ser General raised his voice to call them all to order and attention. They were told they were being called out to their first field mission and ordered into the engines.

"Rebel camps spotted with one hundred or more, and we're the closest compound to the action. We cannot wait; they look to be moving soon. Backup will be coming, but the initial surprise is up to you all."

The Ser General looked right at Essien, and she felt her heart thrill in her chest.

"You will be the onsite lead until backup arrives. You got your name to the top of the board, so you get to lead us in."

Essien gasped and felt the stiffening body language of the men around her, but there was no time for anyone to complain at the selection. The clenched knuckles of their tightened grip around their rapid-fires told her all she needed to know.

A shaky, bumpy ride on a row of engines led them into the darkest parts of the western jungle edging the ocean coast. Essien could hear the sound of their breathing, the snap of twigs, the rustle of leaves, the wet drip of water, and occasionally, the lonesome howl of a night bird. They had been given a set of coordinates along with the information that a large rebel camp had been spotted, and they were to rout them out and capture as many as possible. Hostile combatants were to be killed, but they were to spare any surrendering rebels.

"Fan out in twenty-feet increments, so we can sweep more land," Essien commanded her troops, her heart pounding as she gave her first command. She steadied the weight of the rapid-fire in her hands.

"Twenty-feet increments? That's too far apart," a Soja said.

Essien looked toward the voice, but she didn't recognize the speaker.

Someone else chimed in, "If one of us spots the rebels, it will take a while for us to reach them."

Essien knew her instructions had been correct, yet she heard herself say, "Fine, pick a different distance, but the point is to cover more area. We can't do that walking single file."

"We should split up into groups," Enyemaka suggested.

Essien lifted her rapid-fire to her shoulder. She raised her voice, forcing the tremble out of it. "Fall in line. Space out east and west. On my order."

There was more grumbling now, but Enyemaka fell into line, and that started a chain reaction. The rest of the Sojas began spacing themselves out to either side.

"Minimize noise," Essien said into her earpiece. "Move. Wait for command to fire."

Essien took a step forward through the trees, and then the two Soja next to her took a step forward. She kept walking, and all the Sojas down the line advanced with her. They walked through the trees for so long that the sky began to lighten. Essien felt relieved that she could finally use more of her senses than just her hearing. Up ahead was a wide clearing, and then the trees resumed on the other side of it, maybe twelve stadia ahead into the lightening sky. Essien flinched and swirled at a flutter in the corner of her eye. Through the slivers of space between the trees, she saw a glimpse of what looked like moving bodies in the trees across the clearing, creeping closer from the right. They were not wearing the same uniform as she was.

"Fire across the clearing now!"

The words were out, but she was already lifting her weapon to her shoulder to aim. She felt her unit turn as one and begin firing, without questioning her or debating her leadership in that moment. She saw bodies fall between the distant trees, and then she felt hot shimmers whizz by her as the rebels returned fire. She put her shoulder up against the nearest tree and kept sight of any flickers of movement.

Her rapid-fire let off bursts of fire that thrummed through her whole body. The tree above her exploded, and she didn't even duck. She just kept firing until she couldn't see any more sparks coming at her. She stopped firing, and after a while, the other rapid-fires down the line stopped, too. She breathed through the trembling in her limbs and the tactile echo of the long-range rapid-fire bursting off its rounds in her hands and against her shoulder. She heard leaves rustle, a stick snapped, and a frog croaked.

A blast ripped into the tree in front of her, exploding bits of bark against her cheek.

"Return fire!" she yelled. She sighted into the trees in front of them and fired. She shot at moving sparks and sounds. She kept firing because they kept coming. Her squad followed her, spread out in their standard formation where they could see each other. She covered her portion of the field that she could see and trusted the men around her to do the same.

There was more fire than she'd packed heat to cover. She had not been given time to bring extra rounds to reload. She knew they couldn't stay in the trees firing at line after line of rebels. The intelligence information had estimated the camp had at least a hundred rebels, maybe more. How many had they killed so far? And how did she feel about killing a man for the first time? She decided she didn't have time to consider this and pushed that thought aside.

Essien took a step away from the tree she had used for cover. Pops of bark shattered near her head. She kept advancing, letting her own shots strike every spot that moved. She squatted low to the ground, her rapid-fire tucked up to her shoulder, using trees for cover as she passed them. She kept firing, trying to think of the level of her ammo. She knew she'd started with five thousand shots in the rapid-fire, but she hadn't kept track of how many she'd used. She couldn't stop to check the rounds. She couldn't stop to look at what was left in her team's rapid-fires.

Moans and screams of death filled the air on both sides of the clearing, but she couldn't stop to check on the fallen members of her squad. She kept firing and walking low across the clearing, darting around fallen bodies and hopping over broken branches and sharp banks.

Her squad followed her, continuing to shoot as they crossed the clearing, reaching the line of trees on the opposite side of the clearing. There she saw more bodies on the ground, bullet-ripped trees, and plenty of smoke. She took her finger off the trigger. Somebody down the line kept firing, but eventually they too stopped. The air around them filled with silence.

She kept walking, low, scanning the hidden crevices in front of them. Her boots sank into sand and then the trees ended abruptly within sight of foaming waves and rocking sea vessels at the edge of the shore. They had reached the coast where a beach butted up against all the forest, and now she could see their backup unit cautiously creeping up onto the shore, about fifty Sojas with rapid-fires out but pointed down.

As they approached, one of them called out, "Who's in charge?"

Essien stepped forward. "We need to search the area." Without thinking about whether they would obey, Essien ordered a search team to double back and check for survivors, pointing a finger in the direction with a sharp and authoritative snap of her arm.

"Backup is supposed to lead," the same Soja from earlier said loud enough for Essien to hear.

"We were told to follow the lead of whoever was placed in charge," someone in the backup group said.

"That's me, then," she said, feeling the thrill of the words. "We need to search for survivors."

The Soja behind her stepped up to where Essien was. He said, "We were given conflicting information. Our superior told us to follow backup."

The backup who had been speaking pulled his helmet off and walked closer. Essien saw that he was a sandy yellow color underneath his gear, his eyes a bright green. "I'm Soja Dlamini."

"Soja Ezinulo," Essien said, and they touched palms.

"Our military instructor told us to follow you."

Essien wanted to smile, turning back to her squad mate to see him put in his place, but she repressed it, even as she felt him slinking back, away from her. "There might be survivors. We need to double back and make sure we didn't miss any."

"We follow you."

Essien turned and began trekking back the way they had come. The backup fell in line, yet Essien noticed that only a few of the Sojas from her own compound followed them immediately. As more Sojas stepped forward, the rest slowly fell in line until they were all advancing as one.

Sweeping back over the clearing, Essien saw just how many bodies they had left behind. None moved, and they were all covered in blood, their bodies ripped apart from the impact of the bullets that tore through them. Seeing the carnage made nausea wave up through her stomach. There were so many bodies, littering the ground like fallen logs, and Essien felt the sting of remorse for the first time. Holding the rapid-fire in both hands, she let herself see the destruction she had helped cause. She let herself internalize it, feel it, so that she would not forget it. If there were a safer way to stop the rebels from growing and spreading than this much slaughter, Essien hoped they could find it.

The group searched the battle site thoroughly. No one was found alive.

"Let's continue the sweep," Dlamini said.

Essien fell into line with the rest of them. They crept silently through the trees and watched for any movement. She had been sure they had gotten all the rebels, but what if some had escaped?

The forest was lightening brighter and brighter as they moved. They were about thirty-six stadia into their search when they encountered the ramshackle village, several wooden sheds up against a stone cliff face. The sound of the shore wafted into their ears bringing the smell of salt water with it. There was a firepit in the center of the village and the markings of chairs that had been removed.

The troops approached cautiously, splitting up and searching the sheds. The first one Essien entered was bare and swept clean. The shed was big enough for five of them to crowd in and spread out. The next shed was equally empty. The group met up near the firepit.

"It's deserted. They either knew we were coming, or they weren't actually using this site. It's too cleared out. There's no way they could've cleared that much in the time we've been here."

Dlamini nodded in agreement. From behind them, shouts came. The group jogged toward the sound coming from the shed furthest from the firepit. The Sojas came out with smiles on their faces. One of them was holding a large rapid-fire, a type that Essien had never seen.

"They have a weapons cache."

Essien crowded into the shed with a few others. Inside the shed, the floor had been pulled up like a trapdoor. Below, a set of wooden stairs led down into a storage room. Essien crept down the groaning, rickety stairs, smelling the intense scent of wet dirt the farther into the ground she traveled. At the bottom of those stairs, the room opened up into a large square with crates lined up against walls all the way up to the ceiling reinforced with wooden beams. Inside the crates were weapons of different sizes and powers, an entire slew of other models of rapid-fires Essien had never seen.

"These weapons were produced in a different country," Dlamini said.

"How can you tell?"

He shook his head. "We don't manufacture any of these weapons here. They're all made overseas."

"We'll have to collect all of these to bring back with us."

One of the other backups said, "Let's get pictos of this room first. And then we'll carry everything up."

When Essien's group returned to their base camp, they were carrying all seventeen crates of weapons. The dead were piled and arranged for burial tallies. Essien was glad she was spared the task of dragging the bleeding bodies into the center of the clearing, the overwhelm of the day's events already humming in her mind. She watched Akpari carrying the body of a fallen comrade that had dripped lines of blood down his pale skin and across his facial scar. He tossed the body onto the assembled pile and then stripped off his blood-covered coat and overtunic. As he did, he caught Essien staring at him. The snarl he gave her looked like the closest thing to a smile he could manage.

When all of their dead had been counted and recorded, they had lost forty-six Sojas. One of the dead was from Essien's training team. The bodies of the Sojas were carefully bagged and tagged to be retrieved by the clean-up crew that would soon follow. Their families would receive a certificate of their death and a small remuneration for the Soja's service. The clean-up crew was also responsible for disposing of the rebels' bodies.

They were not counted as they were heaped into high mounds, but Essien guessed they had killed over one hundred men.

The one hundred and fifty Sojas that remained gathered on the shore to prepare for their departure. The weapons crates they had discovered and confiscated were also assembled to depart with them. Essien stopped to listen to the commotion of their movements around the shore. Above the din, she could hear the rumble of engines coming closer; it was their transportation back to the compound. A breeze floated off the ocean, and Essien breathed in deep, feeling secure for the first time in her ability to survive. The fear and overwhelm pushed away, she might as well have killed all the rebels herself with how powerful she felt.

CHAPTER TWENTY-FIVE

◆

I T ONLY TOOK A FEW DAYS FOR ESSIEN TO LEARN THAT SOJA Dlamini was right: the confiscated weapons were from Albion, a nation to the north. Alkebulan had a ban on rapid-fires of higher capacities; weapons carrying more than five thousand rounds were outlawed. The weapons they had found were capable of carrying twice that, ten thousand rounds each. One of them had a high-powered projectile bigger than her hand. The serial numbers on the weapons were traced back to a rapid-fire manufacturer in Alemania, a small state in central Albion. From there, the case of the weapons was pushed up the chain of command, and Essien was no longer in charge.

Back at the compound, Essien overheard her teammates talking about her during evening meal.

"She won't last past the next round of training," Akpari said.

"Essien is strong, ehn, but she is also weak," Keesemokwu said.

Essien ignored both men and silently continued eating her food.

THE NEXT MORNING, ESSIEN WOKE UP EARLY TO GO RUNNING ON the trail that traced into the center of the compound. She set out at a moderate pace and quickly lost herself in the movements. The exertion made salty waves of perspiration drip into her eyes and settle over her spine like a sticky film. The front and back of her tunic were soaked through. She might have been swimming in a chest-high pool of water.

The best time to run, she had found, was before the sun had risen, before the track was full, before anyone else had gotten in mind to go running, too. The trail was surrounded by trees, and as she ran, Essien passed hidden ovals of natural water holes. There were hills around the track that she had to pump her legs harder to climb. She reached the top of the first hill, and the breeze tickled the sweat on her temples. She stared out at the landscape; dark forest trees touched with the pale pink of a rising sun at its very edge. She kept running as the track tilted downhill.

She was climbing the steepest hill on the track when the wind blew the smell of molten musk, like melting iron being tempered with male sweat. A cove of trees ahead hid the path from her view. She knew the track turned around and headed back in the opposite direction just ahead. On each side, the trees were their thickest, planted right up against the path. She could barely see between their tree trunks in some places. Essien pushed her pace a little faster to reach the top in less time. She had just stepped one foot on top of the hill and was preparing to look to the right into the darkness of those trees, but before she could turn her head, the weight of several bodies smashed into her.

"Hey!" she yelled, but her mouth was covered with something that smelled of raw meat and wet clothes. Thick, calloused hands crushed her to the ground, the smell of searing sweat so much stronger now.

A fist to her right eye and her jaw, and more fists hitting her exploded pain all over her body. There was a boot pressed into her back, and she screamed around her gag of flesh.

Her skin was torn, and she felt some pieces of hair had been ripped out of her scalp leaving a throbbing behind where hair had once been. They stopped beating her with their fists and their feet, but Essien was too disoriented to tell how many assailants there were. She was being dragged further into the cove of trees, even as she kicked and thrashed against it.

They couldn't hide in plain sight like this; eventually someone would come along and catch them. But, in the weeks that Essien had come out to this track to run, she had never passed anyone else on an early-morning run. She had never seen another Soja here at all. She couldn't be the only one who ran; *please, don't let me be the only one who runs!*

Hands turned her over and pulled her closer. She was lying in fresh mud; it was squishy around her as they each moved, trying to get a part of her body to claim as their own. Essien peeked her eyes open slightly; she wanted them to think she was unconscious, so she tried to remain as limp and nonreactive as possible as the hands grabbed, pulled, and beat her. The scar running across Akpari's face caught her like the hook in a fish's lip.

The sight of him shocked her into opening her eyes wider. She could see Keesemokwu hunkering down next to him. A black steel knife hung from one of his pants pockets. There was no holster around it, just a free blade with the hilt sticking out of the top of his pocket. *They're going to stab me to death. They're going to stab me . . .*

Enyemaka stood apart from the group, just off to the side, his boots unmuddied, his hands free. His eyes were on her face.

"She's awake." The voice took Essien's eyes off the man behind them to the ones above her.

"Good," Akpari responded. He started unbuckling the pants of her uniform. It would take them forever to undress her in full uniform, pants, tunic, overcoat, boots. Undress her? They were undressing her.

The one above her moved higher on his knees to reach the other side of the overcoat he was trying to pull from her arm. With a sound of frustration, he pulled the blade from his pocket and used it to slice her overcoat and tunic down the middle, revealing a strip of her naked skin. He put the knife down on the ground beside him as he reached into that slit and touched her. His fingers felt sharp as nails scratching through her skin.

Quicker than she'd ever moved, Essien put her hand on top of the knife so close to the side of her head. She pressed it into her palm and made herself grip it tight. She caught Enyemaka's eyes as he stepped forward from his frozen position.

"I want to join not watch," she heard him saying.

Their eyes were on him as he walked closer. She made herself grip the knife and with her eyes on that soft spot underneath the neck above her, she lunged the blade upward. Its sharp edge sank into Keesemokwu's neck, the jag of steel slicing into his throat and pulling a sound like laughter out of him. Blood like hot, salty water poured over her as she pulled the knife out the other side of his neck. Gurgling sounds emitted from his throat as he kneeled in a frozen state above her, blood falling in a triangular shower. The men around her froze, and she locked eyes with Akpari.

Splashes of blood hit Akpari's cheek as she curved the knife toward him in a flash of speed. The tip of the knife sank into the top of his abdomen. Essien pushed herself off the ground, using her shoulder to slam into him and drive the blade until his stomach met the back of her hands.

"Nwaanyi!" he screamed and tried to throw her off.

She fell back, the knife coming with her, along with a hot splatter of Akpari's intestines spilling into her lap. Essien noticed Enyemaka and the others running away, their backs a blur. When she looked away, Akpari tried to come after her with the final strength of his hatred, but his insides were on the outside. He looked down at the gaping wound as he sank on top of the pile in her lap.

"Akwuna!" he screamed weakly, and it was too late. His bowels let go all over her lap, and the life fled from his glare.

Essien turned to see Enyemaka grunting with exertion as he held another Soja to the ground. Beyond him, Essien could see other dark backs running away down the hill, their boots kicking up mud in their escape. Essien counted three of them.

"I couldn't catch them all," Enyemaka panted as he held the other Soja down.

Essien let the knife drop out of her hand as she pushed to get Akpari's shoulders and head off her lap. She stood up, and blood and excrement washed down her legs. Thick pieces of Akpari still clung to her. The Soja on the ground was still struggling where Enyemaka had him pinned.

Though her muscles quivered, and her legs felt like they would dump her right back onto the ground, Essien picked up the knife and walked over to them, her hair pulled free from its ties. Even seeing the knife dripping with another's blood, intestines hanging off her legs, the Soja was still filled with so much rage. He still believed it was her who deserved to die.

She could hear him talking, his words like sharpened arrows tipped in poison. "No matter how hard you fight, no matter who you kill, no matter what you do, you will always be akwuna, less than akwuna. You will always be abaghi uru, a worthless whore. You don't belong. You will never belong."

She had heard enough.

"I can take him back to the Building for Internal Affairs. We can call Command. I know who the others were." Enyemaka was watching her face and jumping between the blank look she was giving and the bloody knife in her hand.

"Move," she said.

He didn't at first, still staring back and forth between the knife and her face, fear and apprehension slicing through his features.

"Move, Enyemaka. Move now."

She stepped forward as she said it, so that he had no choice. He stood and stepped away, leaving the Soja on the ground on his back. Before he could react to try and run, Essien dropped to a kneeling position beside him and plunged the knife into the Soja's stomach. She heard Enyemaka gasp as the Soja began to scream. Essien used her free hand to push the knife all the way through him. Then, she used her knee against the handle to drive the blade deeper until it pushed through his body. His breath left him in a croaking gasp, as the knife sank into the dirt beneath the body.

Essien stood up, pulling the knife with her. A woozy feeling washed over her, and she felt the need to sit down. She looked down at the body in front of her, with its belly slashed open and lying lifelessly in the twilight. She turned and looked at the bodies of the other two, their skin even more pale against all the dark red. Enyemaka's eyes grew wide as she turned to him, and he held up his hands.

"I tried to stop them," he said, his voice louder and shakier than she'd ever heard him. "I tried to talk them out of it. I thought if I at least came with them that I could help you . . ."

"You helped me," she said, and then she tossed the knife blade into the mud where it stuck and stood on end.

The sun was just beginning to break above the horizon as Essien walked out of the trees. She could feel aches hurting all over her body. She clutched the two halves of her tunic top together and moved back down the hill she'd climbed, alone.

CHAPTER TWENTY-SIX

◆

A S SHE ENTERED THE FIRST BUILDING SHE ENCOUNTERED, ES-
sien was covered in blood and various body fluids. The building was
colder than the air outside, and the scent of jasmine flared up like a waft of
beautiful-smelling clouds. She hated it, cloying and sweet in the back of her
throat. She wanted to cover her mouth, but toxic body fluids were on her
hands. As the scent wafted over her, it hit her that she had just killed three
men. Murder was a crime punishable by only one sentence. In Alkebulan,
murder was one of the worst crimes one could commit against another.
It meant a total devaluation of life, and in Alkebulan, murderers did not
deserve to live. There was a certain destructiveness to it, but it was the way
of things, and nobody had yet sought to change it.

Essien thought about the ultimate end for murderers: execution. She
wondered if she might confess now or wait until she had been formally interrogated. When a person committed murder, they were arrested, interrogated, given a trial, convicted, and sent for execution. It was done privately,
and no one was sure how or when executions were carried out. There were
no prisons in Alkebulan; petty criminals paid fines or worked in agricultural camps for a set period of time. The worst criminals were killed, and
their remains were never seen again.

Because of their tough stance on crime, Alkebulan did not have any
repeat offenders, and crime was generally low. Essien wondered what the
news reports would say. She wondered how her parents would find out.
What would her brothers or the Mothers think? If Essien was going to turn
this into something salvageable that didn't end with her dead, she would
have to do what everything in her didn't think she had any right to do at all.

Essien stepped up to the counter and forgot how to utter words for a
second. It was like the world of before no longer existed, and this new world
required a language that she didn't yet know.

"The Ser General needs to know what's happened," she said in a calm voice. She felt cold and hot at the same time. Her voice cracked when she tried to speak again, and she had to clear her throat. "Have Command come to me, please," including the please because nobody in the military ever said that word. Orders were given with authority, and authority didn't ask permission.

The man at the desk wore the identification tag of administrative officials, those who dealt with recordkeeping and certificates. His tag said Ncheonu. He wouldn't know the first thing to do about her. A woman covered in dead men had never walked through those doors nor likely ever would again. His jaw was so low it made him rise from his chair and lean forward over the desk.

Enyemaka came through the doors behind her, and his eyes searched the space frantically until they landed on her. He walked closer, noticing the man behind the desk whose face was screwed up with revulsion and confusion. The man at the desk looked at Enyemaka and opened his mouth to speak but then closed it without saying anything. Ncheonu looked full at Essien, unable to decide whether he should try to help her or be afraid. A drop of blood splattered from her hand onto the floor, disappearing in the darkness of black marble.

Her face, her hair, her neck, even her teeth were stained in blood that had darkened to a rusted orange in some places, a black cherry in others. Her hands were completely red. She shuddered as she looked down at herself and held her hands away from her body, as if attempting to distance herself from them.

A quizzical look came over the man's face. He reached for the phone and then drew his hand back.

"You expect me to call Command . . . for you?"

Essien almost laughed out loud as the words tumbled from his mouth and landed at her feet.

"I have killed three men."

Here was another one who could very easily be disposed of in the same way. She should have kept the knife with her. That thought cut her feeling of laughter short.

Ncheonu frowned, like he wasn't sure he'd heard her correctly. Then he seemed to take in all of her, the blood covering her from head to foot.

He reached for the phone again, picked it up, and dialed. He didn't get an answer, and he hung it up with a slam.

"Maybe an air message," he muttered.

"This is an emergency, Ncheonu." She stepped closer to the countertop. "They need to know what's happened right now."

"You're a murderer," he whispered it like they were dirty words.

Essien shook her head. She wanted to scream at this man with his plastic name tag, but she knew it wouldn't get her what she wanted. She fought the quaking in her muscles as chills and shivers made them vibrate. She glanced over at Enyemaka, who was standing with his arms by his sides, his eyes all for her. She looked back at Ncheonu.

"Call Command, please. He will know how to handle this situation."

Ncheonu looked at Essien's face doubtfully. He wanted to get further information, but the sight of her made his pulse thump visibly faster in his neck. He looked back and forth between Essien and Enyemaka.

"How is that one involved?" Ncheonu gestured at Enyemaka with his chin.

Enyemaka spoke up. "I was a witness. Please, do what she says."

The man finally picked up the receiver again and pressed a few buttons. He got an answer on the other end because he turned to speak into the receiver, so Essien couldn't hear what he said. He hung it up and glanced quickly back at Essien.

"Did you call him?" Essien peered over the black marble desk counter. Her hands touched the cold, smooth surface, and when she pulled them away, there were impressions of her fingers and the tops of her palms in sticky red prints that barely showed. She put her hands down at her sides.

"The Guard will be here soon."

"The Guard?" Essien's voice rose. "You called the Guard?"

The Guard were the ultimate elite Sojas, they were the ones her village whispered about in fear. A Soja had to pass high-level certification exams to be admitted into the secretive group tasked with protecting the President.

"What is the Guard doing here?" Enyemaka asked.

Ncheonu spoke up, "The President was visiting this compound unannounced, as he likes to visit all the compounds occasionally. As you know, the Guard goes where the President goes."

Essien turned to Enyemaka, her body shaking, and her eyes wide with apprehension.

"They're going to kill me," she said, with a whimper in her voice.

CHAPTER TWENTY-SEVEN

♦

FROM BEHIND THEM, THE FRONT DOORS OF THE BUILDING cracked open, startling Essien. She saw Antonious step quickly into the building. The doors seemed to open before he even got to them, and Essien saw them close shut again without his touch.

Enyemaka stepped closer to Essien, whispering to her as Antonious walked through the doors. "I'll tell them what I know."

The shaking took over, and Essien stood there with a tremble showing in all of her limbs, and making her teeth chatter.

Enyemaka said, "I have seen people spared from execution. It doesn't have to—"

But Antonious interrupted, "I saw an air message that you had just committed murder on compound grounds. The Guard is coming, so we don't have much time. You must not resist them, Essien. They will be looking for a reason to kill you. Do not give it to them. Put your hands up and do not move at all. No matter what they do, Essien. Do you understand that?"

"I was defending myself. They were—"

"It doesn't matter," Antonious cut her off. "It matters only that you have committed a crime in the President's vicinity."

"Why are you helping me then? Why not let them come and kill me?"

Antonious responded with a slight smile that made his face look less gray.

"I haven't done all I have to get you here only to let you be cast off at the first sign of trouble. You're a valued Soja, Essien."

A frown indented Essien's forehead. "What exactly have *you* done to get me here?"

Antonious didn't have time to answer as the doors behind them burst open again, and a row of rapid-fires were immediately pointed at Essien's head. Essien watched as the wall of men advanced. She almost couldn't separate one from the next in the red blur of her vision. They were all inside the building now, fanned in a half-circle in front of her, with masks covering their faces. Essien could see herself reflected back in the shiny dark surfaces. As she looked over at Antonious, his eyes were calm and steady on hers. *Put your hands up*, a voice in her head whispered. *Slowly, let your hands rise, and do not fight them.*

She raised her hands, and two of the men came forward from their solid wall of black. They clinched her hands behind her back roughly, and she didn't protest or give a reaction of any kind when they tightened the cuffs against her wrists.

At that point, Antonious gave them orders. "Take her to the Building of Transfers and Holdings. And don't leave her alone. There is to be nobody in or out."

They said nothing to her and seemed to be waiting for something. Antonious turned and left the room. Essien expected the Guard to follow, but they looked at her, their heads turning in an identical swivel.

"Shall we go?" she asked, motioning them forward with her head as her hands were clamped together behind her back.

She could feel parts of her body beginning to ache, like her shoulders where her arms were pulled back so tightly and her side where she'd been kicked repeatedly during the assault. It also hurt her to breathe too deeply, so she was taking shallow, light breaths hoping she wouldn't hyperventilate. Her lip felt larger than normal as she ran her tongue over it. There was definitely a chunk of flesh missing from the inside of her cheek.

Essien tried to take in a deep breath that shook going in, and she wondered about who other people prayed to when they were in trouble but didn't believe in foreigners' gods. The Mothers, Essien knew for herself. She prayed to the Mothers. A stillness spread upward from Essien's hands clamped together, and she smelled silvery-blue water in the middle of the jungle. She glanced outside the doors that were open and saw Enyemaka talking to Antonious, gesturing with his hands.

The Guard had taken their moment of considering her and each other before they parted in front of her and let her walk through the space they'd made to get out of the building. Essien couldn't remember how to get where they were supposed to go, but she let them prod her forward in front of them.

Essien stopped in her tracks, her legs trembling. Her hands were uncomfortably tight behind her back, and she was finding it difficult to endure the pain and hold in her tears. Water flooded her eyes, as the events of the early morning finally started to hit her. Hands yanked her forward, and she was pushed along by two Guard on either side as her delayed reaction flooded over her.

Since Essien could barely walk, as her legs continued to shake and quiver, eventually it became necessary for her captors to drag her along, their gloved hands mired in the blood and fecal matter still dripping from her body. She wasn't certain how far they dragged her, but suddenly there was a building looming ahead, located between trees comprised of hanging green feathers almost touching the ground below. They walked beneath a canopy of splotchy green and gold, and Essien stopped crying long enough to look up. When she did, she saw a verdant green umbrella silhouetted by pale blue sky and fluffy white clouds. A light breeze ruffled the leaves above them as they approached the building entrance. After witnessing the scene of serenity, Essien wasn't crying any longer.

Standing near the entrance of the building, surrounded by Guard in a protective barrier around him, Essien saw the President. He was wearing a dark blue suit with a silver cap. His arms were crossed in front of him, and his face was blank as he stared down at her.

Her throat clenched tightly at the sight of him. She cast her gaze down, her mind racing, unsure if she even had the right to look at him.

Inside the building, she was carried down endless halls and placed on a metal chair inside a metal room with a small metal table and another Soja to stand in the room with her, this time one without a helmet covering his face. Essien knew him from training, but his name wouldn't come to her. She put her head down trying to hide her tear-drenched and blood-covered face, but the Guard rapped on the surface of the table. Essien jolted up and stared at him. He wasn't looking at her anymore, as if he hadn't just used the butt of his rapid-fire to startle her. She kept glaring, hoping the scowl would make the tears invisible. She wanted so badly to wipe her cheeks and wash off the blood.

But Sojas didn't cry. Elite members of the Soja kept stony glares, like Essien's brothers, Idara and Malachum, and her father's father who had served before her. They didn't let their emotions fall down their face in lines like she was doing right then.

Choked sobs that she tried to keep in poured out and bounced loudly against the metal walls of the room. There wasn't any way for her to cover her mouth or put her head down. She was crying now because she hadn't been able to cry in the midst of the attack. She was crying because she had spent all these years wanting to be exactly where she was, and now that she was here, she wanted to be anywhere else.

"THEY WERE TRYING TO KILL ME FIRST."

Essien heard herself say this out loud. She had no idea how long she'd been in the room when it bubbled up out of her mouth. Yet, she realized it too late. The Guard ignored her, but Essien stared at him.

What made men into stones and kept women so soft? If it all boiled down to testosterone, then she could easily inject herself with some. Her health practitioner would prescribe her the dosage, and she wasn't squeamish. She could shoot herself full of masculinity every day, and maybe then she'd fit in and not stand out so terribly that someone would want her dead. Maybe then she'd feel like she'd earned being there. Yet . . .

Part of Essien felt destined to be in the military. Like it had been chosen for her before her time even came. That moment she had picked up that golden coin in the sandy dirt cemented it for her, but why did destiny come with so many hurdles? Did that mean it was not destined at all?

There was that smell again. The same smell she'd noted when standing in the darkest part of night, next to a shimmering pool of water so fluorescent she couldn't help wanting to step into it. There was a clank at the door, and a slice of light from outside cut into the room. Essien tried to use her shoulder to wipe her eyes, but she could only reach the sides of her face.

The door opened wider, and the President walked in. He was taller and darker up close. But everything on him emitted a shine, even the slicked-down waves on his head. Essien stood sharply and tried to lift her hand up to salute him, but her arms were still clamped behind her back. That smell flooded through her nose again, and she tried to breathe through her mouth.

"If my hands weren't . . . Pardon me for not saluting you." Essien looked down at the surface of the table and didn't want to look up again.

"Can we uncuff her?" Essien heard, and it was such a relief to her that she almost sat back down. She kept staring down at the table surface. It was shiny, but not reflective, so she couldn't use it to see what they were doing while she continued to avert her gaze by looking down.

"Soja Enyemaka told me what happened, and he has gone to give his formal statement," She hadn't seen him enter, but it was Antonious speaking now. "Enyemaka is likely your only ally, and you've seen up close and personal what his allyship looked like. He could have reported them before they even got the chance to attack you. How long had he known what they were planning? He could have told you what they were planning and given you some advance warning."

Essien looked back up at all of them crowding into the small metal room. The President was staring directly at her. She wondered what he saw when he looked at her.

She should be executed. Did he have the authority to simply send her home, as if none of this ever happened? There was no way they could just send her home, but there was no way they could let her stay either. Maybe going home was exactly what should happen. How could she remain knowing she was surrounded by enemies? She should have chased down and killed the ones who ran. She should have killed Enyemaka, too. As the thoughts raced through her head, she noted something in the President's eyes. They began to sparkle. And then he queried her.

"Why did you not kill Enyemaka, too?"

She frowned at him, trying to see beyond the dark features of his face into the motive behind his inquiry. How could he know that she had just then thought about killing Enyemaka? How could he know that she had contemplated using the knife one final time, in a frenzy of rage that still bucked inside her? Why would he ask her about exactly what she was thinking?

She tried to shrug, but her arms behind her back stopped the movement.

"He didn't attack me. He tried to help me."

The President kept staring at Essien, and neither Antonious nor the one Guard present in the room spoke. It was so quiet, Essien could hear the dried blood flaking off her skin and hitting the table and floor. Her answer was the truth though. Something in her had relaxed as Enyemaka looked fearful and cowardly before her, eyeing the knife like a cornered chicken. Essien had realized that what she felt about him was being clouded by how she felt for the men she had killed. He had done what he could for her, what he thought best to do.

The President nodded once, as if her answer satisfied him. "And the other men. They were your teammates, but they tried to rape you and take your life."

"I wasn't going to let them kill me. I should have killed the ones who ran."

And then she stopped. She didn't know why she was speaking so freely.

"Why do you think they wanted you dead?" That question hit on exactly what Essien had been trying to work out in the back of her mind.

"Because I'm a woman. Because I'm better than them."

Just hearing it said out loud made wetness collect in her eyes again. She felt ashamed of her tears because this was the President, not a faceless Guard. She should be showing him why they'd allowed her in the military in the first place. And here she was doing exactly what women were pegged for: being overly emotional.

"You have just faced an attempted murder and survived to tell us about it. You have the right to a few tears."

Essien stared at the President in silence as a single line of water made a trek through the blood drying on her face. She wanted to sit down. She wanted the cuffs taken off, but none of the Guard had gotten around to doing it.

"You, take the cuffs off," the President said to the Guard standing against the wall, pretending that he wasn't listening, with his eyes directed straight ahead. The Guard pushed himself away from the wall and pulled a cuff key from his pocket. Essien turned to give him her hands, but she felt him hesitate. There was still blood all over her, so maybe he was squeamish.

Essien heard the sound of metal hitting concrete. She turned to see the Guard bending to pick up the key.

The President kneeled down at the same time, and the Guard stepped back to let him pick up the dropped key.

"Let me," he said.

The President took hold of her hands, still cuffed behind her back, and began moving them around, so he could insert the key into the lock. He didn't seem to care about the blood covering her as he pushed up her sleeves to better reach the lock. Soon, she felt the release of the cuffs, and a lightening of pressure in her head.

The President held on to her free hand while he unlocked the final cuff. The metal cuff fell away and clattered to the floor of the room, but he didn't let her hand go. She turned, so she could look up at him. The blood was dried in thick patches, and her skin showed where the dried blood had started to peel. She liked how his hand felt holding on to just one of hers. She liked it so much she tightened her hand just a little. Then she wanted to take her hand back. Why was he holding her hand?

Essien tried to swallow and couldn't. She didn't know if she was slowly moving toward him or if he was pulling her.

"Did you see what I did?"

He shook his head, and there was only a small space of distance between them then. Up close, she could see that his lips were a soft mauve, gentle curves, with lines and wrinkles over the soft, not quite pink skin. An edge of white teeth showed behind the folds. The quick slip of a bright pink tongue.

"The President, of course, will not handle any aspect of the case, but the incident spot will be photographed for the trial." Antonious' voice was the buzzing of a gnat, and they both turned to him in slow motion.

It felt like her head was moving through boiled tree sap, thick and slow, as she tried to keep her eyes on the President's face and turn to Antonious at the same time. She finally had to force herself to look away, but to do so was more difficult than anything she had ever experienced before. The President was still holding her hand in his, his palm clasped to hers, their fingers intertwined and pressing. Something made her clasp his hand back, even as she wanted to let go. She was holding the President's hand, and it felt like the most natural thing she'd ever done in her life.

Antonious' eyes dropped down and stayed there without saying anything else. The President let go of Essien's hand as calmly and naturally as he'd taken hold of it. Essien felt his release of her hand like an aching hollowness that set free all the emotions she'd been fighting not to feel. The world came back into focus, and she remembered once again who she was and what had happened. She felt like her protective covering had been stripped, and she was naked before them, when a moment before she hadn't been. She could feel a grinding ache begin in her side when she tried to take a deep breath to steady herself. The pain caused her to double over, and she felt the President want to reach out to steady her, but he stopped himself.

"She needs a health practitioner. And the Internal Investigations Team needs to collect evidence. You can have this conversation after she has been treated medically."

Antonious nodded at the President's orders and then turned to Essien, giving her a long, searching look that started by staring into her eyes, jumping back and forth between both of them, before scanning her. He saw that her uniform was muddy, slit down the middle, and soaked in dried blood. Her skin and hair were covered in blood. And there were some thicker blobs of a substance Antonious didn't want to name. She was still holding her side and breathing shallowly.

"I will call for the practitioner and Investigations," Antonious said, as he turned and left the metal room.

The President looked back at her. He looked like he was about to say something, his lips even parted to speak. But he shook his head, a small side-to-side motion that she caught. He, too, strolled from the room, taking the cuffs and the key with him. The metal door closed, and she was left alone.

Moments later, the door reopened, and two Guard entered with a taller man in a white lab coat followed by two more Guard. The Guard were dressed in the standard black-on-black uniform with their faces covered by reflecting helmets. The man in the white lab coat introduced himself as Doctor Nwabueze.

"I'm going to take some pictures and samples for evidence." Essien just nodded and held out her hands. Everything in her felt hollow, like she was waiting for something to pour in and fill her up.

Nwabueze instructed her which way to turn, and his picto capturer clicked and blasted bright light. Essien closed her eyes as the clicks whirred one after the other. The doctor told her to turn; she turned. He told her to take off the uniform top, and she stopped. She didn't want to disrobe. She'd been clutching the two slit halves together around her once she had use of her arms. She could easily slip her arms out of both halves of the uniform top and be naked from the waist up. She didn't want to be naked in front of anyone. She flashed on the knife cutting through her uniform and fingernails scraping her skin, and her hands clenched tighter around the fabric.

"Take off the tunic," the doctor ordered her.

But she couldn't make her hands unclench from where she was gripping them around herself. She wasn't going to take off any of her clothes. She backed away from him and his capturer. She shook her head, still backing away until she hit the wall, which made her yelp with surprise.

The doctor put the capturer down and stared at her. The four Guard stared at her. She started to cry again. It was like her reactions to what the men had planned for her, an attempted rape and possibly murder, flooded out of her eyes, and she fought not to wail. That hollow feeling grew deeper inside her, and she clutched at the top and let tears wash down her cheeks. Essien had never been a crier, and she remembered the President remarking that she deserved a few tears.

The doctor left and then came back almost instantly, and this time he had an assistant and made three of the four Guard leave the room. The assistant was the first woman Essien had seen in the compound who wasn't a cook or a cleaner. She wanted to hug her and put her head on her shoulder. But the assistant was too thin and too short with her hair braided down the back of her head. Essien stared passively as the female assistant introduced herself as Yahira.

"Doctor Nwabueze will take the pictures. I will move you. We need you to remove your items of clothing."

Essien clammed up again and shook her head, backing away from them as much as she could in the small box of a room. There was nowhere to run if they insisted. She wasn't going to take her clothes off in front of them. She couldn't do it. She felt like gagging at just the thought of it. And letting them take pictos, too? She was breathing fast and shallow and was starting to see gray around the edges.

Yahira was patient. She didn't try to touch Essien or force her. She kept talking, "Breathe deeply, Essien . . . We need to take the pictos for evidence. We need the evidence for the investigation . . . slow your breathing down . . . The evidence is on your body. We need to collect that evidence. Try to breathe into your ribs instead of your chest . . ."

Essien felt panicked, but something in Yahira's voice let her see that there was just her and the doctor now. She tried to control her breathing, keeping it shallow still because every deep breath seared her ribs in a vise of fiery pain that she didn't want to keep experiencing. Essien closed her eyes, her bottom lip trembling even harder, and she nodded her head as Yahira's patient pleading finally reached her.

Yahira gently slipped the uniform top down her arms. She held up Essien's legs one by one as she slipped off the pants. The doctor took in a sharp hiss of breath between his teeth, and then his picto capturer kept clicking. There were dark purple patches all over her. The darkest patch was on her side where she'd been holding and scared to breathe. The doctor touched her gently on one of her ribs with his fingertips, and she trembled from that small contact. She was hurt. She was very hurt.

They made her take X-rays, and that's how they saw that four of her ribs and her collarbone were fractured. She had been walking around and sitting there for over an hour while there were broken bones in her body. She didn't remember anything hurting so badly when they were attacking her, but the adrenaline had long since faded, and the aches and pains were worsening.

She was loaded onto a wide engine with no windows in the back. They gave her an injection of something into her upper arm, and she didn't ask what. They made her lie down on a spinal board and strapped her down. As they drove her to the medical center, Essien allowed herself to float into a medically induced unconsciousness. An image flashed into her head, and she fought to push it away. She kept seeing it in her mind, a triangular fountain of blood falling down onto her face and into her mouth. The engine rumbled underneath and swayed back and forth. Essien didn't remember any more of the ride. When she awoke, Antonious was sitting next to her hospital bed.

She thought at first that he was an illusion, that she'd conjured him from her imagination. Then, she smelled jasmine like a sweet caress. She tried to sit up, but her side ached with a dull grind. She touched her chest, and it was encased in a hard plaster wrap. She had been cleaned of all traces of blood and bile, and her hair had been washed and braided into two plaits. She looked again at Antonious sitting at her bedside. She wondered if the President had sent him personally. He was wearing a white formal shirt with buttons down the front and crisp brown slacks. He had one leg crossed over the other, and his hands steepled in front of his mouth, staring at her.

"Take a moment, Essien. You've been asleep for seven days."

Essien blinked at the news. "Seven days . . .?"

"Bones take time to heal, but the sleep was to give you faster healing time. You should be discharged in a few days."

"But . . . why are *you* here?"

"To provide you some very important information. Are you lucid enough to understand me?" He leaned forward in his seat.

Essien took a moment to consider the question. Besides the tightness of the wrap and a general feeling of confusion, she didn't feel anything else. And then suddenly, she remembered everything all at once, and it swelled over her and poured out of her eyes. Her hands were no longer cuffed, so she used the back of her palm to wipe away the falling drops. She made herself try to sit up, and was rewarded with sharp and intense pain emitted from her rib bones.

"I'm trying to sit up, but every time I try, I'm reminded how hurt I am."

"You didn't look hurt back at the base when you were meeting with the President. You held yourself up very well."

Essien stared up at the ceiling, concentrating on not letting the flow of water from her eyes get into her ears.

"I do not wish to cause you more upset." Antonious said slowly, as if he wasn't sure she was listening to him. "But you must know . . . your trial will be held in one month. You will be sent back to your family home under military guard during that time, but you will not yet be discharged. The results of your trial will determine how the military shall proceed."

Essien let his words sink in, and again, she had no initial reaction. Not fear or anger, not sadness or happiness either. She felt nothing.

She said nothing.

She'd known there would have to be a trial. It was to be expected. But she was actually surprised to hear that it wouldn't be even sooner. Instead, Essien was to face her future in a month's time, one of the longer time periods she'd heard offered.

She could hear Antonious rise from his chair and move toward her, and she tried to lift just her shoulders to see him. He was leaning down beside the metal bed, and then the top of the bed was rising. She didn't have to strain to see him anymore, as she was slowly brought to a sitting position. Her pain level spiked like sharp nail pricks along her ribs, but she breathed around it and concentrated instead on Antonious' face. He wasn't an ugly man, just old. He had moles on his warm brown cheeks, dotted underneath both eyes. Essien wondered why he hadn't gotten them lasered away.

She wondered about his position in the military. What did he do for Alkebulan exactly? He almost seemed to be a diplomat or ambassador of sorts. He did the majority of the military's press conferences when the President wasn't obligated to speak himself. He welcomed public figures visiting the compound. He led training for the newly recruited soldiers. And he'd always been an ambivalent guide to Essien, never offering too much help, but just enough to encourage her. She wanted to ask him what position he held, but worried about their separation by military codes of hierarchy. For there was a hierarchy, no matter how flat it might seem with him sitting there beside the bed with a small gold pin on the lapel of his tunic in the shape of Alkebulan. A hierarchy that reminded her suddenly that her hand felt small when held by the President.

"Are you the Vice-President?" she asked spontaneously.

She'd learned about different governments around the world. She'd learned about the Iroquois Nation's government in comparison to Alkebulan. She knew the country on the other side of the Atlantic had a President and a Vice-President. She didn't think Alkebulan had such a role, but she couldn't think of an equivalent. What position did a man hold when he seemed to do all the things that the President couldn't personally do himself? Maybe he wouldn't answer her at all, and that would be answer enough.

"Not exactly," he said, brushing off his sleeves. "Alkebulan only has a President. My position is less . . . standard." It was almost as though he did not want to tell her, and that made her even more curious.

"Are you the President's right hand?"

Merrily, Antonious began to laugh, and it made him clap his hand on his knee. Essien didn't laugh, but she liked that she'd made him laugh.

"I am whatever the President commands me to be, true." His mischievous smile lingered, as she dropped her eyes down into her lap. "When I first met the President, I was a Soja in the military, just like you. And so was he. We served alongside each other, and I knew from that time that he would be a powerful man. He was serious and knowledgeable. Everybody looked up to him.

"As he rose in the ranks, I rose with him. When he became Ser General, I became his General Surrogate. When he became Senior Council Member, I became Junior Council Member. When he became Parliamentary Executive, I became Parliamentary Executive Assistant. And when he became President, well, it was only natural that I would rise with him. He brought me with him, but I worked for it, too."

"So . . . you're a Presidential Assistant now?"

Antonious grinned at her again, but he didn't answer.

Essien asked a different question, one more pressing than what Antonious might or might not be in the country's governmental hierarchy. She knew he was high up, and that would have to be enough. "When will I be transferred home?"

"As soon as your practitioner clears you."

She wanted him to ask her about the murders, but everything still felt distant and unreal. She should have been dead. Only her own determination to live had saved her. Only the power and fearlessness in her own two hands had helped her face death and live to tell anyone about it. Death was a fierce opponent but not a worthy one.

"What happens if I am made guilty?"

Essien stared down at the cream-colored bed covering over her lap. Even after what she had gone through, she still had a desire to remain in the position she had. She still wanted to serve her country and her countrymen. Despite the dull aching in her side, she couldn't shake that deep conviction she had to wear the uniform, to serve alongside those who also felt the same and to avenge her family's hardships at the hands of the rebels. Antonious looked at her like he understood what that was like—being beholden to an entity outside of and more important than yourself.

"If you are found guilty, you will be executed. If you are found not guilty," he steepled his fingers again and stared at her over the top of them, "we shall see."

CHAPTER TWENTY-EIGHT

◆

ESSIEN STEPPED CAREFULLY OFF THE SKYCRAFT ONTO HARD tar, pulling on her military overcoat. The sun was covered by clouds, and the sky was gray and foggy. She peered out over the runway of the transportation center and spotted her mother standing amongst the people present to pick up passengers. Her mother, a foot taller than everyone else around her, had on a white ichafu piled high on top of her head in intricate folds. Her uwe was light blue with silver thread embroidered through the neckline, sleeves, and hem. Essien let her eyes scan the crowd, hoping to see her brothers. There was just her mother, smiling at her with her cheeks almost pressing her eyes closed.

"Nne," Essien greeted her mother. She couldn't run and walking still felt tight and awkward. Her mother gripped her shoulders and kissed both of her cheeks and her forehead.

"Oh, my daughter," her mother whispered. Essien bent awkwardly to pick up her luggage. Her mother held Essien's free arm as they began walking toward the exit.

"How do you feel?"

"I am better than I was," Essien said.

"Your nna has been well but not well enough for a trip so far. I left him in front of the screen projector. He may be awake when we arrive home."

Essien nodded. She had hoped her father would be there to welcome her home, as she did so with little chance of being able to go back to the Soja. She knew her parents would be worried and anxious about her chances of being executed, but at least they'd know for sure she wouldn't be going back to the military.

When Essien and her mother eventually arrived home and walked into the family compound, her father sat upright in his chair, looked her up and down, and then he nodded.

"Nice to see you, Essien." The look in his eyes was soft and gentle, and his eyes were covered by a liquid sheen.

Essien walked slowly into the front room to stand by her father's chair. She took his hands. "I missed you, Nna."

He patted her hands and then leaned forehead and pressed his forehead against the back of her hand. Essien closed her eyes and let her father rest his head against her hands. He squeezed her hands tightly.

"How now, nwa m nwaayni?"

Before Essien could stop herself, she was crying tears that made no noise. She kneeled beside her father, still holding his hands. Essien put her head on her father's knee, and he put a hand on the back of her head. A silent waterfall fell, and she let go of her father's other hand in order to wipe the tears away. She didn't want to talk about what had happened. She didn't want to think about it. She wanted her father to rub her head and hold her hand.

Her mother came into the room and put her head down on Essien's shoulder. For the first time in a long time, Essien felt surrounded by people who cared for her and would keep her safe. She stopped holding in her tears and let herself cry freely.

NEARLY A MONTH HAD PASSED SINCE THE MURDEROUS MORNING, and since she had come home, Essien had spent nearly every day inside her parents' compound. She was typically in her old room, staring at the ceiling, waiting for the arrival of her trial. The first thing she'd done upon re-occupying her old room was to turn the doorknob the correct way, so that the lock was on the inside. She thought of the time her parents had locked her inside the room to prevent her going out while they decided what to do about her joining the military. The lock on the outside made it convenient for them, and Essien had likely given them plenty of reasons to want her locked in.

Essien's father left her alone and stayed in his bed the majority of the days, propped up and surrounded with books, journals, and padlets of writings and calculations. On the bedside table at his side, a near constant burning of spices and herbs filled the air. He seemed happy to have Essien home, and he occasionally called her into his room to share interesting news he had read or seen. Her mother watched her with silent eyes and tried to engage in conversation, but she, too, left Essien alone. Her mother had hired a house girl who came to cook evening meals and weed the garden after the school day, so she did not even need Essien's help around the compound.

The garden was smaller now, only six rows in the closest garden patch. The rest had been turned into bright splashes of colorful flowers with a border of green trailing ivy. Essien smoothed fingertips over the petals of a deep pink flower and wondered who had planted them. The garden had been all harvestables when she had been growing up, and it surprised her that it had shrunk so much. Essien could now kneel down in the dirt without pain, and she could stand to her feet without wincing. Her body was almost completely healed.

Two members of the Guard were stationed outside the front and back gates at all times, trailing her every time she set foot outside her parents' walls. They had not stopped her any of those times, but they kept a close distance. Her mother had tried to coax her into visiting with her childhood friends who still lived across the street, but Essien refused the suggestion with a silent stare and the click of her closed door.

When the letter at last arrived informing her of her trial's scheduled start time, it was slipped underneath her door with the flap still sealed. Essien opened the letter with a slit of her pinky fingernail. The letter showed her time and date of trial—only three days away. For the first time that day, Essien exited her room. Her nne and nna were sitting in the front room, not talking to each other.

"I have a trial in three days," she told them.

Her mother nodded. Her father covered his face.

"Your father cannot travel, and I wouldn't be able to leave him alone. The brothers are far away now. It would be better if someone were with you."

Essien shook her head, "I will have the Mothers with me. If they cannot help me, nobody can."

"Essien, the news reports . . ."

"Don't watch them."

"Your father likes to know what's happening in this country now, since he can't go out and get the news himself."

"I am not hopeful they won't execute me."

Her father's eyes looked wet, and he had to stop and cough before he could speak.

"You are my only daughter, Essien. This country was never worthy of you."

Essien didn't want to cry, but she had never seen her father cry real tears. He was more often happy than sad, even after his accident. Now she looked away so her father could recover his dignity without her seeing him rebuild himself. Her father had lost so much in those fires. She knew he wanted to passionately rail against what had happened to her, to defend her, but his will and might were all but gone. These tears were all he could give her.

"The Mothers be with you," her nne said.

CHAPTER TWENTY-NINE

◆

A N ENGINE PICKED ESSIEN UP IN FRONT OF THE FAMILY COM-
pound before the sun had risen, and she was accompanied by the two
members of the Guard who had been assigned to watch her. The trip to
the Capital was a quick three hours by engine, and she watched out the
window as the village turned into the city. The streets were mostly empty,
filled only with the few people heading to early-morning jobs. They arrived
at the same building where her first hearing had been. She stared out the
engine window at the door of the building where her fate would be sealed,
her heart hiccupping as the engine came to a stop.

Essien entered the room where, once again, the Military Council sat
waiting for her. She was in full black uniform, the uniform feeling tight and
stiff on her neck and wrists. The walls and the floor were a shiny black—so
bright she felt like there was a window—but all the walls were smooth and
closed off from the outside world.

She faced the panel of thirty-two men, two men from each of the sixteen states in the country. They'd each served in the military, she knew,
and as Essien recited their names silently, she remembered that part of her
military academic training had been memorizing all of the military council
members up to the current position holders. She'd memorized the func-
tions of the Military Council and been tested on the Presidents who had
presided over Alkebulan. Now her own schooling had come back to cast
judgment upon her.

The Council sat behind a raised panel at the front of the long, rectangular room with three tables right in front of the panel. There was a chair
sitting in the middle, with no table or stand near it. Behind the empty
chair—undoubtedly meant for her—there were a few rows of spectators
comprised of the families of the deceased. They were all tall, even sitting,
and they all wore angry frowns meant just for her. She passed them with

her head turned away, but she could feel their fury like a palpable smack against her skin.

She took a seat in the solitary chair and noticed that the President wasn't among the men on the panel. Had she thought he would be here to preside over the trial of a violent military criminal? That's how the news reports were describing her and worse.

Antonious was seated at a table near the front of the room. He looked down at his hands clasped over his stomach, and she didn't even try to get his attention. Antonious might have been her only friend in the military. He seemed intent on showing her more of his humanity than he showed anyone else. But why was that? Was it because she was the one of the few women to survive in the military past their first few months of enlistment?

None of that mattered while she was in this room, as her skin was scorched by the stares of the dead's living. The way Antonious avoided looking at her told her that he didn't want her depending on him in this trial. If Antonious wasn't her friend, then she didn't have any at all.

There were news reporters with picto capturers seated in the back of the trial room, and there was the court typist to transcribe everything that was said. While one of the council members announced the start of the trial, Essien let herself look fully at the men who would be deciding her fate. They were all old, the oldest member a grizzled and almost blind husk of a man who had lived for over one hundred years. Some said he was closer to two hundred, but Essien couldn't believe that. No one lived to be that old, even if they had spent their life serving the country.

A council member stood at a podium facing the room. "Essien Ezinulo, you are on trial today for the murders of three of your fellow Sojas. We plan to present evidence today for which you will give an account. Are you capable of speaking truthfully as to the events of that day?"

Essien didn't know if she was allowed to speak, so she nodded. But the recording clerk spoke up, throwing her voice into the quiet room. "You must speak, Soja Ezinulo, so that I can record your words."

"Yes, I can give an account."

And so, the questions began. Rather than coming from one central council member, they came at her from all of them and from what seemed to be all at once.

"When did you notice the men?"

"When they attacked me." Essien fought not to roll her eyes.

"Had you seen these men before?"

"All three were in my practice squad." Her eyes flicked over to Antonious, who held her glance for just a second.

"Did you know these men before they attacked you?"

"I just said that I did. We were on the same practice team." She knew she sounded impatient.

"How did they overpower you?"

"By being very, very violent." She hoped they wouldn't make her describe the attack.

"Did you call for help?"

"I don't remember." Essien scanned the faces on the panel, stern and unmoving.

"Where was your body when they tried to rape you?"

"In the middle of a circle of trees." Essien flashed back to the moment when she'd reached the top of that hill.

"What were you doing while they held you down and cut off your tunic?"

"Trying to figure out a way to get out of that situation alive."

"How were you able to grab the knife?"

"One of them put it down." The black steel knife near her head, and Essien moving quicker than a flash of lightning.

"Which one?"

"I don't remember." Essien thought of the two palbinos, both tall, but only one so scarred.

"Did you call for help?"

"I don't know." She saw Antonious staring again and held his line of sight. He pursed his lips and looked up at the crowd behind her.

"What made you choose to murder?"

"Over my own death? The choice was an easy one." Essien felt uneasiness spread through her stomach.

"Do you regret killing these men?"

"I regret they tried to kill me."

The questions droned on. Essien's leg began to bounce, and she found herself clasping and unclasping her hands. She wanted to stand and walk around the chair. She felt like a spotlight was shining directly on her head, but there weren't any direct lights. She wiped at sweat on her brow and glanced around the room at all the people in the stands. A picto capturer flashed, and Essien frowned.

"When you were being held down, how did you manage to grab the knife?"

"I wasn't being held down. One of them put the knife down, and I grabbed it."

"How did you know how to use the knife?"

"I had two years of military academy training. I've been in the military for the better part of a year now."

"Tell us how you used just a knife to kill three men?"

"Very quickly," She responded, beginning to feel once again like she was under attack.

"How did you grab the knife?"

"*When they weren't looking.*" The frown on Essien's face deepened. The questions were pricking her more and more, like little hornet stings.

"How were you able to take the knife while on the ground beneath them?"

"*They were distracted.*"

"How did you know what to do with the knife?"

"*I received extensive weapons training at the university in Ibadan.*"

"What did you do with the knife after you had killed them?"

Essien sighed. There was no use letting them see her upset. It would only hurt her in the end. She took a breath and replied calmly, "I left it there on the ground."

Essien looked up again, scanning the faces of the council members. They each displayed varying stages of interest. Some scanned papers in a file, and Essien assumed they were about her case. Some of them stared down at her with serious glares. Some looked bored, exhibiting waxing and waning attention as the council members took turns asking the questions.

Essien wondered what was in the files. There had to be information on her training history. She began training at the mgbati ahu when she was sixteen. She'd then spent two years in military academy after finishing her twelfth levels at eighteen. She'd been in the military barely a year yet.

Everything she knew and had experienced came from the military and yet, it was as if they wanted her to say she had taught herself—as if she'd become some savage murderer all on her own. If not for the military, cutting produce in her mother's kitchen would have been the only cutting with a knife Essien had ever done.

"What were the men doing while you grabbed the knife?"

"They were looking away." Essien seeing Enyemaka's face while he distracted the men from her hand grabbing the forgotten knife.

"Did they try to stop you when you stabbed the first one?"

"No. I was moving too fast."

"How did you manage to stab such big men without getting hurt yourself?"

"Skill. Speed. Magic."

A murmur waved through the crowd, and Essien looked behind her at the stands again. She couldn't tell if the mood was darkening or brightening.

"When you had the knife, did any of them try to stop you?"

"Two couldn't have. They did not see me coming."

An hour ticked by. Essien felt physically uncomfortable but not from any pain. Her wounds had healed, but she still felt sore in some places. She realized that she had tuned out as the questions were being repeated over and over in different ways. Essien understood that they were trying to trip her up. They were trying to catch her in an admission of guilt, something they could lay claim to as their reason for doing what they wanted to do anyway.

She told them the part that had been left out so far about Enyemaka distracting them long enough to get their attention off her.

She said, "He saw I was going for the knife, so he had to know what I planned to do with it. Perhaps he should be placed on trial, too, for helping me kill. Maybe he should be the one on trial for letting them get far enough along in their plan to attack me."

Essien did not really want Enyemaka to be tried alongside her, but if it would help her case and keep her from being executed, including him was a smart move. They didn't want to hear her story, how she'd been able to save herself and survive. They wanted her to prove that what she'd done hadn't been a crime at all. She watched the council members' faces as they considered Enyemaka's role in her murders with what looked like interest.

"Let it show for the records, Odibo Enyemaka is present in court today. He is now called as a co-witness."

Essien whipped her head around to look more closely at the spectators she had previously avoided making eye contact with. There were the grieving family members with squares of cotton up to their mournful faces. There were the news reporters with picto capturers and audio capturers. She didn't see Enyemaka among them.

He stood up at the very end of the farthest row back and began walking to the front of the room. He was wearing the standard black-on-black uniform with well-shined boots. Enyemaka walked stiffly, like he'd been sitting too long, or he didn't really want to come forward. He walked up to a podium set up diagonal to where Essien was sitting. He did not look at her once, but she kept her eyes on him. *He'll have to look at me eventually. Unless he's guilty. Unless he's not really a friend.* The coldness wafted off of him like dry ice.

One of the Members began to question Enyemaka, and Essien wondered if he would stand at the podium the entire time. No one had brought a chair for him, and there was only the one in which Essien sat. He began answering their questions without looking at her, his hands gripping onto the sides of the podium. He licked his lips and looked down at the ground.

"What was your role in the attack?"

Enyemaka answered staring at the ground, "I was supposed to be the lookout. I was supposed to make sure if anybody came, I gave them a warning or helped distract the person away."

"Did you know what they were planning to do to her?"

Enyemaka looked up at the panel and answered, "I thought they were going to try and convince her to leave the military. I had hoped that's all they would do, but . . . I think I knew they might try to hurt her if she didn't listen."

Essien had to look away from him then. It was disappointing to hear, though she had figured as much. Behind that short height and small voice, Enyemaka was obviously more calculating than she, but was he really cold-hearted and conniving? He said they wanted to just talk to her, but she'd felt her death in that knife slicing up her tunic. In their hands holding her down and touching her. In their boots kicking her again and again. They were going to do more than just talk to her. So, they'd lied to him.

Or he was lying now.

He got to the part where she had walked up to him with the knife in her hand. "I had Ojo down on the ground, but I let go when she told me to move."

A Member asked, "Why did she kill that final man?"

Enyemaka shrugged. "I do not know. I tried to convince her not to. I told her I would make sure he didn't get away."

Essien shook her head, staring at her hands on the table. She had wanted to know without a doubt that she'd gotten rid of them forever, so they could never plot or plan to come back for her in revenge. She had wanted to eliminate any of them who were a threat to her. He knew that.

He *knew* that.

Essien turned her head to look at the people who had come to see her trial and sentencing, the family and friends of the dead. They glared at her, cried, or held their heads down in disbelief. They were bereaved for their dead ones; she could see their grief hovering over them like a clinging gray mist. She could hear it in the air. One man had slow tears falling in a sheet of wetness across his cheeks. She had taken their family members, and they had come to see her pay for it. They probably preferred that she was the one dead and buried with her parents and brothers crying over her memory in those seats over there. There was a great likelihood that no trial would even have been held; perhaps they would have patted the men on the back for a job well done. Perhaps the country would have rejoiced at her death rather than mourned over it. There were many Alkebulanians who wanted to return to the way things were before women had moved beyond their place in the home and the garden. She still heard their grumbles about military women in the weeks she'd been home on the rare occasion she left the compound. Looking into the assembled crowd, Essien could see both sides in one quick flash of insight. Some were proud of the women who had ventured into joining the military. Others were personally aggrieved and didn't see any right to the gendered changes.

"Was there any discussion of doing more than talking to her?"

"They had been watching her for weeks before I knew what they were going to do. They watched her from the time she left her room to the time she went back into it. Every day. They took turns, but Akpari spent the most time following her around. That's how I found out because I was suspicious about where he was disappearing to every morning. So, I followed him, and I realized that he was following her. I tried to be cool when I confronted him about it, told him I wanted to help. He didn't believe me at first. He shoved my face out of his way. A couple days later, they came to get me early in the morning. They told me they just wanted to talk to her, tell her to leave the Soja, and that's it. But they were excited about it in a way that made them . . . It was disgusting. I agreed to be the lookout thinking that at least with me there, they might . . . I could at least . . ." Enyemaka stopped and looked over at Essien for the first time, the slant toward pity causing his bottom lip to poke out.

Shortly after that, Enyemaka finished giving his testimony and returned to his seat. Suddenly, there was a commotion that Essien could see out of her peripheral vision. Essien could feel cold air blowing toward her, like a rushing wind. Without stopping to wonder where the breeze was coming from, she tipped herself over in the chair, so that it fell to the ground with her in it. As Essien fell, a hand holding a knife jabbed over top of her, missing her head and neck. She saw the hand was coming back around and down and noticed the eyes appeared to be red, as if from crying, but they were wide with eagerness. The individual holding the knife was an old man in a dusty hat and patched overcoat. That knife came down again, and Essien was already rolling out of the chair and backing up toward the tables at the front of the room.

It was a shouting, chaotic mess with other family members trying to push forward, until the person with the knife was finally taken to the ground by members of the Guard. The trial chambers dissolved into a pandemonium of Guard surrounding her with their rapid-fires pointed outward this time, protecting her from any further attacks. The old man was dragged from the room, screaming, "I will kill you, akwuna! I will see you dead!"

As Essien quickly scanned the room, she noticed that Antonious was the only one staring at her . . . with a smile on his face.

CHAPTER THIRTY

◆

AN ENGINE WITH ONLY A DRIVER RETURNED HER TO THE FAMily home, and the two Guard that had followed her for the past month remained behind with her. Before being transported home, she had been told she would be sent a date for her final verdict and sentencing, and that due to the chaos at the trial, her verdict and sentencing would be done in private.

As she walked into the front room, she was comforted to see both her parents sitting together in her father's chair. Her mother was cuddled up next to her father, folding all of her height into the chair with him. Essien smiled at them as she approached the chair, and seeing her smile made them both sit up.

"I don't think I'll be executed, but I won't know until my final sentencing date."

Her mother hugged her tightly, holding the back of her head like the infant she once was. Essien let her mother hold her. Behind her, her father reached his hand up to her. Essien took her father's hand. It was warm and worn smooth after years of working in his fields. Her mother squeezed her, and her father gripped her tight, and Essien knew at that moment that her parents loved her, even when they disapproved of her decisions.

That evening, they enjoyed each other's company and a meal of homemade egusi soup with fried fish and pounded yam. Essien ate two servings and drank two glasses of her mother's hibiscus tea with mango nectar. The red and orange was a beautiful swirl in the glass, and Essien told her mother afterward that dinner was lovely.

In response to the compliment, her mother said, "The house girl, Binye, made the meal. She has evening classes now. She wants to be a birthing assistant. Her mother finally agreed that we might pay for her schooling in addition to her wages. Your higher education was free, Essien. Be grateful.

Not every Alkebulanian child gets a free education after the lower levels. Some have to pay."

As she lay in her childhood bed that night, she couldn't sleep. The hours bled into one another in a dark stretch that left her feeling worse and worse. She opened her window shutters and stared up at the moon. Its cold, white surface revealed nothing. Eventually, she got up and pulled on her overcoat and boots. She needed to do something besides lie still and wait for her future to overtake her, so she left her parents' compound through the back gate.

THE VILLAGE LOOKED DIFFERENT AT NIGHT; IT ALWAYS HAD with everything cloaked in so much secrecy. Every shape took on a new form without the light of day to see clearly. Every branch rattling and leaf blowing was an Akukoifo calling to her and luring her out into the night.

As usual, all was quiet in the surrounding compounds. No one else walked the streets alone at night. Essien noticed again how peaceful village life was; it had been boring and lifeless to her growing up. Now she breathed deeply of the lonely, cool night air and made herself move quickly down the road. She saw no one. The Guard who had been with her since her arrival were no longer a hindrance to her free movement. She'd taken that as a sign of something, but she wasn't sure what. That she wouldn't be losing her head after all? That they knew she was a dead woman walking with no need of protection?

As she walked away from her parents' compound, the stories and tales she'd grown up hearing her entire life came back to her. When she looked up from watching her feet kick dust, she realized she had found herself back at the very same spot to which she kept coming. The same hidden trail running into the densely packed trees making a tight tunnel with a canopy of waving leaves above. Essien didn't hesitate at the edge as she had before. She ducked her head down and pushed through. She looked back, but it seemed the entry was already beginning to close behind her. Then she saw a blinding flash of silver, so bright she felt like it came from everywhere around her.

Even though she could feel an anticipatory skip in her heart, what felt like excitement, Essien was afraid to remember what she had seen the last time she had come into the jungle. Something so supernatural and unreal that she'd kept herself from thinking about it at all. She remembered waking up in the middle of the night, sweating, and feeling hot air flow up her body from her hands. She never could make sense of that feeling, like she was touching something hot that flowed up her hands and into the rest of her body, burning her as it coursed through.

Essien had trouble getting through the stand of trees in front of her. They were so close together, almost growing into one another like a protective barrier. *To keep people out*, Essien thought again as she shoved her way through, the same as she had the first time she'd stepped foot there. She pulled her leg through the space she'd made, and then turned. There was the lake again, an expanding stretch of silver water like a flat piece of sky transplanted into the darkest part of the world. As far away as she could see, the water lay like a prism, reflecting glints of silver and blue from its smooth surface. Essien wanted to slide into the water, but she was afraid, and could feel her pulse thumping. She glanced along the shore, but it was the same muddy, rocky beach that it had always been with trees butted up against each other all the way around. Essien couldn't see the far end of the lake; it wrapped around and disappeared between more trees.

She stared back at the surface of the water. The silvery-blue glowed and pulsed, but she couldn't see more than a few inches below the water line tonight. There were no darting fish, and the bottom was murky and unclear though the lake was perfectly still. Essien knew that water usually rippled and waved, but the lake wasn't moving at all. No wind blew, and no waves gurgled at the edge; even the leaves above it were silent.

Teenaged Essien had been so afraid that it had felt as though her heart had beat inside her mouth. The figure of a man had floated up from the lake because she had touched the surface, disturbing that serene stillness. Adult Essien, now on the cusp of such uncertainty, yearned for any moment of magic she could conjure; seeing the Mothers again would be a blessing. Seeing the floating man-figure was a guarantee.

She leaned forward, the tips of her fingers skimming the edge of the water. It felt warm, like blood sliding out of veins. Water dripped off her fingers, as the disturbance she made began to spread out and away from her. The rings spread and grew bigger, and then stopped, and began changing direction. The water pulsed toward her and she could see the rings spreading from a central point.

"To live or to die?" she heard a voice say, like an ancient whisper from thousands of years ago. Essien whipped her head around, but there was no one. "To live or to die?"

"I come to live," Essien said. Silence. The waves stood still again.

"I come here to live!" Essien shouted it, her voice echoing out just like the rings in the water.

There was no reply. Feeling foolish, she turned to leave. A sound of water splashing stopped her, and she turned.

The silver man hovered over the surface of the water, a man with no face, no arms, no legs, but a man, nonetheless. Essien's mouth hung open as she watched the figure float just off the shore, not even ten feet from the edge. The figure was translucent with a pearl-shimmer around the edges and blue threads running throughout, like the silvery flow of water poured through fingers. She had to touch that figure. She had to see if it was truly real—if her memory of him from her night sweats could be trusted. That's what she'd come out here to find out, she now understood, and here she was . . . here it was . . . here he was.

She stepped into the lake with her boots and kept sloshing forward as the warm, silvery water soaked her knees, then her thighs, then her hips, all the way up to her chest. The bottom of the lake felt like a soft carpet, but she could feel it sloping downward the further in she walked. The water smelled faintly of jasmine, but she couldn't be sure because she tried to breathe through her mouth. She didn't enjoy the smell of jasmine with its subtly clinging sweetness. She was so close now. She stretched out her arm above the water, and her dripping fingertips caressed the very edge of the floating figure.

It was solid, the feeling of skin over bones solid. She floated closer and was able to put her whole hand flat against the figure. It felt like a human's leg covered in a vibrating, gelatinous substance, hot to the touch. Essien paddled in the water and looked up. The face was looking down at her as she touched it.

"I come to live," she whispered, the smell of jasmine like a faint tickle in her nose. The solidness of the floating waterbody above her left a tactile echo that reminded her of the other times she'd come here.

Suddenly, a piercing sharpness hit her from every side, and she was sucked under so violently she didn't have time to take in air or fight back. It happened so quickly that she didn't even thrash around under the surface.

THE SILVER FIGURE CONTINUED TO HOVER ABOVE THE WATER AS the ripples slowly subsided. A bubble appeared on top of the water, settling there for a second, before bursting. The figure began to sink back down into the water and spread out like an oil slick on top. It drifted down into the water until there was nothing but the surface of the still lake, as flat and motionless as it had always been. A silence descended, softer and gentler than before, a silence of waiting with pregnant expectation. The wind didn't blow at all this deep in the jungle. Even the vines hung in stillness.

All at once, the jungle seemed to tremble and crack from deep within its surface. Rocks crashed down from mountain peaks, tree roots pulled up grass and dirt and squirming worms. A lightning flash split the sky in two, but rain did not fall.

No one was awake to wonder what had taken place. No one was awake to touch themselves in the motion of a hasty prayer. The ground shook, but the silver-blue water remained still.

Time passed. Purple and blue wisps raced over the face of the moon. Then, a figure began to rise from the surface of the lake, so slowly as to be almost unmoving. A head of sorts, shoulders, then a second head close by. A second set of shoulders rising up alongside the first. Two figures rising above the lake in a silvery sheen of water that molted and transformed in a rolling wave contained. The second figure was much shorter and smaller than the first. It began to walk forward, stepping across the water as across a solid path. The figure got to the edge of the lake and looked back over its shoulder. Both figures stared at each other with faces that were not faces. The second figure finally stepped off the edge of the water onto solid ground as the first figure, still hovering over the water, exploded in a scattering of water that sprayed in every direction. A drop hit the face of the second figure and was absorbed instantly. Then water fell like a cascade into a puddle, and Essien stood shivering in the cool air.

She took in a deep breath and opened her eyes. The lake was a slick, smooth surface that didn't move. The sky was gaining a light dusting of pink far away over the tops of the trees. She could feel the sun just below the tree line, waiting to begin its climb up overhead. The smell of jasmine was stronger, filling her nose and her lungs, the scent thick on her tongue.

"I hate that smell," Essien whispered. She turned and began pushing her way back through the line of trees, toward the family home.

CHAPTER THIRTY-ONE

◆

Later that same day, a letter was delivered to Essien by a Soja in full uniform. When she opened it, she discovered that her sentencing would be held the next day. *Perhaps it is best not to have much notice. Less time to think about what the end result might be*, she thought to herself. She let her parents know, and after a few tears and a hug or two, the house was eerily silent for the remainder of the day and night. Neither of them knowing what to say, nor wanting to talk about it.

The morning arrived surprisingly fast after a sleepless night. Essien braided her hair back into a twisted bun, donned her uniform and boots, and headed toward the smell of food coming from the kitchen. Her mother had made her porridge with spiced herbs, and although Essien was not hungry, she appreciated her mother's intention and ate a few bites out of thankfulness and obligation. Soon after, her father called her into his room, and her mother followed behind. Essien kneeled beside the bed, so he could reach her.

He held her hands and tried to smile. "You will see me this evening, Essien. We will have evening meal, and all this military madness will have passed behind us."

Essien nodded and kissed her father on the cheek. Her mother hugged her at the door and whispered, "The Mothers grant you life."

Her words gave Essien a chill through her skin. Essien had never known her nne to be religious.

An engine picked her up, and although they were wearing a mask, Essien was nearly certain it was the same driver from before. A few hours later, she arrived at the now all too familiar building, and she was led down the same hallway to the same bright black room. The panel was mostly empty this time. There was just one Council member present and off to the side, seated at the same table, was Antonious. There were no grieving family members to watch from the corner of her eye. There were no news reporters to snap pictos or moving footage. The Guard didn't even cuff her or make her walk in front of them. Everything felt so casual, so meaningless. There was no fanfare at all, and she had expected more people, more pomp for a human life, at least.

Antonious stared at his lap. The Council member stared at her. He was the one from Igbo State, and she had expected him in all of his seriousness and gruffness. She ignored a small internal voice of disappointment that the President hadn't come to this part either, though she knew it was foolish as she tamped it down. The President had much more important matters to attend to, matters to which she wasn't even privy.

Essien was asked to rise, and she did. She felt her heartbeat skip and then beat faster. All of her future depended on this moment. She was asked her name and her occupation, to which she responded. She was then asked if she was ready to hear the Council's verdict, to which she answered with a solemn nod. Essien felt that was sufficient, and no verbal response was required, since there was no court notetaker present this time around.

The Council member then began to read the verdict and sentencing in a monotone and seemingly disinterested manner. "You are pronounced not guilty. You are remanded to the service of the President's Guard. May the Mothers have mercy upon your soul."

Relief flooded Essien's eyes, and she saw the room through a watery blur. She had hoped she would not be executed, but there had still been doubt. Now, she was sure of everything. Her eyes shifted to Antonious, but he wasn't looking at her. He was staring at the man on the panel, a near smile barely widening his lips.

CHAPTER THIRTY-TWO

◆

H ER HEAD WAS STILL SPINNING. ONE MOMENT ESSIEN WAS facing the prospect of a death sentence, and the next she had been invited to join the President's personal Guard—his Uzo Nchedo. Wherever the President went, the Guard went. Whatever danger or threats faced him, the Guard was in line to block or thwart them. They were the highly trained militia she'd heard whispered about, the ones she'd feared would kill her only weeks before. And now she was one of them.

The Guard trained and resided in the President's palatial compound on Capital Island. It could only be reached by one bridge and one mountainside road. Though a curious choice for the crime of murdering three of the President's Sojas, it was a relief to still have breath in her body.

The road leading up to the Palatial Compound stretched like an endless, snaking chain up the side of the Capital Island. When the truck reached the top, the surface flattened out and then sloped up the side of another mountain covered in lush green acres of trees and grassy plains. Essien watched through the windows of the truck as it ate up the distance but didn't seem to get any closer to the compound she still couldn't see. She knew it would be the only set of buildings on the top of the mountain-shaped island.

Essien thought she saw a small village clinging to the side of the steep grades on the way up, but they were moving too fast for her to be sure. She had twenty-five years to spend here, so she figured she'd get to explore it all at some point. Essien recalled the bargain that had come shortly after her life had been spared from execution. The two Guard had taken her into a small room. A military clerk had presented her with a new contract of enlistment. She had been found not guilty on three deprivation of life charges, and now, on top of the thirty-five-year military contract, she had a twenty-five-year contract with the Guard. Even though she'd escaped execution, she was still bothered by the commitment of so many years. She had thought she might still live a life outside the military, like Idara and Malachum. Despite how much she wanted the position, it bothered her to have all her life now committed to the military. It was what she'd thought she wanted, but seeing it spelled out on paper made her feel a strong discomfort. With a sigh of capitulation, Essien had signed the paper showing her agreement with the terms. Immediately after doing so, she was taken to an engine assigned to take her directly to the island just off the coast of Igbo State. She would not be able to return home or see her parents before her transition. From not guilty to Guard enlistment, it was an abrupt and sudden shift in an increasingly chaotic life.

Essien sat inside the engine and watched the bridge they had crossed grow smaller, now just a silver line down below the height they had traveled. Essien gripped her hands tightly together and stared at the shades of green rushing by. All of her life belonged to Alkebulan now, and that was assuming she would live to old age. She was consigned to the President and indebted to the military for over three quarters of her years to come. She realized it bothered her because she had never planned on joining the Guard; it had never even occurred to her that she could be invited to enlist in the elite group. She forced herself to think about something else, a deliberate process. Her parents had likely received news by then of her new assignment. She imagined her father's mouth and her mother's eyes. The image caused Essien to bury her face in her hands . . . she did not see the rest of the ride up to the President's compound.

Essien's mind flashed back to the man at the lake. She shivered involuntarily though she wasn't cold. Everything about her felt different, hyper-real, and super sensitive. She wanted to tell someone what had happened to her in the lake, but there was no one who would believe her. If Enyemaka had not been there to see her kill three men, they probably wouldn't have believed her then either. She felt marked by trouble, like a magnet attracting it toward her. *That is scary*, she thought, as the compound finally came into view around the tall, wide-branch trees. Essien sat up straighter and held tight to the door's handle. There might be enemies even among this new crew of men. She was the first woman ever elevated to the Guard. All of them were called to serve the President, but she wondered how many of them were criminals. Perhaps all of them were. Or perhaps she was the only one.

The truck stopped directly in front of the tall, long, gray compound with concrete stairs leading up to its black wood doors. Essien had not expected Antonious to be waiting for her outside the compound, but in the back of her mind, she had known he would be there somewhere. She was smiling as she got out, and she didn't know why. Maybe it was because she wasn't dead, and she felt deep down that Antonious and the President had everything to do with it. They had wanted her to join his Uzo Nchedo, and here she was.

The thought of the years before her flitted across her face, revealing itself in a small tick of her upper lip. She would try to make the most of this second chance and see it for what it was: paving the way for the next generation of women who might join ranks after her. She would try to open her mind to what it meant to serve as an elite member among the best-trained soldiers in the world. Although, Essien quietly admitted to herself, simply surviving the next twenty-four hours would be an accomplishment.

She was back to smiling again when she reached Antonious. He was wearing the same gray suit that he had been wearing in the courtroom, and somehow it remained shiny and stiff. The same grave features pulled together to study her closely. She couldn't wipe the smile off her face. It was the only emotion she could show trying to hide so many of the others she felt. She would pretend to be excited and joyful as long as she could. Eventually, her smile would slip and everything she hid would come tumbling out of her. Maybe not this day or even the next. She might put up this facade of fake cheer for a month or two even, but eventually, the veneer would crack, and the real Essien would peek through. The Essien who stood beside a lake and didn't know if what she'd seen was real or not. The one who looked at men and wondered if she could kill them. For now, her smile was firm and held tight across her face. She had grown to like Antonious. She thought he may even like her, despite the ever-present grimace he always wore.

"Welcome. Let me show you around. The President will return this evening."

She followed him up the steps of the massive compound made of a dark gray stone with a lighter gray stone trim around the doors and plate glass windows indicating each floor. The building was six stories high. The roof was flat. She stepped between the two doors, which swung open to reveal black marble floors with glittering gold veins, white brick walls, and a light gray ceiling stretching high up, further up than any ceiling she had ever seen, with balconies showing where each floor began. She guessed it was one hundred feet tall from the floor to the top.

"This way," Antonious gestured to her from another set of doors. He seemed rushed, waving his hand at her. She would have time to linger and pause over the home later, but it was the most luxurious compound she had ever been in. She had never imagined the President would spend money on a home such as this. From the news reports she'd seen and the economic policies of his administration, she had thought him more frugal and modest than marble floors and ornate gold doorknobs.

Her boots made a hollow *thunk* against the floors as she sped up, and she could feel the vibration of the floor through her soles. She passed built-in eaves holding framed pictos, some painted, some captures of real scenes. One she caught in passing was an image of a battle with bodies intertwined in heaps and a river of blood flowing out into an ocean of red. Seeing it brought a chill of reminiscence to Essien and she hurried past.

Set in one wall by itself was an open set of doors leading into a room with rows and rows of books all the way up as far as she could see. In it, Essien could see the corner of a dark wood desk and a curved back chair. She followed Antonious through another set of doors and down a long hallway with the same dark marble floor and white walls. The gray ceiling was lower here, maybe fifteen feet high. Essien passed door after door with silver labels on them. These must be the dormitories where the Personal Guard stayed when not on duty.

"The previous positions were vacated suddenly by death." Antonious spoke into their silent walking.

That was news to Essien. She had wondered why they were bringing her in and why the President thought he could use fewer males protecting him rather than more. The hallway of doors felt endless as she walked behind Antonious. The Guard now consisted of one hundred and one personnel: one hundred men and one woman.

"As a result, we decided to upper enlist two newly enlisted personnel, the most promising among the entire military. You will be meeting the second person shortly. A tour of the grounds is also in order, so that you know your way around. You will meet with the President upon concluding these activities."

Essien nodded silently. Antonious was being so formal that she almost didn't want to ask him any questions. But then her curiosity over who the other new Guard might be won out.

"May I please inquire as to who the other person is?" If it was someone she knew, Essien figured it could make her job here much easier . . . or much harder, if they wanted to remind her and everyone else what she kept trying to forget. The second person they brought in could determine if she was doomed to a continuation of what she had just escaped.

But Antonious only replied, "I will let him introduce himself."

They approached a single door at the end of the hallway. The door opened outward, an entrance to the front of an auditorium. There were rows of chairs to the very back of the large room with a platform and podium on an elevated stage to the left. The front of the stage was backed by a wall of curtains that sparkled like diamonds made liquid. The ceiling and floor were white, and all the chairs were black.

The room was empty, but Essien felt eyes all over her, like tangible touches on her skin. There was a faint buzzing she couldn't identify, almost like chatter in a crowded food shop that rises up as a wave of white noise. She walked further into the room, and the sound got louder. It felt just like eyes were creeping all over her, and she couldn't understand why she felt suspended in front of a large crowd when the room was utterly empty.

She stared hard at the chairs that appeared empty to her eyes but felt full of something, maybe a person, maybe people. Essien could feel heat grasping at her as she moved closer, and she could just barely see what looked like a faint outline or glow on top of the closest chair. When she looked at the chair next to it, the outline was bigger, but still there. She walked even closer to one chair, staring at it intently, her eyes squinted to make them focus. Her knee bumped into a knee she hadn't seen and just like that, the camouflage broke.

It felt like a splash of water against her face, and there were suddenly rows and rows of at least one hundred men staring back at her. They were all within a certain age range, not too young, nor too old. They wore the same uniform, a light-gray tunic and athletic slacks with white running shoes.

Essien jumped back, her heartbeat choking her. She then surprised herself by laughing, the merry sound bubbling up from her and out into the wide room. Essien kept laughing even after no one else joined her. The men sat with stony stares looking back and forth between her and Antonious, who now had a real smile on his face. The smile showed all of his teeth to the back of his mouth.

"You shouldn't have been able to see them at all."

"Is this real?" She turned back to the men and let her eyes run over every single face of those present. There were none she recognized. Not every face was hostile, but some refused to meet her eyes at all. She turned back to Antonious and said what she was thinking, "What in Mother's name did I just walk into?"

"Cloaking. The ability to disappear from sight by using one's energetic capacity to influence cellular visibility."

Essien's frown deepened. She felt utterly displaced from one moment to the next.

"Invisible cells?" It didn't make sense to her.

"Have you not seen this before? Surely, you must have to be able to see it now." Antonious leaned into her, as a grin spread across his face.

Essien started to shake her head, but Antonious cut her off. "Of course, you have, Essien. If you can see cloaking, you can see Akukoifo."

His grin widened as she gasped at that word, the thoughts slamming together in her mind. But Antonious had already turned away and was walking out of the room. She looked back at the men, and some of them were still watching her. Every face was a different shade of brown with different levels of sternness etched into the brow and jawline. Rows and rows of dark eyes, dotted with a few pairs of frost blue eyes, but all of them head and shoulders above her. She saw one palbino man in the very last row, and she flashed on the pink jagged scar that bisected Akpari's face. She blinked and shook her head. There was no scar across this pale man's face; he was just another man who looked like a small minority of people in the world. Akpari was not here because he was dead.

More of them looked curious now, as if wondering whether she might be worth something to them as a team. Essien noted to herself that once again she would have to watch what she said, what she did, and where she went. This cloaking, as Antonious had called it, added another layer of mystery and complexity that she'd never considered before. If these men could move like Akukoifo, then she would need to be hyper-aware.

Essien's mind flashed to that silver water man she had found in the middle of the jungle. That had been the weirdest thing she'd ever seen before today. For a moment, she wished that she might see him again and push her hand into his gelatinous body. It had felt like a smooth layer of jelly encasing normal human limbs. Perhaps there was an actual person inside of the quivering sack. Essien shuddered suddenly, a chill spreading down into her limbs. She looked down at the ground and then up at Antonious who had been talking to her while she thought about Akukoifo and how much real-life magic was floating around her.

"Patience is virtuous for those with no time they can waste." One side of his lip quirked higher than the other, and she thought it might have been a smile.

"The tour then?" he asked. She nodded as he turned away, leaving her to glance once more at the men as they stood as one unit, and turned like one entity, to watch the two of them walk out of the auditorium.

Essien followed Antonious again as he took her back down the same long hallway to a set of wide doors with buttons set in a panel. Antonious pressed the top button. The doors slid open, and she stepped into a rise. The second floor was an entire space filled with training rooms and exercise equipment. There was an indoor track made of a bouncy black material with yellow lanes. Essien could see that some of the Guard had come to the location to train. A group of Guard was beginning a run, their stride in sync, all of them keeping the same pace with the same perfect form, bunched together as they began their first lap around the track. They picked up speed as they passed her and Antonious. In a matter of seconds, they were running so fast that their combined mass blurred together into one swift motion. In another section of the training room, Essien saw heavier weights than any she'd ever seen before, and she watched as one man lifted a set of bars with stones stamped 1,000 on each side. There were other rooms, some larger or smaller, with gym mats spread out, a climbing wall, a weapons inventory, and a shooting range. There was also a large room with clear walls and a clear floor, but nothing else. Essien wondered what it was used for, but she did not feel comfortable asking her guide.

Antonious finished showing her around the training area and brought her back to the lift. On the third floor, there were more rooms, none of which would be hers. Antonious told her that personnel were housed according to seniority, with lower ranked Guard assigned two to a room on the first floor, and the higher-ups located on the third floor. Essien wondered where she would be billeted, and when Antonious would reveal her quarters. She felt uneasy about it. Like maybe they had forgotten to include her in their designs, and so she would be relegated to a box of a room and sneaking in to use the men's toilet. She swallowed and tried to pay attention to where they were going, so she would remember her way around.

At the end of the third-floor hallway, there was another auditorium-sized room, this one white with blank walls and individual desks spread out in front of a rectangular blue screen that came to life when they entered. Words scrolled across: *The Greater Unified Alkebulan Republic Dominion, presided over by President Gabriel Ijikota.* Essien stared at the President's name and thought about his imminent arrival. She would be greeting her employer face-to-face in just a short while. She would make sure she shook his hand this time. She hoped he wouldn't try to hold on to her again. It wasn't appropriate, no matter how good it made her feel.

"This is where you will come for daily instructions and verbal training. Any questions?"

"Will my room be on the first floor with the other junior guard?"

Essien's question had come out before she'd thought about its implications. If she had to share a room on the first floor, she would quit right then and suffer the consequences. If they hadn't thought to include a separate bathing room for her, but she at least had a place to sleep, she could manage. If they hadn't thought to make her comfortable at all, this didn't bode well for the next couple decades of her life. She didn't expect them to lavish her with luxury, but she did not want to be in the situation of hopping from the fufu pan and straight into the fire.

Antonious began to chuckle, and it struck Essien how rare it was to hear that sound. She liked how much he reminded her of an old village elder, a grandfather to everyone.

"Do not worry; we have thought about your comfort, Essien. You will not be rooming on this floor."

The fourth floor was barred to her. Antonious let the doors slide open to show her. The hallway was gold, like liquid tiles of molten metal made solid. She started to step out of the rise, but Antonious held up his left hand, halting her abruptly.

"The President's wing. You will not enter this floor until he invites you to."

Essien stared at all the bright metal, like bars flattened out thin and cemented into place with a mixture of powdered gold dust mortar. Everything sparkled richly, even the doorknobs. Although, the door at the end of the hallway was a plain, silvery white.

What a waste, she thought. Why would he spend so much money on home decorations and furniture? She wanted to reach out and touch the floor but resisted. That floor would remain off limits to her forever if it must. She had never lived a life that luxurious, where wasting gold inside a home was seen as tasteful and not just a rude expense. She had never really desired any form of luxury. Especially not this much of it.

"And this is where you'll be staying," Antonious said, as they exited the lift on the fifth floor.

To her surprise, the fifth floor housed a wing that Antonious informed her was entirely for her. She stood at the edge of the lift, on a soft white carpet that felt cushiony beneath her boots. The walls were covered in a soft gray textured wallpaper. Essien reached out to run her hand over it, and the texture felt like the finest velvet fabric.

Antonious stepped back into the lift, and announced, "Dinner is in half an hour," just before he disappeared behind the closing doors. And for the first time in a very long time, Essien found herself alone . . .

ESSIEN TOOK THE LIFT BACK DOWN TO THE FIRST FLOOR. AT THE end of the hallway was the auditorium and just next door, on the right, was the dining hall. Essien could hear loud voices coming from the opened doors, so she took a deep breath and stepped into the doorway. There were groups of men sitting down at the round tables spread around the room. There were twenty to thirty men crowded around one man who was much shorter than they were. *He must be the second recruit.* Essien pretended to feel more confidence than she'd ever felt as she swaggered over to them. She tried to swing her arms more, to give a slight smirk, to show that she was tougher than she actually felt. Her breath shook going in. She stepped around the tallest man in the group, so she could see who this short man was.

Most of the men had quieted and were watching her. The short man stopped talking, too, and turned around to face her. He was wearing a smile at first, but as their eyes connected, the smile dripped off like a melting cream stick. She felt her face lose its smirk and shine.

"Enyemaka."

Essien took a step back. It was the one man who knew exactly what she was, what was waiting just beneath her surface for a trigger to spill out over all of them. She stared at him, her mouth closed. The surprise showed on her silent face as she couldn't think fast enough to respond.

"I see they didn't decide to behead you. Everyone was sure they would."

"Execute the first woman to make it as far as I did? Please."

"Execute the first woman to kill three men on a military compound. Please."

"Maybe it should have been four."

His face changed, and she knew that it was too much, too soon, too late. She put up a hand, and everyone seemed to react to it. A subtle pulling away, a drawing back, suddenly not wanting to be too close. She put her hand back down. She raised it up, and again, they all seemed to move back. She smiled.

"You don't bring up my past, I won't tell you how I can make it your future." It wasn't what she should have said, what she'd been planning to say, but then, she hadn't been planning on the second recruit being Enyemaka.

An older member of the Guard stepped in. "If trouble comes, let it be from outside these walls."

Essien looked at the man, and the look on his face was kind. He made her feel instantly safe. He had gray strands of hair at his temples, and his chest was thick and round like a barrel.

Another Guard spoke up, "They let trouble in the moment they promoted her to this Guard. She can only bring trouble. One woman among so many men?"

Essien couldn't remember anyone's name, so she didn't bother trying.

"I will lead this Guard one day," Essien boasted.

The Guard began to talk amongst themselves, and there were too many conversations to keep track of. She looked down at her hands. If they wanted her to work with people who might harbor ill feelings against her, they needed to figure out a way to protect her. Or give her free reign to protect herself.

Antonious' voice interrupted and kept anyone from responding to her unveiled threats. "Essien, Enyemaka. Enyemaka, Essien. Two recruits to replace our lost men. I see you all have gotten acquainted quite quickly. Shall we retire to a celebratory evening meal now? The meal is prepared in the formal dining room, and we don't have to wait."

They all trailed into the dining room where Essien viewed a long table bisecting the space. She quickly surmised that it had to seat all one hundred and one of them, plus Antonious and the President, and any visitors who might be invited to attend. The table was black, as were the chairs. The walls of the room were covered with white wallpaper in another textured fabric, and the floor covered in white marble with gold veins. One wall was made entirely of thick glass and provided a view over the edge of the island, down into the crashing blue water, and out to a jut of land with a tower of stacked gray stones at its very edge. She stared at that tower, wondering what it was used for, but it was mostly so she wouldn't have to catch anyone's eye.

Essien was shown to a seat next to the one Antonious occupied, at the end of the table. She remained reticent to look around at anything or anyone. She could already feel a multitude of eyes on her and didn't need another reason to draw attention to herself.

Then she heard her name being called by a voice at the other end of the table. The food had not yet arrived, and she realized she hadn't put a thing in her mouth all day. Slowly, all of the faces turned to her. She looked up from her empty place setting and turned her head. So many faces to look past, so many eyes to connect with as she turned. There was Enyemaka's face to cross over, and then her name was called again, drawing her attention to who had spoken.

"Is Essien inhabiting the body we see?" The President laughed, and everyone else echoed his laughter.

Essien stared at him, silent. He was smiling, and she felt a general sense of goodwill passing from him to her, but she distrusted it.

"Sir President," she said, and nodded her head.

He nodded back. "Call me Gabriel, please. And now that I have your attention, perhaps you might answer my question?"

Essien shook her head; she hadn't heard anything he'd said. "What was the question, Sir?" Laughter again, only she didn't laugh, and neither did the President. Gabriel. She rolled the name around in her mind.

"How do you like your sleeping arrangements?"

Essien cocked her eyebrow involuntarily. "Oh, everything's fine, Sir. And very much better than the previous arrangements."

The President kept his smile in place. He looked like he could smile at her forever, and looked like he meant it. His face was so striking that part of her wanted to keep staring at him, as he stared at her. She let her eyes slide away and back out to that distant peak of that tall tower.

"You will find we take the comforts of our personal Guard very seriously. Will the entire floor be good enough for your stay here?"

Essien looked back at him again. She'd been hoping he wouldn't mention that, but apparently, he wanted them all to know she had an entire floor of rooms to herself. She'd kept her answer purposely vague. He had gotten very specific and clearly did so on purpose.

The other Guard jumped their eyes back and forth from one end of the table to the other, and then they made eyes at each other. This was exactly what Essien did not want: attention and animosity. So why would Gabriel draw their attention to her at all?

She stared at his face, trying to see beyond that grin which could be hiding anything.

No, she couldn't trust that smile, not at all.

"I would have been fine with just one room, Sir."

His smile shrank a little, but he kept staring at her. Perhaps he was trying to see into her mind. Their food arrived at that moment, and Essien fell into her plate without looking up again. Dinner consisted of rice with beef chunks and a red sauce, fish floating on top of egusi soup, balls of pounded yam, a bean salad, and fried dough. She ate hungrily and did her best not to focus on anything said around her.

None of the men were timid about speaking. They joked with the President. They spoke freely with him about their own arguments and discussions. The Guard was controlled and stern in public, but here, they were comedic and friendly to each other. Seated next to her, Essien could feel Antonious look at her occasionally, but he didn't try to say anything. The silence was comforting, but she felt a familiar sense of loneliness. Being a single female among all males would never be a place of welcome and belonging. She would always be abandoned to the outskirts or capturing everyone's attention in the center. She wasn't sure which was worse, yet: being invisible or being hyper-surveilled.

A platter of sliced mango was brought out. It was the best part of the meal, and she thought that if the food was this fresh every night, she might survive. When she was done, she wanted to exit immediately. She looked up and saw the President was staring at her. Essien had the feeling that he had been staring at her the entire time she'd been seated at the table. She let all the things she felt for men spill over her face as she looked back at him. He seemed to chuckle, his shoulders coming up slightly.

Gabriel's voice rose over all of theirs, and everyone instantly fell silent. "Following the meal, there will be a demonstration in the viewing room tonight. Please follow Antonious."

Essien got up immediately, while Antonious took his time standing. She would stick close to him as long as she could. When he was nowhere to be found, she was on her own. A lamb among wolves or a lion among sheep, it was up to her.

CHAPTER THIRTY-THREE

◆

THE VIEWING ROOM TURNED OUT TO BE THE ROOM ON THE second floor in the training room with the transparent walls surrounding it on all sides.

The members of the guard filed into the room, following by the President. Behind him were two Guard guiding four men Essien recognized from the day she had been attacked. They looked surprised to see her, staring more at her than at anyone else.

The men were shackled hands to feet and had their heads and faces shaved completely bald. They wore the standard white jumper of the convicted. Seeing them standing there stopped her breath in her chest and made her legs and hands begin to tremble. Essien recalled there had been Ojo, a man she hadn't even really known, and then three or four men who had run away when she'd begun slashing with the knife. She hadn't seen their faces or noticed their heights, and she hadn't had the chance to go after them. Enyemaka must have identified them. Or maybe they'd given themselves up. Either way, there they were in the President's compound.

Gabriel's voice spilled into the suddenly silent room. "These men have been set for execution after being convicted for their roles in an attempted rape. Their trial was quicker than yours, Essien. I commandeered their bodies for the purposes of this demonstration." He turned to the Sojas who had brought the men in. "Place the first sentenced to death within the inner chamber."

The Guard followed his orders. The man they led into the glass enclosure kept flicking glances at Essien, his thoughts running across his face plain as day.

Surprise that she was alive, and he was about to die.

Perplexed at how events had shifted so dramatically.

Resigned to the ending he was about to face.

The second chamber inside the room was closed with a sliding door that separated the large space down the middle. The prisoner remained shackled inside the second chamber. Flashes of his hands on her—grabbing her, bruising her—dashed across Essien's mind, her eyes widened in disbelief.

Gabriel stepped forward. "I would like our new recruits to understand face-to-face what it is they have signed up for and what it is they will be expected to do. This may shock you. This may disgust you. This may even break you beyond repair. I will not give you advance warning of what is about to happen. I only tell you not to blink."

Essien glanced around the training room at the other Guard, some looking eager, their eyes watching every movement.

Inside the chamber, something was happening. The man convulsed and shook violently. Gabriel took his eyes off the man and looked around the room at them.

"This process can be painless, if I were to allow it. It can be simple and easy, no pain at all."

The man in the glass chamber levitated above the ground. Every inch he rose, his face crumbled in terror, foreboding coloring his features. The other Guard moved closer to the glass as the seconds passed, suspending Essien in curious anticipation. She stepped closer, too, the man's mouth open in a grimace, feeling the cool shaft of the knife in her hand that she'd yearned to use on him.

One second, he was a whole man, his body fully intact, mouth trembling in fear; the next moment, there was a burst and a vicious splatter, and the walls of the inner chamber were covered in dripping red. The former Soja was no longer standing in the chamber. He was rolling down the clear walls in red washes that pooled at the bottom and dripped off the ceiling.

"Don't worry about the mess," the President joked without a smile. "The demonstration room is self-cleaning. Bring the next convicted. Would anyone else like to try?"

Essien closed her eyes and shook her head. What horrors were these? Seeing a man splashed across a wall like so much red paint.

"Both of you new recruits will learn to do this and so much more. We start today. Essien, come forward."

What Gabriel said stopped her even as everyone turned to look at her. A few of the Guard near her looked as ill as she felt. From the looks on their faces, Essien could tell they were likely the newer ones. Others were gritting their teeth and working their jaws in silent disagreement. They wanted to have a turn at being monsters. Essien tried to swallow and couldn't. She looked back at the room, but the walls were already clean and clear again. Not even his clothes remained. It was as if he'd never been.

The second convicted man was led forward. Gabriel had likely chosen these men for that exact reason. It would be cruel to ask a man how he'd like to die, but this explosion of body parts into fluids somehow seemed worse.

The second man was placed inside the chamber. Gabriel motioned for her to draw nearer, so she did. When she stood shoulder to shoulder with him, she realized just how tall he was, and she was not. Over two heads shorter than him, she barely came to his chest.

"Close your eyes," he instructed her.

The man had been dematerialized, vanquished, splattered, with minimal effort at all. How was he going to teach her to do something like that with her eyes closed?

She shrugged mentally and closed her eyes to the room. She could feel the President standing next to her like a flaming bonfire. Essien opened her eyes, and he was still staring down at her. The bonfire burned hotter the closer he got to her.

"Keep your eyes closed. Can you sense me standing next to you?" She nodded once sharply. "Good." His voice sounded like a smile. "Now, try to sense the man in the room. He's further away, but you'll be able to sense him, too."

She tried to sense something beyond herself, but the bonfire burning right next to her was too hot and too bright. She couldn't feel anything else around that huge blaze. He must have realized this because suddenly, she was left standing in a draft with only her own aura to sense. It was a faint trickle of electricity, unlike anything she'd ever felt before. Standing next to the President, she could sense the same feeling of air currents and invisible sensations wafting toward her from him. There were fainter vibrations coming from the other Guard. She tried to use this newfound ability to sense further outward. She breathed in deeply and then imagined freeing her consciousness from the confines of her own body.

At first, she felt silly trying to do something so preposterous. How did one push themselves beyond the confines of their physical body while it still occupied a set space? Then, she felt a faint flicker in the direction of the inner chamber. She pushed harder and began to feel more of the flicker grow warmer.

"Good," she heard again.

She peeked one eye open, but Gabriel was staring at the man in the chamber. Essien looked at her former Soja colleague, a man who'd shot rebels alongside her and then turned on her with the viciousness of a caged lion. He was no longer standing but was levitating off the ground. Essien jolted, and the man hit the ground again. Gabriel looked down at her. "You were doing that. The minute you doubted yourself, the power stopped flowing. Try again."

She didn't want to try again. Had she been using her mind to make a man levitate? Was she about to use her mind to explode a man's body all over the glass? She shook her head.

"This isn't right. I thought people were executed more humanely than this."

The President's head tilted as he looked down at her. "This man tried to help others kill you, others whom you killed. You said it yourself, you would have killed them if you had caught them."

"I never said that," Essien protested.

"But you thought about it. Anyone in your position would have."

Essien shook her head and backed away even further. The Guard around her moved away. "Sense him. Try to feel him from this far away. What does he feel like?"

She could feel a faint warmth pulling at her. She breathed deeply and let herself sense the environment outside of herself. Suddenly, she could feel everyone present, like opening a roaring oven. Little fires burning all around her.

"Focus on the one in front of you. Narrow it down to just that one man. Can you do that?"

One flame drew her in quicker than the rest. She let herself sense the flame with stronger certainty. Sorrow. She could feel his sorrow. Regret. He was sorry for what they tried to do. He had only wanted to fit in, not actually hurt her. Looking at her, he was glad she had survived. He felt more regret that he would never get to see his mother and his sisters and explain to them that he was sorry. By not protecting Essien, he had left them unprotected, too.

Essien wanted to ask Gabriel if she was supposed to feel emotions back when she did this. Instead, she wrapped her mind around the feeling of that sorrowful regretting flame, feeling all of it held within her mind.

"Good," a hint of excitement. She was doing it. "Now when you're ready, when you've got your mind wrapped around their aura, use it against them. Turn it inside out. Think of an explosion. Think of flames. Explode the flame. You could douse the flame, too, but I think explosions work best."

Essien felt like gagging again. She could feel the reflex of bile pushing up into her throat. Could she do this? Could she allow herself to feel the full power waiting to be unleashed from within her? If she killed a man using just her mind, wouldn't they know what she was hiding? Wouldn't that give her more power than it might be wise for her to have?

It was the President's voice in her ear, instructing her so patiently. Part of her wanted to win his approval by repeating what he had done, showing him that she was, in fact, the perfect weapon. But if she did that, they'd want her using this weapon all the time.

"I can't do it," she said again and opened both her eyes.

The condemned Soja was dangling in the air, floating within the chamber. His eyes were closed, and his head and limbs were dangling loosely. He had already given himself up to his punishment. By the relaxed look on his face, she thought it might feel good to him, a certainty of death after the deeds he had been planning to do. He was a man who had surely earned his death, but she couldn't bring herself to kill him.

Not like that.

Not when he wasn't trying to hurt her in that moment. The rage that had let her kill Akpari, Keesemokwu, and Ojo couldn't be allowed to rise up in her again.

"I can't do it," she repeated and shook her head.

She couldn't figure out how to put the man down. He was still hanging midair, and she knew it was because of her mind. She started to concentrate on lowering him down to the ground, but he kept dangling. She felt the President take over. Suddenly, it wasn't her power holding the man above the ground, but Gabriel's stronger, tighter grip was wrapped around her too. It felt like an unexpected wave knocked her over and then held her down at the bottom of the ocean.

"You could have burned him alive. But you can also do it like this."

She heard the words in her head, she was almost sure of it, and her skin pricked, perspiring all over at once. She was afraid to look away from the man as he floated in the air. The President's power melded into hers so tightly she could feel it when he thought the word, "Explode."

Instantly, splashes of red hit the clear walls and pooled into puddles at the bottom. She covered her mouth with her hands, as she felt like she had been standing in the epicenter when the blood flew everywhere. She would not be sick. She could take the sight of blood. She would not vomit just because she had seen so much warm red. Her tongue felt thick and useless in her mouth as she watched blood drop in rivulets. Essien stared at the fresh horror and then turned to Gabriel. She expected his face to be stern or smiling, but he looked disappointed. Like he'd expected more from her, and she'd failed to deliver.

His glower sent pricks of disappointment down her spine. She didn't like failing.

"As first tries go, that was only a partial failure."

She had just seen two men killed with nothing more than a passing thought. Did they expect her to do this in the real world? Weren't there laws against this type of barbaric power? Essien would rather a rapid-fire over this any day.

"You will both learn to perform mental firepower, like you have just seen me do, but it is entirely up to you. You must know that it should only be used in specific instances, like execution. Any other use is outlawed. That includes in self-defense."

They were dismissed soon after with the news that tomorrow would begin formal training for the two new recruits. Essien escaped up to her floor, feeling only slightly less guilty as she closed the door of the large bedroom and bathed in her very own bathroom. She slept restlessly that night with visions of bloody walls and jeweled brown eyes.

CHAPTER THIRTY-FOUR

◆

Y OU KNOW HOW TO SHOOT A RAPID-FIRE BETTER THAN ANY other soldier I've ever seen," Antonious praised Essien. She had just finished her preliminary testing, and by Antonious' praise, he seemed to want to use her to goad the other Guard. She had indeed passed every shooting test they had given her, even the test in which she'd needed to load and use a vintage firearm that she'd only seen once before and never discharged.

He stood in front of the largest gathering space on the training floor wearing the same gray ensemble as every other day she'd seen him. Essien and the Guard wore either the white or the gray of their training uniform. Besides these uniforms, Essien had found in her closet the thick black uniforms they wore for outdoor drills, the fancy black uniform for public guarding, the white uniform for cultural ceremonies, and the red, black, and green uniform for political ceremonies. There was also a uniform for hotter summer months made of a breathable black cotton, whereas the uniform for winter was gray and padded thickly with several layers of tunics and overcoats. When Essien had first seen them, she ran her hands over the fabrics and reflected on the fact that it was more clothes than she had ever owned in her life.

Essien knew already that using her performance against the other Guard would backfire on her; it was only a matter of when. She shook her head, knowing already that in trying to help her gain their respect, he was only undermining any efforts she might later make to generate her own. They wouldn't respect her just because the higher-ups told them to. Enyemaka had told her as much before. She hadn't believed it then, but she would be a fool not to believe it now.

"You can shoot any kind of rifle we put in your hand. This is marvelous. No trouble with automatics or vintage models. And not just rapid-fires;

you can fight with knives, swords, and axes too. You're fast, and you have quick reflexes. It's almost like you have a sixth sense. The military was right; you are perfect for this job."

Essien didn't smile at Antonious, her face hanging drops of sweat. She brushed an arm across her forehead and down her chin.

"Thank you," she said, just to be polite, though he didn't seem to realize his pride in her could get her killed.

"You are the best Guard we've ever had." That got a few sucked teeth responses. "Not the strongest or the tallest, but definitely the best with weapons."

She kept quiet as Antonious continued his praise, looking around the room. Enyemaka was nearby with another Guard learning the same moves she was learning. He hadn't spoken to her again since their first day. She looked around at other faces—some looked back with a spark of challenge; others wouldn't meet her eyes at all, their arms crossed over chests puffed up three times wider than hers with disdain.

"Mr. President, what an intriguing surprise!" Antonious' voice got louder, and his face seemed to tighten. "Essien just finished her preliminary tests. She aced every one of them."

Essien and all the other Guard went to attention and waited for him to walk into their line of sight. Antonious' tighter face made his voice higher than it usually was.

"I was just telling Essien how talented she is and how overjoyed we are to have her here to help guard your person and property. She is a most excellent replacement."

"At ease," Gabriel said, his voice directly above her head. She still didn't look at him but kept facing the far wall and staring above Antonious' head. She wasn't supposed to make eye contact with her superiors, and even though this was a completely different branch of the military, her habits wouldn't—couldn't—degrade now.

The President was still the leader of the country, and her nerves alone kept her eyes from meeting his. She'd dreamt last night of eyes the dark color of his, and she couldn't concentrate as she listened to Antonious droning on. She couldn't take her mind off the hot air the President was breathing against the side of her face, or the brush of his shirt against her arm, or the fact that she'd been at his compound for just two days, and she was already dreaming about him. *You aren't a schoolgirl anymore*, she chided herself and straightened her shoulders back to stand stiffer.

Antonious was still talking, but it was Gabriel's voice she was listening for when he said, "I would like you to have evening meal with me tonight. A meal for two."

She looked at him, sharing a quick meeting of their eyes from a short distance. Essien then looked around her at the other Guard and back to the far wall above Antonious' head. Gabriel had looked just as serious as he always did, but he was the type to kid and joke, even with her. She'd seen him be charming and effusive with Guard and sometimes with her. However, Essien could tell he wasn't joking now.

He was still breathing on her, and she didn't know how to answer, or if she even could. Why did he want her to have dinner with him alone? Why her? She took two steps away from him, so that she couldn't feel the warm air breezing out of his nostrils onto her ear. She finally turned to look at him fully. He was wearing a flashy overcoat with bright yellows, oranges, and reds. His slacks were a bright blood red. She knew then that he had been to the mainland, as he usually wore the black on black of the Guard when he was at the compound.

"I am here at my President's command," she said softly. She didn't want the other Guard to overhear her or him. "Permission to get back to training, Sir."

She was here to train and be a Guard; she would focus on that fact. As long as he would let her. She couldn't deny his request, but she could pretend he hadn't made it.

Gabriel was silent above her, and she had the overwhelming urge to look up at him. Already, she could feel herself thinking about him in a way that a Guard wouldn't think about their protectee. She could smell his scent now, a spicy fragrance that made her nose tingle.

Her fellow Guard were paying her too much attention. It was military training all over again. She didn't need this distinction; everyone already looked at her as weaker and less capable. She didn't need the President's favoritism added to that scrutiny.

She would have to be so careful.

The mood in the gym fell to one of suspicious curiosity, everyone waiting to see what Essien would do. They all wanted to see if she would live up to her reputation. Essien knew firsthand what their perceptions could do to her. Looking around the gym, she caught Enyemaka's eye. He was studying her face, and he didn't look away when their eyes connected. He was the only one who knew what she was really capable of.

Antonious began to fill the room with a more animated style of talking than usual: "As I was saying, we will teach you to use your mind as a weapon, but we will not neglect teaching you to use your body as a weapon. Next, Essien and Enyemaka, you will learn our traditional style of fighting, engolo. Neither of you is tall or physically imposing, and you never will be. So, we have to teach you how to fight against people who will always be bigger, and if it came down to it, to win without weapons."

Essien scoffed at that, and a snort came out of her nose. "I'm always armed, Sir." She had commented before thinking. She had to stop doing that. Antonious wanted her to brag, but it wouldn't make her any friends.

But he was shaking his head at her. "What if someone were to take your weapons? You've been lucky before and gotten to keep them and use them before your opponent could take them or use theirs. But what if someday you're not so fortunate?"

Essien felt prickled by just the thought of not having weapons.

"Mental firepower?"

Antonious shook his head again. "You can only use mental firepower in restricted situations. Weaponry of the mind is limited and exhaustible. We never rely on it."

Then she had no answer. If she didn't have at least a knife, she could be easily overpowered.

"What will you rely on without weapons? Luck?"

Essien shook her head. "My skills have never been luck, Sir."

She didn't feel like she was bragging or being boastful, but she saw one of the Guard turn his lip up slightly. A few others shifted uncomfortably from foot to foot. A couple crossed their arms over their chests.

"If not luck, then what?" Antonious stared at her with an intensity she did not like. He didn't look like a friendly grandfather anymore; he looked like a gaunt-faced judge. "Tell us, what made you better than the three men you came up against?"

"Power, Sir. I'm better because I'm more powerful."

Antonious and the President both let go of laughs that didn't include her at all. It was the first time she'd ever heard the President laugh. It filled the training chamber like the clang of bells tolling.

"Prove it then." Antonious made a motion toward the shiny black mats they'd pulled out of a back closet. Four of them were laid end to end in the middle of the floor space creating a larger area. "Today, we begin practicing hand-to-hand combat . . . so you can learn to fight without the use of a weapon."

Gabriel took off his overcoat, slipping effortlessly out of the sleeves, and shook it out to lie on top of a stone-lifting bench. He sat down on the bench and rested his elbows on his knees. Without the overcoat, he looked more relaxed. It still felt unnatural to have him there. Essien tried not to watch him out of the corner of her eye as he looked at her.

Antonious enlisted the help of the other Guard in teaching Essien and Enyemaka the basic moves of dambe and engolo, the traditional fighting styles. The moves required power and speed. With proper strength and skill they could control an opponent, with greater strength and skill they could be used to kill. The other Guard continued their own workouts in different groups around the training area. A few of those called over to help seemed overly eager to help Essien get into position and demonstrate bodily how she should move.

"I got it," she told one as he tried to move her leg to show her how she should kick. She wore pants, but it felt like he was touching her bare skin.

Essien got smashed into the mat again and again, tasting blood in her mouth and having to kneel with her head hanging down while she tried to recoup. The military had never taught her about grappling and fist fighting. It had always been assumed that she would have weapons at her disposal. And knowing there were weapons she could use simply by thinking a thought made hand-to-hand combat seem all the more useless.

Antonious seemed determined that this lesson would be ground into her like a knee in the back of her head, or like the slice now present in her lip. Knocked down over and over, she got up again and again. Essien kept going, twisting and slippery with sweat, until she became fast enough to avoid her opponent's long arms and large legs.

When she used one of the moves that they'd shown her to pop out an arm and a knee of an opponent with a satisfying sucking sound, the practice was officially over for the day. The Guard screamed out curses as he rolled around on the floor. "I hope your hair falls out, and your teeth rot in your head, wicked girl!"

Essien stood up from a crouched position and wiped a dribble of blood off her chin. She stared down at the fellow Guard she'd hurt. He was squealing and trying to hold his knee with a dislocated elbow dangling from one of his arms. She suppressed her own smirk knowing they would all hate her with the strength of their entire species if they caught even a glimpse of it. She'd had no problem using those moves to hurt them once she'd decided she didn't want to play fair anymore because she knew they'd have no problem using such moves on her. Maybe because she knew they wouldn't die or become so much blood dripping down a wall. Hand-to-hand combat could prove useful after all.

Gabriel walked over to them. The side of his body brushed Essien out of the way as he moved onto the mats to kneel beside the man who had just gotten his arm and knee disjointed. He put one hand on the man's arm and the other hand on the man's knee, whispered something in Igbo that Essien couldn't quite hear, and they all heard a crack louder than popping the joints had been. Essien stared after him as he grimaced to his feet, toughened like leather, with the help of three other Guard.

Gabriel turned to face her. "Why did you pop his bones out?"

She felt bolder, knowing there was nothing they could teach her at which she wouldn't excel. She'd never popped out a man's joint before and already she wanted to do it again. "I wanted to show myself that I could do it."

"So, you were putting into practice what we wanted you to learn proving that you had learned it?" Gabriel didn't seem angry at all; he seemed more proud of her than angry. She nodded and then looked at Antonious. He was looking at her, but he wasn't smiling anymore.

"When we teach you to snatch a man's throat from his neck, would you also need to practice that on us, too?"

"I won't kill anyone here, Sir. But if someone on your team tries to kill me, I will definitely kill them first."

"I assure you, Essien, working for me, your challenges will not come from within the walls of this compound."

She looked down and nodded, trying to appear chastised, but she really wanted to ask when she could learn to snatch out a throat. It would probably be just as bloody as exploding a man to death, but to Essien, less frightening. There was something primitive about using hands to kill, whereas using the mind was an altogether different type of battle. She ran her tongue over the groove in her bottom lip, tasting metal, and wondered what other feats she might soon be tested with.

CHAPTER THIRTY-FIVE

◆

THE PRESIDENT CALLED HER DISOBEDIENT TO HER FACE THAT evening.

Essien sat diagonal to him at the long dining table overlooking the cliffs, the remaining chairs empty and pushed in. Essien gritted her teeth, and a vein in her temple throbbed. She sipped her water and tried to keep her own emotions from rising up to challenge him.

"You take orders well, Essien, but only when you want to. That does not make for a good bodyguard."

"I was following orders by being able to do what Antonious taught me. One day, if I have to do real hand-to-hand combat, now you know I can," Essien told him, trying to smooth the annoyance from her tone. The reprimand stung and dug under her skin.

"This work relationship is not starting out very well. You've been here only a few weeks, and I am beginning to ask myself if my safety is worth my sanity."

"Sir, I am here to keep you safe and to be as objective as I need to be regardless of emotion or attraction . . ."

The President's attention snapped to her face. Her voice trailed off then because she didn't know if she could make herself sound as sure as she was trying to be.

"It's true you have proven yourself to everybody, Essien . . . everybody except me."

"How else would I have to prove myself?"

"I don't know, Essien, but injuring my Guard is not the way closer to it."

"If winning your approval was a part of my position description, I would be trying to do that."

"Eat your salad, Essien."

"I'm not hungry anymore."

"It's shredded cabbage; you love cabbage. Please eat."

Whether she liked it or not, the directive to eat was another form of an order. She was stubborn and contrary, but she couldn't see a good enough reason not to eat the salad. She wondered how he knew she liked this particular salad more than any others—with spicy suya, grilled so it was crisp and oily, and stewed fish that had been fried first, and red rice with onions sliced not chopped, and . . . she had never discussed anything unrelated to training with him or around him. She had never commented to anyone how much she liked eating the shredded cabbage with the grilled spicy meat or how she hated chopped onions but loved them in thin slivers. She had never told Gabriel anything about herself not concerning her job or her military service, and that information he already knew.

Yet, there were small details he knew about her, which she had never told him herself. Like this being her favorite salad. She thought again about how he often seemed to be reading her mind, saying the things she had only just thought to herself. Coincidences all? They both sat in silence while she ate the rest of her meat and salad as quickly as she could.

"How was the meat?"

"Delicious."

"Not too tough?"

"No."

"And the soup?"

"Loved it."

"A glass of palm wine?"

"No, thanks."

"Would you like a dessert?"

"I'm full."

"I do not care for sweets, but I can have something made for you."

"No, thanks."

"Not even fried dough? I know that you like fried dough." Gabriel smiled; Essien frowned.

"How do you know what I like?" She tried to sound casual, but what she really felt came through anyway. Staring at her face made his smile deepen.

"I've read your military file."

"That information isn't in there."

"How would you know?"

He was right; she'd never seen her own military personnel file. She'd never asked to see it and couldn't think of a reason why she'd be allowed to. The files were for senior level officials and higher. She was just a captain, and here, she wasn't even that. The Guard didn't have a hierarchy.

"I should be getting back to my room."

"You want your beauty slumber?"

The President made a joke, and she didn't laugh. She stood up and set herself into a salute. He had no choice except to dismiss her. His plate was almost full, but he had drunk three glasses of palm wine, finishing a bottle by himself. He picked up his fork to resume dining as she walked away.

THE NEXT DAY, ESSIEN PASSED GABRIEL'S OFFICE WITH ITS DOOR sitting wide open. It was usually closed, and as she passed, she could hear his voice loud and booming. The closer she got to the open door, the more she heard of what he was saying.

"If Alkebulan demands it of me, I will serve until my dying day."

He pounded his fist to the desktop to mark his point as Antonious nodded. Essien glanced into the room as she passed, unable to resist the itch crawling up her spine to turn and peek. Gabriel stood in front of his desk, Antonious sitting in the chair in front of it.

Both heads swiveled to see her.

Essien turned her gaze and continued walking.

◆

CHAPTER THIRTY-SIX

FOR HER FIRST ASSIGNMENT OUTSIDE THE COMPOUND, ESSIEN would be accompanying the President at his annual speech to the Houses of State and Tribal Councils. They had arrived on the mainland in the presidential procession, all the Guard in their official uniforms, including the helmets. Essien had to braid her hair flat to her head in order to fit the helmet.

The State and Tribal Council House was in a low, long building at the end of Lagos Street. There was a festival going full steam in the middle of Lagos, the Capital of Alkebulan coinciding with the President's planned speech. The crowds were so thick that no engine could get through the streets. Vendors loudly hawked their trade, and the crowd moved sluggishly as families stopped to inspect their wares and chatter amongst each other, dancing in the streets in some places.

As the President exited the engine, the Guard took up their posts surrounding him. Essien was posted at the rear, the sounds of festivities and revelry flooding her ears. Enyemaka was somewhere in the crowd; she had caught only a brief glimpse of him when they unloaded from the engines. With the President walking in a protective bubble, their procession made its way toward the Council House where he would give his speech. All sixteen states and over forty-three hundred tribes were represented there. The Guard at the front of the formation moved people out of the way with a flick of their hand, clearing a wide path. Guard posted on the sides of the group made sure civilians didn't get too close to the President. The Guard at the rear made sure no one snuck up behind them, while additional members of the Guard threaded their way through the crowds to take up posts around the perimeter.

People began noticing the President and his dark entourage of protection and shouted out greetings. "President Ijikota, the Igbo President!"

Gabriel waved back and smiled. Their movements came to a complete stop as people crowded closer, pushing others forward to catch a clearer sight of him. The President kept his grin in place, but the Guard was all seriousness around him, prodding people out of the way more forcibly now.

Essien remembered being a young adolescent girl and seeing the President for the first time. He had been in a procession similar to this one, long and snaking down the main village street. The crowd then had not been as large. The President went so many places and saw so many crowds, that his visits and revelers likely blurred together, but Essien wondered if he remembered that day.

It took their full transport procedures just to get through it all. Guard moving ahead and clearing a path, scoping all sides for threats, establishing a secure perimeter, and then motioning the President forward; it was a slow and methodical inching along. The military procession finally arrived at the Council House, and the President was ushered quickly into the building. From inside the first wide corridor of the legislature, they could still hear the shouts and instruments of the revelries raising up outside. The sound pounded in Essien's ears and shook the floor beneath her feet.

The Guard split up into groups. Essien fell into line with the group tasked with securing perimeters and watching entries and exits. The Guard pushed open the ornate black wood doors with their golden handles. The carpet inside the main floor of the assembly hall was light gray and soft as suede, the room partitioned into rows with comfortable armchairs in embroidered black fabric. The tribal and council members were all seated by tribe, but Essien could see where the sections blurred, and the attendees sat conversing together in mixed tribal groupings. It was far too noisy for Essien to hear much of what anyone said, all their voices buzzing together and mixing with the noise from outside.

Essien followed among the last of the Guard as they climbed a set of stairs to position themselves one level above the audience. The Guard spaced out along the rounded second story balcony with its wide windows letting in all the light but none of the sounds of the street. She thought about how easy it would be to subdue every single person in the room if she needed to. She remembered what it felt like to focus her energy on one person, and suddenly she could look at everyone below her and see a full body halo around them that blazed with colors. Some of them blazed brighter than others. Essien tried to blink it away, but the new power remained, coloring her vision. Essien's eye was drawn to Gabriel, his flame stretching upward like a blue-and-green shadow encasing him where he stood on the raised platform at the front of the room below, talking jovially with council members. Looking down at her own body, she could see the faint outline of a red and gold aura surrounding her.

Seeing auras was new to Essien, and seeing the blazing colors engulfing those around her startled her. What did it mean?

She remembered how it had felt to stand in the middle of an explosion, colors everywhere. Essien quickly shut her mind off from those thoughts. She didn't know if she was still meant to see the translucent shields overlaying everyone around her, but they still sprang up every time her eyes roamed over the gathering. Essien looked around the Council House and noticed two Guard on the floor below standing around another councilman who was gesturing at the stage with his hands up. His face was thinned down with anger, leaving his lips just a slash across his mouth. Essien stepped closer to hear the man was yelling, his distinguished accent from a faraway tribe. "I have not heard anybody, not a single citizen of this country, ask for a life-term presidency! He wants us to believe it was Alkebulan's idea and Alkebulan's decision, but that is false. He is doing what he wanted all along. The people had no say in it!"

The Guard had their hands out, directing the councilman to move down the aisle between the chairs and toward the doors. The man had Gabriel's attention now, too. He watched from the stage, surrounded by other tribal council members, as the councilman was physically escorted from the room with two solid hands on each of his arms, likely be taken to the enforcement center for an interrogation.

Why would a councilman speak out against their own President? And in chambers at that? Essien's contemplations were interrupted when a council member on the raised platform began inviting everyone to find their seats, clearly resolved to put that unpleasant business behind them. There was a noisy rustling as everyone got settled. Essien tried to pay attention to the crowd both inside and outside but found herself listening to what the councilman on the stage was saying. "May the President never die and bless us with long rule and prosperous times."

At that, Essien began to wonder at the hyperbole of it. What would happen if the President really never died? She knew it was impossible but imagined what it might be like to be stuck with one President forever. She wondered how the country might get rid of a ruler who had been in power for much too long. As Antonious introduced the President to come to the stage, Essien felt a gust of wind blow up her back, like the motion of something big running up behind her, making her hunch her shoulders in anticipation of a collision that never came. She looked around the balcony, heart racing wildly, and leaned over the railing to glance below as Antonious began to speak under the auditorium lights. The other Guard were in their positions at regular intervals, and the council members were all seated with their attention on the stage as Antonious read out the President's accomplishments in chronological order.

She looked at the Guard posted in the aisles of the main floor and along the walls just below the balcony. Some were paying attention to the crowd, like she was, but most of them were watching Antonious and waiting for the President to speak. Their guard was down, but that gust of wind blowing over her from seemingly nowhere had put Essien on high alert.

"President Gabriel Ijikota!" Antonious' voice rose in fervor until the applause drowned him out. Essien glanced down to see the President, smiling, his teeth and eyes glistening, step up to the podium. Antonious clapped him on the back and stepped aside.

"How now, countrymen." That got some laughter and some applause, and Gabriel stood there beaming until it died down. Essien had never seen him smile this much, and she found herself staring more at him than at the room.

"A fine room of citizens, if I do say so myself. A fine time to be leading in this era of Alkebulanian history. I am humbled at the praise you lavish upon me. I aim to be worthy of it all."

Essien shook her head, realizing she was distracted. The crowd outside was still churning out chants, but a larger mass of people was making its way up the main street that ended at the Council House. The group was moving determinedly straight, and Essien saw signs in black and red paint. NO MONARCHY FOR ALKEBULAN, in bold letters on one sign. DEATH TO THE PUPPET PRESIDENT on another. This wasn't a part of the festival. A crowd that size with signs looked like trouble.

Without alarming anyone in the assembly hall, Essien slipped out of the doors leading to the front entrance, pressing a button on her earpiece to bring her radio to life.

"I need backup at the Council House, in the hundreds."

An immediate response, "Headed your way. Eight minutes until arrival."

Essien quietly took the stairs to the first floor and exited the building. The crowd was growing, and a handful of Guard were moving people away from the Council House, shoving them away from the entrance steps. The singing had died down, replaced by a growing swell of angry chants from the new crowd pushing through, their signs held high.

Three of the Guard were advancing up the middle of the street with their hands out. Essien realized they were heading toward the large protesting crowd, and she hurried up the street with her hands out to show she wasn't holding a weapon either.

When Essien reached the other Guard, one of them whispered, "See if you can get them talking. Try negotiating."

Essien was surprised they were giving her the lead considering the glances they'd given her before. She turned back to the crowd and recognized it was mostly women, but there were men in the crowd, too—a mixture of city and village folks, some wearing traditional garments and others wearing thin shirts and casual slacks.

She raised her voice and shouted, "We want to negotiate. What are your demands?" Too many voices began to yell at her all at once, and she had to put up her hands. "Who's your representative? Who's your leader?"

"I organized this protest today!" A man standing at the front of the widening group came forward. The front of the crowd pressed back to let the older man through. He was wearing the traditional dress of village chiefs, men who governed the rural districts by ancestry and wealth rather than election. His tunic was heavily embroidered and dangled long threads from the ends. His head was adorned with a tall cap, wrapped all around with cords of gold and silver. He carried a black staff with silver wire wrapped around its length. "My name is Berechi, and we came to tell the President that we don't want him in power for life! We want to choose a new President every year, not be subject to the same corrupt thieves living out their lives! He became corrupt when he went on this mad mission to make himself a monarch!" With that, the assembled group increased their shouts and cries as they protested the idea of a monarchy.

They'd come en masse to make noise and wave their signs, not to cause any real damage. She thought about letting them pass her and head up the street. There was anger, she could hear it in their voices, but it didn't have the tinge that violence usually had.

Essien thought of her father and the field burning. He had not been a political man, but politics had almost taken his life. No one was ever charged for burning the fields, though it was attributed to political unrest. Her father often answered her questions with, "I don't do the job of politicians." Essien remembered when the President was elected, her father had said, "If he's a man of the people, he'll listen to what they have to say." Essien suddenly found herself missing her father. He wasn't a political man, but he'd paid attention.

That swell of nostalgia made Essien abruptly consider how important it was for her countrymen to have a voice in their government. It should matter to the President, too. She had lived in his compound for almost three months, had been in the military for going on five years, but she had never stopped to consider the President's political leanings beyond the smile he flashed in pictos.

Essien could see the uniforms of reinforcements working their way around the mass of people, the black and gray of the Sojas standing out in the colorful crowd. The green of local law enforcement officers. The black on black of the Guard, backup on its way as she had known it would be. The reinforcements appeared from side streets and alleyways and began edging around the outermost parts of the crowd. The Sojas all had their helmets on, with face shields down, and their rapid-fires out but pointed at the ground. By the time the crowd realized they were being distracted and slowed, the reinforcements had them completely surrounded.

A local enforcement officer began making announcements over a voice projector. "You must leave the area immediately. Any who do not immediately disperse will be arrested and taken to the enforcement center for interrogation."

The crowd's energy changed. Essien could see auras blazing bright in stark reds and dark blues. Some of the protesters began to turn and file away. Essien knew the majority of those present would not risk being arrested, but there were ones who would. Essien moved forward, keeping her rapid-fire pointed at the ground, concerned about the remaining crowd getting out of control.

Several protesters began to shout, "No monarchy for Alkebulan! Death to the puppet President!"

Venders along Lagos Street had started closing up their stalls and leaving the area when the Sojas arrived. Shopkeepers closed their doors and peered out through the windows as the enforcement officers began to advance on the remaining crowd.

A row of engines was making its way up the crowded Lagos Street with Sojas in front moving the crowd to the sides of the streets. More announcements were made from the voice projector: ". . . You will be taken to the enforcement center if you do not leave the area immediately."

Then Essien heard over her radio, "The President finished his speech. The Councils are preparing to vote on the legislation. The President is exiting via Akoko Street. Guard on site, remain in your positions until the protesters have been cleared."

Essien felt a sense of relief and then wondered what might have happened if she hadn't seen the crowd heading for the Council House. Could they have overpowered the Guard? Could they have penetrated bulletproof glass?

The officers were starting to make arrests of anyone who refused to leave or self-identify, and scuffles broke out before her eyes; red, yellow, and green auras colliding together as she tried in vain to blink it all away. Already, there were people being led toward the waiting engines. As the first engine filled up, more protesters began shouting. Essien could hear staccato echoes of "Let them go!" emanating from the crowd around her, and she caught a glimpse of Berechi being led toward a waiting engine. Seeing the older man being put into one of the engines made Essien recoil. She imagined her nna being in the crowd, fighting for something he believed in, only to be cuffed and taken for an interrogation. It made Essien feel dizzy.

Soon she found herself at the top of the Council House steps and watched as an engine full of arrested protestors drove through the almost empty street.

"... his plan to make himself a king..." she heard a protestor shout.

Essien kept watching the last engine drive away until she couldn't see it anymore.

PART THREE

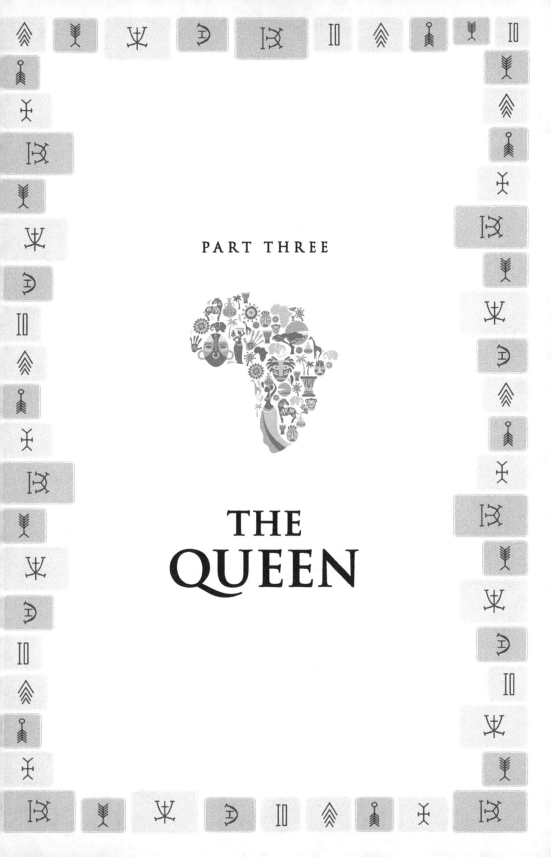

THE
QUEEN

CHAPTER THIRTY-SEVEN

◆

THE EVENING MEAL HAD ALREADY BEEN SERVED WHEN ESSIEN and the other Guard finally returned to the compound. Antonious was there, standing at the doors to the formal dining hall.

"Guard, evening meal has been kept waiting for you in the dining hall." Essien began following the other Guard, but Antonious called out to her. "Essien, a moment."

Essien sighed and turned to follow where his outstretched arm was guiding her. The other Guard flowed around her and entered the dining hall. She caught sight of Enyemaka for the first time in days. On separate details for the Council House speeches, she hadn't even thought to look for him—wouldn't have recognized him anyway in full gear and helmet. He looked back at her now, and his face was as still as a stone.

Essien entered the formal dining room alone, where she had been coming to have her meals regularly now. The President was seated at the head of the table. A plate was covered for her at her spot at his left hand. As she took her seat, Gabriel let out a sigh while he looked into his glass of palm wine.

Essien spooned rice and soup into her mouth and avoided saying anything. She knew that she felt uneasy because of the protest, and she imagined that might be what kept the President so silent next to her, too. Despite the protests, he'd still gotten everything he wanted even though it was the Council voting for it: a lifetime appointment to the presidency that he didn't even have to fight or go to war over. He'd only had to flash that smile one last time, have his Guard usher his opponents to the side, and sweep his hand charismatically to put it to a vote on the floor.

If that protesting mob hadn't come up the main street, would she be feeling this unsettled? Would she have stopped to think about the political implications of the new policy on unlimited presidential terms at all? Would she have even noticed what was happening?

She hadn't told the President what the protestors said, but he could read about it in the written report she would be required to file; that is, if he actually read the reports that were delivered to his office every day.

Essien thought that perhaps the crowd's grievance had some merit. She wondered why the government's first instinct was to subdue and disband the protestors rather than meet and discuss their concerns with them. Her first instinct had been to willingly help in squashing their dissent. That protest had meant something, Essien realized. Those people had stopped what they were doing to make their voices heard, and she'd lied to them. She had been an agent in service to keeping them silent and cowed.

She worked for the President, so that automatically meant that she supported his policies, his government, and his person, but what if she found that she didn't? She had never stopped to really think about this aspect of her military service—her own principles and morals. She had called for backup because, from where she stood, a large mob being allowed to come right up to the Council House would have been a failure of her position as Guard. But as a citizen of Alkebulan, she was also considered a constituent with rights and demands of her own. That's what she'd been taught in her childhood history classes. Alkebulanians had rights, and their government was merely a protector of those rights.

If the government began to transgress those rights, what could be done to stop them? At what point did the laws and policies of a government cross the line? At what point did her citizenship and military service collide? What happened if the government no longer served the interests of the citizen? Was her service nothing more than propping up the government at the expense of the people? And what if the protesters were right about their apprehensions?

There had never been a lifelong President in their country. Individual tribal leaders, usually the eldest member of the wealthiest or largest family in the tribe, ruled the village tribes until their deaths. There were always contentions and strife in those situations over which family was the richest or which family had the most members. She had heard of villages being razed and people slaughtered over tribal affiliation. It was nonsense to her. As far as anyone knew, they were all connected through the Mothers, so it shouldn't matter which tribe each had been born into.

Essien's own family had a tribal history dating back hundreds of generations. Her mother had told her stories of great gatherings that once occurred between the tribes in Western Alkebulan. How they had traded languages and cultural works and even their marriageable daughters and sons. Her mother made those times seem prosperous and peaceful compared to what Essien learned in school. She'd learned that pre-Unification, the tribes were always at war and shifting factions, so it was never clear who was safe and who wasn't. She'd read in one textbook that many tribes saw all other tribes as enemies. Her mother's stories told her a different side. Essien knew also that the elder ruled the tribe until they passed on, and the position then went to the next eldest or wealthiest person in the tribe. Essien knew there might be an ancient precedent at work with the Presidency being declared a lifelong term, but it made her feel cautious and weary.

The President spoke up finally. "Essien, I want to thank you for today. You kept the proceedings from being interrupted, and that was invaluable to me."

For the first time that night, Essien looked directly at Gabriel's face. She found herself noticing how thick and pink his lips were against his dark skin. She noticed that his jaw was a sharp line, always clenched, even when he smiled at her, as he was doing now. His eyes were large in his face, with the longest lashes a man should be allowed to have. She felt again that feeling that reminded her why she didn't like to look at his face very often; she liked it too much. She wanted to appreciate his thanks and feel glad that he was praising her, but everything about the entire situation felt off-putting, down to her own emotions about it. Not to mention the mandatory meals, which only she attended every night. It kept giving her a niggling pressure in the back of her mind that she would ignore as long as she could. Ignore it for the same reason that she didn't like to look directly at his face.

"Essien, I know that you can speak, yet here at evening meal, you never say a word. Is it Antonious that makes you nervous? I can ask him to leave us if you would prefer."

Antonious laughed, "Oh Sir, I believe it is you who stops her tongue."

Essien let herself smile a little, more for them than because she actually felt cheerful. No, she didn't want Antonious to leave.

"I'm not very talkative."

"You must talk about something... What would you like to talk about? What would interest you?"

The President put down his spoon and fork. He put his napkin on top of his plate and pushed it away. He leaned his elbows on the table, steepled his fingers, and rested his chin on his folded hands. Essien looked down at her plate, burning with embarrassment at having his full attention when that was exactly what she both did and didn't want.

"What happened to the other Guard?" she asked.

The President's eyes shifted over to Antonious, and Essien turned her head to follow that glance. Antonious had pushed his plate away, too, and he was staring down at his lap. He looked up as Essien looked at him.

It was Antonious who responded, "We thought you might like the opportunity to get to know your employer better without the other Guard present. You are the newest Guard, and we thought you might have questions or concerns that you wouldn't want the other Guard to overhear."

Essien started to nod as if that explained it, but then she said, "What about Enyemaka?"

Antonious' eyes shifted from her to the President. Essien's head followed that glance.

The President shrugged, "I invited him, too. He said he would rather have dinner with the other Guard."

They were lying to her. She could feel it. She just didn't know why they would lie about something so simple. And if they'd lie about a dinner, what else might they lie about?

She was already shaking her head before she could stop herself. "I'm not buying it." Then she remembered who she was talking to. She tried to apologize. "I'm sorry, Sir, I didn't mean—"

He waved her words away with a flick of his fingers. "Gabriel, please. And I want you to speak freely, Essien. I cannot ask you to speak and then punish you for what you decide to say. You are worried about the other Guard getting their dinner, I assume."

He was still chiding her, but gently. She thought back to that fourteen-year-old girl who had dragged her father out of a burning field. His collapsed body so much heavier than anything she had ever carried before. Such determination to see him live. It was the spark that drove her. She wanted to serve, protect, and most of all, prevent tragedy. She had bolstered her broken spirit with the desire to one day become so powerful, no one would dare attack her or her family members.

"Tell me about your father."

Essien's eyes snapped to the President's, and she widened them at him.

"I was just thinking about my father."

The President smiled, "I have a gift for reading minds."

Her forehead wrinkled into frowns. "What kind of gift allows you to read my mind? And if so, why didn't you use it today to predict what those protestors were going to do?" She thought back to every conversation she'd had with the President since meeting him face-to-face. He always seemed to be responding to her thoughts, since her words were few.

"I will depart dinner early this evening," Antonious spoke up. And then he was gone from the dining room.

The President was still sitting and staring at her. She made herself reach for her cup of water and took a sip while staring at him. She steeled herself in a concerted effort to remain seated because everything in her wanted to get up and leave that table. But doing so would leave her questions unanswered, and that nagging feeling that haunted her mind since before she'd arrived would keep trying to push its way into her consciousness. That feeling that had dogged her since the President had held her bloody hand and not let go.

"Mind reading is not a perfect science. And it's not the same as being psychic."

"So, you can't read everyone's minds, only some? How can you read mine?"

The President looked down into his glass. "I was eight years old the first time my Nne Nne took me to the lake in the middle of the jungle."

Her eyes locked onto his like ballistic missiles, and she didn't blink or look away. He had to look away first, dropping his eyes down to the table for a second before bringing them quickly back up.

"My Nne Nne was old by the time I was born. So old, I think she may have been over one hundred years. But she was strong and small. Like you. She took me on a trip outside of our village, and the journey was so long I cried when she made me keep going. She had to carry me there the first time. We made it to the lake, and the second I saw that glowing, silver-blue water, I ran and jumped in. My grandmother didn't even try to stop me. I jumped right in, feet first, and then I died."

Essien stood up from her seat so abruptly it rocked back on two legs and fell flat with a clatter. The President stood up, too. She felt a panic fluttering in her chest, like she wanted to run from the room. She looked down at the seat and didn't know how she'd gotten out of it or how it had fallen.

"After that first time I died, my Nne Nne took me back to the lake every month, always on the full moon. We made that same journey to the lake every month until the year I turned eighteen. By then, I had died one hundred and twenty times."

Essien started to say something, but she cut herself off before the words came out. She just stared at him, not blinking, not moving, and saying nothing. He kept quiet and watched her. She put a hand against the table to steady herself and stared down at the cream-colored cloth. She covered her mouth, feeling nausea roll up into her throat. She wouldn't be sick, she told herself. She wouldn't vomit in front of him.

"You're telling me I died when I went into that lake?"

"I was eight years old when I died the first time. At least you were much older when you gave yourself to the lake."

She started to shake her head. "Gave myself to the lake? What do you mean I gave myself to the lake? What does that have to do with you reading my mind?"

"You see the Akukoifo."

Essien pursed her lips and nodded. She crossed her arms and then uncrossed them to let them fall.

"Ancient Akukoifo speak of a man so powerful he could control water. He once kept water from reaching the continent at all, and many people had to leave to find water during that drought. There was also a woman. A woman so powerful she could sit next to the sun. She once used the heat of the sun to scorch all the earth into dry, sandy hills. The woman went to war against the man for control of the continent, but neither of them won. Instead, the war of water against fire can be seen in the deserts of the north and the powerful ocean waters in the east and west. Neither managed to take over the continent completely. Neither managed to gain complete control."

Hearing these stories again seemed to give them a new meaning. A meaning much deeper than any she had ascribed to them when she was younger.

She began to imagine him as that man and herself as that woman. Two beings beyond earthly limitations, far removed from the physical and mental barriers that limited ordinary men and women. She imagined herself as a blazing fire and him as a wave of water, the two elements crashing against each other forever, water trying to douse flames, flames boiling water into steam.

"I've heard all these stories before," Essien told him. "I know about the Akukoifo. I still don't understand what this has to do with you reading my mind?"

"We became Akukoifo when we died in that lake."

She shook her head. "That's impossible, Sir."

"Call me Gabriel." There was a force to it this time.

Essien looked away, trying to keep her mind clear of thoughts. "You can read my mind because you are . . . a god?"

She looked at him to see if he thought this was as ridiculous as she did. Yet, he nodded. She shook her head and turned to go. Then she stopped and turned back around to face him. She didn't know why she did it, but some will outside her own held her in place. She could feel herself wanting to leave, but she was standing there in front of him with her eyes stuck on his face.

"Why did you bring me here?" She suddenly felt like she was surrounded by enemies.

"I am not your enemy, Essien."

"How do I know?"

"You're alive, aren't you? Didn't you ask me to live? Didn't you come to me to live?"

The pupils of his eyes glowed with a silvery light, shining against the dark brown of his irises. She kept staring into his eyes as the very bottom began to spiral down into itself like a staircase leading into his mind. Walk with me, those eyes begged. Come with me, they commanded. Essien went with him down into that bottomless descent. She couldn't have resisted even if she'd thought to try.

Essien saw him in her mind as the silver-blue man floating on the surface of the water. She pictured the trees swaying and the branches bending in a closed circle around the lake. Then she saw a second silver figure. It was smaller and she knew it was herself. The figures merged into one, becoming larger and spreading out until the silver mass exploded and evaporated into a sweet-smelling mist that floated through the trees.

She watched the mist spread into a thick cloud that floated over the entire continent, a storm brewed and then spread water over every inch of land.

She saw herself kneeling before the President as he placed a shiny, golden, jeweled crown upon her lowered head. She saw him hold her face in his hands, pulling her closer. She saw herself rising on tiptoes to meet that kiss, wanting it more than she had ever wanted anything else in her life.

Then she blinked, and she was back standing in his dining room.

Her voice trembled, "You are the President of Alkebulan. I am just a Guard. How can you tell me that we are anything besides what we are?" She suddenly felt more physically exhausted than if she'd run three hundred stadia in the heat.

"Ask for the truth, you will get it from me, Essien. You may ask me anything, and I will tell you."

So many questions. So much confusion. This news felt like a weight pressed against her eyelids. She wanted to sleep.

"I know you have had a shock, Essien. I will give you a few days to think over what I have shown you."

She shook her head. With her teeth gritted tightly together, she shot at him, "Whatever it is you think I am to you . . . Whatever it is you want from me. I do not consent. I do not agree. I came here to do a job. Let me do that job, Gabriel. Do not ask this of me. Do not force this on me."

She heard him sigh, like a washing of pure mountain air blowing through whispering leaves. She felt herself falling forward and down into the deep well of stillness inside him. It was a stillness she knew had come from many deaths. She was standing in the formal dining room, but in her mind, she was everywhere and nowhere. She felt herself being pulled and tugged by him into a deeper trance of calm and serenity. It felt comforting; like being wrapped in warm blankets and rocked to sleep. She wanted to stay there forever.

But it was a lie. She had a job to do, which required danger and pain, a job she once thought she had chosen on her own. But had she? What was reality, and how could she tell? It was too much for her. She started to push against the comforting lies, but that feeling of calm grew stronger, drifting her out of consciousness.

She awoke in her bed, in the smallest room of her floor of suites. The light seeping into the window was still a deep purple as she turned and saw something glint on the top of the bedside table. There, shimmering in the early morning light, lay a golden crown. It was larger than what she'd seen in the vision. It had jagged edges and shiny bits of diamond embedded in a row. Above the diamonds were different colored gems set in various arrangements, showing images of something she couldn't quite make out. She reached her hand out to touch the crown. It was cold, rough, sharp, and smooth under her fingers. She wanted to pick it up, but tiredness sucked at her, and her hand fell.

When she opened her eyes again, it was daylight, the sun a bright yellow smear outside the windowpane. The table beside her bed was empty, and Essien noticed that her training uniform and boots had been freshly washed, pressed, shined, and set out for her.

CHAPTER THIRTY-EIGHT

♦

E SSIEN SLIPPED INTO THE AUDITORIUM JUST MINUTES BEFORE
the start of the training session. She wore her military cap pulled low
over her forehead, with her hair tucked up into it. As she took a seat, she
noticed Enyemaka seated in the row in front of her. He noticed her, too. He
jingled his knees and clapped his hands together until the Guard next to
him eyed him and then turned to face him fully.

"Don't be nervous, eto eto. You will be terrible today, that is a fact. Just
accept it now, and your expulsion will go smooth."

Enyemaka chuckled, but he didn't respond. Essien leaned in because
she could hear a faint whispering. It was like something she could overhear
but not make out. Enyemaka turned around to look at her, the muscles in
his neck straining. When their eyes met, the whispering grew louder, and
she could make out words and sentences. Essien realized it was Enyemaka's
thoughts that she was hearing, and she was so startled that she slapped a
hand over her eyes as if that would stop what she was hearing.

Enyemaka was thinking about the tests he needed to pass just to qualify for the military and how he'd failed them all the first time. His father
had laughed in his face when he had returned home that evening, down-
trodden and droop-faced.

"We are short men, Enyi. We do not put ourselves in the way of danger.
We run, and we run fast. Learn from me, your father, now eighty and still
quick." Enyemaka had laughed then, too, so his father's boisterous laughter
didn't sound as pathetic as it felt.

The next day, Enyemaka had begun lifting heavy stones in the recruitment center. He'd begun running further distances, reaching villages several dozen stadia away in his daily runs. His father punched him gently
with gnarly fists as he began to thicken around the arms and chest. His
mother had new tunics and slacks made that would fit around his back

and thighs. Everyone watched silently as Enyi finally grew into Enyemaka. He was still gentle and sweet with his five little sisters, but a hardness had grown over him.

When military recruits came again the following year, he was there to try again. He barely made it through. He had been one of just fifty men accepted from his village, and he had been number forty-nine in rankings. His childhood friends had jeered that a half man with short legs would be the first to die on the battlefield. Enyemaka took a perverse delight when he learned that he would be on the engine that would take him to the Capital, while they would remain behind.

Antonious stepped up on the platform, and Essien pulled away from reading Enyemaka's mind. But doing so was like walking through a cobweb and trying to get the sticky webs off. The more she brushed at them, the more they clung and seemed to be everywhere.

Antonious actually had a smile on his face today. He looked pleased with himself, like he was about to reveal something that they had all been waiting to hear. He put his hands on the podium and leaned in.

"Today, Guard, we will continue with our mental tracking. We must establish mental connections with our two new recruits before we can advance them to the next level of advanced tracking."

Enyemaka looked back at Essien, but she didn't give him the slightest register of recognition, looking just above and to the side of where his eyes were.

"Let me ask our new recruits: What is mental tracking?"

A silence settled into the room.

Essien knew what tracking was. She'd come across the ancient practice while studying in the Soja academy. At the time, mental tracking hadn't seemed like something she could use as a weapon, but then she'd seen that explosion of bloody body parts dripping down a glass wall and had since modified her stance. No, mental tracking was likely more powerful than any rapid-fire she would ever use. But Antonious looked right at Enyemaka as he waited for a response.

"Mental tracking is the ability to use auric fields to track a target," Enyemaka spoke up.

"Very well," Antonious said. "Do either of you know how mental tracking is performed?"

"I don't know how to do it, but you can track an individual using the same mental faculties that would allow you to explode a convicted criminal, but you must be careful not to confuse the two." A few Guard chuckled or laughed out loud. Essien did not.

"Any questions before you are dismissed to the training room?"

There were no questions, of course, and all the Guard filed up to the training floor. From the corner of her eye, Essien could see Enyemaka trying to get her attention. She walked faster, slipping in between Guard who were walking slowly. She didn't want to see him or hear any more of his thoughts. There was a faint whispering coming from all around her, and she tried her best to ignore it.

Essien sat cross-legged in a large circle of the other Guard in one of the training rooms. She was supposed to be grounding herself and linking herself to the other Guard in the circle, but so far, she felt nothing. She had her eyes closed, and her chin slightly lifted, breathing deep enough to make her chest and shoulders move up and down. She started breathing slower, and a tingling began in her toes and spread upward. The tingling moved lazily up her calves, over her knees, into her groin, up her stomach, into her lungs, creeping slowly up her neck. She could feel that tingling drifting into her brain, and then suddenly, it felt like a veil was pushed back, and she could see and feel so much more than she had just moments before.

Bright flares of energy pulled at her from points all around the circle. She kept her eyes closed but moved her head around. Every person around her was a flare of energy, like she'd seen in the assembly hall, drawing at her from all sides of the circle. She tried to focus on Enyemaka, by turning to face where he was sitting. When his energy hit hers, the flare in front of her blazed bright red for just a second, and Essien brought a hand up to shield her eyes from the brightness. She felt Enyemaka look at her, too, and the blaze settled to a cool white. Essien felt her energy stretching and linking with the flares swirling in and around her, and realized with a jolt of astonishment that she was using mental tracking.

Antonious' voice dropped into that static stillness, "Well done, Guard. You have accomplished what we call group linking. Every one of you now knows the psychic trace of every other member. This link can be easily turned off and on. It can also be blocked. We will not teach you how to block the link as this would be extremely harmful to group dynamics, but many of you will learn how to do this naturally. Let us practice turning off the link now."

Essien didn't want to turn off that buzzing connection she felt between herself and everyone else. It felt like she had discovered a world that she had been taking for granted, but one that she could barely wrap her mind around.

Without meaning to, Essien thought about Enyemaka again. Then, with what felt like a shift of her inner poles, she was suddenly across the room and looking at herself. Essien could see herself blazing brighter than all the other auric flares, hers stretching all the way up to the ceiling and seeming to envelope those around her. Enyemaka tried to hold tighter to their connection, scrunching his face in concentration. They both felt it when she turned to look at him like a push of air against his forehead. He sent a small push of energy against her, just to see what she might do. Essien's inner poles shifted again, and she was back in her own head, looking out of her eyes. She sent her energy back to Enyemaka, but this time, it was waves and waves of skin-shivering currents flowing over him, not meant to hurt, but warning him that she could.

Enyemaka popped his eyes open, and Essien was staring directly at him. Her head tilted slightly, considering him from head to toe. Their tall flame slowly untangled itself and began receding away from each other. She felt the release of pressure as their connection closed, and water leaked from her eyes. Their linkage was disconnected, and the other Guard had already begun to rise from their seated positions on the floor.

Essien pushed herself from the ground and headed quickly for the exit. She wanted to be alone, so she could think her own thoughts and exist in her own body. But as she made her way toward the doors, the President stepped into the training room and leaned against the wall next to the exit. He was wearing the white of the Guard training uniform. His eyes gleamed as he took in the fullness of the training room before him.

His sudden appearance made Essien stop mid-step, and she nearly stumbled as Antonious walked over to greet the President. The two touched palms and exchanged some words between them. Then they both turned to look at Essien with identical stares.

Enyemaka walked over to her, stepping right into her line of sight. They were the exact same height, small for someone of any gender. She liked that his height matched so perfectly with her. When he crossed into her line of sight, Essien seemed to snap awake from a trance, and when she looked at him, something like gratitude softened her face.

Enyemaka blurted out in a tangled rush, "Have evening meal with me?"

Essien had not eaten in the main dining room for weeks and knew the other Guard would have noticed. She knew they would wonder about it and make assumptions. Her eyes slid away from Enyemaka to stare behind him. The President was talking to Antonious, and when she looked at him, he turned to meet her eyes. Essien did not like having meals with the President. It made her feel singled out, isolated, and something else that she couldn't quite name. If the goal was her being in the Guard, then didn't she need to bond with the group? Essien felt a boldness well up inside her that wasn't there a moment before.

"Follow me," Essien said. Then she was leading them out of the training room, past the President and Antonious, who were still watching her. Her pace was swift, her steps staccato. She could feel Enyemaka forcing himself to keep his eyes on the back of her head and not lower. He followed her as she led him to the main dining room without saying a word.

The press of all the Guard made the dining room feel inadequately small. She stopped just inside the doors and glanced around. They were at the very beginning of the meal, so no one had yet sat down. Enyemaka led her to the serving table at the far end, past all the tables. They proceeded to fill their plates with the meal of the day, consisting of fish filets with crispy tails, floating in a thick yellow sauce. Essien felt Enyemaka watching her put everything on her plate before he led them confidently over to a table with very few other Guard sitting nearby, his own plate in hand. He sat, she sat, and they began eating their food.

"Where do you eat in the evenings?" he asked.

She looked up at him and accidentally spilled sauce on the front of her uniform. She used her finger to quickly swipe it away and lick it off. Her eyes met his when she put her thumb in her mouth. She kept staring at him.

"I eat evening meal in the President's formal dining room."

"Oh."

Essien couldn't help hearing and feeling what Enyemaka was thinking. Even though the link had been closed down, it was still there, like a faint undercurrent of buzzing. He did not know what else to say, and he had not imagined she might confess so easily. He wanted to ask her what it meant but kept quiet. He could figure it out. He looked around the dining room and tried to imagine any of the other Guard being offered the same arrangement. He couldn't see it happening. He felt again that feeling he'd felt in wanting to protect her back in the Soja. It was fear, a fear so deep that Essien didn't understand it at all, even as she was able to read his mind. It was as though he knew more than he could express. He had protected Essien against the men who had assaulted her, but even he knew there was no way to protect her against the most powerful man in the country.

"Thank you for . . ." She didn't finish the sentence.

Maybe she didn't know what she was thanking him for after all.

Maybe there was a lot she wanted to thank him for, but she didn't know how.

She put more food in her mouth and looked around the room to see if anyone was staring at them together. There were a few eyes, but not too many.

"You don't have to thank me," he told her, his voice gone low. "It was no problem. You look like you could use a friend."

Her eyes snapped up to meet his. "Do I?" Her bottom lip was oily from the sauce, and her tongue darted out like a pink caress to lick it away. Enyemaka looked down into his bowl.

"You always look scared," he said without looking at her. "But . . . I can see why you might be scared."

"I am not afraid of anyone or anything." There was an edge to her voice that he'd heard before. He was making her defensive, and he didn't want that either.

"You should be afraid," he said, still looking down at his plate. "The President is a very scary man."

"I do not think so. He would never hurt me."

"Hurt, no, maybe not. Use you? Yes, he is using you."

"He is using you too."

He could hear the combativeness in her voice. Making her mad was the last thing he wanted to do. Enyemaka felt annoyed with himself that he couldn't just ask her what he wanted to know. He had never been overly emotional or one to react too strongly to events in life, especially the misfortunes of others. But there was something about Essien, how she was his exact height, how she had a way of narrowing her eyes or widening them and going from harsh to innocent in seconds. Perhaps it was how she was so good at everything, or how she could be so powerful it made his brain ache.

He knew what she had been through. He had seen it with his own eyes and imagined it countless times afterward. He knew also that she could defend herself because she had done it before. He remembered witnessing how she had become a different person with that knife in her hand. How her eyes had looked like glowing embers deep inside a roaring fire, as though it wasn't her looking out at him anymore. He recalled how fast she'd moved, too. As he recalled it all, Enyemaka considered for a moment that maybe he should be more afraid *of* her than for her.

Essien thought to herself, *maybe you should.*

"The President is keeping you close for a reason, Essien. I'm afraid of what that reason is."

Essien shook her head, dropping her fork. "What do you know about any of it? How could you possibly know what's going on?" She was surprised to hear the tears forming in her voice.

"Essien, I'm sorry. I don't know what's going on. But you can tell me."

Essien dropped her eyes quickly. "I'm the first woman to be promoted to the Guard. I'm the first woman to make it this far." She lifted her eyes suddenly, and there were no more tears. "On the outside, people just see a small, Igbo woman, but I am so much more than that. All I wanted was to join the Soja and carry a rapid-fire. That's it. I got all this instead."

They shared a smile. Essien sensed that Enyemaka still felt uneasy, but whatever it was that burdened her, he would not be the one to hear it.

"If you want to talk, Essien, please, I am your friend. Can you believe me on this?" Essien looked away from him without answering.

A large group milled around a table near the entrance; a game of bones was being played on the cleared space. There was an outburst of laughter, male laughter at something only men would find funny. Both Enyemaka and Essien looked over at them, and then their eyes slid to each other. There were so many words behind her eyes, words just waiting to spill out to him. Enyemaka used a piece of yam to clean his bowl and slurped down his tea. He clanked his utensils down and then stared at her. Their meal was almost over.

He took a deep breath, leaning forward with his elbows on the table. "Essien, I want to warn you."

"That's your thing, is it? Warning me?"

"Only if you will actually heed the advice this time."

Her eyes were on his face, but they were calm and serious. Like she already knew what he was about to tell her. He plowed on anyway, ignoring the real emotion underlying his warning.

"The President is trying to seduce you, Essien. If you value the future of this country, you must resist him."

She frowned. "What do you mean?"

"I failed you before, but I will do what I can to protect you here." He said it without any emphasis, like stating the weather or the time.

"What does the future of the country have to do with me?"

"Do you know Akukoifo magic?"

She stared at him for a few seconds, and then she nodded once and kept nodding.

"I have never believed them, but . . . now I do . . . because of you . . . because of how powerful you are . . . because of how powerful I know he is. Legends speak of a marriage between the most powerful man and the most powerful woman in Alkebulan. The story tells that the man and woman will be joined together for eternity, their union causing them both to become immortal. In their immortality, they will forget what it is to be human and become cruel monsters, who slaughter people for fun. Their joining will destroy Alkebulan, turning the country into ruins."

Essien opened her mouth to respond, and then her eyes slid away from him again. She quickly shifted her eyes back.

"I will not let that happen. I will not let him use me like that."

Enyemaka shook his head, "If he succeeds in seducing you, Essien, the Alkebulan our ancestors fought to create will be over. He will destroy this country, and everyone with it. And you will help him do it."

As he finished his statement, Enyemaka noticed Essien was staring at something behind him. He turned around and glanced across the space of the dining hall. He saw a few remaining Guard finishing their meals at the round tables. He saw the cooks scraping the last of the food out of the giant metal serving bowls onto platters. And at the door of the dining room, he saw the President and Antonious standing in a circle with a small group of Guard. As per usual, Antonious was doing the talking, his hands gesturing wildly with his words, but the President had his arms crossed, and he was staring directly at Enyemaka.

Essien rose from her seat and gathered her plates. "Thank you for telling me," she told Enyemaka as she stepped away from the table.

She marched confidently over to deposit her dishes, and then walked straight toward where the President stood just inside the doorway. He stepped aside for her as she walked through the doors, his gaze remaining on Enyemaka still seated across the room.

CHAPTER THIRTY-NINE

◆

A FEW WEEKS LATER, THE GUARD WAS GATHERED IN THE training room after their mid-day meal. Antonious told the Guard, "Today, you will be paired to practice tracking. One partner from each group will be placed at different locations in a practice field. The other partner will need to locate their partner using mental tracking, and then locate their partner physically using their mental map. Form pairs amongst yourselves, and then we will proceed to the training site."

Essien immediately looked around for Enyemaka, but she did not see him. She stood on her tippy toes, attempting to make herself a few inches taller to see around all the high shoulders. When she still didn't see him, she ended up settling on the nearest Guard to her, a veteran of ten years. He had small teeth and large gums, and Essien tried not to stare at their pink color almost starting to cover his teeth.

She looked around for Enyemaka again, wondering if he had avoided her on purpose, like she usually did to him. She craned this way and that as Antonious led the group out of the training room, down the stairs, and to a line of waiting engines. Essien tried to locate Enyemaka using her sense of auras. She closed her eyes and opened herself to that constantly buzzing undercurrent. Essien remembered the feel of his energy. There he was, sitting all the way at the back of the engine. He must have gotten on first. Enyemaka gave a little pushback, but his energy was weak and barely there. Then the connection was closed, like a clamp on a lock. Essien wasn't sure if Enyemaka had done that or someone else. It had felt too powerful to be Enyemaka.

THE SUN BLAZED LIKE A FIERY FROND SPREADING LEAVES OVER all the sky. Essien climbed down from the engine and tried to shield her eyes. There was a great hedge stretching away from them to the edge of the field where the grass turned brown. The hedge boxed a large space divided with more hedges. It was literally a maze. The Guard gathered at one end with Antonious' short frame in front of them. He was giving them instructions, and Essien was half-listening, attempting to catch sight of Enyemaka again. Now that she'd found him, she wondered about that pushback she'd felt from him. When she'd opened herself to the buzzing around her, she'd felt his energy like a small buzzing gnat, barely there at all. She wondered how he would do in this sort of challenge.

"Each partner must pass this part of training as mental tracking is one of the most important tools we use in the Guard," Antonious was saying. "You have two hours. If you do not pass, you will be immediately demoted back to the Soja." Antonious eyes squinted at the seriousness of the task. "A Guard who can't track his mark is a Guard who can't find his own President in the dark."

Essien's ears tuned in, and she realized she needed to concentrate on her own performance. She turned to her partner and his stern face.

"Should we link up now?"

They had been practicing this skill for weeks now, but it was already second nature to her. One minute, Essien was squinting to avoid the blazing sun, and the next she could feel the energy markers blazing all around her. She glanced around the edge of the field, and she could sense Enyemaka standing just a few feet away. His energy was still a small, blinking white dot; it was not at all powerful. She pushed a bit of energy in his direction, but his aural signature remained weak. Essien pushed more energy his way, closing her eyes to get a better feel for his faded impression.

Suddenly, Essien was staring out of Enyemaka's eyes from where he was standing across the field. It was like she could still see him at the same time she was inside him. The sensation made her dizzy, and she tried unsuccessfully to pull away from the intense connection. Enyemaka turned those eyes toward where the largest energy marker blazed like a tall, sky-reaching bonfire—toward Essien. He began to smile at seeing her face in the distant crowd but stopped himself. He rolled his lips in to keep himself from letting that joy slip out. *Just at seeing her face, ehn. Making girl-love*, he chided himself. He nodded at her and then turned away as his partner was led away to be hidden inside the field. He shook his head to help himself focus, jumped up and down, swinging his arms. He would pass this test easily, and then he would rush to ask Essien to have evening meal with him again before she could disappear.

Half the Guard was led away to be dispatched into the field beyond the hedges. Enyemaka could hear the wind blowing through the tall trees, the leaves rustling in the movement. A loud horn sounded, and the Guard bolted into the field as the dividers fell. The hedges were taller inside the field, and there were openings at irregular intervals. He watched other Guard pelt past him, barreling ahead with top speed. No one stopped to ground themselves or plan a path using their mental map. Enyemaka knew he had two hours to locate his partner, but the faster he performed, the better he would be scored and ranked. He needed to do better than he had been doing so far.

He tried to sense his partner, remembering the static feeling of their energy. He couldn't sense it. He poured more of his own energy out into the field, trying to envision the entire space before him. There . . . a weak flame that might be him. He took off running, sprinting to make up for the time he'd taken to use his mental map but dead ended at another hedge. He turned another corner and another, other Guard bolted past him.

It was harder keeping a connection with that weak signal when he was running, but he couldn't stop. He headed in the general direction he had sensed it. Other Guard were now shouting and jumping up and down as they found their targets and could celebrate.

Enyemaka kept running.

He had smashed through a slim opening in a high hedge wall when he finally stopped to establish the connection again. But what he sensed was impossible according to the mental map he'd created in his head; that weak spark was on the other side of the field, back through all the hedges where he had just run. He let himself use more energy than he ever had trying to be sure he wasn't misreading his own tracking, his forehead wrinkled with concentration. But that weak spark kept jumping, even as he tried to pinpoint it in one spot.

Sweat slipped into his eye and stung.

He wiped his eyes but got dirt into them instead.

Across the field, Essien felt him close his eyes and try to direct the energy he was pushing around every corner of the field, now yelling for his partner. But what was that other feeling she felt just behind it? Another aura greater than her own pressing in on Enyemaka. But whose?

Enyemaka didn't seem to notice this at all. He could only feel his time ticking down.

He was passing fewer and fewer Guard now. He slipped through a hedge and then turned and went right back through it, the branches scratching at his face and arms. No matter how much energy he used in concentrating, his partner's signal never got stronger or closer. The sun seemed to be leaning down on his shoulder. The front of his uniform top was so damp with his sweat that Essien patted her own collar is if it were hers that was dripping. The connection lay like a film over her own vision as she found her partner, and they high-fived.

Essien and her partner made their way out of the maze to join the growing group of Guard who'd already completed the exercise. Essien turned back to the tall hedges and felt Enyemaka searching the field in a systematic method, moving up and down, from one side of the field to the next. When he hit a hedge, he crossed through it and did the same thing on the other side. He got all the way back to the entrance, and there had been no sight of his partner anywhere inside the field. Everyone else had already located their partners and exited the hedges.

Enyemaka turned and was about to begin the same search method in the opposite direction, but at that moment, a horn blew letting him know he was out of time. Essien felt the blare of the horn right down to her bones, and she could feel that he did, too.

The first thing Enyemaka saw when he exited the field was his partner coming through at the same time with the gall to look embarrassed.

"When you didn't come for me, I tried to find you."

Enyemaka gaped at him. "We were running past each other the entire time?"

He sucked his teeth and shook his head. He kicked the ground with the toe of his boot repeatedly.

Enyemaka didn't want to look at anyone else, but he finally let his eyes pass over everyone around them. He saw Antonious was doing his usual animated talking, and most of the Guard were talking excitedly, bumping shoulders, and pounding each other on the backs. Enyemaka and his partner were the only two with frowns. He was about to turn and complain when he saw Essien again. The locking of their eyes broke their connection, and Essien felt such disorientation as she realized she was alone in her body and seeing through her own eyes again.

Essien watched as Antonious signaled to Enyemaka and his partner to wait. The rest of the Guard filed back into the engine to return them to the compound, while Essien remained in her place, her eyes on Enyemaka and his partner as Antonious looked at the two with regret.

Essien could sense Enyemaka feeling like he was moving in slow motion, even as she no longer saw through his eyes. Enyemaka felt like everything around him was surreal and just out of his reach. The feelings coming from him left her disoriented all over again, and she couldn't figure out how to put up blockers between them.

Enyemaka felt sorry for himself; Essien recognized the feeling vibrating in her chest. It was an immense pity that weighed him down, and in turn weighed her down. The hanging of his head as Antonious spoke to him said it all.

He was being banished. Demoted. Dropped back down to the ranks of Soja.

A short while later, up in her room, Essien lay across her bed, face down, her eyes squeezed shut so tightly that it took her a few seconds to realize she was alone in her own body once more. She had felt everything Enyemaka had felt. His frantic energy growing in intensity as he desperately searched the field. Yet, Essien had also felt a more powerful energy the entire time, concentrated directly on Enyemaka, keeping him from sensing his partner. She'd felt it like an iron lock that couldn't be broken. Essien also noted that she couldn't reach Enyemaka around it either. Enyemaka had been head-blind and sight-blind. Essien knew there were at least two sources of power that could accomplish that level of deception, and she had thought she could trust one of them but now knew she could not. It could only have been Gabriel behind the ordeal.

CHAPTER FORTY

◆

Essien had always dreamed. But she began to have specific and repetitive dreams—dreams that came to her every night and felt more familiar than anything she experienced during the day. They felt like memories of past lives or visions of a future existence. They felt so real to her, like something dredged up from the oldest parts of her brain. What she saw in her dreams every night started to feel more important to her than her rise in the Guard.

The dreams themselves weren't significant to her own life. She never saw people she had met before. But the images still haunted her in wakefulness. She dreamed about a woman with her face and a little girl who grew too fast, that were both present in all of her dreams. Sometimes, there was a man with the President's face, only it wasn't him. That's what she told herself in the light of day, that it wasn't the President she dreamed about every night, but some other man whom she hadn't yet met. The dreams kept coming to her, and with each dream, her understanding of the story grew. Essien realized that the woman was the Queen, and the girl was the Queen's daughter, born of Akukoifo magic.

One night, she dreamt of the Queen and the girl in a nighttime jungle of familiar smells. Spicy trees and damp undergrowth amidst the clear sound of flowing water. They walked through a jungle that was loud in its quietness. It was the darkest part of the night, and Essien wondered why the young girl was out of bed so late. The Queen led the girl beneath a wide canopy of low hanging branches with gently swinging vines. There were natural benches under the canopy made of water-smoothed fallen trees with firm sides. On the other side of the canopy, the trees opened to reveal a clear stretch of silvery-blue water. The moon hung above that empty space, full and expectant. It felt like the air itself hummed around them. The Queen led the girl into the water, silvery splashes climbing up their tunics as they sank waist deep and then chest deep. She helped the girl to float, the water swirling around them. The sounds of wet ground, creaking branches, and whispering leaves grew louder and louder. The Queen rose out of the water, droplets sliding down. She led the girl out of the water. Standing on the edge of the lake, dry and shining in the darkness, the Queen began to speak.

"Once upon a time, there was a girl, just like you. Her name was Day. She was a beautiful girl who hated being a girl. You see, the girl had many brothers, big, strong, tough brothers who made her feel small and useless. Day wanted to be like her brothers. So, one day, she hid herself in the garments of the night and walked in a crowd with her brothers. She got close enough to challenge her eldest brother to a race. Not knowing it was his younger sister, the eldest prepared to run. Just as someone yelled go, Day threw off her garments, revealing herself, and then began to run as fast as she could. She ran so fast that she left her stunned and laughing brother waiting at the starting line. Day won the race, and she won the respect and admiration of all but two of her elder brothers."

The little girl asked the Queen to tell her the story again, like she always did, but the story would never be told the same. The dream spilled into other nights of the Queen and the girl running through the jungle holding hands, being chased by something, a white misty shape always behind them, but never getting close. Then the park again with the rock benches, and the moon hanging over the Queen's head like a crown. The little girl swimming and splashing in the water, drinking mouthfuls of it with her head back.

The stories the Queen told were always different, but always about the girl called Day. Sometimes, Day made her brothers so angry that they wouldn't let her tag along with them no matter how much she begged. Other times, Day was a mischief-maker who succeeded in showing off her dubious charm and winning their approval. Story after story was told, stretching like a timeline in the dreams that started and ended so abruptly.

Essien began to pine for the end of her own waking hours, so she could return to the dreamscape. In her dreams, the girl aged and grew bigger, but the Queen stayed the same. The Queen's stories shifted and began to tell the story of a Day who was fierce and powerful, a Day who made men afraid to venture outside after the sun came up.

"Day was a fighter. She believed in conquering her opponent no matter what it took. She made staffs from great Marengo trees. She carried a whip made of scorpion tails. She drank poison from red toads. Any man who dared to come near her would find his death in her staff, in her whip, and as her last defense, in her lips. She was a force on Earth like no other.

"Day was more powerful than anything. But she forgot the most important lesson of a fighter: never get close to your enemy. Day let herself get too close to the Night. Her enemy struck when she was vulnerable and unarmed. Day thought she was winning, gaining the confidence of Night, but all along, her enemy was learning and studying her, too. When Night came to snap chains around her, Day was taken without a fight. She was captured and imprisoned in a cage of moonlight. She was not allowed to enter the light at the end of the night for thousands of years after that."

The girl began to cry when she heard that story—large, loud tears that made the jungle ring with their mournfulness. The girl's cries felt like burning ashes blowing in the wind. Essien watched the Queen wipe away tears that glittered like diamonds.

Essien realized that she was dreaming, and the girl's cries faded as she began to wake. As she lay in her small room in the President's compound, Essien couldn't decide if the prick of hurt the girl felt was from the tale of Day's demise or because that was the last story about Day her mother had to tell.

Essien didn't dream about the girl and the Queen again after that.

◆

CHAPTER FORTY-ONE

THE SUMMONS CAME IN THE FORM OF A LETTER BROUGHT with a knock upon her door. A Guard handed Essien the message from the other side of her entryway. There was no envelope, just the slip of white paper with black type that instructed her to report to the President's office as her first task of the day. Essien stared at the words, and a soft feeling of dread thrummed into her.

Reading the words in her hand brought Gabriel to mind in a whoosh, and suddenly Essien could see him, like she hovered in front of him or just above him. He was standing in the middle of a stage, wearing a white agbada embroidered with sparkling silver all over. His hands were stretched out wide, and his head was tilted back. His lips were moving, but Essien couldn't hear what he was saying. It was as if she was too far away. She closed her eyes and blinked them rapidly. Gabriel remained below her, but his eyes were open now, and he was staring at her. His face was blank, but his eyes were squinting, as though he were trying to see her more clearly, too. A smile broke across his lips and Essien tried to break away. She couldn't feel her body standing in her suite. She couldn't see anything else around Gabriel, just his figure standing in one spot, arms spread wide, his eyes on hers. His lips were still moving, and now, Essien could hear him.

"When the galaxies were still swirling purple ribbons of gas and dust, the Mothers were there, stirring that primordial soup, adding just enough seasonings and sauces to bring creation to life. Whether by word or will, the power of the Mothers flows out and out, and there is nothing that can limit or contain them completely. The power of the Mothers protects us all, granting us their inordinate ability to wield on Ala-ani as they wield the otherworld, eluigwe."

"I don't know how to stop this," Essien said.

In front of her, the Guard said, "Stop what?"

Essien turned her head, and she was suddenly back inside her suite, standing before the uniformed Guard she'd trained alongside too many times to count. He stared back at her as she breathed heavily, her chest expanding out.

"Never mind," she said, as she shook her head, and then watched him retreat down the hall to the lift.

Essien closed the door and squeezed her eyes closed, attempting to slow her breathing. She hadn't experienced body jumping since Enyemaka had failed his promotions test. Essien had been desperate to break the connection then, as she had been now, but it had been easier this time. She breathed deep and tried to concentrate on the present. She didn't want to get caught in someone else's body or mind again. The sensation was paralyzing, and Essien was afraid of it happening when she needed her own arms and hands to protect herself. Being able to see auras and connect with Akukoifo was intriguing, but Essien couldn't risk the more negative effects, like possibly exploding someone's body into red rain.

She was secretly haunted by what she had learned. She didn't think she would need Akukoifo magic to stop an attack in real life; there were powers she knew she had that she refused to ever use. The burning feeling of energy floating just beneath the surface of her skin made her afraid of the powers she had yet to discover—powers that the President had attempted to show her. Essien began to consider that perhaps those powers might be more useful in this world after all.

THE PRESIDENT'S OFFICE WAS COMPRISED OF SLEEK DARK WOOD flooring, dark wood desk furniture, and walls covered in books arranged by color. One bookcase contained all red books. Another bookcase contained all blue books. Another shelf was a mixture of green and yellow books. Essien stared around the room with a desire to read every single book on the shelves. The President's mahogany desk was in the center of the room on top of a white rug, and there were large cabinets located just behind the desk. The President sat in a tall, black, wing-backed chair that framed him wearing the silver and white tunic she'd seen him in before.

"Sir?" Essien asked as she stepped into the doorway.

The President smiled at her, and it flexed his face just enough to show his laugh lines. "Essien, come in."

Something shivered its way upward and then downward inside Essien's belly at the sound of his voice, and she recoiled from it. She swallowed and took a deep breath, walking closer to the desk until her boots stepped on the white rug. "You have orders for me?"

"Essien." The President stopped, silent as he quietly observed her. "There was an assassination attempt on my life today," he finally said.

It was Essien's turn to be silent. There was that thrumming of dread in her belly again. She felt her chest clenching, her body tightening all the way up to her teeth, but she remained quiet, stewing in her own thoughts brought on like a deluge at these words.

"You can read the details of what happened in the eventual report, but the Guard who were with me were very valuable today, as you all are every day."

Essien swallowed, flashing back to the magic of leaping out of her body earlier that morning. "It was during your speech, wasn't it? During your speech about the Mothers, about creation. You were wearing . . . this."

"I was. I wanted you to see. And you saw."

Essien choked on her response, trying to parse what she'd seen in that flash with what Gabriel was now telling her. "I regret not being there," was all she managed to speak into the silence. But the feeling in her stomach was so much more than regret. What was it? She pushed the thought away and wouldn't allow herself to consider it again.

Gabriel chuckled; the sound was a soft rumbling that purred into her thoughts. "It wasn't your rotation. Even you need time to rest. And what would you have done differently than your peers anyway?"

"I'd have used all the tools and techniques I've been taught by your military. I'd have used the skills I used on you not so very long ago."

Silence.

Then Gabriel let out a loud rumble of laughter that hurt Essien's ear. "Or we could just find the rest of their numbers and kill them. Those who didn't die at the hands of the Guard right then and there."

Essien studied his face for a tell, any tell, but found none. Narrowing her eyes apprehensively, she watched him watching her. "You can do whatever you wish to do." Her words unfolded slowly as she considered them. "You have that power. Government channels or Akukoifo, you have it. All you have to do is will it."

"As can you, Essien," Gabriel said with an emphasis on her name. He leaned back in his chair, fingers steepled over his stomach. "Try it now."

"Try . . . what now?" Again, her eyes narrowed in disquiet.

Gabriel reached forward over his desk, a thoughtful smile playing at his lips, and touched her hand with his own.

Essien whooshed forward, out of her body, and when she looked around, she was crouched low in a dingy, dim room. A splintered door was only a few paces before her, and she felt herself walking forward. The door gave easily. The hallway now before her was long, paved with light-colored wood adding a flash of brightness in the dim space. There were no windows in the room or the hallway, just the walls leading to an open doorway. The building, perhaps a house judging by the tattered furniture strewn haphazardly about, smelled old and musty, and a layer of gray dust coated everything. Essien breathed deeply and then let all the air out of her and continued forward.

She reached a large room at the end of the hallway, still low to the ground. Four bodies lay in various states of abrupt end, not exactly a circle, but each of the bodies appeared to have fallen exactly where they stood. Two of them were half lying on each other. The other two were sprawled out nearby, their rapid-fires scattered around them like macabre decorations. Essien could see one bullet hole in the sides of each of their heads and a spreading stain of blood on the other side underneath them. She stared at the sight, their pools of blood widening and expanding until she had to take a step back to avoid the red puddle.

Essien whooshed back into her body, disoriented and off balance. She saw that Gabriel had removed his hand from hers and was leaning back into his chair again. Her chest heaved with the shock and exertion of the sudden jump, with the jolt of seeing the four dead bodies, still warm and oozing blood.

"Was that the men—?"

"As I said before, as can you, Essien. All you have to do is will it."

She knew and had known since he exploded her attackers into red rain what abilities Gabriel possessed, what abilities he could teach her to wield, which she had adamantly refused to learn. The ability to read minds and switch consciousness, to move men or destroy them. Everything in her was certain of how much power Gabriel hid from everyone, especially her; some alarm in her knew that he was capable of anything, and everything, and only some strong will kept him from directing that great capacity at her, at them all.

He eyed her face for a second and then casually steepled his fingers in front of his nose and mouth.

She swallowed and tried to ask a question. "When did you—?"

"I wasn't there in the flesh, but I didn't need to be. Neither would you need to be."

Essien couldn't look away from his face. "What are you saying?"

"Things have a tendency to happen for me . . . concerning me. If someone means me harm, they tend to die. If someone threatens me, they die. I'm sure you've noticed that happening to you, too. These four men were threatening me, so, of course, they had to die. And I hear your thoughts now, that they should have been brought in and tried. Thrown in confinement or formally executed. But trust me, killing those men now served a greater purpose."

"What purpose was that? What part of the law was being enforced with you killing them like that?"

"My threat had a more immediate effect than trying a bunch of petty criminals. Their group may not even make another attempt now. They should realize that this Presidency doesn't just have sharp teeth for display. We use them."

Essien shook her head and planted her hands on the desk, leaning toward him. "How did you get it to look like they did it all at the same time? How did you—?"

"There are tools that you have forbidden us to teach you. Maybe now you will reconsider."

Essien frowned. No, she would not. She didn't want to be able to commit murder on a passing whim. She'd seen him do it, and she didn't want to become that callous toward human life. To be able to think *die* and watch a person's life explode out of them. Essien didn't want that much power at her fingertips.

But she remembered the hot sear of fire in her hands before the cool waters of the lake had quenched them. Maybe those powers were already there.

CHAPTER FORTY-TWO

◆

S HE TRIED TO SLEEP BUT TOSSED AND TURNED FITFULLY. SOME-
thing inside her felt uneasy and apprehensive, like she was standing
on engine tracks and could feel the engine barreling toward her, but she
couldn't move out of its way.

The next day, she was issued another summons, delivered to the room
before she could get dressed for the day. The summons was from the President—requesting her presence at dinner that evening.

THE PRESIDENT SAT WITH HIS BACK TO THE DOOR, AS PER USUAL,
when she entered the hall for dinner that night, the light streaming in over
his slick, tightly curled hair and the gaunt lines of his face. She stared down
at his bowed head from behind as his golden writing point scribbled across
a leaf spelling out words that she could read over his shoulder. He didn't
look up at her as she stood there, so she let her eyes spill over his large hand-
writing. They were military commands; she read the words *search* and *sei-
zure, checkpoints,* and *rebel village razing.* When he finally looked up at her,
he smiled gently and pushed the papers away, extending his hand to gesture
for her to sit.

She noted that the spot right next to him always seemed to have a
warmer temperature range than everywhere else in the room. She knew
the heat was emanating from Gabriel, but she thought it might be because
of her, too. Whenever she sat this close to him, she couldn't help sensing
a great wall of restrained energy wafting off him like a powerful phero-
mone. A restraint that made him seem always poised for sudden action.
The feeling that he always guarded himself with her, every single word and
phrase, made her still somewhat uncomfortable, but now she noticed it
more acutely after the shocking revelation in his office days before.

He had on a pleasant smile, but Essien didn't buy it. Eating with him had become an accepted part of her reality at his compound. He was intrusive, true, and demanding of her, but he let her ask him questions. He gave her more freedom than any of the other Guard had, so she had convinced herself that his orders and demands didn't bother her as much. Even though they did and likely always would.

Essien thought of her family and all the time she had missed with her parents. She should go to see them soon, perhaps the next time she was offered reprieve. She didn't say anything out loud. Instead, she stared at him as their food was presented, and he began slicing, spooning, and sipping. She wondered what it was about him that still terrified her because at moments like this, he seemed so tame.

She wasn't afraid of him, not in the way of thinking he would harm her intentionally. He'd had ample opportunity to do so, but he had been nothing less than gentlemanly and presidential. Still, she knew that he could harm her in more ways than physical, and she'd seen this up close and personal more than once. The fact he chose not to sometimes made her feel unusually safe around him even as she knew that she shouldn't. She never said anything to him about the feeling of danger that kept catching her unawares, another one of the many things she never brought up with him. She couldn't tell him that sometimes just the sight of him walking toward her made her heart pound inside her chest like an anxious anvil waiting to hammer her to a pulp. She couldn't talk to him about how often she dreamed about a man with his face and what those dreams turned into each night. She couldn't tell him that her fear of him had everything to do with fear of herself. She remembered that he had probably read the thoughts in her mind already.

"I asked you to dinner tonight to remind you that you're coming up on your one-year anniversary with us soon, if I calculate correctly. I knew it was just the kind of thing you would overlook."

Still, she sat silently. Gabriel smiled mischievously, as if he'd anticipated just that response from her.

"It's on September fourth, your one-year anniversary here. And the Guard may have been informed that something big is supposed to be happening on that day."

Essien looked up at him now. "The festival."

"That's correct."

"But . . . why that date? Why have it on *my* anniversary here?" Essien was asking herself, but Gabriel gave her an answer she wasn't expecting.

"We announced a festival and parade set for the same date. It's the first we've had in a while. A lot of work and effort is going into preparation; a lot of people from other nations are going to be there."

"Will it be safe?"

"Metal detectors, the Guard, Sojas, and skycraft. The Guard will handle it, Essien. Don't you worry."

"But did you make that date such a big event on purpose?"

"If I say 'yes', will you refuse to attend?" he laughed, teasing her.

"Why didn't you tell me before?"

"Because I thought I might be able to surprise you with something."

She didn't like the way he said that and wondered what it meant. Immediately, she was reminded again why she felt uncomfortable around him sometimes, and how right she was to feel that way. He had kept his word to her and never touched her again. Still, moments like this reminded her of unwanted truths. Namely that he often behaved like a man trying to please a woman, and she was that woman.

"Surprise me with what? Another possibly hostile situation to defuse just like at the Council House?"

"No, actually. An award."

"An award? What for?" Essien nearly forgot herself in her casual tone, but Gabriel didn't seem to mind.

"An award to honor your service as the first Alkebulanian woman to join the Guard, of course. Did you think such a distinction would go unnoticed?"

Essien did not believe she needed to be awarded for anything and squinted her eyes at him over her plate.

"You must not do what it is you are planning to do."

"Awarding the first woman of Alkebulan is not only about you, Essien. This is a triumph for the country, for the people, for me, even. Choose to see it as another task in your service to Alkebulan if you wish."

"Don't I stand out enough? You want me front and center even more?"

She couldn't do her job guarding him if she was up on a stage with thousands of eyes on her and picto capturers going off around her. The less she was in the news, the better. People might know her face from when her trial was on the nightly news reports, but she hoped not very many would remember. If the President insisted on drawing attention to her, that might change quickly. But she could see in his eyes that the matter was already a done deal.

Essien's eyes fell on the leaves he'd signed and pushed away. She scoffed and gestured to them. "And what is that? Your plans to . . . raze whole villages?" At his raised eyebrows she jerked her chin toward his now-closed leafbook.

"I saw you writing it. What if you raze the wrong villages? What if innocents are harmed? What if angry people attack the festival that you'll have raging while elsewhere fields burn?"

Gabriel's teasing smile disappeared. "No one is truly innocent. Not once they are born into this world. The festival will go on. And you will be celebrated. We shall give the people something to celebrate. Don't you agree?"

She didn't, but the turn of his head back to his plate let her know that such an answer would go unheard.

CHAPTER FORTY-THREE

◆

T HE MORNING OF THE FESTIVAL, ESSIEN WAS AWAKENED BY A knock on the door that roused her from her sleep and out of bed. When she opened the door, still in her bedclothes, a Guard handed her a package and then quickly withdrew down the hall. Inside the package, a silky slip of fabric spilled out. It was a short black dress with thin straps. There was also a pair of sandal stacks that would raise her height at least five inches. The accompanying note read, "Dress as a civilian, and do not bring weapons."

Essien stared down at the type and felt anger thrum through her. She had not been expecting these types of orders. She had finally accepted that the event was happening whether she wanted it to or not. Having to attend without the protection of armor and armaments made her more upset than having to wear a dress. The shoes and the dress slipped to the floor as she rushed out of her suite, toward the lift, and pressed the buttons to take her down to the first floor.

She met the President in the hallway outside the auditorium. He was with Antonious and a few other Guard. He seemed so casual, leaning up against the wall with his arms crossed over his chest. He was nodding to one of the Guard when she walked up.

"I will not go without weapons, Gabriel." The weapons seemed the easier battle of the two. The military already dictated what she wore on a daily basis; this was simply one more occasion for specified attire.

"You will be surrounded by weapons, Essien."

"I want to be carrying my own."

"You will go unarmed, as ordered."

"Are you trying to set me up?" she yelled at him. Her voice echoed into a silence in the hallway. Something hard clenched in the President's jaw. "Do you mean to have me killed at this festival?"

"The people of this country love you, Essien."

"I've been attacked by the people of this country once already. They do not love me any more than they love you. I do not want to go without at least one weapon on my person."

He stared down at her, not saying anything. She noticed that the black short-sleeved tunic and slacks he was wearing were in a similar material as the dress she was expected to wear. She froze, growing self-conscious as she remembered that she hadn't stopped to get dressed in her uniform.

She plowed on. "I do not think this award will entice them to love me any more than your village razing will entice them to love you."

Gabriel pushed away from the wall and told her as he walked back into his office, "You can bring one weapon."

"And the stacks? What if I have to run?"

"Surely you can run in stacks?" he smiled, and she realized he was joking with her.

"I have never worn stacks in my life, and I won't start as a sworn Guard in the Udo Nchedo. Do you want me to break an ankle, too?"

A quirk near his lip let her know that she had won. "Fine. I did not mean to presume. Wear boots if that suits you. But at least the dress?"

Essien shook her head and left the President in the hallway to go and find the smallest rapid-fire that might fit underneath the dress.

THE TRIP TO THE CAPITAL WAS SILENT. SHE SAT NEXT TO GA-briel in the back of an engine that swayed them into each other as it lurched into the city. She'd come down to the first floor wearing the flimsy dress like a dark whisper against her skin. She'd substituted open sandals for the stacks. The President was wearing shiny loafers with a gold buckle. The sleeves of his tunic were rolled up, revealing gently muscled biceps.

Essien eyed him wearily and looked away as he tried to catch her eye. The other Guard followed them in engines in front of and behind them. Essien wasn't paying attention to the ride outside the window; she'd seen it enough times already—only, from her viewpoint as a uniformed Guard. She wondered about the award ceremony and the threat of attack that made her feel sweaty with paranoia.

When the engine stopped, she got out first. They were parked in an alley between two tall buildings that led into a courtyard.

"Walk next to me," she heard. She sighed and looked back at the President. He wasn't smiling, but she could feel that same energy vibrating like a subdued electrical current.

It was her first time going out with the President in anything except her uniform. Standing right next to him, out of uniform, made her feel like the target on him was now solidly on her, too. How many people still despised the idea of women in the Soja, let alone the Guard?

She kept staring up at him and then out at the crowd of men in the Guard that surrounded them. The dress was short, above her mid-thigh. She tugged at the hem. Most of the Guard avoided looking her in the eye, standing in a protective circle around her and the President, but a few of them stared back at her defiantly. She saw deeply indented foreheads and a few disdainful sneers. She fought the urge to put her hand into her pocket where it allowed her easy access to grip the butt of a small rapid-fire attached to a holster fitted around her hips. On the other side, she had a sheathed knife six inches long. She brushed her fingertips against the harsh shapes as her dress stirred slightly.

"Gabriel, I feel naked."

"I can assure you that you are not." He was smiling when he said it, but she took several steps to be further away.

"I don't want people to notice me. Everyone will be staring at me."

"You look fine, Essien. It's okay if you are a civilian for this one day."

"I am not a civilian. I will still be searching the crowd. I will still be checking for visible weapons. I will still be watching out for the slightest threat to you. I wish I had more weapons on me."

"Smile and enjoy the day, Essien."

"How am I supposed to enjoy this? This isn't work. I should have been one of the Guard today, Gabriel."

She felt him wanting to put his arm around her through the motion he suddenly made toward and then away from her. The feeling emanated out of him into her, and she wouldn't have felt the desire to be consoled rise in her if he hadn't first reached out to her like that. She felt it almost as a shock a second later when his arms were holding her shoulders and her waist, squeezing to test how small she truly was compared to him. It was the second time he had ever hugged her.

She waited for it to feel wrong or uncomfortable, for that panicky state she'd once lived in full time to set in.

Nothing happened.

She pressed her face into his chest and locked her hands together behind his back. If she let herself, she might stand like that forever. She finally stepped away from him, and he tried to keep her pressed against him.

She didn't look at him again as she started walking further down the alley, which signaled his Guard to start walking, too. They hesitated, though, and she noticed it. Gabriel trailed behind her. He probably noticed it, too. The President didn't hug his Guard.

Her sandals clicked as she walked faster. She reached the courtyard and the smack of so many people was sudden. The wide-open space was packed full of families with small children, groups of teenagers, and elders craning their necks to see. The Guard reached her, and she could feel the President walk up behind her. She turned to look up at him, but Gabriel was watching the crowd, a smile ready in wait upon his face.

The Guard led them around the metal detectors and across the boisterous plaza. As they made their way, they passed vendors lined up in orderly rows, and Essien could smell roasting meat in the air. Small red, black, and green flags flapped in the wind as they dangled from ropes threaded in the canopies of trees and off the peaks of buildings. The mass of people jostled for space, while groups of men in the identifiable dark green of medicine men hovered around the edges of the plaza.

"How now, President Ijikota!" Voices began cheering together, their merriment rising above the plaza like a cloud. The Guard remained tight around them, a wall of black preceding their advance through the crowds. They passed the vendors in a bubble of black, the crowd pressing in on them from all sides.

Essien saw people selling caps, hats, shoes, shirts, crystals, and jewelry. There were also dozens of food stalls and games for children. She even caught a smell of the sticky sweet aroma of chopped fruit. In another life, she'd have stopped to buy some mango.

At the end of the festival grounds, a steel stage had been erected with chairs lined up in a row near a wide podium. Essien climbed the stage and then turned back to look at the President. Antonious was whispering something into his ear.

"Sit in one of the chairs near the end," a Guard instructed her, pointing at the spot she should take. The President sat in the first chair behind the podium. There were various officials sitting in between them. The crowd had followed them and were filling in the rows of wooden benches lined up in front of the stage. The Guard lined up in front of the stage facing the audience, a wall of protection between them.

Antonious walked up to the podium and began trying to get the growing crowd's attention. He raised his hands and fluttered his fingers. He tapped the voice projector, making sharp static emit from the speakers placed around the audience space. Essien glanced over at Gabriel, but he was wearing his public smile, while his eyes moved back and forth over the audience, raising his hand to wave at them.

All of the spaces in the first few rows were filled to bursting, yet still people poured into the seating area. Antonious tapped the mic again.

"Countrymen, thank you for joining us here today. This is a significant event, the celebration of an historic moment in our country's history. I'd like to invite to the podium, President Ijikota, the first President in Alkebulan's history to preside over such an occasion. Join me in welcoming him up as he honors our awardee."

Antonious led the applause, and it thundered in the space for several seconds after Gabriel had stepped up to the podium. He stood there and smiled, waving his hand. Essien felt herself zoning out, her eyes darting across the crowd searching for opportunities of threat. She couldn't turn off her training, it was so embedded into her, but she was shocked out of her focus on the crowd when she heard the President say, "We created this award because we wanted to honor the first woman to join the Guard. She has demonstrated a steadfast commitment to this country and protecting its people. She has gone above and beyond in her duties. Today, on the one-year anniversary of her promotion to the Guard, we celebrate her accomplishments. May she continue to rise in the ranks. Who knows? Maybe one day she will be in my position," he added, with an affectedly light-hearted jest. He waited for the subsequent laughter of the crowd to die down and then raised his head and turned to Essien. "It is with great pleasure and great pride that we present Essien Ezinulo with the Onyinye Izizi, an award for our first woman Guard."

Essien watched the faces of the crowd while her accomplishments were read out. It sounded like a description of someone else, not anyone she recognized. Gabriel turned to her over his shoulder again and beckoned her up. She stood on shaky knees as the President handed her the award framed in white wood. She stared at it but didn't take it; she didn't want it. The award was handed off to someone else while the nervousness jangling through her legs made her eager to sit. Never fond of public speaking, she hurriedly sat back down before they invited her to the voice projector.

She looked out into the crowd and surveyed the faces of those present. Most of them were smiling and happy, but not all of them. A few faces in the crowd wore the frowns and grimaces she had come to expect from her brief time in the spotlight during her trial. Essien wondered whether her parents would smile or frown if they were here. This thought drowned out all of the speakers who came next. When she glanced back at the podium, it was empty. Gabriel was standing up in front of his chair, and Antonious had a hand resting on his shoulder. Essien waited for one of them to exit the stage, but they were engrossed in a conversation. And so, tired of waiting, Essien took it upon herself to make an exit and walked briskly away from the stage.

The Guard settled around her, and it was a subtle reluctance that Essien could convince herself she didn't feel. She could hear the President trying to catch up to her, his steps clambering down from the stage. She walked faster.

The bubble of Guard around them allowed her to move in a circle of empty space with the crowd rushing past just outside of their protective barrier. It made her feel out of place and awkward to be the one protected rather than doing the protecting. She glanced at the crowd around the bubble of men, imagining that crowd turning violent and trying to attack her or the President in an assassination attempt. She didn't have that many weapons, and she didn't have on any protective layers.

She would be so easy to attack.

It was almost too foolishly easy.

She shouldn't have imagined it.

There was a stop in the flow of movement. Essien sensed an angry buzzing energy in front of them as the Guard went into high alert, spacing themselves out without leaving any gaps. They didn't need to speak to step shoulder to shoulder and unharness their rapid-fires. The metallic click of rapid-fires moving to point at the ground made Essien tense up. She peered around the shoulders of the line of tight defense to see a group of men, mixed ages, not moving out of the way to let them pass. Essien noticed the men were all wearing white or cream-colored tunics with gold caps. She couldn't see if they were carrying weapons, but nobody should've gotten into the festival grounds with weapons of any kind. Gabriel had assured her of this.

Shouts reached her, and she couldn't recognize the language, so that Essien had no idea what they were shouting. Essien wanted to step forward past the press of the Guard, but they wouldn't let her. If she'd been in uniform, they'd have let her push past them to confront the threat directly. They wouldn't have been able to disregard her rank. Now they elbowed her back like an annoying distraction.

Gabriel caught up to her, and his bubble of Guard merged with Essien's to form an even larger circle. He used his grip on her elbow to push her even further behind him.

Essien wanted to know what was happening up ahead of them, so she did something she had never gotten used to being able to do. She remembered the feeling of a large crowd growing outside the Capitol Building. She felt that energy rumbling up toward them, like the whoosh of a growing bonfire. It was enough; she made a connection.

The first thing she felt was anger like the oppressive heat of the sun shining from everywhere. The stand of men in front of them was angry about centuries of transgressions. Hostile, their thoughts leaned toward murder as retribution.

She knew that they were all carrying swords, and that another thirty of them were further away in the crowd and moving quickly toward them. She tried to hold them all in her mind, to see if they were enough to cause violence. Sweat beaded on her upper lip, and she felt heat flush over her skin in the chaotic shouting around her. She knew instantly that at least half of them had come here with the intent to kill or be killed. She knew the men in the crowd were just a small portion of their total numbers. It was enough information for her to understand the situation better than the other Guard charged with protecting her.

She felt Gabriel react to what she had just thought, and he turned toward her.

"Don't," he said to her between gritted teeth.

"Don't what?" she asked. "Wasn't this your plan all along?"

But there was no time for him to respond. Suddenly, the bubble was receding and pulling back. The Guard were changing direction to avoid the men rather than forcing them to move by storming through. They didn't know that they were already surrounded.

How had knives gotten through the metal detectors? The detectors were supposed to scan every entrant to the fair. Knives the size the men were carrying should have set off every machine. There was only one possibility: someone had let the men in with those weapons.

She tried to stop moving with the tide around them pushing and urging her forward, but Gabriel's hand gripping her arm got tighter, and he kept tugging her behind him. She felt like they were running away, a cowardly move.

"No casualties today, Essien," he told her.

But Essien was staring at something over his shoulder.

She saw the man with the sword raised up over his head, the look of pure glee and rage on his face sending shivers down Essien's skin. The suddenness of the man's appearance was wrong, and Essien couldn't figure out where he had come from. There seemed to be a space in the bubble, a Guard not where he should have been. The man with the sword had on a white tunic, his beard the same color and blending into his chest.

Two Guard quickly realized their mistake and turned back to see the man in between them and the President. They had been so concentrated on getting themselves out of harm's way that they had momentarily forgotten that the safety of their charges came first. They hadn't seen the man with the knife slip past their barrier, and as they turned and saw him, Essien knew that they were frozen wide-eyed behind their helmets.

The man was heading toward Gabriel, moving so quickly that his tunic billowed around him. His arm was reared back, and there were people in the crowd noticing and pointing, their screams punctuating the moment. Essien knew she could step in the way of that man with his long knife glinting. So she did, stepping around Gabriel so that she was in the man's way. Her hands flew up in a protective stance, and she felt the blade slice into her shoulder. His arm reared back to hack at her again.

She could feel that the space behind her was empty, and she stepped back into it. Her hands covered the man's hands as he tried to switch directions to swing the blade at her again. Essien stepped forward and to the side, pulling the man even further away from Gabriel and off balance, the knife the man was holding suddenly pointing toward his own abdomen as he fell. The knife fell with him, and Essien kept her hands on the man's hands as he fell. The knife scraped into his lower abdomen and continued to sink through until it scraped against his spine. The surprised look on the man's face settled her. He knew he was dead. A rivulet of blood poured over his dry lower lip, and Essien snatched the blade out of his loosened grip.

She stared down at the man on the ground as the Guard realized they were in trouble. Several began to radio in for reinforcements. There were at least one hundred and fifty of their men in the crowd, but it would take time for more of them to reach their position. Glancing around, Essien knew that the crowd immediately surrounding them was full of hostiles, their blades out in the open now.

Essien knew she couldn't wait for reinforcements. She felt the men who had drawn their swords pressing forward. The Guard surrounded the President in a tight mass, leaving Essien by herself with the stolen sword stained in its owner's blood. *So much for being a civilian.* She was on her own outside the circle, and the Guard didn't even pretend to protect her anymore.

Without the Guard's protection, two more men moved in to continue the battle with Essien. She almost laughed at how stupid they were and how easy it was going to be. Killing men shouldn't be this easy.

She heard a shout from behind her and tried to turn, but a harsh blow to her forearm knocked the knife out of her hand. Essien screamed a sound that hurt her throat as she felt the ache of that strike down into her bones.

She looked up from her wounded arm to see another man in white advancing toward her.

Everything seemed to slow down, as if seconds stretched out into longer spans of time. Essien felt her hands burning, like fire was being pulled through her fingertips instead of blood. Her hands hadn't burned for so long, now the sensation startled her with its ominousness. She saw mouths opened in screams as people ran in all directions. She saw the President trying to come to her, pressing against the barrier of the Guard's backs, his mouth moving in words she couldn't hear or read. Then a blaze of heat spread out from her, like a wall flamed up right before her face, a wall of burning air like a consuming crush searing right through the men as they kept coming, unknowing what she was and what she could do.

Maybe Essien herself didn't even know what she was or what she was capable of.

The flames were hot, so hot, but they did not burn her. She could feel her assailant's flesh peeling against the assault of her flames, the char spreading. She wanted to stop.

The fire, like a raging press, surrounded her on all sides, and she could not feel or see anything except the flames rising up around her like her own personal fire Guard.

One moment Essien was surrounded by fire, and the next, water like a dousing gush, drenched over her. Essien blinked the cascade out of her eyes and saw Gabriel standing in the clouds of steam floating around them. Piles of ashes turned to lye, scorched earth, and the remains of badly burned bodies surrounded them. She couldn't quite read his face to determine if he was angry or pleased. But she could hear the voices around her. Voices of fear and shock, the click of picto capturers. Her head darted around at all the faces, but nobody looked combative anymore. Everybody looked downright scared of her, their eyes wide in their many shaded faces, their mouths moving, some whispering behind their hands.

Essien stepped forward and stumbled on a body, its burnt flesh disintegrating into ashes and mixing with the water under her foot. There was not enough left of the body at her feet for Essien to determine anything about them. Suddenly, all the Guard were pointing their rapid-fires at her. She froze and glanced to Gabriel. She had been trying to protect him from this mob after all. He was still staring at her. She tried to put her arms out to her sides, so they would know she was unarmed, but even as she did it, she knew it was a lie now. She felt that ache again, like a bone-deep scar in her forearm, and she tried to raise her arm to see. There was a deep, wide gash that showed the layers of her flesh down to white with blood gushing out of it. Once she looked at it, it gave a sharper throb, causing her to wince.

Essien looked at Gabriel, and he was mouthing words that she couldn't hear. She felt them slide over her, like a cool breeze across her skin. The Guard lowered their weapons. Gabriel stepped up beside her, and the Guard moved with him.

"You're hurt," he said. He touched her shoulder, and she let herself scream again as a piercing, stabbing pain throbbed in time to her heartbeat.

"Get me out of here," she managed to say between her teeth held tight together.

Essien tried to look over her shoulder, but turning her neck made streaks of heat shoot deep into her spine. She'd felt the blows in the moment, but she hadn't felt them immediately afterward. Now the adrenaline was fading.

The crowd had thinned down with the majority of the plaza evacuated. A few concerned citizens remained, their faces a mix of worry and panic.

Gabriel made a hand signal to his Guard. He gripped her uninjured arm and began moving as the Guard fell into a circle around them, and they began again to make their way toward the exits. Essien watched as more Guard jogged into view. The reinforcements had missed the action.

Essien felt lightheaded and didn't think she could walk much longer. She looked down and saw bodies crumbling into piles. She tried to stop, and Gabriel squeezed her so tightly she almost forgot about the other pains.

"Gabriel, what did I do?" She could feel that heat rising in her hands again. It was following her emotion, and she was afraid of it. "Gabriel, I can feel it again. Stop it, please!"

Her palm was so hot, she thought her bones were melting inside her skin. She looked down at her hand, red and orange flames superimposed over the center of her palm, the color moving up into her fingers. She watched, horrified, as the flame grew bigger and hotter in her palm.

"Gabriel!"

She put her hands out toward him, and the movement inadvertently gave the flames a direction. She watched as the fire grew more solid and real, the flames flickering in reds and yellows. The fire ballooned to life in the air between them, and Essien clenched her palms closed into fists. The fire began to eat up her arms.

"Help me, Gabriel. I don't know how to control this."

There were dozens of eyes upon them from the assembled crowd. With a flexing of power that Essien felt in her throat, Gabriel held them all transfixed as he reached out to her. The crowd had become completely unmoving, petrified into stillness at his hand. Gabriel held Essien's hands in his own, and water fell through her fingers into a puddle on the ground. The fire flared out, and smoke rose from her fingertips.

"You need a hospital for those wounds. I don't think I should try healing them here. There are too many eyes upon us. They've seen too much already."

Essien nodded. As she glanced around at the people surrounding them, their eyes staring back at her glimmered silver-blue. She looked up at Gabriel, and his eyes glinted with the same shining light.

Essien knew then that they were truly a god and a goddess among their people.

CHAPTER FORTY-FOUR

◆

T HE WATER WAS COOL AGAINST ESSIEN'S SKIN, AND SHE SHIV-
ered. When Essien opened her eyes, she saw the sky like white cotton,
thin trees stretching hopefully upward, and circles upon circles of Akukoifo orbiting above her. Their translucent figures floated lazily, dipping
down and back up, skirting around the edges of her vision and coalescing
into a misty collective. She moved her head around and landed on Gabriel's
face. She started to push against the comfort and serenity.

"Ssshhh," Gabriel's mouth right next to her ear. "You're badly hurt."

Her voice was a whisper. "The lake?"

"Yes, I brought you to the lake."

"Mothers."

"The Mothers have already seen you."

"Hurt."

"The water will heal you."

Essien's eyes wanted to close. She could feel herself sinking. Strong arms
adjusted to lift her and keep her head above the surface. A sharp ache in her
arm made her open her eyes and push against the softness.

"Hurt," she said again.

"Your hands wouldn't stop catching fire," Gabriel said. "The water helped."

The stinging in her arm was getting worse. She tried to lift her arm, but
it was so heavy.

"Hospital," she whispered.

"I thought the water would help the wounds, too."

"Hurt," Essien said again, and this time, the word ended with a sob.

GABRIEL WAS SEATED BESIDE THE HOSPITAL BED. ESSIEN LAY
restlessly unconscious from the drugs they'd given her for sedation. The

nurses had tried to increase her dosage, but he stopped them with a look and a word.

When they were gone, he spoke to Essien in a low monotone, barely moving his lips. She could feel that he didn't want anyone else to overhear him; he wanted to touch her but gripped his own hands together instead. He studied her face and wished she'd open her eyes.

"You have saved my life more times than I have saved yours. You have helped me much more than I help you. I know that you could kill me and every single one of my men if we gave you a reason. I know that you're a killer, that you enjoy killing, and that is what scares you. I enjoy it, too. More than anything else . . . well, except for one thing . . . There is still something you need to know that I do not know how to tell you."

She could feel a tightness in her back and arms even without moving. She opened her eyes.

"You were never in any danger, Essien."

Her throat felt dry, or she'd have called him a liar.

"I can hear you, so do not try to talk. I want you to know, I did not set you up. I did not mean for us to be attacked."

She didn't believe him. Every feeling of trust he might have created in her had bled out of her, literally. *Legends speak of a marriage between the most powerful man and the most powerful woman in Alkebulan . . . immortal . . . Their joining will destroy Alkebulan, turning the country into ruins.*

Enyemaka's warning whispered in her mind, and she wondered if the President could hear it. Was he listening to her thoughts even now? Because of Enyemaka's ominous warning, his foretelling whispered memories to Essien of stories her mother had once regaled her with in childhood. She knew what the President wanted from her. He wanted to reign as a King, and that meant only one thing for her.

Essien thought about that award being handed to her. Perhaps that was just Gabriel's first step toward achieving his ultimate goal. Himself in complete power, and her power an adjunct to his own. There was no way he could erase the horrors she'd committed from the minds of the people. Even after freezing their bodies and minds until they could make their exit, Essien knew the damage had already been done. She could see it in the fear screaming in their eyes. She imagined her mother had already heard, and her brothers were probably learning of it even now.

"No one will have heard about the festival. According to all news reports, a small scuffle broke out amongst fellow revelers and a trashcan was set on fire. No one was injured or harmed."

Essien stared up at him, blinking rapidly.

"We confiscated phones and issued vouchers for replacements. Your aim was spectacular. If you had killed innocents, there might have been a greater outcry, but you did not—only rebels, troublemakers, and radicals. There was another way; yes, I know how you prefer not to use magic."

She took in all of him. The wrinkled gray tunic and black slacks. The lack of jewelry on his fingers or wrists. The person he truly was didn't scare her, not any more than she scared herself. It made her wonder how far was too far for them to go. How far his powers could reach to erase minds and retell history.

"You manipulated information to protect me, but you didn't do it for me. You did it for yourself."

"I planted information, yes. I had the site cleared and cleaned, made sure no one had any pictos to go along with their stories. I did it to be sure you would not be harassed for your deeds. I would have done it for any of the Guard."

"Liar."

She had clearly lost all sense of military decorum. She could feel herself not caring what he did to her after this. He had already turned her into something she didn't recognize and didn't know how to live with. Or maybe it wasn't he who had turned her into this monster; it was simply her proximity to him. It made her shudder to think how near the prophecy foretold in legend came to becoming real. Essien thought of flames like a wall, and her hands grew warm, causing her to press them down on the bed covering in an effort to extinguish them.

"The waters made me this. You. The Mothers. And now, you want me to continue on as if it hasn't happened. As if I didn't use fire flowing out of my hands to kill people." She glared up at him from her hospital bed and knew she couldn't let him turn her into nothing but that flame. "How many?" she asked, wiping at her eyes.

He did not answer right away, a moment of confusion sweeping across his features, but then he realized the meaning of her question.

"Fifty-eight, including the men you killed with the knife."

"Fifty-eight lives. At my hands. Just like that," she grimaced with a snap of her fingers.

"You controlled yourself wonderfully, Essien. Not a single commoner in that number."

Essien covered her eyes. "What have you done to me?"

"It is not I who has done it. You are chosen. You chose life at that water's edge, Essien, and life you've been granted. A life far beyond what you ever considered. Your power scares you, but eventually, it will erupt in a way that even I cannot begin to imagine. I thought I knew what you were capable of, but I would hate to be wrong and limit you."

"This power *should* be limited," Essien said, almost yelling. "How much worse should this be allowed to get? When I am capable of killing thousands? Millions?"

Slaughtering people for fun . . . turning the country into ruins?

She tried to sit up, to press away the intrusive thoughts. Essien looked for the controls to raise the head of the bed as Gabriel stepped away from the bed.

"Theoretically, you could wipe out every person on Ala-ani, if you wanted to. But why would you want to do that?" he grinned, a smirk playing at his mouth.

"I do *not* want to be a goddess if this is what it means."

She looked down at her hands. They looked foreign to her now, like weapons she'd never handled before. She noticed grooves in her hands that she'd never noticed before. A scar here, a mole there. She moved up her forearm expecting to see a tight, painful scar, but there was nothing but shiny new skin that needed to grow old. She stared up at Gabriel and didn't have to ask him; he could hear what she was thinking.

"With the complete activation of your godhead should come the ability to heal wounds, all wounds, even life-threatening ones. Eventually, you won't even scar. Whatever else may come, we shall see. I do not know exactly how the Mothers have blessed you or even if they bless us all the same."

She trembled as adrenaline coursed through her. "I believe you now. I didn't before, but I do now . . ." Gabriel smiled, a mere widening of his lips. "You have to let me leave the military, the Guard. I can't control this, Gabriel. I will cause more damage and more harm to people."

"I can help you control it, but you will have to give me permission to connect with you in a way that might be shocking for you . . . it is called—"

"No," Essien said. "Let me go home. I'll be near the lake, and I can—"

Gabriel stopped smiling.

Essien was afraid to say "yes." She didn't want to know how much more powerful she could get. She didn't want to give him any more power than he already had. Not if it meant more people would die by her hands. Not if it meant he could control her through helping her control herself. She couldn't give anyone that power willingly.

CHAPTER FORTY-FIVE

◆

W HEN THE QUEEN CAME TO HER AGAIN, ESSIEN KNEW SHE
was dreaming.

They were high up in a tower with one window, and when she looked over the edge, Essien could only see the tops of tumultuous gray clouds below. The woman had the same face as Essien, still youthful, but her long ropes of hair had strands of silver and gold running through it. She moved with a slow elegance, like her bones were light and hollow and only her slowness kept her grounded. Essien knew that the woman was the Queen of Alkebulan, and that she had been Queen for quite a long time.

The Queen looked over at Essien, and Essien felt herself being sucked into her eyes, down into a tunnel of shining blackness. She hit the bottom, and she looked out through the Queen's vision. Everything looked so fresh and crisp, like she could look beyond this millennium into the one before, or even the one coming after.

The Queen blinked, and Essien was standing on the edge of a dark cliff. Above her, the clinging gray clouds were misty and moving fast. The tower was gone from her view, and she was left alone on the edge with a steep drop before her. Hundreds of feet below, she could see a gathering of men large enough to stretch like tiny ants for miles. There were thousands. She could feel their energy sifting up to her, fragrant as teakwood, and just as slow burning.

She knew that the men were waiting for her. The fate of the country's future from now unto eternity rested solidly upon the decision about to be made. And it was up to the Queen to decide. Essien cast her eye to the furthest distance across the chasm. There she observed yet another gathering of men, similar in size and severity. Another gathering of men waiting. But not for her.

The Queen knew that whatever happened next between these two great armies, it would be a civil war. They were all members of the country's elite Udo Nchedu, highly skilled fighting units that the Queen herself once belonged to. And they were gathered to help her battle the country's greatest living enemy: the King.

The King.

Through the Queen's eyes, Essien could feel the force of his power butting up against her own, invisible in the air but just as tangible as a wall. One hand held on to the precarious safety of the ledge, and she opened eyes that had never been closed.

Then the Queen was no longer standing on the edge of a cliff but catapulted high up to float above it all. Her men, the strongest, fastest, bravest soldiers in the country had been ready to fight for months now. They didn't need to practice, but at night, she could hear clanging metal and feel reverberations from the energy echoes they were using.

They were waiting for her to decide, but she needed a sign. After everything that had happened, all the centuries between the Essien she was and this crowned woman, she couldn't tell if it was her battle to win or to lose. She still felt unsure, and she knew the Queen wouldn't give the order until she was sure.

Standing so high up and looking down, she didn't know what it was she needed to occur or what she needed to feel before she could resolve her doubts and act. Doubts that kept her motionless floating in the sky, her men in limbo beneath her. Even the enemy's soldiers were glancing over at her side, waiting for her decision. Even her enemy depended upon what she determined to do. She couldn't begin to imagine what kind of sign would be sufficient to pit limbs of these men's bodies against each other, but she hoped she'd recognize it when she saw it.

Uniting thousands of warring, disparate tribes into one continental nation had taken muscle and mental strategizing unseen before in thousands of years of human existence. A war of turning son against father, mother against child, sister against brother. This was a war like that one, destined to be just as deadly. Yet, this one was at her hands. This one depended on the command of her word, the strength of her own actions.

She knew that in this vision she had been fighting against her dark and powerful enemy for some time now. Even battles of silent judgment and unspoken resentment were wars unto themselves. This was a battle that had been long coming, a battle of facing the enemy and realizing suddenly like the dawning of a liquid sun, that the real enemy was herself all along. The Queen knew that she was fighting against herself and sending her men to fight against their neighbors, their families, their friends. Their enemy looked just like them, though their causes opposed each other.

Essien tried to sense the country's fate beyond her own soul and sinew. She threw herself outside of her body, and it was like she unzipped her skin from the neck down and stepped out of it. Her newly naked self had no form and could scatter in a million directions like droplets of water falling from the sky. Her past kept filtering and coloring her emotions, so she couldn't rightly predict how the war might end. Either option was open before her like the great sweep of an empty canvas. Either she would win, and the paleness of death would recede from the continent forever, or she would lose, and that paleness would swallow them all whole. No one would be spared.

Once she made her final judgment, the battle would break out and spill over into civilian lives. Nnas and nnes would see their sons fighting and their daughter in the midst of them both. She knew this would end in a collapsed heap of the bloody bodies of brethren. She shouldn't fight this war; she couldn't fight against him, not if it could cost so many lives.

Her spirit floated high above that earthly landmark, higher still above the earth itself, its size a speckled marble resting in her lined palm.

A clear clip of wind breezing over that field where her men stood, facing across where others of her men stood on the opposing side brought her back, down and down, sinking through violet layers until she was sucked back into the Queen's eyes. They were all her men, each of them connected to her and to each other by an invisible cord of stretching veins, pumping her into them, them into her, yoking a chain around everyone on the continent. She followed those veins as they spanned across gulfs wider than mere distances, their rushing energy pushing past her as she tried to hold them all in her mind at the same time. She sought those veins to their beginning and came back to herself. She knew then that this was a battle she should not and could not win. This was a battle in which she would lose more than just her men.

The sky suddenly darkened, the sun covered by black-edged storm clouds. Essien felt the decrease in light like a caress of fingertips across the back of her neck. She looked out over the field and saw a shape forming on the other side of the clearing. A shape made of dark flecks and shiny glints, whirling around and around, growing faster and faster. She watched as the shape began to fill out, becoming more solid and weighted. It was a man forming out of the mystifying darkness and walking out of its clinging grip.

The man walked a dozen steps before she realized who he was, why he was there in this field, and what he expected her to do. The man walked to the very end of one side and looked up, his head hinging back to rest against his neck. Their eyes met. Essien leaned further out, wanting him to know that she knew she couldn't win, and she was ready to give up; she was ready to submit to him.

An arrow made of foaming black smoke shot up at her from an unknown origin. It chinked into the stone next to her head. Attached to the arrow was a billow of white paper. Essien peered closely as writing formed on the smooth surface. The letters revealed an answer that only she would understand, which only she would know the significance of.

I come to live and to die, had been written in silver letters. No end mark, just the seven words without adornment. Stark and real. She had made her decision. The decision had already been made for her, centuries ago.

She put her foot over the edge of the window and let go of the ledge. It was as though she fell down into him, or out of that dimension and into an entirely new consciousness of being. Time sped up or slowed down, and neither of them cared. They were two becoming one and then multiplying into many. Their existence became a melding moment of eternal consequence, and Essien knew that she had made the right choice.

◆

CHAPTER FORTY-SIX

ESSIEN AWOKE, AND IT WAS AS IF SHE HAD NEVER BEEN SLEEPING. She sat up in her hospital bed and noticed Enyemaka was in the spot that the President had occupied the last time Essien's eyes were open. A smile spread over Essien's face before she discouraged herself. Where had he come from? How did he know where to find her? Although, in that moment, she was delighted to see him, to feel the pull toward him that felt so nourishing rather than the pull toward Gabriel that threatened to consume her in its midst.

"How now?" she greeted him with a weak joke in her voice. "Did you hear about the burnings and come to rescue me from him?"

Enyemaka didn't smile back. He leaned forward in the chair. "I have a minicraft upstairs on the roof waiting for you. If you come with me, I can make sure he will not be able to find you again."

Essien instantly dropped her smile. At first, she stared at Enyemaka silently, and he stared right back.

"How?" Her voice choked coming out.

"Come with me, and I will show you."

"Is it safe? Can you really—?"

"There will be time for explanations later. You must come with me now or lose this chance forever," he cut her off, gently.

She slid out of the bed on the side opposite of Enyemaka, still wearing the thin hospital-issued uwe. As she contemplated where she might find her uniform, Enyemaka peeled off his tunic top to reveal a second tunic beneath. He tossed the one he had removed onto the bed, and Essien smirked as she retrieved it. Enyemaka did the same with his slacks, slipping them down to his feet, revealing a second pair underneath. He put the removed pair on the bed. Essien was already pulling the uwe off, not caring that Enyemaka watched. The pants were tighter on her than they had been on

Enyemaka. She rubbed a hand over her arm where the deepest wound had been. The scar there was almost completely healed, the skin soft like baby skin. She walked around the bed, and Enyemaka was pushing a pair of slippers toward her.

"I had to steal these off a shelf out there. No shoes that would fit you."

Essien slipped into them. She had her military ID card, which she always kept with her. That was it.

"Gabriel will never let me go," she said as she stood beside the bed. "We know that, both of us. If there's a prophecy, then—"

"Who are we to say that prophecies cannot be broken? With the world at stake, with our people at stake. Should we not try?"

Essien hesitated, suddenly missing the feel of golden edges twirling between her fingers, the slight weight of a pouch around her neck. She remembered the coin and wished she had it still.

"I am offering you a rescue." Enyemaka's tone was firm but gentle. "To keep you safe and save this country from him. I told you before, but you didn't believe me. You are the only one who can make the legend true. Without you, he doesn't become King. Without you, all the moves he's made to secure a crown up to this point will be fruitless."

"And I don't become Queen."

"Maybe. Maybe not. But we must try this. When I heard you were healing here, I knew this could be your chance, your way out."

"I need someone to teach me to control this power. You don't know how bad it will be if it gets out of my control."

Enyemaka stepped around the bed. He put his one hand over her hand still gripping the bed railing. "That person doesn't have to be him. In his hands, your powers only magnify his."

Essien let go of the rail, and Enyemaka wrapped his hand around hers. He turned toward the door, opened it, and continued to hold it open, encouraging Essien to pass through it. Essien stepped into the hallway, afraid to look at anything besides Enyemaka's face, afraid to feel the pound of adrenaline rushing to her temples. Was she running from her destiny? Or running toward a new one?

Enyemaka closed the door behind them, walking her toward the end of the hallway where posted signs showed an alternate exit. She followed, letting him lead her without looking back. They went up instead of down the stairs, climbing up five floors. They went all the way up to the roof. Enyemaka opened the stairwell door, and she felt the sun like the gentlest kiss upon her forehead. Outside of the stairwell, on the rooftop, the blades of a minicraft flapped in the wind ready for liftoff. Enyemaka ran toward the waiting craft, crouching low to avoid the rotating blades, and Essien followed him. They climbed in, and the minicraft began to lift off the rooftop as soon as their feet stepped off. She realized as the small skycraft rose higher and drifted further away from their liftoff point that Enyemaka had linked with her. She was getting his thoughts in her mind like a casual breeze through a window. She also realized at the same time that he was still holding her hand. She started to let go.

He held tighter and turned to her. "Don't. The contact helps with blocking."

"Blocking?" A term she hadn't learned yet.

"Think of metal or a sealed lock... some tangible item that is impenetrable."

"Fire?"

Enyemaka shook his head. "Fire can be doused with water."

Essien thought about Gabriel, and Enyemaka's grip tightened. "Your thoughts can draw him near. Blocking can keep him out, but if you don't help me, he will find you before we can land anywhere. You must think of something that cannot be penetrated or overcome. Think of that, wrap its essence around you, your mind, the people with you. It can be expanded to include an entire building, or a block. I imagine someone powerful enough could obscure an entire town ... or more."

"How did you—?"

"You're not the only one who learned to harness the powers of the mind, Essien. I have felt you connected to me before. And now I'm connected to you."

Essien nodded, thinking of how she had imagined her skin being covered in indestructible scales before. She did this now, closing her eyes and thinking of herself as completely covered from head to toe. Suddenly, she could feel the blocking, like a wall erected all around her, which kept her in and kept everything else out. She could sense Enyemaka's hand in hers, the vibration of the minicraft beating against gravity, and nothing else.

"Just like that," he said. "Don't think about him. Think about your shields. Keep your thoughts elsewhere."

Essien kept nodding. She focused her glance outside the front windshield of the minicraft as it hovered higher and higher. She thought of metal, even as she wondered what dangers awaited her and Enyemaka— even as she wondered if she'd made the right choice in fleeing the vision she'd seen, the connection that held her bound to the Alkebulanian President. The thought of the crown he'd left beside her bed flashed into her mind, but she pushed it away.

Essien strained to catch a glimpse through the minicraft's front windows, hoping she might gain an idea about where they were heading, or see into the future somehow. But all Essien saw were thinly stretched clouds and endless blue space ahead. She closed her eyes and fought to think only of metal surrounding her and not of a crown adorning her head.

ACKNOWLEDGMENTS

◆

GRATITUDE: TO APPROACH LIFE WITH A PROFOUND SENSE OF thankfulness for everything, from the simplicity of fresh water to drink and clean air to breathe to the more complex moments of finally publishing a work that has been in the making for over ten years.

I'd like to start off by thanking my mother and father, Marinel Williams and Uzoka Anofienem. From a very early age, they instilled in me a love for written words and a passion for excellence. I remember the bedtime stories my mother would read to me and the collection of advanced works by Black authors that my father helped me build starting at age eight. I remember being banned from reading *Flyy Girl*, *The Women of Brewster Place*, and *Beloved* because of the very adult content I was consuming at such a young age. I am convinced that my hyperlexia led me to the creation of this story you have in your hands and the unquenchable thirst I had to tell it to the world.

Next, I'd like to thank two of my earliest readers: Ginger Gayden and Tonye Jaclyn Bobmanuel. Ginger, my sister and cousin, was one of the first people I allowed to read my stories. These were poorly written, drama-filled short stories and novellas that referenced people I knew or wished I knew. Tonye, my elementary school best friend, loved reading my stories too. I remember carrying my freshly printed pages to her house for her to read and give me feedback on. Her enjoyment at seeing herself represented in a character was amazing to experience. What Ginger and Tonye gave me was fuel that would sustain my writing career for several decades to come. Knowing there were people out there who would want to read my words and would fall in love with my characters kept me going through periods when I didn't have the energy to write at all.

An especially grateful thank-you to my writing buddies, who at different times throughout the life of this novel have met me everywhere from Starbucks and Dunkin Donuts to cafes and local libraries, to help inspire me toward productivity and actually sitting down to write and to edit: Eboni Rafus-Brenning, Tom Moore, Abbey Lenzie, and Ashley Jackson.

Additionally, I'd like to thank my agent, Felice Laverne, and her entire team at Art House Literary Agency. She saw something majestic and exciting in my manuscript at a time when I was absolutely tired of reading it. They helped me to rediscover the passion I felt about this story and the hope I had for how this story might resonate with readers in the future.

Finally, I'd like to thank my editor, Ryan Smernoff at Turner Publishing, for making this book the literal reality you have in your hands. Thank you for believing in the vision and helping me to see even more clearly and authentically.

Another important moment of thanks goes out to everyone I met during my time at the University of San Francisco. Specifically, the creative writing program cohort class of 2017. These individuals read this work when it was in its infancy. They gave me comments and pages of critiques. Whether I read or incorporated these critiques in the final product, I want to share my appreciation for their connecting with the work and providing their thoughtful and passionate feedback. Their encouragement helped push me to keep editing and keep querying to get this book out into the world, so they could see the final product. A special shout-out to Rose Heredia and Ebonie Ledbetter.

To that end, I'd like to send a special thank-you to the professors and instructors I had along the way. These educators taught insightful and applicable classes on everything from poetry and poetics to editing long fiction and the business of being a writer.

To Beth Nguyen, thank you for teaching me everything I needed to know to get this book into the world. From querying agents using the letter templates you provided to being firm and self-assured in my persona and identity as an author, I feel that Beth's contributions to my progress have been so central and foundational that this book wouldn't be in your hands without her words and mentorship.

To Karl Soehnlein, thank you for comforting me that time I cried and making me feel that the story I had to tell was just as worthy as the books we read in your class. Thanks for encouraging me to experiment with my story and to push the envelope on what was possible with words on a page.

To Stephen Beachy, thank you for the reality check and all the little tidbits and feedback, of which I absorbed and incorporated into every page of my book. I was still thinking about your advice as I went through the process of editing what felt like the 100th draft.

To Micah Ballard, thank you for accepting me into the USF Creative Writing program and holding that spot for me! I cannot imagine what my life would be like right now if I had not reached out to you that day to see if you'd let me take back my program offer rejection, one of the stupidest decisions I was ever about to make.

To Lewis Buzbee, thank you for your sage words of wisdom and feedback on my manuscript that has become this first edition in what will become a multi-book series. Thank you for modeling what it looks like to have a good sense of humor about my writing and to only take myself seriously enough to realize that I should never take myself too seriously.

To Nina Schuyler, thank you for the precision of language that you encouraged me to embrace. Thank you for exposing me to quietly beautiful stories with subtle messages that continue to evoke a response in me to this day.

To Brynn Saito, thank you for helping me to finally hear and listen to the sounds that language can make. Thank you for inviting me to become the poetry in prose and to remember that prose was first poetry, and it still can be.

To Dave Powell, thank you for helping me to realize that I am in fact a poet. Thank you for inviting me to live through the senses, to reimagine the logical and rational, and to take pride in the way words look on the page, not only how they sound.

Finally, I'd like to give ideological and philosophical thanks to the writers and authors who preceded me, who guided me, and who welcomed me with open arms into this wonderful world of writing.

To Octavia Butler, the writer whose lineage I did not know I was growing up into, whose out-of-this-world creations spawned in me my own dreams of new suns.

To Toni Morrison, the writer whose magic with words I aspire to emulate, and whose accomplishments I could not even begin to approach.

To Laurell K. Hamilton, the writer whose character, Anita Blake, has gotten me through all of my adolescent and early adult years with a wit and wisdom that resonates so much with who I am.

GLOSSARY OF IGBO TERMS

◆

ABAGHI URU
Worthless

AKUKOIFO
Spirit guides

AKWUNA
Prostitute, slut

ALA-ANI
Earth

ARA
Madam, ma'am

DAMBE
Traditional style of fighting

ELUIGWE
Heaven

ENGOLO
Traditional style of fighting

GELE
Traditional Igbo headwear worn by women

IHEBUBE
Blessing

INDOMIE
Noodle dish with eggs and peppers

MGBATI AHU
Gym

NNA
Father, dad

NNE
Mother, mom

NNENNA
Grandmother, father's mother

NWA M NWAAYNI
My daughter

NWA NWANNE
Nephew

NWAANYI
Woman

NWANNE NWOKE
Brother

NWANNE
Sister

NWAODO
Pounding stick for making fufu

NWATAKIRI
Child, little girl/boy

NWAYI NKE NĒLE IME
Midwife

ODIBO
Servant

PALBINO
Albino

SOJAS
Soldiers

UMU NWOKE
Sons

UWE
Traditional Igbo dress

UZO NCHEDO
President's personal bodyguards

ABOUT THE AUTHOR

◆

DIDI ANOFIENEM is a freelance writer and teacher. She is originally from Houston, Texas, born to a Nigerian father and an African American mother. She chooses to identify herself as Black. Didi received her MFA from the University of San Francisco. She currently lives in Los Angeles.